The "fiction dragon" logo is a trademark of Drake Books & Media.

Book design copyright © 2019 by Drake Books & Media
Cover design by Selena IR Drake
Author photo by Robert Berry.

Drake Books & Media
901 62nd Avenue NE, Suite B, Minot, ND 58703
Visit us online at www.DrakeBooksMedia.com

Published in the United States of America

ISBN: 978-1312833418

PUBLISHER'S NOTE
The characters and events in this book are fictitious. Any similarity to real persons, living or dead, is
coincidental and not intended by the author.

The views and opinions expressed by the author are not necessarily those of Drake Books & Media.

Other Books by Selena IR Drake

Dragon Diaries:
Ascension
Culmination

The AEON Files:
The Archfiend Artifact
The Lycan Pharaoh
The Lullaby Shriek
The Bone Prophet
The Sovereign Flame

WEIRD Chronicles, Episode One
How to Author
How to Character

sirdwrites.com
DrakeBooksMedia.com

To my mom, dad, and brother – Thank you for all your help and support through the many years I spent writing.

To my friends and muses, Matt G. and Sabrina S. – Thank you for the many inspirations and good times.

To the late Anne McCaffrey – Thank you for the dream.

It is within the deepest, darkest recesses of our minds that we discover the hidden truths about ourselves and our potential.
– FROM "CONVERSATIONS WITH AMOREZ"
BY DJURDAK ZA'CAR

I was cold in the deep of this night. My breath was loud in my ears, almost deafening in the constricting silence. Clouds billowed out through clenched teeth and hung in the air as if waiting to be snatched away by the twisted forest that surrounded me. The ancient, leaf-bare trees were the color of freshly fallen snow. They crowded together, bent and twisted and gnarled. Hideous and monstrous shapes looming in the brooding shadows. Their appearance could birth fear in even the bravest of warriors. From misshapen root to barren and tangled canopy, the trees glimmered. It was as if they were lanterns, each aglow with ghostly light from a strange and internal source. A silver mist danced like ghosts between the tangled trunks. It covered everything in a fine layer of sweat and shrouded the dangers of the dirt path before me. Though no moon was out to direct my trek through the dreary depths of these woods, the ghost-light of the trees helped to guide my groping steps on the uneven ground.

I trudged along; the mist roiling like fire in my wake. The moist air was thick with the scent of earth and a dour spice that I could not name. The soggy ground absorbed the sound of my footsteps. The dampness seeped into my tunic and leggings. The black, Fey-weave clothing was like ice against my skin. It left me longing for a thick cloak and a warm fire, neither of which I had access to here. I plodded on. My determination to escape the forest outweighing my discomfort. Yet no matter which way I turned, the same trees seemed to surround me. Tears of frustration stung at my eyes, threatening to fall. My vision blurred, and I tripped over an exposed tree root. I crashed to the soggy ground with a cry. I lay there a moment, clearing my head and wiping my eyes with the back of my hand.

A stirring in the trees not far off made my breath catch and my hackles rise. I became aware of a presence drawing nearer. Uncertain of its intentions, I quickly pushed myself to my feet and was off again. I dared to move faster over the irregular terrain. The trees seemed to reach out to me, clutching at my hair and sable clothing. Perhaps they desired to hold me prisoner for the one rapidly closing in.

There was a fluttering of wings right behind me and I did not dare to look back. Had the tangled mess of roots and branches not formed such a hazardous route, I would have sprinted in order to escape the beast. The screech of an eagle pierced the night, and all I could think was: There were no eagles here. Then the creature in pursuit fell back, called out again. I rushed onwards, focusing on the careful placement of my steps. There was a whoosh of air that reminded me of a giant fire igniting, then a red-orange light sent the shadows of night skittering away. A moment later the fiery light faded slightly, moving away. I watched out of the corner of my eye as a glowing ball of fire moved to my left, darting and dodging passed tree after tree. It rapidly gained speed and with another screech, turned right sharply.

The creature wove a path between the trees just in front of me and a spectral echo whispered, "Tabiki ni heile."

In an instant the creature's snaking course through the forest was alight with crimson flames. Unable to stop in time, I threw my arms up over my face and dove through the wall of fire. There was half a heartbeat when, suspended in midair, I felt the flames lapping at my skin as if they wanted to devour me. The instant I was free of their grasp, I tucked myself into a ball and hit the ground with a rolling somersault. Back on my feet, I paused briefly, observed the dancing inferno. There was no heat from this fire. In fact, it was as cool as the air around me. Perplexed, I slowly reached out. My fingers caressed the tongues of the leaping flames. Feeling no bite, I reached further and let my hand bathe in the heatless inferno.

The sound of wings fluttering returned much louder than before and a gentle heat permeated the bone-chilling air. I forgot the fire in an instant and whirled around only to find myself facing the glowing creature. I did not move. Nor did I breathe. I just stared at the beast before me, utterly afraid. It must have realized how fearful I was of it, for it cooed softly and slowly backed away.

A gnarled branch creaked as the creature settled upon it. The red-orange light around the beast began to fade much as a fire would die down to embers. With the fiery glow melting away, the inferno at my back vanished into memory along with it. At last I could see the creature. It was a bird; the same shape as a hawk, but nearly thrice the size as any I had ever seen. Its beak was hooked and golden and its eyes were as blue as the sea. Red and orange and yellow feathers shimmered across its body like heat waves on desert sand. Its tail was longer than my arm, and tipped in purple and blue.

A phoenix, I marveled.

The firebird studied me with its glowing, cerulean eyes. It was a long, tense moment, in which neither of us moved. Then the bird opened its golden beak.

"Esté imlít lerra rité mertuác jidó. Arx et cólaz ni Kohnbenai rahn…"

The spectral whisper continued for several more verses, emanating from the phoenix. I hung on every word, trying in vain to translate the message. The words were as foreign to me as a fish in the desert. I did not understand a word of what the phoenix said but sensed it was somehow important. When at last the whispered verses were swallowed by silence, I began to speak—to ask the meaning of those cryptic words. Before I had uttered even a single sound, the firebird screeched and vanished in a blast of searing hot flames.

In a flash the world around me changed completely. Night became day. Dark became light. Cold became hot.

I found myself standing alone amid mountainous dunes of sand as red as blood. A few scattered rocks of black basalt littered the ground like gravestones. The sky overhead was deep violet despite the twin suns fixed at their zenith. Their heat combined to scorch the land laid bare beneath them.

There was no foliage. No drop of water. No lick of wind. No whisper of sound. This whole land was dead and deserted; a crypt. Yet my senses were screaming at me, warning of something out there, waiting. The sea of red sand and black gravel seemed to scream of an evil presence lingering in this space. It was as if an angry spirit had been trapped here for untold eons, feeding on its own lust for revenge against whoever locked it away.

A soft growl was the only warning I had before an enormous spear struck the sand half a heartbeat after I threw myself out of range. I hastened over a dune and pivoted on the balls of my feet to face my attacker head-on only to be dismayed at the sight before me. It was not a spear that had been used against me; it was a spade.

The head of the weapon was half again as tall as I was, jet black, and edged with what looked to be bone as sharp as any sword. It fed into a rope-like tail that was as thick as the oldest spider palm trees. It was covered in needle-like spines and jet black scales that seemed to absorb all the light around it. And the tail was attached to a fearsome, onyx and crimson beast. It was taller than a mansion, and standing boldly on four enormous feet that were armed with talons longer than I was tall. A pair of torn, bat-like wings – held aloft and wide to give the beast an even more fierce appearance – sprouted from its shoulders. A long neck gave way to a wedge-shaped head where long, ivory horns swept backwards over a spiny frill that had evolved to protect the beast's neck and throat. More horns, smaller, yet sharper, grew along the beasts snout and lower jaws and a ridge of bone guarded its amber eyes. My breath was stolen by the mix of evil and absolute hatred in the beast's hardened gaze.

I gawked at the monster, and all I could think was: I am going to die here.

The enormous, sable and scarlet beast angrily yanked its tail spade free of the sand, sending up a cloud of dust. It flexed the individual blades, testing them like a seamstress would her scissors. It took a step towards me and…

…A loud chorus of bells suddenly rang out.

*She knew not how she had come to find herself at that holy place, nor could
she recall anything prior to her waking.*
– FROM "THE SECOND KEEPER"
BY THERA ONYX

I erupted from the tangled bed sheets, gasping for breath. Tendrils of my hair clung to my face and neck. Sweat dotted my brow and dared to run down my cheek. It was… It was a dream, I told myself, just a dream.

With each resounding boom of the bells, I replayed the dream in my mind. I wanted to commit it to memory it before it faded into nothingness.

The twisted and ghostly forest…

The heatless inferno…

The phoenix…

The unknown language…

That monster in the desert…

It all felt familiar. Yet when I tried to remember where or when I had come across that language, that strange forest, or those creatures I realized that I knew nothing of myself or my past. I did not even know my name or my age, nor did I have any clue about where I was.

The last bong seemed to last forever as it faded into silence. At last, I cast my gaze about the room I found myself in. It was narrow, but long and housed over a dozen small beds. Each bed was adorned with plain, green and white sheets. At their feet sat wooden lockboxes with iron hinges and filigree flowers. Soft green curtains affixed to free-moving metal frames provided the individual beds with a modicum of privacy. The floor was a grid of contrasting tan mud tiles while the walls were white stone blocks polished so smooth they shined. There were three unmarked wooden doors; one of which was on the wall farthest from where I lay while the other two were side-by-side just meters away. The ceiling was high, and a quartet of matching, large chandeliers had been spaced at equal intervals throughout the room. Windows with stained glass accents allowed light to spill into the room.

Beyond the glass, I could see a trio of stark white obelisks piercing the early morning sky like apparitions. Standards of violet and black barely woke in a soft breeze. The light of the twin suns barely broke the horizon, casting an ethereal glow in the deep cobalt sky. This glow reflected off the white marble of the obelisks, turning them jewel-like. It was breathtakingly beautiful, and yet the ghost of a memory told me that I had been here before.

But where is here? I asked myself. I knew the name, yet it eluded me like a word teetering on the tip of the tongue. Then another question arose to plague me: How did I get here?

A loud bong suddenly tore through the silence. It made me jump in fright and lose my train of thought. More bells began to ring out with the first, marrying their various tones in a sepulchral chorus. All I could think about was how terrible their melody was for this beautiful morning. In their resounding echoes, a new sound emerged. This one signaled movement, and lots of it.

I tossed the covers aside and left the warmth of the bed. The cold of the stone floor on my bare feet made me grimace and shiver. I quickly but quietly slunk to the closest window and peered out. A courtyard lay far below the window, and countless people of various ages spilled out over the stone slabs. Everyone in the courtyard appeared to be in a hurry as they converged on a location I could not see from my viewpoint. They were all dressed similarly, with soft gray tunics hidden beneath violet vests and flowing, black robes. The boys wore black slacks while the girls had pleated, black skirts that settled at their knees. Black, skin tight leggings kept their legs warm against the morning chill. Some of the elders in the rush wore violet stoles edged in silver ribbon. The vestments bore a pentacle; the sigil of the priesthood.

One girl stood out from the rest. Not because she wore the boys' slacks or crossed the yard at a more leisurely pace, but because she was about half a meter taller than everyone else. Her hair was deep amethyst in color, and tied back in several tight braids. The end of each braid was bejeweled with small, colorful beads. A pair of painted feathers was affixed by her left ear. Her face was more angular, with high cheekbones and a dainty nose. Even her ears were different; longer and ending in a point instead of rounded. It was plain to see that she was nothing like her companions.

There was a soft rattling, like a key in a lock, to my left. I looked over my shoulder in just as one of the two doors along the wall was pulled open. In the doorway stood a man who appeared to have no more than thirty years on him. His hair was dark auburn and long, kept out of his face by a small and neat tail that left most of his hair free. His eyes were the same green as the crescent sigil on his simple, cream smock. He was a Healer.

And he smiled warmly upon seeing me by the window. "I am delighted to finally see you up and about. How do you feel?"

"Confused," I admitted as I turned away from the window. The Healer nodded. I motioned around the room, "What is this place?"

"You are in the Healers' Wing of the Temple of Five Souls."

That was the name that had eluded me earlier – the Temple of Five Souls. I thought. Aloud I said, "How did I get here?"

The Healer stared at me for a minute, a soft frown tugging at the corners of his lips. "We're not sure," he said at last, and moved into the room. I watched as he went to the wooden lockbox that sat at the foot of the bed I had occupied. He unlocked it with a small key hidden within the folds of his smock. Finally, he turned to me and gestured towards the lockbox. "One of our third-year students, Ríhan, discovered you washed up on shore during an outing. He and a classmate immediately brought you here. This was all you had in your possession at the time."

I crossed the cold mud tiles and peered into the box. Laid neatly within it was a worn, leather satchel with frayed embroidery on the front, some copper and silver bits the size of my thumbnail, a pair of strange bars the length of my forearm that had begun to rust, and a tattered, old book with a title I could not

read. Everything was alien to me, like it belonged to someone else. All of it…
save the book.

Despite knowing nothing about it or its author, I somehow knew that that
book was the most important thing in that lockbox. The brown leather
wrapping had aged, turning great portions of it almost black. The runes
embossed into the hide were barely legible from the wear and tear of what
might have been centuries. I picked it up, untied the leather lacing that kept it
closed. The pages within were thick parchment, jagged and uneven along the
edges. Runes similar to those on the cover filled the pages. I yearned to read
the stories they spoke of, but I could not recall how to translate them. Intricate
sketches inked by a deft hand appeared throughout and I wondered, Was I the
artist?

"Curious thing, that," said the Healer with a wry smile. "Practically
everything you had on you was ruined by your time in the water. Everything,"
he paused to point at the book in my hands, "except that."

He is right, I realized as I looked the book over again. There are no signs of
water ever touching it.

"Might I ask you something?"

I nodded as I sealed the book and retied the lace.

"How did you come to be in the Eastern Ocean?"

I could only shrug. "I do not recall anything prior to waking this morn."

The frown on the Healer's lips grew deeper. "You do not remember your
name? Your home? Your life?"

I shook my head negative upon each query.

The chorus of bells rang out for a third time that morning.

I grimaced at their song. "What is it with that dismal annoyance?"

"The bells?"

I nodded.

"They sound at specified intervals in order to keep students and staff on
schedule throughout the day. Another toning is played to sound a death, and a
third is played to sound a warning of danger either by weather or by invasion,
which is a useless concern here; no one would attack this Temple."

I found his optimism at that rather naïve. This place would be no challenge
to sack, and was suddenly surprised at myself for thinking such dark things. I
could not help but wonder what I had gone through in my life to immediately
see the foolishness of the Healer's thinking.

He continued with his explanation. "That one we just heard was actually
the second breakfast sounding, which means that everyone should be in their
seats in the dining hall for the morning meal. Since we are not, we will have to
wait until the meal is over before we may enter. In the mean time, however,
best we get you cleaned up and presentable. The Palavant and her Matron will
want to meet with you right away."

"Palavant and Matron?"

Surprise then belated understanding flashed in his verdant eyes as he
looked at me. "The Palavant is the highest ranking priestess for the Five Souls.
She leads this Temple, and her voice even carries into the court of the King,

where laws and other things are decided. Palavant Celestia has been in her ranking for nigh on sixty years now. Her assistant, who is one of the most promising and devoted Archbishops, is the Matron. More often than not, Matrons are elected by the Archbishops to become the Palavant when the one they serve passes into Havel, but that is not always the case."

The Healer bent to remove the other things from the lockbox. He picked the leather satchel first, examining it with a trained eye. "These stitches have not held up very well against the water. I am sure our leatherer can craft you something better to replace this one. He probably won't even charge you," he paused long enough to reach back into the box. This time he came away with a small handful of silver and copper bits, "though it appears you have enough coin to buy his entire stock of wares." He opened his hand to show me, and I glimpsed the glint of a pair of gold pieces in the mix. "This sort of money could mean that you are a Highborn. If that is the case, your Lord Father and Lady Mother could be looking for you. Perhaps some of the travelling priests have heard something." When I did not move to retrieve the coins from his hand, he put them in the satchel. Finally he removed the last of the things from the box: the strange bars. He said nothing as he looked them over and placed them in the bag. "Well, then," he said, putting on a cheery smile, "let's get you a room so you can freshen up and put on something more appropriate for meeting the Palavant."

Upon his words, I looked down at myself and realized I was clad only in a short tunic of drab green and a pair of loose, white slacks. The Healer handed me a pair of slippers to wear, then led me through the door at the farthest end of the room. I stepped into the hall just as a young priestess strode by, escorting a woman fresh from the road. The woman was about my height, and had auburn hair that was short and messy. She wore spectacles with glass so dark I could not see her eyes, yet I got the distinct impression that she was looking right at me. As we passed each other, I glimpsed the sigil of the clasp which had fixed to her white cloak: a golden hammer encircled by a ring made of silver olive branches. I could not recall its meaning.

The beginning of the Second Age of Humes on Ithnez was marked with the finished construction of the new capitol city in AR 50. Though it was given a Hume name, the city was forever know by the title given by the Dákun Daju, Bakari-Tokai.

– FROM "THE CHRONICLES OF ITHNEZ, VOL. XII"
BY MERLIN SINGER, COURT HISTORIAN

Many leagues upriver from the Temple of Five Souls was the capital of Ithnez, known today as Bakari-Tokai. It had been built many centuries ago when the arcane technology of the Earthers still functioned. The city stood half on water and half on land, held level and unsinking atop a magnificent plate supported by enormous, stone pillars driven deep into the ground and lakebed. It was the crowning achievement of the long-forgotten architect.

Recent centuries had annexed in more and more surrounding acres until the city covered an area of one hundred and sixty square kilometers. Most of the new additions had been farmsteads and plantations at one time. Now they were mansions for the wealthy of the merchant class or guesthouses for visiting royalty. One section of the city housed the wyvern stables and barracks, while another was home to a school and a small Temple. A tower that seemed to scrape the sky stood by the docking ring and served as the armory. A great portion of the land had been dedicated to the largest free garden on Ithnez, and people from all walks of life were welcome to come and admire the collection of fauna.

Walls of brick and mortar surrounded the additions, but these newer walls were not nearly as strong or as tall as the original two. The original portion of the city, today called Old Town, had been roughly ninety square kilometers; vast for the era. Enormous walls had been erected by the Earthers and their technology. They were craft of black stone and metal and nearly ten meters thick and fifteen meters tall. One stood guard over the Old Town while its twin kept a constant vigil over the black marble palace at the city's heart.

The House of Za'Car, the planet's first and current ruling family, had kept the city beautiful and flourishing, a challenging task after the destruction wrought by the Tyrant King's reign. The gem of Bakari-Tokai was the marble palace constructed in the central square amongst luscious gardens and sculpted fountains. It was outside the ebony walls of this palace that the rendezvous was set.

A tall man paced the shaded cobblestones impatiently. His face, though shaded with stubble from a two-day beard, was young with high cheekbones. It betrayed nothing of his true age. He was clad in studded leather boots and pants that had been dyed a deep, marbled chocolate. A sage-green tunic with long sleeves and hand-sewn gold embroidery was tucked in to his pants and a crisscross of studded belts held everything in place. A long vest of black leather lined with white fur kept him warm against the early spring chill.

Godilai must have been delayed, he thought as he listened to his boot heels knock against the stones. He stopped his pacing to set his crimson gaze at the obsidian tower jutting into the sky. No lights could be seen through the stained windows. That was the only good sign so far– it meant it was still too early for the guards to patrol the library level. He sighed and ran a hand through his unruly black hair, feeling some of his impatience leave him. He took to pacing again.

"Where in Havel could she be?"

"You have no idea how large the palace truly is," said a voice that came from above like wind. "And the Grand Library is much larger than we expected."

He loved her voice. It was so calming and gentle. He looked up at the woman half hidden in the dark of predawn. Her cyan gaze seemed to glow in the dark as she peered at him through long, snow-white bangs. She was a Dákun Daju, beautiful, strong, smart– deadly. Only her eyes betrayed her hardened exterior.

"You are late, Godilai."

The Dákun Daju snorted and leaped to the ground. She landed without a sound and stood to her full height—an entire meter taller than he. She wore a jet-black leather bustier and matching leggings so snug fitting they appeared to be her skin. Several belts wrapped around her hips and both thighs, holstering weapons of all sorts, which he believed to be tipped in poison. Her feet were wrapped in cloth boots that silenced her footsteps.

She pulled down the cloth mask that covered half of her face, revealing an angular face and pointed ears. Her ears helped to hold back her long, curly hair, which was half-tied up in a high tail. After a moment to observe the man, she freed a tattered book from the sack on her hip. "I only found what you sought a moment ago, Dimitri. As I said, the library was bigger than what you said it would be."

"Were you seen?" Dimitri asked as he stared at the book in her hand.

"You insult me with such a stupid question."

"You will have my apology when you turn that book over to me," Dimitri said, raising his gaze to her eyes.

Godilai smirked and tossed him the book.

"What do you need that old thing for anyway?"

Dimitri ran his fingers over the runes stamped into the leather cover. He paged through the ancient leaves. "I need better light to read this," he muttered.

Godilai scoffed and crossed her arms. "Those pages aren't in Standard. Like the cover, they are written in Kinös Elda. Even if you have the light you seek, you wouldn't be able to read it."

"And do you read these runes?" Dimitri asked, glaring at her through a black veil of hair.

Godilai shook her head. "Only few can."

"Then we must find someone who can."

The Dákun Daju sighed. "Pay me my dues, and I will take you to one who does."

"Is this…person in Bakari-Tokai?"

Godilai dipped her head in the smallest of nods. Dimitri smiled and tossed her a pouch of coin, which she caught in a flash.

"Lead the way."

The old gods now are gone,
In their place, the Five have dawned.

– FROM "THE CHANT OF SOULS"
BY PALAVANT MIRANDA

I stared at the nude woman in the large looking glass before me, committing every one of her features to memory. She could not have seen much than twenty years. She stood barely over a meter and a half tall, with dainty feet and long and shapely legs. Her skin was slightly tanned and smooth, with the exception of an angry scar which ran from below her right knee clean up to her hip. It looked so much like lightning that I wondered if she had survived being struck by a stray bolt during a storm. Her stomach was toned and flat, and her breasts were full and round. Her hair barely reached her shoulders and was straight as an arrow. It was as black as ink with blasts of an unnatural, bright red here and there. Her face was soft and unmarred, save for a beauty mark by her left eye. And it was her eyes that truly captured my attention the most. They were a rich, emerald green that shifted to sparkling gold in the middle. That verdant gaze bespoke power and betrayed a wisdom well beyond twenty years; a wisdom now secreted away from me, along with the rest of my life.

I resisted the sudden urge to punch the mirror. Not knowing anything about myself or where I had come from was far beyond frustrating. I could not even recall my own name though I had been trying all through my bath. It was there; like a fossil shrouded in dust and silt. I could feel it, so close yet so far out of reach.

With a growl, I spun away from the mirror and scanned the room the Healer had lent me. It was tiny (I could cross the space in three swift strides) and sparsely furnished; only a small bed, a dresser that had obviously seen many years of abuse, and tiny desk with a missing drawer occupied the space. There was one window, framed by iron shutters that were fit for a prison. The only blessing the room had was its own private bath. Aside from that, it was perfect for a criminal.

But I am no criminal. I thought, frowning. Then, with a sigh, I moved towards the bed, where the Healer had set the satchel and laid out garments for me. I was disappointed to realize that the clothes were a selection of underthings and the uniform of a girl student. I donned the under clothes and the grey tunic, but refused the skirt in favor of the white slacks I had woken up in. The bells started to ring as I stepped into a pair of slippers and left the room.

I stood in the hallway totally lost. Both ends of the hall looked alike, and I could not remember which way I had come from the Healers' Wing. I had expected the Healer to wait for me or at least send someone to help me navigate through the Temple's labyrinth of corridors and stairwells. Instead, I was left alone to fend for myself.

A scoff escaped me as I turned left and started walking. I would either run across someone who could guide me or I would find my own path. Either way worked for me. So I rounded the closest corner and took a flight of stairs down a level.

I was not sure how far I had walked, but the bells had long ago turned to silence. I was still navigating the halls. At last, I spotted a mosaic I had seen before. The Healers' Wing would be right around the corner.

"Are you sure it's her?" A voice I recognized as the Healer's echoed down the quiet hall. I froze, wanting to hear what he was talking about and to whom.

"I have no doubts, Adrian," came the reply. It was the voice of a woman I did not know, yet somehow it sounded familiar; like the ghost of a dream. "The resemblance is unmistakable. She is the one I have been searching for."

A silence settled over them, then voice of the Healer spoke again. "Then, you should know tha—"

The chorus of the bells swallowed their conversation, and I bid the morbid tones a thousand curses. I spent several moments straining to listen to their conversation, only to hear nothing but the cursed bells. When at last the song retreated, silence had swept through the trio.

"That does explain a few things," said the woman softly.

After a moment, another woman spoke. "Well, I am just glad—" A coughing fit suddenly overcame her. As I listened to the raspy hacking, I wished that I could do something, anything, to help ease the fit. Then it occurred to me that I did not even know the woman; why would I be so quick to help a complete stranger? Finally the coughing stopped, but it left the woman breathless.

"I wish you would let me cure you, Celestia" said the other woman.

"No, Zamora," the voice I now knew to be that of Celestia said between gulps of air. "The Gods call to me to join them in Havel. I will not prolong Their waiting with a cure for this ailment." She took a moment to clear her throat and calm her breathing. "Besides, you have lived enough for both of us, old friend."

I heard the trio chuckle lightly.

"You two had best be on your way," said Celestia. "You have an afternoon class to prepare for, Adrian, and you look weary from your travels, Zamora. I, meanwhile, have an appointment to keep. I shall see you both again for the midday meal."

Fond good-byes were murmured, and two sets of footsteps strode away. I lingered in my spot a while longer, trying to figure out what I had just overheard. Before I had even a moment to sort it all out, I heard footsteps approaching. I cursed my rotten luck at the interruption, and quickly stepped around the corner. I almost bumped noses with the Healer, who gave a surprised yelp at my sudden appearance.

"Oh! You startled me," he said, placing a hand over his heart and breathing deeply.

I muttered an apology.

He nodded. "Sorry I was not waiting for you when you finished your bath. I had a quick meeting to attend, but I am glad to see that you found your own way back. I see you do not like skirts though." He put on a goofy grin. "That's alright; I can get you a boy's uniform a bit later. For now though, it is best that I get you to the Palavant. She is eager to meet with you. Are you ready?"

I said I was, though in truth I had no desire to. I just wanted to be left alone to figure things out. I needed to know who I was, yet I found myself quietly falling in step behind the Healer as he turned around to go back the way he had come. We passed before a door marked with the green crescent – the Healers' Wing – and took the stairs down. We turned at the landing and made the final descent unto the ground floor of the Temple. Then the Healer turned left and traced a trail over a floor of enameled tiles. The clay blocks had been laid out in a mesmerizing, flowery pattern of bronze and black and cream with a splash of turquoise to form tiny accent pieces. As we walked to the end of the hall, I admired the pattern and wondered how patient the Temple's architect must have been to see it laid properly.

"I am not certain how long the Palavant intends to speak with you," the Healer said as he stopped. I looked up from the wondrous floor to see that we stood outside a pair of large doors. They had both been stained dark chocolate, but a wash of gold made the doors sparkle beneath a silver pentacle crest. "Anyway," the Healer smiled at me, "I have classes to teach starting next period so I won't be free to help you through the Temple. I will be sending one of my students to meet up with you though."

"Alright," I replied and stepped up to the doors.

"I shall see you at the midday meal." With that, the Healer walked briskly away. I watched him until he disappeared up the staircase. I turned back to the doors, knocked thrice. One of the doors creaked open, and an extremely tall girl with violet hair tied in several braids stared at me. Her rose-colored gaze was intense and cold, and her angled face betrayed no emotion. It was as if she were stone.

After a moment, she opened the door wider and moved aside. I stepped over the threshold and took in the office of the Palavant. The floor was more of those enameled tiles from the hall, only this time the pattern was more subtle. To the left, a marble hearth was alive with a roaring fire that made the room uncomfortably hot. Knick knacks and a glass time piece decorated the mantle. Large windows covered most of the wall opposite the door. Thick, gray curtains blocked out the light of the suns, and dancing shadows filled the room. The remaining wall space was decorated with a variety of tapestries and paintings and shelves with leather-bound tomes. An oversized, mahogany desk with intricate scroll work was situated opposite the hearth. Behind the desk, in a high-back chair that reminded me of a throne, sat an old woman who I figured was the Palavant. She was clad in white robes that had been embellished with golden embroidery and jewels. She looked pale and sickly, but her hazel eyes seemed to sparkle with the mischief of a youth. Something in those eyes felt familiar; as if we had met before when she was much, much younger.

At her elbow stood a woman of about thirty years. Her skin was the same rich chocolate color as her hair, and her eyes were strikingly blue. Her robes were simple and black and decorated with the stole of her fellow priests. In fact, I would have mistaken her for an ordinary priestess if not for the lace collar she wore. It looked to be made of platinum, but the way it settled over her shoulders told me that it was fabric; a rarity called moon silk. It was an expensive accessory.

How in Havel could I know that? I asked myself.

The old woman's gaze shifted from me to the strange girl by the door. "Thank you for your report, Zhealocera. We will definit –" a severe coughing fit stole her words away. It took the old woman several minutes to overcome the assault. The younger of the two was hard pressed to make sure her senior drank a tonic after the coughs died away. When at last she could breathe again, the Palavant thanked the rose-cyed girl – Zhealocera – once more. "We will definitely look into making the security changes you recommended, especially with the High Prince Valaskjalf coming for the Festival of the Phoenix."

The girl gave only a ghost of a nod, then strode from the room.

"Dákun Daju," said the Palavant with a half smile. "They are neither overly friendly nor full of words, but they are dedicated to what they do."

"Is she the only one at the Temple?" I asked, glimpsing the door she had passed through.

"Her cousin, the Queen of Katalania, paid her entire tuition upfront," replied the priestess in black. "Zhealocera has dreams of becoming the first Dákun Daju in history to be a Lady Knight of the Dragonsworn Brigade, and to do that required an education from this Temple."

"Another stupid rule of our racist High King," the Palavant muttered. "He would do everything in his power to ensure that anyone who is not a Hume cannot serve the royal family or be privy to military tactics. Little does he know that his son will be under the protection of a Dákun Daju while he's here."

"When is this High Prince due to arrive?"

The priestess in black looked at me like she could not believe what she was hearing. "The Phoenix rises in four days' time. He will be here before that time."

"Phoenix…" I whispered, and my dream came back to me in a flash. The strange words spoken to me in a spectral whisper echoed in my mind. It was a warning. Something terrible was going to happen.

"So," the Palavant began and I was yanked out of my reverie, "I had heard that you have no memory, not even your name or family. Is this true?"

I stiffly nodded.

"I am afraid the only help I can offer you in this case is your name. I hope it will serve as a stepping stone as you work towards discovering yourself completely."

"So we have met before."

Her silver eyebrow curved upwards. "You remember me?"

"No." I shook my head for emphasis. "I know you are the Palavant because I was told, and when I look into your eyes, I feel like we have met before, but it is like looking at a dream of a dream shrouded in heavy fog."

The Palavant nodded in understanding. "In that case, I am Palavant Celestia the Third. This Archbishop beside me is Matron Serenitatis. And you, my dear, are Xyleena, a Daughter of the Temple."

Xyleena. I silently repeated, and a swell of excitement filled me. The largest of the many puzzle pieces had finally slipped into place. Perhaps with this knowledge, I could begin to fill in the rest of the mystery. Still, something she said was nagging me. "What exactly is a Daughter of the Temple?"

"It is a title given to orphan girls who have taken the vows to live as priestesses of the Five Souls" said Matron Serenitatis. "Many of them take up the road to become traveling priests, who spread the word of the Gods to towns and villages without a proper Temple. Some of them even return to their home towns to become part of the existing parish or to establish one."

I am Xyleena. I am a priestess. I repeated that chant to myself, then aloud said, "So, since I am a Daughter, that means I am an orphan?"

A strange look flashed across the Palavant's face. It lasted for only an instant, but I could tell she was hiding something as she spoke. "I am afraid that I cannot be certain of your parentage or origins, Xyleena. Perhaps if you were to meditate in the Sanctuary of Zahadu-Kitai, you will find the answers you seek. You might also remember more about yourself if you attend some of the classes here. If you would like, I can certainly schedule you in for lessons."

I did not have to think long on that choice. What better way was there of learning about a world you no longer knew? So the Palavant and Matron sent me away with a list of classes offered by the Temple. I told them that I would have my selections made by the end of the mid-day meal.

With that, my meeting with the Palavant ended.

It has been said that, in his search for retribution, Agasei looked upon the face of Wind and, there, found inspiration.
– FROM "A TYRANT'S HUMANITY"
BY PRINCESS UNÉ SHARVÍN

Dimitri sat in a secluded corner booth and stared out a window at the midday commotion. The citizens of the city were always worrying about meager things in their petty lives. This was something he hoped to soon rectify. With a sigh, he moved his crimson gaze to his surroundings.

Godilai had led him to a small tavern called Luna's then left him to find someone who could read the ancient runes of Kinös Elda. Oddly enough, as he studied his rustic surroundings, he saw the runes carved into the woodwork. There were too many people present for him to investigate the embossed wood. So he sat. And he waited.

A fight suddenly erupted amongst a trio of drunkards. Dimitri watched them roll about on the floor exchanging blows. They spun under another drunk and knocked him off his feet, turning a three-way brawl into a free for all. Dimitri watched, entertained, as the drunken patrons fought each other. Other customers managed to escape the frenzy of flying limbs as the fistfight turned into an armed battle. One of the drunks who started the fight screamed in agony and rage as the sword of another severed his hand.

"Nan dasai nevoa!" The voice of a young woman rose above the shouts and swearing.

Almost immediately, the combatants were caught in a thick, black fog. They stopped fighting and danced around, unable to see. Dimitri's gaze was drawn to the Dákun Daju woman standing in the doorway. He could not tell what color her eyes were over the distance between them, but her face betrayed rage. Magenta hair fell like water over her shoulders and covered but a small section of the sheath of a sword wider than the length of Dimitri's own forearm. Like every Dákun Daju, she was clad in armor that consisted of a blood red leather bustier and snug-fitting burgundy leggings, both of which were adorned with overlapping plates of flat black steel. Leather bands around both of her muscular biceps and thighs sheathed a number of throwing knives. She wore cloth boots to silence her footsteps and allow her to move silently, thus telling Dimitri that she—like Godilai—worked as an assassin.

"All of you, out of my bar this instant!" she roared.

Dimitri snorted. He was not about to leave, no matter what kind of death that Dákun Daju threatened him with. He watched as she stepped aside to kick the drunks out. When the last of them was sent rolling in the dirt, Godilai entered. She looked amused at the antics of her fellow clansmen. The two of them spoke for a moment before Godilai pointed in Dimitri's direction. He took this as his cue and strode toward the two Dákun Daju.

"This is the Hume I spoke of. Dimitri, this is Luna Graves."

"It is a pleasure to meet you," Dimitri said, exposing his throat in the honorary display of Dákun Daju greeting. He looked into Luna's stark-white eyes.

Luna crossed her arms as she spoke. "How is it you came to be schooled in our ways, Hume?"

"My mother was Dákun Daju. She raised me."

Luna snickered. "A Hume-aju."

Dimitri resisted the urge to rise to the insult.

"So, what is this relic you wanted me to read for you?"

"Dimitri paid me to scrounge the Grand Library for some ancient book," Godilai explained, taking a seat at the nearest table. "As it turns out, the cursed thing is written in the ancient form of Kinös Eldic runes."

Luna quirked an eyebrow at Dimitri. "You want me to read a book to you?" She unstrapped the gigantic sword from her back and sat opposite Godilai. She propped her feet up on the seat next to her and sneered at Dimitri. "How much are you paying?"

He expected that. "How much are you asking?"

"Let's say…two thousand bits." Luna watched as Dimitri weighed the leather pouch at his belt.

"Make it one thousand bits."

"Fifteen hundred."

"Twelve."

"Done." Luna held her hand out.

Dimitri took a minute to count out twelve gold-plated coins then slid them across the table to her.

Her long fingers curled around the pile. "And just where is this old book?"

Dimitri gingerly laid the book on the table before him. "This is it."

"Interesting…" Luna lowered her feet from the chair and turned the book toward her. Her fingers brushed the embossed runes of the cover. "Meo Resuko. My Diary."

"You paid me to steal a diary from the library of the high king?" Godilai shot a look at Dimitri. "I thought you said this book was a source of great power. Now it's just a stupid diary?"

"If you would give her a chance to actually read what the diary says, you will learn just how special it really is." Dimitri finally took the seat next to Godilai. "Please, Luna, continue."

Luna flipped through a few pages during the silence that followed. Many of the runes had long ago faded into the aged and brittle parchment. With a sigh, she returned to the first page.

"Meo namae wa Agasei DéDos. Esté buko wa meo resuko, bó et tel né rité sterim et Kohnbín Nírigone."

Godilai looked at Dimitri. "Et Kohnbín Nírigone?"

Luna looked up from the page. "This book was written by Agasei himself. He says it is the key to finding the Shadow Dragons."

"See, Godilai?" Dimitri smirked at her. "This stupid diary is the key to the Shadow Dragons and ultimate power."

"You plan to release the Shadow Dragons from the gate?" Godilai faced him with a cold stare, but her cyan eyes betrayed amazement.

"I thought only the Dragon Keepers or their heirs could control the dragons," Luna said, looking into Dimitri's eyes.

He smirked in response.

"How did you even know about this book to begin with?"

"My mother told me about it as she lay dying from a wound caused by a Hume's blade." Dimitri's hands slowly turned to fists at the memory of his mother's death. "I swore to her that I would find my father's diary and have my revenge on the entire Hume race."

"Your...father?"

"Agasei is your father?"

Dimitri looked at the two women. "Yes."

"But the Dark Keeper died over four hundred years ago," said Godilai. "How could you be his son?"

"Immortals cannot die. My father is merely entombed and locked away, maybe beyond the Dragons' Gate, as well. And I"– Dimitri's eyes glinted mischievously– " am four hundred and thirty-two years old."

"Impossible!" Godilai hissed.

"It is more than possible." Dimitri growled. "The dragons are immortal and through them so is my father and anyone in his bloodline. I have seen the ages come and go. I have lived things that have long been history. And I have spent the last century searching for this diary. Finally, I have found it! And with it I shall unleash the Shadow Dragons."

"And just how do you plan to do that?" Luna asked, looking up from the page she had been reading.

"With that diary, that's how," Dimitri answered, glaring at her.

Luna sighed and pointed to a line on the page.

"Agasei did not write this."

Dimitri leaned in to read the green ink scribed in the margin of a page.

He knows not where the Dark are hidden.
The key lies with Amorez, written.

"What?" Dimitri roared.

Godilai snatched the diary away from Luna and read the ink for herself. "It is in standard...and the ink is centuries fresher than the rest. I wonder who could have written that."

"I can't believe..." Dimitri slumped back in his seat. Guilt settled heavily over him and he sighed in defeat. The promise he made to his dying mother would now be nothing but empty words. "After all those centuries of searching, my own father's diary turns out to be absolutely useless."

"Well, it is not completely useless, Dimitri. After all, it did tell you that the key to finding your father's dragons does not lie within these pages." Said Luna with a half shrug. "You will just have to find the key Amorez had."

Dimitri shook his head, disheartened.

"Watch, it will be another diary," Godilai muttered, shoving the book away.

Realization struck him like a ton of bricks and he exclaimed, "Godilai, you are a genius!"

She looked at him coolly. "Yeah, and your point is?"

"Amorez kept her own diary as well. I am certain that if the key to the Shadow Dragons is hidden with Amorez as that little riddle states, her diary is where we will find the route to the Dragons' Gate."

"Hold on there." Luna said, moving Agassi's diary off the table. "Even if Amorez actually kept a diary of her own, where would she have hidden it? I don't know about you two, but I do not want to spend the next century looking for it."

Dimitri scoffed. "I doubt either of you would live that long anyway." He raised his hand to silence Godilai's retort. "And I know for a fact that Amorez kept a diary, as well. During my search for my father's, I found many records that mentioned Amorez's handwritten account of the events leading to the rise and fall of the Dragon Keepers. However, the records never gave a specific description or location of where the diary might be found."

"You did not happen to see any books similar to this one in the Grand Library, did you, Godilai-sortim?" Luna asked.

Godilai shook her head. "I did not really have the time to look, but there were many ancient-looking, leather-bound books."

"Curse it all." Luna sighed. "Where else besides the Grand Palace could we find an expansive library that would include ancient texts?"

"I have been in pretty much every library in the world except the Grand Library and the Temple of Five Souls," Dimitri replied. "Though some of the books in those libraries are old, not one of them is written in Kinös Eldic runes."

"I'll bet ten million bits that Amorez's diary is in the Temple of Five Souls." Godilai banged her hand on the table for emphasis.

"Why do you say that, Godilai-sortim?"

"Do you not remember any of the old tales, Luna? Amorez was a Temple Monk. It would only make sense that she would hide her diary in the one place she would call home."

Dimitri frowned. "The Temple Priests do not allow just anyone to search their rare books. I have petitioned for access at least a hundred times in the last four hundred years, and not once was I granted permission. So how do you propose we gain access?"

Dimitri rubbed his temple, feeling a headache coming on. He had spent the last few hours reviewing the layout of the Temple of Five Souls. His Dákun Daju companions shot down one idea after another. Forcing their way into the

Temple library was now completely out of the question. The security of the Temple was dwarfed only by the security around the ruling family.

Impersonating traveling priests would not work either. The Dákun Daju– or anyone appearing as one– would never be granted access to the rarest books. If not for his crimson eyes, Dimitri might have attempted that. What other options did they have?

"Any other ideas?" Godilai asked, sounding bored.

A sudden trumpeting from outside interrupted the meeting. Luna leaped over the table they were seated at and raced to the door. She pulled it open and stood in the doorway as another blast of trumpeting sounded.

"What is that ruckus?" Dimitri growled.

Godilai joined Luna in the doorway. "The high prince is on parade. I wonder what he's showing off this time."

"Aside from his gold wyvern? Nothing." Dimitri leaned back in his seat. "The so-called high prince is a joke. If my father was still the high king, the-"

"That is it!" Luna exclaimed.

"What is it?"

"I know how just to get into the Temple. But it will take some acting on your part, Hume-aju." Luna grinned and turned to face Dimitri.

He cocked an eyebrow in question.

"Yes. Yes." Luna's grin widened the longer she looked at him. "The resemblance is uncanny."

"What resemblance?"

"Dimitri, do you not recall that the high prince has been scheduled to appear at the Temple of Five Souls for the Festival of the Phoenix?" Luna's exclamation took both Dimitri and Godilai by surprise. "And you look almost exactly like Valaskjalf. All you would need is a haircut, an armed royal escort, and a gold wyvern. You could walk right into the Temple!"

Dimitri crossed his arms. "There is a flaw in your plan, Luna. Where do we find this armed royal escort? Prison?"

"How much money do you have?" Luna asked, sealing the door with a slam as another blast from the trumpets sounded.

Dimitri snickered. "Enough. Why?"

The Dákun Daju pointed her thumb towards the door. "There is a Judge out there, probably riding with the prince. He'll get you an army if you pay him enough."

"And exactly how much is enough?" Godilai asked, glancing out the window.

A burly, old soldier paced between the houses. He was short, balding, red-faced, and atrocious. His plain, plate and chain armor was marred with old signs of combat and an enormous axe was strapped to his back.

Godilai's lip curled in disgust. "Disgusting Hume."

"They all are," Dimitri muttered.

"So says the Hume-aju." Luna smirked when Dimitri's growl reached her ears. "So, are you going to buy him, or should we forget about those Shadow Dragons?"

Dimitri sighed. "Very well. Bring him here."

Luna jerked the door open. "Hey! Ugly!"

"Brilliant, Luna," Godilai muttered, trying hard not to laugh.

Dimitri, on the other hand, was almost doubled over with laughter. A moment later, the old Judge barreled into Luna's tavern. Luna back flipped out of the way to avoid being bowled over. The fat man roared in rage and reeled around to swing his giant axe at Luna. She caught the blade between her fingers and smirked.

"You are pretty quick for an old man."

"And you are soon to be one dead Dákun Daju whore!"

Luna's white eyes narrowed dangerously, all amusement wiped from her expression. She released her hold on the axe blade and rolled away as the Judge swung. Luna jumped up on the bar only to back flip over the Judge's head. She found her giant sword and unsheathed it in time to block a blow from the axe. She pushed against the weight of the fat Judge, forcing him to slide back across the floorboards with a harsh squeak.

"You're not just ugly. You're weak!" Luna shouted. She shifted the force of her sword and caused the Judge to fall backward. Luna moved her sword to rest its blade at his jawbone "And I am not a whore."

The blade of the axe crashed into the wooden floorboards, sending splinters flying. Dimitri shifted his crimson gaze from the golden axe to the pinned Judge, then to Godilai. She had not moved during the scuffle. He doubted that she would have even bothered to assist Luna. He knew he would not. Luna was far stronger than any Hume and could handle herself perfectly fine against one old Judge.

Dimitri sighed and returned his gaze to the Judge. "Let him up, Luna. Now that you're done playing, we have work to do."

"Playing?" The Judge's deep baritone vibrated the hairs of his overgrown mustache.

"If she had been serious, you would not be living," Godilai said, sitting at the table she previously vacated.

Luna sheathed her sword with a scoff and sat opposite her clansman.

"Then there must be a reason why you let me live."

"What is your name, Judge?" Dimitri asked.

The old Judge found his footing at last and managed to stand. "I am Vincent DuCayne, one of the commanders of High Prince Valaskjalf's Dragonsworn Battalion. And you would be who?" The Judge gripped the handle of his axe.

Dimitri smirked. "I am Dimitri DéDos, son of the Keeper, Agasei, and heir to the twelve Shadow Dragons."

Vincent's blimp of a face somehow formed a frown. "What do you take me for? Agasei had no son, and if he did, the boy would have died of old age centuries ago."

"That would be true if I was not made immortal through my father's blood." Dimitri looked into Vincent's hazel eyes and saw the obvious distrust. "All right. Since you still do not believe me, how is this for proof: In the year

AR sixty-seven, there was a war between a city of Dákun Daju and a large battalion of Humes. Though the war lasted just three months, both sides lost thousands. Among the fallen was a Dákun Daju woman named Solahnj, who had a son. When Solahnj died, the boy brought the Dákun Daju forces together and led them in a slaughter of most of the remaining Hume soldiers."

"Yeah, I read about that massacre in school. So what?"

"So, the boy who led the Dákun Daju to victory was me."

The Judge still looked as skeptical as ever. "That is not possible."

Dimitri sighed in frustration. "How about we make a deal, Vincent? Assist me in proving my birthright to the world by finding and freeing the Shadow Dragons, and it will be within my power to give you anything you have ever wanted."

"Anything?"

Dimitri nodded at the inquiry.

"Money? Power? Women?"

"Yes."

"So…" Vincent released his axe, "what is your plan?"

"Luna, will you please fill him in on your idea." Dimitri smiled and joined the duo of Dákun Daju at the table.

"Four days from now is the Festival of the Phoenix. Since Prince Valaskjalf will be attending the festival, it is the perfect opportunity for us to sneak into the Temple to retrieve a particularly important artifact. We will have Dimitri here impersonate the high prince so we can have access to the Temple's rare books room. We need you, Hume, to pretend Dimitri is your prince."

Vincent rubbed his chin. "I'm curious as to how you intend to take the high prince's place. He travels with troops from the Dragonsworn, all of whom ride fighting wyverns."

"You command the Dragonsworn, do you not?" Godilai asked.

"Only a small brigade. About one hundred men."

"That should be more than enough." Dimitri nodded. "We will waylay the prince's escort during his trek to the Temple. Your men will do nothing or face death by Dákun Daju blades. We will proceed to the Temple in the prince's stead. The question for you, Vincent, is what road will Valaskjalf take when he and his escort ride out?"

Vincent answered after a pause. "He is to ride a-wyvernback via the main road to Sindai then take the ferry to the Temple island."

"Good." Dimitri untied the leather pouch from his belt and tossed it to Vincent. "That is just a taste of the wealth you will obtain when I rise to my birthright."

Vincent opened the pouch and dumped the pile of gold coins in his hand. He smiled. "You are most generous, my Prince."

My father once told me that the habits of evil men are their own undoing. It is because of this wisdom, that I know we are going to succeed. We will save this planet.

– FROM "CONVERSATIONS WITH AMOREZ"
BY DJURDAK ZA'CAR

The Palavant's door clicked shut behind me. I stood in the hallway, facing a smiling boy and the cool and aloof Dákun Daju, Zhealocera. The two looked like they were practically polar opposites. She was taller than him by head and shoulders and half a torso, which put him at just about my height. He had a dull brown mop of curly hair that fell into his chestnut colored eyes and his skin was a pale peach in color. Zhealocera was as skinny as a rail, while he had a bit more meat on his bones. They both wore matching school uniforms, but the badges on their collars were different. Her collar was emblazoned with a sword and blazing sun while his depicted a triangle with an eye in the center.

The boy was the first to act, stepping closer to me and extending a hand for me to shake. "Good morning. My name is Ríhan. Healer Adrian sent me to help you find your way through the Temple."

I slowly reached out and shook his hand, and all the while wondered where I had heard his name before. Then it occurred to me, The Healer mentioned that a boy from the Temple had discovered me washed up on the shore. This must be him. "I am Xyleena."

"Nice to meet you, Xyleena. This here is Zhealocera," Ríhan said as he pointed his thumb at her. "She is a Dákun Daju, and generally not very talkative."

Her rose colored eyes fixed on the back of his head, as if her icy glare would smack him upside the head if she stared long enough. He smirked as if sensing her gaze upon him, but did not turn to face her.

"So, do you have any thoughts on where you would like to begin your tour?"

I produced the scroll that the Matron had given me. It contained a list of all the classes offered at the Temple. "Can you help me with this?"

His chestnut gaze flicked over the rolled up scroll. "Choosing classes, eh? That must mean you plan on sticking around here for a while. Do you know what job caste you would like to join?"

"No."

"Oh." He frowned briefly, but his smile came right back in full force. "How about interests? Do you like the arts? Or perhaps healing? Maybe you are more into a quiet life of a Philosopher."

I caught Zhealocera rolling her eyes at that.

Ríhan went on dreamily, "Nothing beats sitting in a quiet room reading the ancient texts and learning all about the little details of history that no one ever pays attention to."

"That is your ideal profession," muttered Zhealocera in a voice laced with boredom. Her rose colored eyes shifted to me, and I could almost feel her chilly gaze inspecting every millimeter from head to toe. At last she said, "She has the eyes and posture of a warrior who has seen much battle, not the appearance of one bent over ancient tomes with long faded words."

I look like a warrior? I thought. But that does not make any sense. The Palavant had just got done telling me that I was a traveling priestess; not a battling one. Though, if I really was a warrior, that would explain the grim thoughts I had earlier this morning about how easy an attack on this Temple would be.

Zhealocera must have read the confusion on my face for she asked, "How much of yourself do you remember?"

Her words pricked Ríhan's curiosity, and the smile on his lips faded to a look of concern. When I quietly admitted to knowing nothing of my past except what little the Palavant had revealed, the odd pair looked at each other for a moment, then returned their attention to me.

Ríhan's smile was back. "Then we will just have to help you remember."

"I have an idea that may be of assistance to you," replied Zhealocera. She had my full attention in an instant. "I suggest signing up for classes such as: zoology, to learn the creatures of this world; geography, to learn the lands and people; runic studies, so that you can be sure to read; definitely history, for obvious reasons; and make sure to sign up for martial combat. I can tell that you have been in battle, so perhaps sparring with a worthy opponent will jog some of the memories you are missing."

"That is only five classes, Zheal," Ríhan piped in. "She needs at least six to have a full schedule with an off hour; seven if she does not want a break. I would suggest something spiritual, such as theology, especially since you mentioned that the Palavant had named you a Daughter of the Temple. As a priestess, you should definitely know about the Five Souls. Though I would recommend having that class scheduled at the end of your school day. Most of the priests and priestesses in charge are dull and tend to drone on.

"And if you want a really fun elective subject for your seventh class, I would suggest astronomy. For three nights out of each seven-day, you can go out to the astrolabe and learn about all the star constellations in the sky and planets in the Rishai System. It is a fun class that starts about an hour after dusk and lasts about two to three hours."

Zhealocera shook her head. "I will never understand you Humes and your obsession with the sky and naming everything. This planet, its twin, and the three moons did not even have names before your ancestors arrived. After their landing, everything had names; even a rock formation in the desert was given a name."

"Naming things makes it easier for us to reference or picture in our heads, and understand," Ríhan said with a shrug. "Besides, Dákun Daju name things; their cities for one. True, the names are more descriptions, such as the City of Long Winters or the City of Thundering Falls and my personal favorite the legendary City of Thieves, but it is generally the same concept."

Zhealocera fixed Ríhan with an icy stare but did not reply.

"So," Ríhan clapped his hands together and rubbed them as if warming them over a fire, "where would you like to begin your tour of the school?"

I had almost forgotten about that. "I am not sure, but I was told there is a leatherer here that can craft me a new pack. I would like to stop there."

"Ergen's workshop is next door to my martial combat class, which I must attend after the next bells sound," said Zhealocera. "Perhaps you would like to start there; meet with Enforcer Maaz, and decide if his class would be appropriate for helping to return your memories of your glorious battles to you."

Ríhan shuddered. "You Dákun Daju and your love of fighting."

"It is in the heat of battle that the true character of a man or woman can be discovered and judged." The words escaped me before I had even realized it. Ríhan was taken aback while Zhealocera nodded approvingly. Without a word, the Dákun Daju spun on her heel and strode away.

"I will give you one thing, Xyleena," Ríhan said as he and I started down the hall after Zhealocera, "you are full of surprises."

The mid-day bells had sung their dismal chorus only moments ago. Ríhan and I stood with our backs were to the northernmost wall of the massive dining hall. The two of us had been the first to arrive in the hall, as if his guided tour had been planned that way. I had asked him about his timing, and he had laughed and said it was purely luck that we happened to be passing the dining hall just before the mid-day bells rang out.

We were at the very end of a long row of tables and farthest from the double doors that led to a main hallway (the best spot to sit according to Ríhan). In front of us were four more rows of tables, identical to the one we were situated at. To my immediate left was a pair of smaller round tables, which were set up around a pentagram-shaped stage that housed a single round table. Two more round tables stood on the south side of the stage, mirroring the pair closer to me. Each table had already been dressed and set for the mid-day meal, and the silver glinted with the light of the suns that filtered through the overhead windows.

Another stage, a little higher than the pentagram-shaped one was against the wall opposite the main doors. It stretched the width of the room and was wide enough for three people to walk abreast. An enormous hearth stood atop the stage and fixed to the wall. A trio of tapestries depicting water and ice hugged the white stone walls behind it. Pass-through windows with wide, marble counters sat on either side of the mantle. The false walls that had been down when Ríhan and I strode in were now up, and I could barely make out parts of the kitchen beyond. The kitchen drudges were beginning to move the heavy platters from the counters to the tables. There was fruit and greens, roast meats and fresh-baked bread, and drinks and desserts. The mix of spices and seasonings and sweet glazes made my mouth water in anticipation.

"Technically speaking," Ríhan muttered as the room began to fill with students and teachers and priests, "since you are a Daughter of the Temple, you should be at one of the round tables closer to the Palavant's stage, not here at the rows with the students who have not graduated yet."

"Should I move?" I asked as I watched everyone file into the room. I had been looking for Zhealocera; instead I found that strange woman that I had crossed paths with outside the Healers' Wing earlier this morning. She still donned the white cloak affixed with the sigil of a golden hammer and wreath of silver olive branches.

I saw Ríhan shrug out of the corner of my eye. "You can if you want to. I would do it soon though; once the Palavant enters, you won't be able to switch."

"You see that lady with the red hair and white cloak?"

"The Judge? Sure. What about her?"

Judge. That is what rank the sigil on her cloak stood for. My eyes were glued to her as she moved across the room. I lost her momentarily as a group of students rushed past her, but she reappeared at the round table that had been set on the stage.

Ríhan continued, "It is very rare to see a Judge here at the Temple. Most of them are situated in Bakari-Tokai or other major cities, where they work in tandem with Enforcers as upholders of the High King's laws. Why are you so interested in her?"

I forced myself to look away from the woman. "I have seen her twice already, and both times I got the distinct feeling that I know her."

"Maybe you do," he offered. "After all, you knew the Palavant, but you had no recollection of that. Perhaps you do know the honored Judge. If that is true, then she may be able to help fill in some of the missing pieces."

My muttered response was swallowed by the chorus of bells. Students and teachers and priests alike all rushed to their places, and stood patiently behind their chairs or benches. Silence descended upon the room as the last, echoing bong died away. After what felt like an eternity to an empty stomach like mine, Palavant Celestia strode in through the double door entrance. Matron Serenitatis and an Archbishop were right beside her, helping to guide her through the rows of tables and up to her honored seat atop the pentagram-shaped stage. After she was seated and comfortable, she lifted a tiny silver bell from the table in front of her and jingled it.

The entire room exploded with noise movement. I had barely a moment to sink onto the bench beside Ríhan when one of the drudges handed me a large platter leaden with meats. Ríhan was quick to spear a good selection of the slices for both of us before I was forced to pass the platter along. A deep bowl of creamy, mashed tubers followed the meat. Then a bowl of mixed vegetables. Then a platter of breads, and then another platter, and another. When at last the plates and bowls ceased coming, I discovered that a mountain of food had covered my plate. As hungry as I was, I was not so sure I could eat all of it.

I must have been looking at the heap in awe for Ríhan started to chuckle.

"Make sure you save room for dessert."

I shot him a look that hopefully relayed my dismay. He just laughed harder.

The room quieted as mouths were put to work chewing and drinking. After a while, the conversation started picking up again. The boy sitting in front of Ríhan leaned in to ask, "Hey, Ríhan, can you help me with my Kinös Elda homework? I'm having troubles with the possessives."

"Ah." Ríhan nodded in understanding. "Possessives are a cinch. I can show you a few examples during your study hour today."

"What is Kinös Elda?" I asked.

The boy across the table looked at me in shock, like he could not believe what he had just heard. Ríhan, on the other hand, smiled and said, "Kinös Elda, or Nature Tongue, is a very rare language today, but in the times of the Earthic Landings, it was originally developed in order to communicate with the Dákun Daju, and later used by the Sorcerers for magic."

"Can you speak it?"

Ríhan nodded, "Speak it and read it. Fluency in Kinös Elda is a requirement for graduating to the rank of Philosopher. I am in my fifth year of study, so I am able to help students like Timney, who is in his first year."

"I would love to hear this strange language."

"Meoja rité ker chiiripan tehr zāto," said Ríhan, then he translated. "We will have pie for dessert." And pointed at a kitchen drudge, who was making her way over to me with a huge platter full of tiny pies. Before I could move to assist her with her load, she sat the platter on the edge of the table. The pies were quickly dispersed along the row, then another drudge with more pies arrived.

As I indulged in the fruity sweetness, I thought about Ríhan's quick blurt of Kinös Elda. It reminded me of the words spoken to me by the phoenix in my dream. Try as I might, I could not remember the long string of words, but I did recall something from that dream.

"Does 'tabiki ni heile' mean anything?"

Ríhan licked the fruit syrup off his fingers as he looked at me. "Yeah, it means 'wall of fire.' Where did you hear that?"

Before I could answer, the Palavant stood and rang her silver bell. Silence quickly swept the dining hall, and I dared only to whisper, "In a dream."

"I have a special announcement this afternoon," the Palavant's voice, though hoarse, echoed off the stone walls of the hall. "A visit from the High Prince, Valaskjalf, has been confirmed. He shall be here with soldiers of the Dragonsworn in time for the Festival of the Phoenix. Because the High Prince's visit is a rare treat for this Temple, chores will be assigned to each dorm in order to make preparations. Each dorm's deacon will be given a list of those chores, so please see them later today for the assignments. For any questions or concerns, please speak with Matron Serenitatis.

"Enforcer Maaz has had to leave suddenly for a family emergency, so his classes will be overseen by a very…" she paused, searching for the right word to use, "unique substitute. I expect all students and staff here to treat her with the respect she deserves."

I glanced at the faces of everyone at the round tables, looking longest at the white-cloaked Judge. The strangely familiar woman was chuckling lightly at the Palavant's words. I guessed that the Judge knew the substitute of whom the Palavant was speaking.

"Lastly," my attention was torn away from the Judge as the Palavant spoke again, "Professor Urgeon has asked me to remind everyone that glasshouse plots will be coming available later in the spring for anyone interested in starting their own garden this year. Please speak to her if you would like to reserve one." After a moment's pause, the Palavant raised her silver bell and jingled it lightly. The dismal bonging of the Temple's larger bells immediately tore through the silence. As if one mind, students and staff rose to their feet and began to file out of the dining hall.

Ríhan paused just long enough to speak to me, "I have classes that I must attend now, so that means you are left to your own devices. Perhaps you should visit one of the Gods' altars. They might be able to help you find who you are. Oh! And don't forget to pick up your new pack from Ergen's Leatherworks."

He was gone before I could thank him. I sat in my spot on the bench and watched as he and the others quickly vanished through the large double doors. When the thunder of footsteps finally faded into silence, I sighed. The sound seemed to echo in the vastness of the room and I was once again reminded of my dream and of the strange book in my possession. Perhaps Ríhan was right; I should visit the altars of the Gods for answers... If only I wasn't so afraid to.

Dimitri was glad for the suns' rising. Their warm light melted the frost that had overtaken the petite camp in the night. The air grew warmer and, at last, he could stop shivering. He and his two companions did not dare to start a fire. The blaze and smoke would give away their position to anyone wandering the road. As a result, they were reduced to eating hard bread and salted pork for breakfast. Dimitri grumbled about the conditions as he ate.

Godilai and Luna chose to ignore him. Godilai lounged in a tree, keeping her cyan eyes on the road for any travelers. She whittled a bone as she kept her silent sigil, an act Dimitri thought rather macabre. He wondered where the bone had come from, and what Godilai's steady hands were turning it into.

Luna asked Dimitri's question before he could. "Where did you get the bone?"

He listened to the answer, intrigued.

"It is the jaw bone of the last Hume I killed." Godilai's voice was just above a whisper.

Dimitri swallowed past the lump in his throat. Why was he so afraid of that woman? He had faced many foes in battle and never once showed fear, much less felt any. So why did Godilai have such a power over him?

He dared a glance at her. Long, shapely legs covered by snug, black leathers crossed at her ankles. Her back was straight, even as she leaned against the tree trunk. His gaze lingered at her breasts, and he felt heat rush to his face. His gaze rose to her face. It was soft and angular, half hidden by hair as white as snow and framed by her pointed ears. She really was beautiful.

Her cyan eyes met his. It was a look so powerful it made his blood boil. Dimitri suddenly realized why he reacted to her so strangely. He was in love with Godilai.

Her gaze returned to the road, and she smirked. She leaped from the tree and gathered her swords. Dimitri followed her example and reached for his weapon.

"Here they come," she whispered. "Luna, take the other side."

"I wonder how many of his men will attack us," Dimitri whispered as he saw Luna vanish into the bushes on the opposite side of the road.

"If that fat Hume did his job correctly, none." Godilai sunk into a crouch as she waited for the escort to draw closer. "However, I doubt this fight will be that easy."

"Agreed."

They lapsed into silence as the wyvern riders drew near. Vincent was in the middle beside the high prince. As expected, prince Valaskjalf was astride a gold wyvern and covered in golden armor. With a single link from his armor, a slave could buy his way to freedom. And Dimitri would soon wear the same armor—the perfect disguise.

Dimitri breathed slowly and loosened his muscles. He counted the soldiers—three against sixty. He had faced worse odds. This battle would be over quickly, however. They only needed to worry about the gilded prince. Godilai whistled a bird's song. Luna answered. As one, the three of them burst from their camouflage. The soldiers shouted in confusion, and their wyverns stumbled. Dimitri streaked passed them. His target was the prince.

Many of the soldiers realized what was happening and forced their wyverns under control. They watched as Dimitri charged the prince. Valaskjalf unsheathed his sword and prepared to defend himself. He noticed that only five of his escort joined him against their attackers. All five were quickly dispatched, leaving Valaskjalf to battle alone.

"Surrender, Valaskjalf. You cannot win," Vincent said, thumping his wyvern on the neck to calm it.

Valaskjalf removed his golden helm and glared at Vincent. "I never would have pegged you for a traitor, DuCayne."

"The real high prince stands before you, Valaskjalf, ready to once again claim his throne."

"What are you talking about? My family has ruled Ithnez since before the fall of Agasei. There is no other heir to the high throne."

Dimitri ignored the glare of the Gilded Prince as he introduced himself. "I am Dimitri DéDos, sole heir of High King Agasei and the Shadow Dragons." Luna had been right when she said they looked alike. Dimitri felt like he was looking in a mirror.

Valaskjalf scoffed. "Referring to Agasei as high king is a joke! He was nothing more than a power-hungry murderer, and Amorez ended his bloodline by killing him."

"You are wrong!" Dimitri shouted. "I am Agasei's son and the sole heir to the throne and the Shadow Dragons. Like my father, I will use my dragons to claim my birthright and I will kill any who stand in my way."

Valaskjalf reined in his wyvern, preventing the creature from lashing out. "Would you kill me and my family for believing you will never achieve that goal? Amorez beat your father, and she will defeat you!" Valaskjalf paused as his wyvern wheeled around. He dug his heels into the creature's ribs and forced it to be still a bit longer. "You will never be King of Ithnez. The people will make sure of that, even if Amorez doesn't strike you down first."

"Amorez?" Dimitri spat the name. "That wench is dead."

"Oh? And where is it written that she has indeed ventured beyond the Gates of Havel? You know as well as I that no such record exists."

"If she were still alive, don't you think her presence would be known?"

"Is yours?"

Valaskjalf and Dimitri glared at each other.

"What is your choice, Valaskjalf?" Vincent broke the silence. "Will you surrender? Or do you want to meet your ancestors in Havel?"

Valaskjalf pointed his sword at his commander. "May the Five Souls forever curse you and your bloodline for this treason, DuCayne. As for your question of surrender, my answer is heile pricé!"

The sky darkened immediately. Dimitri dared a glance upwards in time to see clouds as black as night explode with orange and yellow and red fury. The sky writhed and twisted, whirled and spun. It picked up speed, moving faster and faster until a tornado of fire touched down on the road behind the prince. It swept over Valaskjalf, leaving him unharmed. It struck the force of traitorous soldiers, drawing them skyward and melting the flesh from their bones until only black ash remained. An ebony snow fell softly around the stunned survivors.

Speechless, Dimitri watched the tornado dance over the land, consuming everything it touched. He looked away from the fire storm in time to see the prince drive his wyvern into the forest. Dimitri swore and sprinted after him. The few remaining soldiers from Valaskjalf's escort ushered their wyverns to follow.

Dimitri was immensely grateful for his Dákun Daju blood. It let him easily catch the escaping prince. Valaskjalf wheeled and swung his sword, striking Dimitri in the shoulder. Dimitri loosed a pained yowl and slowed his pace slightly. When Valaskjalf's wyvern passed him, Dimitri came up on the left and shoved his uninjured shoulder into the creature's side. The wyvern released a panicked cry as it lost its footing and rolled into the mud and leaves of the forest floor.

The crash threw Valaskjalf from his saddle. The prince lay in the mud, groaning. Dimitri slid to a stop and backtracked to stand at the prince's feet.

"If you had chosen surrender, you would have lived." Dimitri snatched Valaskjalf's sword from the ground. "Now, you die!"

"Hydíca semít!"

A spike of razor sharp ice exploded from the ground, nearly impaling Dimitri before he leaped into a tree.

Valaskjalf jumped to his feet. "Medícté!"

"How is it you have come to know magic?" shouted Dimitri. "Are you a Sorcerer?"

"No." Valaskjalf shook his head. "No blood but Hume flows in my veins. I am merely well schooled."

"Since you have such talent for magic, I will extend this offer to you just once—join me. Teach me the magic you know. In return I will allow you to live and command my army."

"Very tempting, but no." Valaskjalf took a fighting stance and watched as Dimitri left the safety of the tree.

"Then you leave me no choice, Valaskjalf."

The prince scowled. "May your death come slowly and painfully."

Both men stared each other down, waiting for their opponent to flinch. Dimitri adjusted his grip on the prince's stolen sword. If not for Valaskjalf's knowledge of magic, Dimitri would have a complete advantage. He watched Valaskjalf's lips, wary of any spell that might be uttered.

Valaskjalf took a step to his left. Dimitri mirrored him by stepping to his right. The prince took another step, then another and another. For each of his steps, Dimitri moved the opposite. Irritated by the prince's attempts to circle around him, Dimitri lunged.

The prince's own sword sliced the air, barely missing as Valaskjalf ducked. He kicked Dimitri's elbow, causing him to lose his hold on the sword. Dimitri flipped out of range and freed his double sword from its sheath on his back. Valaskjalf retrieved his sword from the ground in time to deflect Dimitri's blow.

"Daréta suahk!"

Lightning ripped the air at Valaskjalf's command, nearly striking Dimitri before he threw himself sideways. Both fighters were forced to cover their ears at the explosion of thunder that followed. Valaskjalf was the first to recover and wasted no time in lashing out at his would-be murderer. The prince's sword sang as it sliced the air, connecting with Dimitri's flesh. Dimitri cried out as the blade split the skin between his eyes. Hot blood gushed from the wound and rained to the ground.

Dimitri looked up, squinting through the blur his vision had become as the blood coated his face. Valaskjalf was above him, sword poised for a killing stroke, and Dimitri could not find his own weapon to parry. Dimitri somehow managed to roll away just before the blow landed. He got to his feet and wiped the blood away. He still could not see clearly. He muttered a curse as a low whistle reached his ears. He heard a gasp and a sickening crunch, and then the prince fell to the ground.

Godilai's ghostly voice came from somewhere to his left. "You look awful, Dimitri."

"How long were you going to wait?" Dimitri frowned, relaxing his guard slightly.

"Half a heartbeat."

"Let me heal that for you before you pass out." Luna was standing before him now. She placed a finger over his wound. "Medícté!"

Her finger traced the wound across his nose and to his cheek. There was a disgusting slurp as the wound healed. Dimitri blinked, finally able to see again.

"That is so much better." Dimitri sighed in relief and wiped the remaining blood from his face.

He found Godilai standing over prince Valaskjalf. The jawbone she had been whittling was jutting out from the prince's neck. Dimitri watched as she yanked the bone free and began to strip the prince's body from its armor.

"We will need a convincing story to explain your new scar and the blood on the armor." Godilai said as she peeled the breastplate away.

"We will have one ready before we reach the Temple," Vincent said, entering the clearing.

The seventeen remaining soldiers of the escort followed him. Each of them was visibly upset about the death of their prince but did not dare make a move to avenge him.

"Here is the pri—the gold wyvern." A soldier lead the creature to Dimitri's side then retreated.

Luna held the breastplate ready. "Put this armor on, Dimitri. We need to hurry to make up the time here, or the ferry will leave Sindai without us on board."

Dimitri looked down at Valaskjalf. He sighed then allowed Luna and Godilai to assist him with the armor. One thought rang clear in his mind and he muttered, "I should have studied more magic."

*I had no desire to take a Dákun Daju as my wife, especially
after losing my greatest love. Yet, I knew that if I truly wanted
to set things right in this world, I would have to make peace
with my enemy, and by doing so, form an alliance which
would stand strong against the real injustices of this world.*
                                    – FROM "THE DIARY OF AGASEI"
                                              BY AGASEI DÉDOS

The bells had just begun their second tolling when finally I found the
correct room. The first thing I noticed upon entry was the lack of desks. In
fact, the only surface in the room, aside from the floor, was a long table at the
opposite end. Weapons of all kinds were spread over its surface. Zhealocera
stood before them, almost as if she were actually admiring the craftsmanship
of the blades. I knew she really wasn't; everything was Hume crafted, and she
would never allow herself to admire something that was not Dákun Daju.

Since there were no desks in the room, the students sat against the walls. I
chose to sit on the floor in the middle of the room. The other students pointed
at me a few times and whispered among themselves, something I had grown
used to. Aside from Ríhan and a handful of other orphans, every student in this
school had been sent to the Temple by their parents to get an education. They
were all alike; pompous brats. I could not stand them.

When I belatedly realized the teacher was strangely absent, I began to
wonder what was going on. The door suddenly slammed open, jarring me from
my thoughts. In walked the most remarkable woman I had ever seen. She had
no footwear and long claws grew from the toes she walked on. She was clad in
white and grey leathers and some light armor. She had long, flowing stark
white hair with long bangs that half-hid her angular face. Sharp, unnatural
amber eyes glowed red in the light. And at the very top of her head were two
wolf-like ears.

Everyone was silent as this bizarre woman strode into the room and paused
in front of me. She towered over me and her amber eyes seemed to study me
for a moment. I saw here smirk briefly before whipping past. She had a tail! A
fluffy, white tail! I couldn't believe it.

At the front of the classroom, she stopped and turned to face the students.
"I am Freya Latreyon. I shall be your dueling teacher while Maas is away."
Freya's voice was quiet and demanding with a sort of growl. She watched,
unblinking, as three students rose from where they stood. "Is there a
problem?"

"You're a Demon." said a girl, pointing an accusing finger at Freya.

"Yes, a Wolf Demon to be specific." Freya crossed her arms. "Does that
fact bother you?"

"You are a freak of nature! I refuse to be taught anything by your kind!"
screamed another girl. She and the other girl stormed from the room. Freya

yawned, showing her sharpened fangs.

"Anyone else with racial issues better leave the room now. I will not put up with it or have it interfering with the rest of the class."

"My parents shall hear of this atrocity; a Demon in the Temple, indeed!" The last student who was standing snubbed Freya before calmly walking from the room. The rest of the students remained seated on the floor.

"Very well then… Let's begin with introductions. We shall go right to left and stop in the middle."

Zhealocera stood from her spot. She bowed to Freya, allowing her two long braids to fall over her shoulders as she did. "I am Zhealocera Hoshino, a Dákun Daju Enforcer-to-be."

"Now that is a surprise." Freya smiled as the girl sat. "I had not expected to see a Dákun Daju in the Temple."

"And I had not expected to be taught by a Demon." Zhealocera returned the smile. Freya waved for the other students to continue. One by one, they stood and told their names. Before I knew it, it was my turn. I stood and bowed to Freya.

"I am Xyleena, a Daughter of the Temple." I sat just as the door opened again. In walked the white robed Judge I had seen several times yesterday.

"Ah! Perfect timing as usual, Zamora." Freya laughed. Every student in the room started to whisper to each other about the Judge's presence. Zamora glanced down at me as she stepped past. She stood beside Freya and leaned against the table. "I see you have all learned of Judge Zamora's presence in the Temple."

"Yeah. I didn't exactly keep my presence here as secret as you did." Zamora winked at the Wolf Demon.

"You haven't changed a bit, old friend."

"Excuse me, but how do you two know each other?" A boy at the back asked. Freya and Zamora looked at him, then each other.

"We go way back." Freya smiled.

"Ah, but that is too long a story to weave in one class period that should be spent teaching." Zamora said with a laugh.

"I requested Zamora's presence here this morning to demonstrate dueling. After our little spar, I will have all of you will all try out various weapons until you find what you are comfortable with."

"Shall we begin then?" Zamora asked. She flung off her Judge's robes, revealing snug, black leathers and well-forged silver bracers, greaves, and breastplate each engraved with magnificently detailed scrolling. Freya motioned for me to vacate the middle of the room. Both teachers took up their arms; Freya a spiked chain, roughly a meter and a half long, and sickle fused as a kusarigama and Zamora two hooked, short swords called dueling blades.

They both moved to the middle of the room and took their stances. All eyes were on the duelists, waiting. Seconds ticked by like minutes, but neither moved.

In a burst of superhuman speed, Freya struck. The blow was blocked by Zamora's blade. They circled each other and attacked again. Zamora got off two hits, one deflected by Freya's chain, the other landed just above her elbow. Her wolfish eyes watched as the blood ran down her arm. She did nothing to staunch the flow. The two old friends continued their dance of blood and steel. Nothing else seemed to matter to them, just their opponent. Steel met steel with resounding clashes that echoed in the room. Each moved in a well-timed ballet of attack and parry. This display truly was the most ancient sport.

As soon as it had begun, it was over. Both fighters stood apart, breathless and smiling. Each wore cuts and blood from the other's weapon, but none were serious. The on looking students were as silent as a crypt as they watched their teachers shake hands. Then a chorus of cheers and applause erupted. The two duelists turned to their spectators and bowed.

"All right, students!" Freya's voice rose over the din. She waited as the clapping and cheers died away. "Now that you have had a view of the action, it is your turn to grab a piece of it. Line up along the wall and find a weapon on the table that you feel comfortable with. After you have chosen, return to the center of the room and sit. If you have any questions, feel free to ask either me or Zamora."

I found my way into the crowd at the table. As I waited my turn to select a weapon, I studied Zamora. Something about being in the presence of the Honored Judge ate away at me, and I knew that we had met her before. Zamora must have sensed my gaze, for she turned to look into my eyes. Unbelievable! She had the same eyes as me; deep emerald green that shifted to gold.

"Did you have a question, Xyleena?" Zamora asked, finally looking away to sheathe her weapons. My gaze traveled to the Judge's belt where her dueling blades were sheathed.

"I was just wondering if it is difficult to fight with two weapons." I returned my gaze to her face as she leaned against a wall to think.

"It does take ambidexterity and a good deal of skill to dual-wield, but after you learn the correct techniques, you tend to have better odds than a fighter with a single weapon. You can attack twice to his once. Down fall of dual-wielding is the lack of shield to absorb heavy blows. If you decide to go with two weapons, you have to be quick, both physically and mentally to stay ahead of your opponent."

"So dual-wielding is a sort of double-edged sword." I said as I reached the table. I caught the smirks of both teachers before I diverted my attention to the weapons. There was a wide selection of hammers, axes, scythes, staves, swords, and more. I was breathless at the selection before me. I knew I could not handle the larger weapons because of the weight. And the chained weapons would probably do more damage to me in the long run. So it was either staves or daggers for me.

I picked a dagger from the table and weighed it in my hand. Something on the table caught my attention. I lay the dagger down and shuffled a few other weapons until two shimmering bars were revealed. As I studied these strange bars of metal, I remembered that I had had something very similar in my pack when I was found on the beach. I quickly dug into the new bag on my hip and removed both of the mysterious, metal bars. With a quick flick of my wrists, the bars unfolded. They were a pair of razor- bladed fans. Though rust had started to claim the blades, I could still make out the flowery pattern emblazoned on the leaves. I felt a grin creep along my lips. These are my weapons. I left the table and smiled at Zamora.

The Judge did not return the smile and shot a look to Freya.

"Those tessens are tough weapons to work with. How do they feel?" Freya asked. Her eyes held a strange look.

"I can't quite describe it, but I feel like I have mastered them already."

"Good. Looks like you and Zhealocera are the only two determined enough to seek dual wielding. She will be your sparring partner. Be careful though. Dákun Daju are far from gentle in a fight." Freya smiled briefly and turned away. She shot Zamora a look over her shoulder before congratulating another student's choice on weapons. I glanced at the Judge, curious to know what that look was about. Zamora appeared distracted as she gathered her robes before leaving the room in a hurry.

Freya called for the students' attention. "You are all allowed to keep the weapons you chose today as your own so long as you do not abuse them. If you threaten another student with them or bear them outside this class room or the training grounds, you will be expelled. Do I make myself clear?"

A loud round of 'Yes, Professor' made Freya smile. The bells sounded their dismissal, so Freya waved for the students' leave. I lingered behind the others, watching Freya as she straightened out the display of weapons. There was a familiarity about her as well; similar to the way I felt around Judge Zamora. I wanted to ask if we had met before, but the way she and the Judge were exchanging looks told me that I would not get any clear answers. Instead, I chose to turn and walk away.

I will find my answers elsewhere.

The proposed Temple was the size of a small city, and included many fortifications and weapons turrets for defense. The Arch Bishops and I set those plans aside and drew up something much more accessible and far less threatening in appearance for we wanted to invite anyone into our walls, not scare them away. Naturally, the king and his generals called the security of it into question. Finally, after a lengthy debate, we had all settled on building the less threatening Temple, but the king decreed it be built somewhere that could be easily defended.

– FROM "CREATING PEACE IN A HOSTILE LAND"
BY PALAVANT MIRANDA

Dimitri watched as the island grew ever closer, admiring the way the waves crashed upon the jagged rocks in such a way to form a rainbow mist to shroud the sandy coast. A long dock of white detra wood jutted several meters out from the beach. It connected to a cobblestone path that lead the way up a carved cliff side filled with exotic fauna. The path climbed about two hundred meters upwards and eventually ended at the iron gates of the Temple of Five Souls.

The ferry would reach the dock soon. Of that, he was grateful. He had grown irritated with constantly playing High Prince Valaskjalf to the crew. The annoying pests never stopped asking about the battles he won or the women he kept for company. If Godilai and Vincent had not been there to intervene, Dimitri was certain he would have killed the crew.

Then there was the gold armor. He had worn the armor for the better part of two days now, and it had quickly become uncomfortable. It was a bit too snug on him, and parts of the plates dug into his joints. He was sure there would be bruises. Dimitri sighed. All that hassle for a measly diary. He snorted. The diary was the key. Without it, the Shadow Dragons could not be released.

"Do not lose your temper when you are in the Temple," Godilai whispered, suddenly beside him. "You must act exactly like Prince Valaskjalf in the presence of the Priests. Failure to do so will jeopardize the reason for our appearance here."

Dimitri shot her a glare. "You don't say? I will worry about my part in this façade. You just steal the blasted diary."

Godilai growled. "Watch what you say, Hume-aju." She stormed away.

Dimitri punched the railing, leaving an impression of the golden gauntlet's knuckles. "The sooner this is over, the better."

"Prince Valaskjalf, we will be docking soon," the captain of the scant ferry crew announced.

Dimitri waved for him to leave.

"Are you all right, Your Highness?"

Dimitri rolled his eyes then faced the captain. "I'm just feeling a bit ill."

"Ah!" The captain nodded. "The sea flu. I'm sure you'll be yourself once we've landed."

"I can only hope," Dimitri muttered, turning away. He heard the captain's footsteps recede. "Idiot."

Dimitri remained at the railing as the ferry made its final approach. The captain barked orders, and the crew hopped to their work. Soon enough the ferry was docked at the island home of the Temple of Five Souls. As Dimitri and his "royal" guard made their way off the dock, a woman in a white cloak passed him. He caught a glimpse of the look on her face; it betrayed recognition, and he was left to wonder if he had met the woman before.

Vincent handed him the reigns to the gold wyvern. "We are running late for your audience with the Palavant."

Dimitri hopped into the saddle with little effort and pulled the reigns to turn the beast around. "Then let us be off."

"Very well, your highness," Vincent said as he mounted his own wyvern.

He gave the command and the royal guard took off, leaving the ferry crew and the puzzling woman. It was not until they were at the stone bridge that marked the halfway point up the cliff side that the woman in white was forgotten. Dimitri sighed as he relaxed in the saddle and took the time to observe the island from this new perspective. The road at other end of the bridge forked, forming a path down into a ravine. Tranquil turquoise water shimmered like a jewel as it reflected the sun's light. Several children and some adults—each in garb fit for school—were gathered on one of the beaches, probably for a lesson since the water was still too cold for swimming.

Dimitri was forced to look away as the road curved and began its final climb to the summit where the Temple sat. During the ascent, Dimitri paid close attention to the soldiers that made up his escort, wary of any sign of nervousness to the challenges they were about to face. He was surprised to find that not one of them appeared to be second-guessing their decision to join him. So they rode on, listening to the cacophony of noise that was the waddle of armored wyverns making their way along the cobblestones.

It was several minutes before the escort reached the apex of the cliffs. Dimitri scoffed at the whistle of one of the soldiers as he gazed upon the white marble Temple, apparently for the first time. Dimitri allowed the men to admire the view while they drew nearer. At long last they arrived at the gates to the Temple grounds and a Lord Knight astride a cobalt wyvern rode up to greet them.

"Welcome to the Temple of Five Souls, High Prince Valaskjalf. How was your journey?" The Lord Knight reeled his wyvern about so he could walk with the escort into the grounds.

"Uneventful and tiresome," Dimitri replied. He gazed around the grounds.

The Priests were already preparing for the festival. Crimson banners depicting a gold phoenix rising from a pool of flames were draped from window ledges and lampposts. Red and gold ribbon-like standards were set in holders high atop the pinnacles of the Temple, taking the places of black and purple ones. A group of Knights assisted the Priestesses with positioning a large torch in the yard outside one of the prism-shaped Temples. Others still were busy cleaning the walkways or planting flowerbeds. They glanced up from their work as the escort rode passed.

"You will have plenty of time to rest before the festival, Majesty." The Lord Knight smiled over at him. "And the cooks have prepared a special meal for your arrival—glazed Aoao with stuffing and all the fixings. Good eating, that."

Dimitri smiled. "Indeed it is. I can't wait." He did not realize that the Temple had such an exquisite menu. His mouth watered at the thought of the glazed pork awaiting him.

"How fares Palavant Celestia?" asked Vincent.

The Lord Knight's mood turned somber. "She has grown deathly ill. Her doctors do not expect her to see her ninety-third year."

"That is terrible," Vincent said with a frown.

Dimitri nodded in agreement, though he really did not care. The dealings of the Palavant never interfered with his affairs, and he did not care about the passing of an old woman.

"Here we are, Majesty," the Lord Knight said, reining in his wyvern. He dismounted and strode to the heavy oak doors of the central building.

Dimitri and his escort dismounted their beasts as well and followed the Lord Knight.

"This is the school portion of the Temple. The five separate Temples are all built around this building. Then the Priests' and students' dorms form the outer ring. Wonderful craftsmanship of the white marble, hmm?"

Dimitri nodded. "It must have taken a long time to construct this place. I wonder how the ancients pulled it off."

"Same here. Ah! Here we are." The Lord Knight stopped outside another set of oaken doors. "This is Palavant Celestia's room. She wanted to speak to you when you arrived. After your meeting I'll take you to the guest quarters so you can rest and wash up before dinner is served."

"Thank you," Dimitri said, slowly passing through the doorway.

The room he stood in was uncomfortably warm and dimly lit. The fireplace was raging, and thick curtains blocked the light from the windows. Dimitri removed his helm and wiped sweat from his brow.

"I apologize for the warmth," a weak voice spoke from somewhere to his left.

A curtain was pulled aside, scattering the shadows. Palavant Celestia stared out the window. Dimitri studied the old woman. She was pale and covered in wrinkles from her long years.

"Is there a reason you wished to speak to me?"

Dimitri watched as she slowly shook her head.

"I merely wanted to see if Valaskjalf made it here without incident." Celestia finally looked him in the eye. "It would seem that he is lost."

"What do you mean? I am right here." Dimitri frowned.

Again, Celestia shook her head. "You cannot fool me. The Valaskjalf I know does not stand before me."

"You are more ill than your doctors admit to anyone. Maybe you should lie down, Palavant."

"I think I would know my own nephew. Tell me—" She let the curtain drift close.

Panic streamed through Dimitri, and he was hard pressed not to show it.

"What have you done to Valaskjalf?"

"I am Valaskjalf Za'Car, High Prince of Ithnez," Dimitri said firmly.

He could barely see Celestia shake her head.

"Why do you not believe me?"

"There is a long list of reasons. The first of which is—" She was forced to stop as a coughing fit racked her body. She was left gasping for air when it finally passed. "Your general appearance. You have red eyes, and your ears are pointed like a Dákun Daju."

"Blast," Dimitri muttered as he touched the tips of his ears.

A sad smile crept over the Palavant's face. "Just tell me the truth. What have you done to my nephew?"

Dimitri sighed and dropped his hands to his sides. "He is dead."

The old woman nodded slowly. "And will you now kill me for knowing your secret?"

Dimitri did not answer.

She sighed. "I know why you have come, doppelganger. You should know that the path you walk will only lead to your own destruction."

His hands turned to fists and he shook as he exploded with barely contained rage. "You are wrong," he said through clenched teeth. "I will succeed in my conquest and nothing will stop me."

"You are half right," said Celestia, moving to the bed in the corner of the room. "You will succeed in unleashing darkness, but you will be defeated."

"How could you possibly know the future? Hmm?"

Celestia remained silent.

"Very well," he sighed, crossed his arms. "Who do you think can actually defeat me?"

"She who bears the Light."

Dimitri frowned at the Palavant's answer. "Amorez?"

"No. Amorez's blood."

"You are not making any sense!" Dimitri exclaimed. "Amorez has no bloodline."

She looked him in the eye and smirked knowingly. "Are you sure of that?"

Dimitri closed the distance between them in a heartbeat. "Tell me the name!"

"No."

"I demand to know!" His hands flew to her frail shoulders, gripping them so tightly they were liable to break. "Tell me!"

"Never."

"Tell me!" He shook her violently, over and over and he felt her old bones give.

The Palavant made no move to stop him, nor did she cry out. Dimitri roared in rage and shoved her away from him. She fumbled back, collapsing on the bed in an unmoving heap.

"Stupid old woman," hissed Dimitri. "I will find out eventually. When I do, Amorez's blood will die." As he stormed from the room to find Luna and Godilai, he heard the old Palavant moaning something that sounded like a prayer.

It was discovered that the Rishai Bisolar System included six planets. Of those six, only two were actually suitable for human life; However, there was one planet in the system that had the scientists aboard the Haven intrigued. This planet, the last in the system, was called Minerva, and was the first gas dwarf planet ever discovered.

– FROM "AN UNTITLED SCIENCE LOG"
BY UNKNOWN

I sighed and looked past Ríhan to the Palavant's table. What was taking so long? The dinner bells had rung half an hour ago, and we were still waiting for the Palavant to appear. Even High Prince Valaskjalf was growing impatient by the wait.

This was the first time I could recall actually getting to see the high prince with my own eyes. He was really handsome! He had unruly black hair that half hid his face and ears. He was dressed in a ruby tunic that had gold embroidery hand stitched throughout. I found myself wishing for clothes like that.

The Palavant's door finally creaked open. I peeled my eyes away from the prince, but the Palavant was not there. One of her assistants stood in the doorway. She looked grief stricken. She moved her lips to speak, but no sound was heard. Suddenly she burst into tears and fell to her knees. Several teachers and priests were at her side a heartbeat later.

"Oh, Gods, please don't let it be…" I barely heard Ríhan's whispered prayer.

My gaze swept the room. Almost everyone in the room students, teachers, and drudges were praying as well. The only one who seemed immune to the grim possibility that the Palavant had passed on was the high prince. He sat there, watching the circle of people gathered around the assistant. His face and demeanor were strangely void of any reaction.

From the circle of teachers around the assistant, Matron Serenitatis stood. She slowly took a breath and moved to stand beside the Palavant's empty chair. "Palavant Celestia has…has gone to join her ancestors." She bowed her head. "May she be well received in Havel."

I watched as Ríhan collapsed heavily onto the bench and hung his head. Though he tried to hide it, tears slipped from his eyes and broke upon the wood of the table. I slowly sank down to the bench and listened to the wails and cries of the others. Unable to cry myself, I bowed my head and whispered a prayer to the Gods, asking that they look after the soul of a great woman; the mother to many.

"Everyone." One of the Archbishops . She was tall and thin, with skin the color of ivory, a sharp contrast to her black robes. Her auburn hair was curly and long, falling like a curtain to her waist. She had a warm aura and a friendly—but sad—smile. When she had the attention of most everyone in the room, she spoke again. "I know it is difficult to see beyond the sadness right now, but please, for Celestia's sake, eat and be merry. The Rising of Zahadu-Kitai is a happy time—a time for new beginnings. The Festival of the Phoenix will usher in a new time for all of us."

The meal progressed with light conversation, often in whispers that I paid little attention to. I did catch a few snippets, most of which consisted of a debate on which of the Archbishops would be elected as the new Palavant, or would the Matron take over. One thing that struck me as odd was how the high prince did not say a word. He just sat there, eating and staring off into space. Maybe he was too shocked.

"Xy, are we still meeting in the library for our study session?" Ríhan asked. He looked guilty. "It feels…weird to continue on as if nothing has happened."

I nodded. "Everything will be all right. Just give it some time."

"All wounds heal if given time," Freya said, suddenly behind me.

I had not even noticed she had entered the dining hall. She had probably received word of the Palavant's passing, and chose to show her respects by joining the main hall. I looked around again and saw that even Zhealocera had snuck into the room. The Dákun Daju stood by the door, her arms crossed and face as void of expression as the high prince's.

"Some leave scars." Ríhan muttered as he pushed his plate away.

I returned my attention to him in time to catch him wiping his eyes with the back of his hand. I nodded. The passing of Palavant Celestia would leave a scar that would last a long time.

"We will just have to limp on then," I replied solemnly. "Until we find our feet again."

Ríhan sighed.

An unnerving silence suddenly swept the room, and I looked about in concern. I belatedly realized that the same ivory-skinned Archbishop who had spoke before was standing, her hand raised to win everyone's attention. Matron Serenitatis stood beside her.

"Students and teachers, before you retire from the hall this night, I wish to speak to you." She let her hand fall back to her side. "For those of you who do not know me, I am Archbishop Noralani. I have been an Archbishop for nine of my forty-seven years."

Wait a minute! That name, Noralani, I know that from somewhere. I whispered, "Who is Noralani?"

Freya tapped the top of my head, reminding me to be quiet.

"My fellow Archbishops"—she motioned at the table where she sat—"have taken a vote. The results of this have placed me in the position to act as Matron while Serenitatis takes up the reigns of the Palavant. This shall last until the end of the election, when the new Palavant is decided. Does anyone here wish to argue their choice?"

I could not imagine anyone wanting to argue with the Archbishops. To my greatest surprise, Ríhan raised his hand. Serenitatis pointed to him. He slowly stood.

"I do not argue the vote of the Archbishops," he said.

I breathed a sigh of relief.

"I am just curious to know if you plan to become one of the candidates for Palavant."

Noralani smiled. "I am still debating on entering or not. I hope to gain some experience acting as your Matron before I make my final decision."

I, for one, hoped that she did enter the election. From what little I had seen of her today, I got the feeling she was more than capable of handling the role. Her youth was the only problem that I could foresee. Then again, that could make her more appealing—and approachable—in the eyes of the younger crowd who could vote. I wondered who else would enter.

Serenitatis bade us all a good night and took a seat next to Noralani at the table. Teachers began ushering everyone else out of the dining hall. As I joined the line to exit, I noticed that the high prince had vanished from his honored seat. I did not see him anywhere in the room, so he must have either left early or took a side exit. The way that that man was acting filled me with a terrible foreboding.

Something is amiss here.

Dread filled me as I looked around at the ghostlike trees. I was back in that endless forest again. This time I did not dare to wander or run through the twisted wood; I knew what was out there. It was coming. No. It was here.

"Esté imlít lerra rité mertuác jidó. Arx et cólaz ni Kohnbenai rahn…" The spectral whisper echoed off verse after verse.

I knew it was a warning; there was nothing else it could be. I begged the voice to speak in Standard so that I could understand, but it kept repeating the words in that cryptic language. Over and over, again and again, those same strange words echoed all around me. I covered my ears, trying to block out the voice, but I could still hear everything. It was as if the creature was penetrating my mind, forcing me to remember the words of its warning.

"Xyleena?"

I bolted upright with a gasp. It took me a moment to realize I was seated at one of the many tables in the Temple's vast library. The pile of books I had been referencing had served as my makeshift pillow. Ríhan sat across from me, a look of concern in his hazel eyes.

I leaned back in my chair, stunned. "What happened?"

He shrugged. "One moment you were reading one of your books, the next you were hunched over, eyes closed, and muttering something about warnings."

It was that dream again, I realized.

"Are you alright?"

I flashed a smile. "Can you write down a translation for me?"

"I can certainly try." He took out a fresh leaf of parchment. The moment I saw that he was ready, I began to recite the words of the spectral whisper. His pen flew over the paper. Though there were moments where he hesitated over a word, he managed to translate every verse the first time through. When he was done, and the ink dry, he passed the leaf to me.

The blue ink stared up at me from the page.

This great world will die soon,
As the deeds of Darkness spread.
He will rule with mighty hands,
As his beasts destroy these lands.
Only she who bears the Light,
Can take on this ancient battle.
The twelve pieces she must find,
Will aid her in battle heat.
When at last the twelve are one,
He will lose his blackened soul.
She will cast his beasts away,
And Light shall win this day.

"That is a very interesting riddle," said Ríhan, pointing the end of his quill at the parchment.

I nodded in agreement as I read the words again. It just did not make sense. There had not been any news about "dark deeds" recently, much less a rumor about a girl with light. And what are the twelve pieces?

With a frustrated sigh, I rolled the parchment up and shoved it into the bag at my hip. I caught a glimpse of the strange book I possessed. Even days after being fished out of the water along with me, the leather-bound tome showed no signs of damage. I debated asking Ríhan to translate it. My argument with myself was interrupted by an ear-piercing screech. I winced at the sound and looked around for the source. Other students were looking around as well. It was only when Ríhan pointed to the farthest wall of the library that everyone seemed to calm down.

I peered over his shoulder to see Judge Zamora and a librarian standing at a rusty gate. I knew that that gate was always locked. Some of the rarest books in the world were kept behind it, and entering the room beyond required special endorsements. I had even heard of someone petitioning repeatedly for over a decade to be given permission to enter. I wondered why they would open it now, and for a Judge. As I watched the happenings, Zamora disappeared into the room beyond the gate while the librarian stood guard.

After a few minutes, Zamora returned. She looked worried, and she shook her head when the librarian asked her something. The librarian turned to lock the gate again while the Judge strode away. Just as Zamora exited the library, Zhealocera entered. The Dákun Daju paused for a moment, casting a glance at the door through which the Judge had left, then moved away from the door. She spotted me and Ríhan and quickly made her way towards us.

"What is the Judge still doing here?" she whispered the moment she was at our table.

Ríhan looked up from his papers. "What do you mean?"

She pulled out a chair and sank into it. "The Temple Knights were talking about a woman in a white cloak being down at the docks when the high prince arrived. I figured the woman of whom they spoke was Judge Zamora, and she was taking the ferry back to the mainland."

"Maybe she changed her mind or forgot something," I offered with a shrug.

"Or maybe someone else is wearing a white cloak," Ríhan said flatly.

"Speaking of the high prince," I paused to make sure I had their attention. "Do either of you get the impression that he is acting suspiciously?"

Ríhan shook his head negative.

"I have yet to see him personally, so I cannot say," Zhealocera answered. "What gives you the impression that he is acting thusly?"

"Just the general way he was acting tonight at dinner. He did not react in any way when the news of the Palavant's passing was announced, then he vanished from the hall before we were excused from the meal."

"Hmm."

Ríhan scoffed. "So what? I would not call his leaving early or a lack of reaction suspicious activity. He is the high prince; he has probably been trained from birth to not make a hysterical scene of himself in public. Plus, who would want to stick around and be harangued by admirers when you are as famous as he is?"

I could not deny that Ríhan had a very good point. Maybe I am reading too much into the way the prince is acting.

"Well, either way, I am one of the many on duty to guard him tonight." Zhealocera looked me in the eye. "I shall keep a keen eye on him, and if he truly is acting suspiciously, I shall report it appropriately."

I nodded in thanks.

"What brings you to the library, Zheal?"

"I came for you." Her magenta gaze shifted to Ríhan, who looked aghast. "More accurately, I came to pick your brain for information."

Ríhan sighed in relief. "What sort of information?"

"Acting Matron Noralani – Her name; why does it seem familiar?"

"I was wondering the same thing." I admitted.

"Wow, I can't believe you two. I take it back; I can believe you," he pointed at me, "but you should know the source of that name, Zheal. The Archbishop – or Acting Matron, whichever you prefer – is named after her ancestor, Noralani Ithnez. The first Noralani Ithnez was the daughter of the man who helped to save the entire Hume race from extinction, Aadrian Ithnez, for whom this planet was named."

"Whoa. So the Archbishop could actually be queen if she wanted to usurp the Za'Cars?"

Ríhan nodded. "Noralani the First's son, Aadrian Ithnez II, was offered the chance to rule when the Earthers established their first settlement here. He declined, which opened the way for the Za'Car family to rule, and – aside from a brief interval when Agasei DéDos took over the throne – they have been the ruling family ever since."

Agasei DéDos. I hung onto the name like a hound to a scent trail. Though I could not recall the face or deeds of the person who bore this name, a terrible chill set in over me. I loathed that person to their very core; I have always hated... him... That is right; I remember now, Agasei was a man. Whatever the exact reason, this deep-seated hatred towards him was personal, and it went back centuries.

"Thank you for filling me in on your Hume history." Zhealocera's voice brought me back to the present. She stood, turned on her heel, and was gone before Ríhan could reply.

Ríhan shook his head, bemused, and muttered, "That's a Dákun Daju for you." With that, he returned to his studies.

I was content to watch him for a while. My thoughts eventually returned to Agasei, and the mysterious book I had tucked away. The two were somehow connected; of that I was certain. I so badly wanted to ask Ríhan what impression he got from the book – Could he even read the contents. – but I could not. It was as if some sixth sense was screaming at me: Do not reveal the book!

The clock on the wall chimed; it was an hour until curfew. Time to retreat to my quarters and retire for the night. I just hoped that I was not plagued by that dream again.

*Moonwhisperer, who had been staring solemnly into the blaze
this whole time, met my gaze and whispered, "What great feat
would you attempt if you could not fail?"*

– FROM "THE UNSUNG"
BY J'VAC TAIG (TRANSLATED BY B'REG KUNGA)

Midnight was Godilai's favorite time of day. The time when most of the world dreamed. It was the hour of monsters and thieves. Tonight was a rare night. Not one of the three moons was out, and Bedeb would not break the horizon for a few more hours. Apart from firelight, the world was completely black.

Godilai lurked in the halls of the Temple. She moved like a shadow, silent and unseen. She darted past the patrols, who would turn and wonder if they had imagined movement. Finally, she reached the fifth floor– the library. The entrance was watched; Two Priests and a Knight conversed just left of the door. Godilai scowled and sunk deeper into the shadows. She would have to bide her time.

"So Archbishop Serenitatis is acting Palavant?"

The Knight's voice reached Godilai's ears. She growled, remembering the conversation with Dimitri after his meeting with the old Hume. He really needed to learn how to control himself. One would think an immortal would have learned patience. That was untrue in Dimitri's case.

"…and hope she wins the election. She has done many great things in her life so far."

"Wasn't she the one that urged the high king to take action against the bligen poachers?"

"That was her all right. I was glad when the king was finally swayed to help the bligens. Their fur may make nice coats and rugs, but I like seeing the wildcat in the wilderness. They really are gorgeous."

Idiot Humes! Move! Godilai glared at the trio.

"She was also the first Priestess to head a committee. The Committee of Excellence in Education, if I remember correctly."

"That's the one."

"Serenitatis really does have a good record. I'm with you two. Serenitatis for Palavant!"

"That is, of course, provided she runs for the position to begin with."

"She will. I can feel it."

"You three are still yappin'?" The Lord Knight who had escorted Dimitri to Celestia's chamber earlier approached from the right.

Yes! Get them out of the way! Godilai watched him with great interest.

"Sorry, sir. These two Priests were just telling me about Matron Serenitatis. She would make a great Palavant."

"So I've heard, Lee. Nevertheless, you have security rounds to patrol. I suggest you get on with them."

"Yes, sir. Of course."

"Good night, Lee."

"Good night, Scott, Catharsis." The Knight nodded his respects to the two priests before leaving them. He strode toward Godilai.

She readied her dagger and hoped she did not have to use it. It would make the next few days difficult to bear should there be an investigation. Luckily, the Knight turned away from her and disappeared down the stairs she had just used. She breathed a sigh of relief.

She moved her gaze back to the library doors. At long last, no one was there. Godilai waited a moment longer for any noise, any movement. Hearing nothing, she bolted from her hiding spot and streaked to the library doors. They were locked, but she was prepared for that. Removing the small tool from her belt, she easily remedied the blockade. Finally, she was in.

"Annoying Humes," Godilai muttered as she took in the space. The room was as long as the ferry that had transported her to the island. Several shelves leaden with countless books and tomes filled the space. A number of round tables with chairs were set between many of the shelves, more were stationed by a counter where the librarians would normally stand watch. Behind the counter was the gate behind which, Dimitri told her, was the rare books room.

In a few quick strides, she was at the counter; One deft leap and she was over it. She paused a moment to inspect the blockade and found such a meager defense useless. She tested the gate only to find it locked. She sighed and picked the lock.

Godilai winced at the ear-splitting screech of the aged metal as the gate swung open. She hoped no one had heard the noise. Deciding not to test her luck, she slipped inside the tiny room. It was pitch black within, but she was prepared for that. From one of the many hidden pockets on her bustier, she pulled out a hand-sized cylinder. A quick crack in half, a rough shake, and a soft glow of blue light emerged. It sent just enough of the darkness skittering to the corners so that she could see the books. She scanned the titles; Many were so worn from age that they had become illegible. When a quick scan left her with no results, Godilai began pulling books from the shelves. She made her way half through the collection before she realized one was out of place.

"R112...R114...R115... Damn! Don't tell me someone has it."

A loud clang made her jump. She quickly extinguished the light and wiggled through the opening of the gate. It squeaked as she brushed against the metal bars. She swore, shoved the rod into her pocket, and ducked behind the opposite side of the counter as a lantern scattered the shadows of the room.

"Who goes there?"

From the voice, Godilai could tell the intruder was a young male; more than likely Hume. She could easily slip out of hiding and kill him if needed. For the moment she would bide her time as he investigated the source of the noise that had summoned him.

There was a quick succession of taps, probably his weapon against the gate. "You are supposed to be closed," said the boy. "Scared me out of my wits with your racket, you did. Listen to me! I'm talking to a gate!"

Godilai shook her head in annoyance. The boy sighed and closed the gate. Once again it protested the movement with a harsh screech. Godilai winced at the sound.

"Dang, that needs fixing," the boy muttered and turned to leave. He paused when the gate creaked open again. He cursed it and forced it shut again. "The librarians will deal with you tomorrow."

Godilai listened as the boy's footfalls moved away. The light of his lantern vanished. She only breathed when she heard the lock click. She collected herself and left her hiding spot. She was not about to sneak her way back to Dimitri through the halls. The patrols would probably find her this time. She sighed and looked around the room again.

"Window or fireplace," she muttered to herself.

She rolled her eyes and moved to the window. She was surprised to find that it was not locked. She pushed it open and studied the task before her. There was a narrow ledge just outside, then a sheer drop of two stories.

"That is almost too easy."

Godilai lowered herself out the window. She balanced on her toes as she inched away from the escape route. Finally, she was able to close it. She glanced over her shoulder and, with a click of her tongue, pushed away from the cold marble. She twisted and flipped her body as she fell toward the lower level. She landed perfectly and dusted herself off. She whistled a tune as she walked to the edge of the roof. Another jump later, she was strolling along the Temple grounds amidst stalls and pens set up for the Festival.

"What are you up to?" called a girl's voice.

Godilai found its source leaning against a wall and half concealed in shadow. After a moment, she stepped into the light of one of the torches. Godilai was taken aback at the girl's appearance. Violet hair and a cold, magenta stare; she was Dákun Daju. Then Godilai spotted the Warrior's badge on the girl's shoulder, and she knew she had to take care for the girl could raise an alarm before Dimitri could obtain the diary he needed.

"Now there is something I did not expect." Godilai exposed her neck in respects to the young Dákun Daju. "What is your name?"

The girl hesitated only a moment. "Zhealocera. You?"

"I am Godilai."

Her magenta gaze shifted to the rooftop where Godilai had just been. "And what were you up to on the roof?"

"Stargazing." Godilai swore to herself when the girl's gaze snapped back to her. "Tonight is a great night for that."

"Uh huh." Zhealocera crossed her arms, and Godilai knew her story was doomed. She did not want to have to kill such a young clansman. Her only hope was if someone came to interrupt the girl's constant stream of questions. "What are you doing here?"

"I am here to guard the high prince, Sortim. Surely you have been informed of his presence here."

"I was not made aware of any Dákun Daju guards in His Majesty's ranks." Zhealocera frowned.

Smart girl. Godilai forced a smile. "So far there are only two of us. He keeps that fact hidden so other Humes do not lash out at him."

"Who is the other one?"

"She is Luna Graves."

"And is she with the high prince now?"

"Yes, of course." Godilai quirked an eyebrow at the girl. Where was she going with these questions?

"And you say you were stargazing? What kind of guard are you?"

Godilai sighed. "I was allowed a break. Is it wrong to leave my prince in the care of others for a few minutes?"

"It would be," Zhealocera smirked, "if you weren't lying."

"What are you talking about?"

"You would have had to have been raised by Humes to be fond of stargazing. Yet you spat the word Hume with as much hate as any other Dákun Daju. That suggests Humes did not raise you. Therefore, you are a liar."

"So what?" Godilai clenched her fists.

"So I suggest you tell me what you were really up to before I notify the Knights."

"Silence, girl," came Dimitri's voice. Godilai was immensely grateful for his appearance.

He stepped from the shadows of the building Godilai had been headed for. Zhealocera moved her fiery gaze to his face as Godilai bowed to him.

"Forgive me for not returning in time, My Lord. I was delayed at meeting this young sister of mine."

Dimitri quirked an eyebrow at Godilai's greeting, then looked at the girl he had ordered to be silent.

"Ah! You found another Dákun Daju." He feigned his enthusiasm well. "I did not know there were any residing within the Temple. What do I call you?"

"I am Zhealocera."

"Truly a pleasure." Dimitri smiled. He turned his attention back to Godilai. She read his eyes; he was annoyed. "Come, Godilai, I need your wisdom to help me solve a problem."

"As you wish, My Lord." She bowed again and prepared to follow him.

He smiled at the girl, "Good night, Zhealocera."

"Good night, Prince Valaskjalf." Zhealocera turned on her heel and walked briskly away.

Godilai glared at the girl's retreating form.

"What was that all about?" Dimitri asked, his voice barely a breath above a whisper.

Godilai was impressed that this Hume-aju knew the secret techniques even full-blooded Dákun Daju have trouble mastering. She would never admit that to him. "The girl saw me jump off the roof and fired questions at me until you showed up. She is a smart one; did not believe a single word I said."

He sighed, looked sidelong at her. "Is she a threat to our mission?"

"Probably not, but I would be wary should she report this night to her superiors."

"Should we persuade her to join us?" She detected the skepticism in his tone. "Another Dákun Daju on our side couldn't hurt, could it?"

Godilai shook her head. "Do not invite her, Dimitri. I do not trust her."

Their conversation lapsed into silence. Eventually, and as if one mind, the duo turned to walk into the building that housed their sleeping quarters. Godilai found herself impressed with Dimitri once again when she learned that she could not hear his footfalls.

Outside the door that served as the false prince's room, Dimitri spoke. "So, were you able to find the diary?"

Godilai faced him. "It was not there."

"What?"

"I looked twice. The books jumped in order from 112 to 114. I am guessing someone beat us to it."

"Are you absolutely sure?"

Dimitri's scowl deepened as she nodded.

He swore, cupped his chin in his hand as he thought. "I need that diary."

"Use your influence as high prince to see if you are able to find out who checked it out. I shall steal it from them during the festival tomorrow."

Dimitri was quiet for a while. Finally, he said, "That might raise too many questions, but I will try."

"If all else fails, you could always force that person to hand the book over."

I could not find the peace to sleep. I did not want to. There was too much on my mind. So I stood at the window of my room, staring out as the light of the suns slowly started to shift the sky towards blue. The past few days had been a maelstrom of activity and confusing puzzles. Freya, Judge Zamora, the Palavant… they were all familiar to me. I even recognized the high prince – or the man claiming to be him at least. Why did I know them? What part did they play in my past?

Gods! I wish I could remember something!

And then there was the riddle passed to me by a phoenix in my dreams. Upon thinking of it, I looked away from the horizon to locate the desk. Though I could barely see in the dim, I knew that resting on the surface was the piece of parchment with Ríhan's blue ink. I had already committed the words to memory. Still I pondered the meaning of its warning.

Even more curious was the book I had laid beside the parchment. I had unlaced the leather to gaze at the pages within. I still could not read the writing, but the various sketches within were intriguing enough to occupy my mind. There were images of landscapes, diagrams of creatures, and portraits of people; all of which whispered of familiarity. Again I wondered if this… this… diary – What other word would describe it? – was mine.

The bells tolled.

How long have I been standing here? I wondered and looked out the window again. The suns had risen to paint the sky with a medley of color. It would be a beautiful day; perfect for the Festival of the Phoenix. I looked to the square below, where row upon row of wooden stalls or gazebos had been set up for the various vendors. A few people were already up, putting the finishing touches on their displays before the throngs of visitors would come to the island to pay homage to Zahadu-Kitai, the Goddess of Spring. While they would come to beg Her for good fortune in the months to come, I would ask Her for answers.

Activity in the square was growing. I had better hurry if I want to get to the altar before it is full. I thought, turning away from the window. I quickly cleaned up, changed into a festive tunic and black slacks. I donned my leather satchel and placed both the book and the riddle within. Then I left my room.

The hallway was silent. I expected that. Being a holiday, almost everyone would be sleeping in. That meant that only the Knights would be wandering the halls on their patrols. I doubted they would stop me on my way to pray to the Goddess. One floor down, I passed two Knights, both of which wished me a blessed new year. I returned their greetings. Another floor down, no one. On the main floor was a surprise. The moment I stepped of the landing, Prince Valaskjalf strode past me. I caught his gaze when he glanced back at me, and I could have sworn his eyes were crimson. I did not stick around to find out why he was up so early and wandering around without an escort. That man creeped me out enough as it was; I did not need to be around watching his every suspicious move.

Outside in the yard, things were much different. It was a flurry of activity as the final preparations were being made. Decorations were going up. A band was gathered on the main stage, testing their instruments for a long day of playing. Candied rolls and spiced meats were being set to bake or broil in the fire pits. Their sweet and spicy smell made my mouth water. Breakfast would have to wait though. I needed my answers, and I had finally worked up the courage to visit the altar. No sense in delaying further.

I turned left, meandering my way around stall after stall. Many venders greeted me and I bade them good morning in return. Once passed all of the stalls, I could see the pyramid that was the Sanctuary of the Goddess of Fire. I admired the red and gold glass orbs sitting atop the pillars that lined the walkway to the portcullis. The enormous doors had been propped open, inviting visitors in to pray to the Goddess.

At the threshold, I paused. This is it, I told myself, No turning back. I took a deep breath and stepped through. I was greeted with an unlit corridor wide enough for two chariots to run abreast. A moment to let my vision adjust to the dimness and deeper into the pyramid I went. My footfalls echoed off the marble. The tangy scent of incense assaulted my nose. The air grew hot. After what felt like ages, the hallway spilled out to a large, circular room. A stone walkway, that doubled as seating during a large assemblage ran the diameter of the room and spiraled downward towards the altar. At the very center, amidst a ring of raging fire, was an enormous statue carved centuries ago from a single ruby. It depicted a bird rising from fire, with wings aloft and head facing forward as if to look at everyone who entered.

I could almost feel the Goddess watching me as I moved towards Her statue. I stopped a few meters away from the inferno ring, dropped to my knees. There, under the visage of the Goddess of Fire, I closed my eyes and prayed.

I sighed and opened my eyes. The world had gone pitch black. I rose to my feet and looked around but could not make out any shapes in the darkness. Reaching out, I felt nothing. No walls. No floor. Just dead air. It was as if the world had fallen away and left me in a void.

"Hello?" My call echoed over and over. The dead air seemed to move. "Is anyone there?"

"Ake it ja bemu ne meo?"

A spectral whisper reached my ears. My breath caught. I knew that voice; it haunted my dreams.

"Are you Zahadu-Kitai?"

My voice echoing back was my only answer.

The air moved again. Crimson light suddenly exploded, scattering the darkness and blinding me. I covered my eyes until I could face the brightness. Floating within the aura of light was a beautiful bird. She was smaller than I imagined, and could easily perch upon my arm. Her tail was twice as long as her body with shades of blue that matched her eyes. Her wings shimmered with a rainbow of colors before the feathers turned into flames. She was a phoenix.

She had come!

I bowed to her.

"Ake it ja bemu ne meo?" the voice repeated and I could not help but notice that the mouth of the phoenix never moved.

"Forgive me, Daughter of Fire, I do not speak those words," I spoke softly, feeling guilty that I could not speak to Her in the Nature Tongue.

Her azure eyes studied me with an ancient knowledge. "You have forgotten much, child. Why do you call to me?"

I swallowed the lump in my throat. "I know you are busy, Zahadu-Kitai, but I beg for your guidance."

"And what is it that you seek?"

I thought it over for a moment. Face to face with the Goddess of Fire, I was totally lost at what to say and there were so many things I yearned to ask Her.

"How about we start with the warning I have been sending you in your dreams."

"That was really you?"

The phoenix seemed to laugh. "Yes, child, it was me."

I felt honored that Zahadu-Kitai Herself had taken the time to send me a message that, until recently, was entirely cryptic. I was immensely grateful that Ríhan was able to translate it. "You spoke of dark deeds beginning soon and a girl with light. And then the twelve? What did you mean?"

"Tragedy will soon strike. You will begin to realize who you are then."

I mulled her words over in my head. Tragedy? That must be the dark deeds She had mentioned. But… what about the girl with the light? Who was she – or… who will she be?

"A good question," said the phoenix, and I was stunned. She could read my mind! "But what about that bizarre book in your possession? I would think you more curious about that."

"What about it?"

"It is the key."

More cryptic answers. "You are not going to tell me what this so-called key unlocks, are you?"

I could almost sense Her smile. "I cannot give away everything, child."

The crimson light began to fade, and with it, the phoenix. "Fate still has much in store for you."

"A great adventure awaits," I muttered.

"You have no idea." Her final words echoed as the constricting darkness swallowed her light.

*There are many strange features on this planet. The most
inexplicable of all is almost due north of Arcadia, on the
continent called Mekora-Lesca. It appears to be a thick fog,
yet it does not move or dissipate. It has been named the Myst,
and a scientific outpost has been established within it so that it
may be studied.*

– FROM "THE CHRONICLES OF ITHNEZ, VOL. IV"
BY ORN TERSON, COURT HISTORIAN

The old woman looked at Dimitri through thin spectacles. It was obvious
that she was not expecting such a visit so early in the morning, this day of all
days. He did not care if he was disturbing her sleep or her meal; his need for
Amorez's diary was of far more importance. Still, he forced a smile and
apologized for disturbing the librarian.

"I would like to pay tribute to another special lady on this day," Dimitri
explained. "Is there any way I could make a personal vow on the Diary of
Amorez?"

"You are the second one to come asking about that particular tome, Prince
Valaskjalf." The librarian fidgeted with obvious discomfort. "I will tell you
exactly what I told Zamora, I am truly sorry, but the Dragon Diary was
removed from our care several years ago."

He could tell that she was being honest. It was news that he did not want to
hear, so he did not have to feign disappointment. "I had really hoped to make
that vow. I don't suppose there is a record of who has the diary?"

She shook her head meekly.

He sighed in frustration. "Alright. Thank you."

"Good day, Your Majesty." She curtsied.

Dimitri left her standing in the doorway. He began to wander the Temple's
labyrinth of hallways slowly, biding time to think before he would have to
break the news to Godilai and the others. If there truly were no records of who
removed the diary from the Temple, then tracking it down would be nigh on
impossible. Without the diary there was no way for him to achieve his dream
or keep his promise. There had to be a way to free the Shadow Dragons from
the confines of the Dragons' Gate. There just had to be!

Dimitri stopped at a window. Gazing out, he could see the Temple's
pinnacles reaching up into the cloudless, azure sky. It was as if they were
reaching for the large flock of birds far overhead, begging them to come down.
Far below and oblivious to the flock, people from every corner of the world
were gathering. It would soon be time for Zahadu-Kitai to rise; after a hard
winter, spring was finally here.

Dimitri did not care that it was a beautiful spring day, nor did he care about
the birds or the people. In fact, they only infuriated him more. How could the
Gods grant them happiness and a sunny day when he was so miserable?
Without the Diary of Amorez, he could never hope to unleash the Shadow

Dragons and keep the promise he made to his dying mother...

> *The group of hunters made their way home, traveling swiftly as the late evening sky betrayed a growing storm. Dimitri sniffed the air, loving the scent that signaled the coming rain. Something else tainted the smell. He inhaled again, long and slow, and detected a faint hint of blood and smoke. Panic gripped his heart and he rushed forward, ignoring the calls of his fellow M'Ktoah. He hollered back to them, warning them of the threat carried on the wind. They did not hesitate to chase after him.*
>
> *In mere moments they were upon the bridge that ran over the Thundering Falls, sprinting towards the heart of their burning city. Corpses of Dákun Daju and Hume alike littered the walkways, and blood slickened the old stones. Ferocious fighting could still be heard in a few sections of the city, and Viktohn freed the M'Ktoah to spill the blood of those who dared attack their brothers and sisters. Dimitri raced over the bridges as fast as he could, heading towards his home in hopes of finding his mother. He was still several meters away when the soft call of his name stopped him dead in his tracks. He found his mother in a pile of rubble, run through by a Hume's blade and barely clinging to life. It was then that she told him of his birthright and gave him the diary of his father. He vowed to avenge her, and, as she slipped from the world forever, told her that he was now a M'Ktoah. She was dead with her honor once again intact. She had smiled.*

A tear slipped from his crimson eyes. He sighed, miserable, and wiped the tear gently away. His temper flared when he heard footsteps quickly approaching. Another wretched Hume he would be forced to interact with. He took up walking again, hoping that the act would sway any passerby from speaking to him. A young girl in an obvious rush stopped abruptly when she spotted him. Her cheeks flushed and she curtsied. Dimitri froze, looked at the girl's white dress. White. White! He suddenly remembered the woman in the white cloak he had seen at the docks. She had been familiar to him, but he could not put a name to her face.

So he asked the girl. "Do you know of a woman around here who wears a white cloak?"

"You mean Judge Zamora?" she asked, her voice quiet as a mouse.

Zamora? No, that was not right. The mystery woman had a different name; he was sure of it. He rolled the name around in his head a moment. Zamora... He recalled the old librarian also mentioning the name when he asked about Amorez's diary. Realization struck him like a ton of bricks. Dimitri laughed in jubilation and kissed the girl in white. "Thank you!"

He heard her blubber something unintelligent as he sprinted down the hall. He raced around the corner, ignored the Knight that told him to be careful when he skipped down the stairs four at a time. Before he knew it, he was back at his quarters. Bursting through the door had his Dákun Daju companions up in arms at an instant. They relaxed the moment they realized it was him.

He made sure the door was sealed before moving further into the room. He spotted Vincent seated on the lounger by the unlit hearth, a half bottle of ale in his hand. Luna and Godilai were at the dining table adjacent from him, cleaning their array of weaponry. Dimitri moved to the windows, pulled the shutters closed. Then he made his way to the table where a pitcher of fresh water had been pushed aside to make room for the weapons. He poured himself a goblet full and downed it.

Luna would have given him a lash of her tongue for his abrupt entrance if he had not stopped her with a raised hand. "Amorez is here."

All three of his companions were dumbfounded. In their silence, Dimitri poured himself another goblet full of water.

Vincent was the first to speak, "What do you mean, 'Amorez is here'? She could not possibly be right here, right now."

"Do you remember the woman in the white cloak on the docks yesterday?" he asked, not expecting an answer. All he got was an 'uh huh'. "I could not put a name to her face at the time, but I knew I recognized her. That was Amorez!"

"If she was heading for the ferry," Luna crossed her arms as she spoke, "then I doubt that she is still on the island."

"One would think that, true." He nodded, flashed his companions a smile. "But the head librarian mentioned that someone else had come to the library looking for the diary – it was not there. Plus, the way she looked at me... she recognized me, which must have been her reason to return and check the library for her book."

"Did you ever find out what happened to the diary?" asked Luna.

"Unfortunately, someone removed it years ago and the Temple apparently has no record of who it was."

Godilai visibly frowned. "If Amorez was looking for her diary and it was already gone, then she does not have possession of it either. Where is the good news in this, Dimitri?"

"Simple." He pointed at her, clicked his tongue. "We know Amorez is here on the island; we capture her and force her to tell us where she hid my dragons."

"Capture Amorez?" Vincent guffawed.

Dimitri glared at him until his laughter died away.

"Let me get this right," the Judge sat forward in his chair, "You plan to capture the Legendary Dragon Keeper, the woman who not only survived the War, but led an entire army against Agasei. The woman who single-handedly slayed your father and locked his dragons away. One of the most powerful Sorceresses and most skilled warriors the world has ever seen." Vincent paused to look Dimitri in the eye, "You want us to capture her?"

"Well, when you put it like that…"

"You are out of your mind, Dimitri!" roared Luna. She hoisted her giant sword, strapped it to her back.

Dimitri grabbed her arm as she made way for the door. "Now wait just a moment! Hear me out."

She tore her arm from his grasp. Her eyes narrowed dangerously, and she spoke through gritted teeth. "Speak quickly, Hume-aju."

"Listen, Amorez was known for being a goody-goody; she would never allow an innocent person to die if she had the power to stop it."

Godilai scoffed. "So?"

"So? So, we have literally hundreds — no, thousands of people gathering right here at the Temple. We use them as innocents, threaten to kill them all if Amorez does not do as she is commanded."

"And if she does not?" Vincent kept his eyes locked on Dimitri while he put the bottle to his lips and took a swill of the ale.

Dimitri shrugged. "Kill them. It makes no difference to me."

Silence fell as the trio thought about the plan Dimitri had just put forth. He intently watched each of his companions as he took a sip of water. Godilai was sharpening her dagger on a honing stone as if nothing was going on, but Dimitri read her eyes. Her cyan gaze was distant, as if she were strategizing each possible outcome. Luna was a bit harder to read, but her rigid stance and crossed arms, Dimitri knew that she did not agree with him one bit. Vincent, on the other hand, was an ease to understand. Of course the Judge was completely against it; to him, Amorez was practically a warrior goddess and unbeatable.

It was Godilai who finally broke the silence. "If killing them now does not force Amorez out immediately, it will certainly send the message, 'We are willing to do anything to get what we want'. Word will spread quickly, and she will eventually give herself up."

"Now you get what I am saying."

Luna relaxed. "It is… a good plan."

"Unless she decides to fight back," muttered Vincent.

"Take a hostage," Godilai flatly retorted the Judge's argument. When he opened his mouth to speak again, she flung the dagger at him. It whistled a breath away from Vincent's ear and stuck to the wall behind him. To Dimitri she said, "How do you intend on threatening the people in the crowd?"

"Today is a day of fire," he said with a smirk. "What better way to celebrate than with the biggest fire they have ever seen? Or you two ladies can have some fun slaughtering them."

Vincent pipped up, "What about me?"

"Alright," Dimitri sighed, "three ladies."

Godilai's eyes laughed and Luna scoffed. Vincent, on the other hand, rolled his eyes in annoyance.

"I guess it's gather your weapons, boys and girls," Vincent grunted as he got to his feet, "we are about to start a war."

We had barely been on the planet a week when the first natives appeared. Although we had anticipated interaction with local life, these Dákun Daju were the last thing we expected. Though very similar to us – bipedal tool-users with set language skills – we had not expected them to be so… savage. They towered over us, and had wild hair and wilder eyes. Their weapons were displayed proudly, as were their scars. They were terrifying.

We tried to communicate, to explain our reason for settling the island, but they did not understand our words, nor did we comprehend theirs. We did, however, understand their swords and spears quite clearly: We were not welcome.

Night after night, we lost good men and women to raids. We tried again and again to speak with the leaders of the Dákun Daju, but they only saw us as weaklings unfit for their attention. Finally, after nearly a month of constant losses, our newly appointed king declared the Dákun Daju too great a threat to attempt a peaceful resolution. That is how the war between our races truly began.

– FROM "THE CHRONICLES OF ITHNEZ, VOL I"
BY ADJIRSÉ DÉDOS

I bolted upright, startling the person shaking me. I took a moment to catch my breath and take in my surroundings. I was back in the Temple of Fire, and an Archbishop was trying to wake me. He studied me with great concern, as if I had contracted some terrible disease. I nodded to him and glanced upward at the colossal statue. I could not suppress a frown as the Goddess' words replayed in my mind.

Tragedy will soon strike.

"Umm…are you okay?"

I blinked in surprise at the inquiry. "Perfectly fine." I said as I got to my feet. "Sorry I startled you, Archbishop."

He smiled sheepishly at me. "You were in a very deep meditation, child. Are you sure you are well?"

"Yeah, just having a rather strange conversation."

I left him staring at me, his mouth agape. As I made for the exit, I thought about my brief interaction with the Goddess. I wish I had asked Zahadu-Kitai what had happened to me before I was found on the beach three days ago. Perhaps it was in her 'You will begin to realize who you are then' that came with her warning of the coming tragedy. I so wanted to know more of the little details. Like what the book in my pack unlocked or what the tragedy was going to be. Maybe I could prevent it.

At the threshold of the pyramid, I glanced back, towards the statue of the Goddess. Are you sure you could not give me even a little hint? I sighed, stepped out of the pyramid. I did not make it very far. All the yards were packed with people dancing, eating, talking, and bartering. I chanced a look at the suns. It was about noon, and the Festival of the Phoenix had officially begun. I groaned; it would be hard to find my friends now.

"There you are! I've been looking all over for you." Ríhan ran up to me from somewhere in the crowd.

I threw myself at him in the biggest hug I could manage. He was nearly bowled over in the process.

"Uh…what happened to put you in such a mood?"

"We need to find Zhealocera. I have something to tell the both of you," I said, releasing him from the hug.

"I think I saw her over with one of the wine keepers. How about I meet you over there with some pies and sandwiches? I am starving."

I smiled. "Sounds like a plan to me."

"Great!" He kissed my cheek before running off.

I felt myself blushing. And I could have sworn he was blushing too. Why had he kissed me? More importantly, why did I want him to kiss me again?

I chuckled, a smile found its way across my lips. I turned in the direction of the wine stalls and began my search for Zhealocera.

I searched one wine stall after another, looking for a head of purple hair that would mark Zhealocera's presence. Finding none, I moved on to the last wine stall, a shabby-looking, open-walled tent. A huge crowd had gathered around one of the tables, shouting and roaring with laughter. I noticed money being traded and figured there must be a gambling competition going on.

I sighed. It looked as though Zhealocera was not here either. I was about to leave when I heard her voice.

"Throw the bloody dice already!"

"What the– ?" I spun around to search for her again, only to see the crowd at the table.

"Zhealocera?"

Her head popped up over the crowd, and she smiled when she spotted me. "Xyleena! Come on over. Let my friend through, you filthy animals!"

Several of the onlookers laughed and parted to grant me access to Zhealocera. I hesitated a moment, watching as my friend sat back down. I took a deep breath and walked up to her, curious to know what she was up to. I stood behind her and watched the table. There were four overturned cups and a rather large pile of money on the table.

"Um…Zhealocera, what are you up to? You realize you're surrounded by Humes, right?"

"Drunk Humes. They are much more amusing when they are drunk. Not to mention easier to win money from." Zhealocera laughed. "As for what I'm up to, it's a gambling game based on the dice."

I looked at the table again. "I thought students were prohibited from gambling…and I do not see any dice."

Zhealocera smirked at me. "I am not your average student. And the dice are under the cups. Players are given five dice each and place bets on how many of each number dice there are, but they can only bet one number. Whoever is correct at the end of the round gets the pot. If no one is correct, a new round starts, and the pot grows."

"I see… When you are done with this round, do you think I could steal you away? I have something important to talk to you about."

She quirked an eyebrow at me. "Sure."

"Twelve fives."

The bet stole her attention away.

"Six sixes."

"I'll bet…seven sixes," Zhealocera said.

"Eighteen ones!"

I could not help but chuckle at the drunken man who called that bet. I watched as all four players lifted their cups.

Zhealocera whooped. "Seven sixes! I was right!"

The crowd cheered as she gathered the money from the center of the table.

"Better luck next time, boys!"

"Wow," was all I could say as she dragged me away.

We escaped the crowd just in time to see Ríhan enter the wine keep. He seemed to sigh in relief as we walked up to him.

"This looks like a good spot to talk," Zhealocera said, leading the way to a quieter portion of the pavilion.

From here, we could see the musician stage and hear the music without being deafened by it. It was a lively tune that had many in the crowd on their feet dancing. Zhealocera sat down at a table and waved the barkeep over as Ríhan tossed her a sandwich and pie. She nodded her thanks as we sat down opposite her.

"What can I get ye, ma'am?" asked the barkeep.

"Three glasses and a pitcher of Katalanian red butter wine." Zhealocera flipped him a coin that was more than enough to pay for the drinks.

He thanked her and scurried away to fill the order.

"Where did you get money like that?" Ríhan asked, noting Zhealocera's full money pouch. "Surely you don't earn that much working security for the Temple."

She winked and bit into her sandwich. "So what did you want to talk to me about?"

I smiled. "I did it."

"Did what?" my companions asked simultaneously.

"I finally spoke to one of the Gods."

"Wait, you actually spoke to Them?" Ríhan asked, stunned.

"Yes, Zahadu-Kitai and I had a conversation."

He was about to say something, but opted for taking a bite of his sandwich instead.

"So," Zhealocera swallowed the bite she had taken, "what did She say?"

I was about to regale them with the whole story when the barkeep returned with our drinks. We thanked him, and he scurried away again. So I began my tale of this morning's little adventure. They both listened intently, not once interrupting to ask a question until I had finished.

Ríhan looked skeptical. "So Zahadu-Kitai visited you but didn't really tell you anything helpful?"

"Yes She did," Zhealocera said and took a long draught of her drink. She smacked her lips, then continued, "She warned you of something bad about to happen, and told you that once it does happen, you will know who you are. She also told you that that book you mentioned was important, though She was not specific as to why."

"Let's not forget that She dodged the question about the girl with the light." Ríhan pointed out.

Zhealocera put her glass of butter wine down. "So? Like Zahadu-Kitai said, She cannot give everything away. What we do know is that the girl with the light will be found in the future, and is of less importance than the book."

"I don't see how that really helps," muttered Ríhan.

"Change of subject," Zhealocera poured herself another glass of wine. She pointed at me. "You know how you said the man walking around as if he were the High Prince was acting suspiciously?"

I nodded.

"I ran into him last night." She leaned in closer. "Apparently, he has two Dákun Daju bodyguards."

Ríhan laughed. "Yeah right. The High Prince – actually the entire Za'Car family save Djurdak and Aadrian the Firsts – is known to be racist against your people. There is no way he would have Dákun Daju bodyguards."

"I caught one of them sneaking around after curfew last night. Her name is Godilai, and she mentioned another who goes by the name Luna Graves."

Why would Dákun Daju come here? I wondered. "Did she say why she was sneaking around?"

"Stargazing." She scoffed at that. "An obvious lie. Then the Prince showed up, all friendly like, but his eyes betrayed him."

"I know your people excel at reading emotions through the eyes, but why did the High Prince's eyes affect you so?"

"At first I thought it was just the way the light was hitting him, but his eyes really were red. That means that the man going around claiming to be the High Prince is really a Dákun Daju. And that is not all; Some travelers were on their way here when they came across what looked like evidence of a massive wildfire. They also discovered a man's body further in the woods where the fire had not touched. Apparently the man found dead looks like the real High Prince."

"Whoa!" Ríhan's jaw dropped.

"So we were right about the bad feelings we got from the guy claiming to be the Prince. Have you told anyone else about this news?"

"You mean have I reported it to the acting Palavant? No. I have not. I did not think about it. I probably should, now that you mention it."

I nodded. "She needs to know that there is a good chance that the man claiming to be the High Prince is a Dákun Daju and a murderer."

Zhealocera sighed and stood up. She flipped Ríhan a coin. "Thanks for lunch." Then she was gone.

"I was not expecting that," Ríhan said, setting the coin on the table.

It was a silver piece stamped with a face of a queen I could not name.

"That is quite a bit of money. More than enough to pay for eight sandwiches and pies. Where did she get all of it?"

"She won a few rounds of dice," I answered with a smile.

He stared at me dumbfounded. "She was gambling?"

I merely shrugged and drained the rest of my glass.

He cleared his throat. "So…um…you're not upset that I kissed you, are you?"

It was my turn to be dumbfounded. "Why would I be upset? I thought it was sweet."

He blushed. "I'm not sure why I thought it would upset you. I just…uh…I don't know."

I smiled. "You can kiss me again if you like."

"Well…I…um…I…" His blush deepened to an impossible color.

I smiled and leaned in to plant a kiss on his cheek. "You are so cute when you're flustered."

He smiled back and put his arm around me. We sat in silence, listening to the musicians play and enjoying each other's company.

All of a sudden, the music stopped. I glanced toward the stage in time to see the would-be Valaskjalf ascend the stairs trailed by two Dákun Daju women and an ugly old man.

"What are they up to?"

"I don't know," I frowned as an unknown sensation came over me, "but I don't like it."

That indescribably feeling crawled up my spine. I noticed several people now had their full attention on the stage, but many more were still bartering or chatting. I watched as the would-be high prince raised his hand to the air. I saw his mouth move then bolt of red lightning shot straight up from his fingertips. A blast of thunder followed suit, silencing the entire festival. All eyes were on the stage.

"If you value your pathetic lives, you will obey me!" he shouted and stomped his foot for emphasis. "Dragon Keeper Amorez or the Judge Zamora, whatever name you prefer these days, reveal yourself now and I shall spare the lives of all these pathetic Humes!"

The entire crowd, Ríhan and myself included, was stunned.

"Why would he be after her?" I wondered aloud. Some unknown force was screaming at me, Check the diary. I quickly undid the clasp on my satchel, flipped the top up. Sure enough, the book was still there.

"Amorez died centuries ago," Ríhan sounded doubtful of that.

"She faked it, made up a new identity to hide her existence as she has been doing most of her life," I stated in a mater-of-fact. How I even knew that was unknown to me.

The false prince had apparently grown irritated with the lack of response and continued to shout. "Not convinced I won't do anything to these worthless Humes? Fine! Should you choose not to reveal yourself, I will destroy the area."

Ríhan started pulling me away from the table. I let him.

That same unknown force screamed at me again, this will be the tragedy! And I knew it was true. I gripped Ríhan's wrist firmly, started to pull him away. "We have to get out of here. Now!"

Ríhan made no protest.

The man's patience had finally worn out. "You asked for it! Heile pricé!"

The two of us paused just outside the wine stall. I watched in dread as dark clouds instantly converged overhead, blotting out the midday sunslight. Deep down inside I knew what this was; I had seen it before.

I screamed, "No!"

The clouds swirled faster and faster. They exploded with a yellow and red light, and at last the tornado of fire was spawned. The man directed the spell into the crowd. They could not escape fast enough. There was no hope to save them. All I could do was watch the massacre. It made me sick to my stomach, yet I could not turn away. The tornado danced across the grass, sucking anything and everything into its inferno, melting them into nothingness. Ash rained down on the people scrambling to escape– ash that had once been their family, friends, and loved ones.

"By the Gods!" screamed a woman as she shoved passed me. The movement was so sudden that I was sent careening to the ground, spilling the contents of my satchel all over. I rushed to stuff it all away again, hoping against hope that no one saw the book.

Then I heard the man shout, "Godilai, Luna, after that girl! She has the diary!"

I looked to the stage; He was pointing… at me! Spotting me, the women leapt off the stage.

"Oh, Gods. No!" I was on my feet and running as fast as my legs could carry me.

Ríhan was right there beside me, urging me on. I did not dare look back to see if the two Dákun Daju were behind. I just focused on escaping.

Ríhan lead the way through the Temple Gates. "Hurry!"

Several Knights swarmed out to stop our pursuers. I heard the clanging of metal on metal and the cries of the Knights. I knew the Dákun Daju were winning.

Ríhan and I sprinted on. We followed the road over the bridge and down towards the docks. My sides ached from the exertion, and I could not seem to catch my breath. We reached the beach, spotted men at the docks. I was not sure if we could trust them, so we turned and followed the shoreline. A memory of a nearby cave flashed in my mind. If we could make it there, maybe we would be safe.

"Hydíca tabiki!"

A wall of ice erupted from the ground in front of us. We slammed into it. The ice cracked, then shattered. Ríhan and I crashed into the sand.

The magenta-haired Dákun Daju drew her gargantuan sword. "Give up now, girl!"

"No!" Ríhan threw himself at her only to be kicked away as if he were dust.

"Stupid, Hume! Do you think you can stop us?"

"I will if I have to." Ríhan got to his feet again and stood in front of me to shield me. "You won't have her."

The Godilai woman released a cold laugh. "Is that not sweet? You are far too weak to stop us, boy."

"No, Ríhan!" I screamed. I jumped to my feet and sunk into a fighting stance I recalled from a lost memory. This seemed to greatly amuse the two Dákun Daju.

The magenta-haired one laughed. "My, aren't you a funny, little Hume! You really think you can hold your own in a fight against us?"

"Try me!"

Both Dákun Daju were quiet for a moment.

"Do it, Luna." Smirked the Godilai.

She must be the one Zhealocera caught sneaking around, I thought. Godilai was the name.

"Very well. No weapons." The one known as Luna stabbed her sword in the ground and sunk into a fighting stance.

I held my breath as I watched her size me up with her colorless eyes. She sneered. "I won't go easy on you, Hume."

"I never expected you to." I kept my voice even and low. I watched her, waiting. She was as motionless as stone and only her hair dared to move in the soft breeze.

Ríhan took a step, stealing her attention for a heartbeat. I lunged at her and managed to land a punch in her face. She reeled on me as if insulted and launched into a full-on barrage of punches and kicks. She moved so fast I could not block a single blow!

"Stop it!" I heard Ríhan scream, but I did not take my eyes off Luna. To do so could prove fatal.

"Quit blocking with your face, girl! You will never win like that." Luna mocked.

She lunged at me again. This time I was able to grab her hair, yank her back, and throw her into the ground. I slammed my foot into her face hard enough to hopefully break her nose and render her unconscious.

"Look out!" Ríhan shoved me out of the way just in time to avoid Godilai's deadly blade. I stared at him from the ground as he closed his eyes in pain. Blood ran down the length of Godilai's sword and dripped into the sand of the beach. She had run her entire sword right through Ríhan!

"No!" I roared and threw myself at her.

She scoffed and caught me by the throat. I heard Ríhan collapse.

"Foolish," she muttered, yanking her sword free. "Now I will kill you."

"I demand that honor, Sortim." Luna growled, wiping blood from her nose. "She will pay for the insult she bestowed upon me."

"Very well." Godilai threw me to Luna's feet. "Just be quick about it."

"How do you want to die, little Hume?" Luna chuckled, grabbed the pommel of her sword.

I chanced a glance at Ríhan. An aura of blood grew around him, soaking the sand. I wailed and slammed my fists into the ground.

"You...will... pay...for... killing him!" I launched off the ground, attempting to kick Godilai's head.

She grabbed my foot and twisted it before throwing me away. I splashed into the cold water.

"Stupid girl!"

I leapt to my feet with a deafening scream. The Dákun Daju paused in astonishment, and then rushed forward with their weapons drawn. As they closed in for the kill, images flashed in my mind: hundreds of festivalgoers now naught but ash and Ríhan who would never live the life he dreamed. As I thought of their fate, an inexplicable power swelled within me, growing stronger and stronger until it threatened to consume me. And with but two words, I let it explode.

"Heile pricé!"

The sky darkened in an instant and a rumble echoed all around me. The two assassins froze, a look of complete horror on their faces. Lightning flashed and a wall of wind buffeted the three of us as it plummeted from the black clouds. With the wind came a surge of heat, and a funnel of green fire dropped from the sky. It touched down on the beach only meters away and blasted the area with such heat that clouds of steam billowed off the frigid water. The Dákun Daju immediately changed course, darting away from me and the inferno I summoned. I waved my hand in their direction, and the blazing tornado gave chase. The vortex danced across the beach as the assassins weaved to and fro in an attempt to escape. They were fast, but my inferno was faster still.

As suddenly as the explosion of power had come, it was gone. The tornado vanished with a roar as my knees buckled and gave way. The last thing I remembered was the cold embrace of darkness... then nothing.

*It took nearly a month for everything on the Haven to be
stripped down and transported to the settlement. Once it was
deemed unnecessary to return to the starship again, Aadrian
Ithnez II activated the ship's self destruct sequence. The
resulting explosion could be heard half the world away, and
pieces of the ship rained down from the heavens.*
– FROM "THE CHRONICLES OF ITHNEZ, VOL I"
BY ADJIRSÉ DÉDOS

"What in Havel do you mean she escaped?" Dimitri roared, wheeling about
to face Godilai and Luna. The quartet had reunited in the old Palavant's
quarters to go over what had happened. Both women stood, seething, before
Dimitri, only the old woman's desk between them. The fat Judge was leaning
against the wall closest to the door, obviously fearful of Dimitri's wrath. He
would use the door to escape quickly.

"She used magic," Godilai said quietly. "A spell that no Hume should even
be able to handle."

"And she fought like a Dákun Daju," Luna added, rubbing her nose.

"You mean to tell me that two pure-blooded Dákun Daju assassins were no
match for a little girl?" Vincent doubled over in laughter.

Luna and Godilai glared at him.

Dimitri sighed and sank into the Palavant's chair. "She is no ordinary little
girl. Of that, I have no doubt. But how in the name of the Five Souls was she
able to beat both of you?" He stared out the window, ignoring their excuses.

Much of the festival crowd had been killed in the firestorm he had
summoned. The scant few survivors were either forced into serving his team
or hiding somewhere on the island. And still there was no sign of Amorez. The
only other thing that bothered him about that whole ordeal was the purple-
haired Dákun Daju girl. He had last seen her disappearing around a corner of
the Temple flanked by two figures cloaked in white. He could not help but
wonder who was under the cloaks.

The unknown girl had him vexed most of all. Who was she and how did
she come to have the diary of Amorez? He remembered seeing the girl around
the Temple a few times. There was an air of familiarity about her when he had
actually looked at her. She seemed insignificant, yet she possessed the key to
finding the Dragons' Gate. Why?

"She will not escape a second time." Luna's muttering pulled Dimitri from
his reverie. He turned away from the window and listened to his team.

Godilai leaned over the elaborate wooden desk. "It is highly likely that she
did not survive the tax of energy the spell required. It is possible she is dead
and her body washed up on shore somewhere."

A smile found its way to Vincent's lips. "If that's true, then all we need to
do is have these Temple rats search the beaches here."

Godilai glared at him. "Think, you rotund imbecile. The current would have carried her away from the island."

Luna sighed. "Which means she could have washed up anywhere along the Anakor River."

"That is a lot of beach to search," Vincent grumbled.

"Given the amount of time the girl has been in the water, I doubt she could have gotten farther than Beldai or Sindai," Godilai said, glancing at the map on the wall for reference.

Dimitri sighed and reclined in the chair. "Here is the plan: Vincent and Luna, you two go to Beldai and check for the girl. Godilai and I will search for her in Sindai. Whether you find the girl or not, we sail out of Sindai at the beginning of next week."

Vincent scratched his head. "Three days to search two large towns? I'm not sure if that is enough time."

Godilai stared into Dimitri's eyes. "I am more interested in knowing why we will be sailing out of Sindai."

"I plan to find the Feykin." Dimitri rolled his eyes amidst protests from his team. He raised a hand for silence. "There are two reasons why I must find them."

Godilai crossed her arms. "Insanity is one of them."

Dimitri frowned. "I am not insane." He pulled his father's diary from a hidden pocket on his coat. "There are runes so old on these pages that not even Luna can translate them. I am hoping that a Feykin can."

"That's one reason. What is the other? More magic?"

"You just reminded me of a third reason. Thank you, Vincent." Dimitri smiled. "Amorez has allies amongst the Feykin. It is possible she ran to them in hopes of rallying them against us. We cannot afford to let that happen."

"And how do you intend to convince the Feykin otherwise if she has already beaten you there?" Godilai asked.

Dimitri hauled himself out of the chair; realizing that fire spell had worn him out more than he liked to admit. Slowly walked over to a table and lifted the lid on a small box. He paused to admire the treasure within: a simple necklace of three teardrop shaped stones embossed with scrolling glyphs. They were fastened together with black twine that was woven into a steel chain. He removed the amulet from the box and showed it to them.

"This was in the desk drawer. I recognized it from a sketch in my father's diary. Luna, please read the description my father left." Dimitri tossed Luna the diary.

She caught it and turned the pages until she found the sketch. "This is the pendant I stole from her. It is infused with an ancient power and allows one to control whoever wears it. There is a ring with... I can't make out the runes." Luna looked up from the page.

"What does that mean?" Vincent asked.

"The amulet allows mind control," Godilai answered. "But from the sound of it, a ring must also be used."

"My father gave my mother the ring, which she passed on to me. Now that I have the amulet, I can complete the spell."

Luna closed the book with a slap. "And you are going to waste it on a Sorcerer?"

Godilai sighed. "Terrible idea. Why not use it on Amorez herself?"

Dimitri nodded as he returned the amulet to the box. "I thought of that, too. Chances are slim that the spell will work on her, as she may have developed some kind of ward against mind control over the last four centuries. I intend to use the amulet on a Feykin so we can utilize the powers of a Sorcerer."

Godilai frowned. "What if Amorez already reached the Feykin? What good is one Sorcerer against many?"

"Hence why—if presented with an opportunity to do so—I intend to use it on Amorez. However, if she is not on the Sorcerers' Isle, a Feykin would make a wonderful substitute."

Vincent shifted his weight from foot to foot. "So…we're still wasting our time searching two towns for that girl with the diary?"

"Yes, because we still need Amorez's diary to unlock the Shadow Dragons," Dimitri explained with a sigh as he returned to the desk.

"Well, then what are we waiting around here for? Let's get going!"

Godilai smirked. "The ferry does not arrive for a few more hours, Vincent. Until then, how about we play with these Temple rats?"

"Do as you will to them," Dimitri said, sitting in the chair.

He listened as the three members of his team left the room. He sighed and closed his eyes for a much needed nap.

A heartbeat.

Another.

Blue trickled in, just a tiny bit. Then nothing.

Another heartbeat. It sounded so faint, yet it echoed over and over. I forced my eyes to open. A great expanse of blackness surrounded me. I floated in it like a wraith lost between worlds.

"Am I dead?" My whisper echoed back. I shivered, suddenly as cold as ice.

Xyleena.

I reeled about, searching for the one who had whispered my name. No one was there, just an endless expanse of black. I must have imagined it.

Xyleena.

I jumped back when a light suddenly flickered to life before me. It mesmerized me as I watched it materialize into the familiar shape of my best friend. Ríhan stared at me with sad, hazel eyes. I reached out to him, grateful for his presence in this void, but he pulled away as if I had burned him.

You let me die. Why did you let me die?

"Never! I would never let you die, Ríhan." I felt tears sting my eyes.

Still, he continued to face me with an unreadable stare. I thought you loved me, Xy.

"Oh, Ríhan! I do! I do love you. I will always love you."

He slowly shook his head and backed farther away.

"I'm sorry. I'm so sorry."

It is all your fault. You killed me!

"No!"

"Calm down! It's okay, girl. I'm not going to hurt you."

My eyes slammed open with a scream, and I struggled against the hold on me.

"Calm down!"

I stopped struggling long enough to face the one keeping me in bondage. A strange woman leaned over me, her features full of worry. She released her hold on me and backed away far enough for me to look her over.

She had light-grey hair spiked up almost mohawk-like and protruding from a violet bandana. She looked young, despite her grey hair. Her onyx eyes stared at me as I studied her. She wore a sleeveless tunic the same color as her bandana and loose, black trousers. Bizarre symbols were tattooed on her muscular biceps.

"Who are you? And what is this place?"

"My name is Teka Loneborne. You are in a clinic in Sindai. I brought you here for medical attention. Do you remember what happened to you?"

I frowned as the memories flooded back. "You should have just let me die."

"Why would I do something like that?" She crossed her arms and watched me as I slowly got out of bed.

"I would have been in a better place."

"Well, I could kill you now if you wish. Would that make you happier, girl?"

"My name is Xyleena. And if you are going to kill me, do it quickly. I have stuff to do."

She scoffed. "You won't be doing much when you're dead."

"I'd be with him again. That's all that matters."

"Ah, so you lost the one you loved?"

"Ríhan– " I choked on a sob. "I killed him."

"You killed him? Yet you want to join him in Havel? That doesn't soun—"

"We were attacked. He…he gave his life to save me." I cried and did not bother wiping the tears away.

Teka sighed. "You didn't kill him. The ones who attacked you—"

"Dákun Daju…I could have defeated them."

"A lone Hume girl against multiple Dákun Daju? You've got guts! But why would they have attacked you to begin with?"

"Their boss is after the book I have."

"Hired Dákun Daju? Their boss must be rich. And why would they be after a book?" I heard her move around.

"I don't know." I sighed and finally wiped my tears away.

I looked at Teka to see her flipping through pages of an old book. I instantly recognized it and leaped at her to swipe it back, but she was far faster than I was.

"Hey! That's mine!"

She closed the book and met me with an unreadable stare. "I know it's yours. I found it on you when I dragged you out of the Anakor. The question is, why is it so important to you, and to the guy who hired the Dákun Daju?"

"Give it back to me, and I will tell you what it is."

Teka quirked an eyebrow at me before gently handing the book over. I sighed and held it close to me before checking it for damage. There did not appear to be any.

"So what is it?"

"This is the Dragon Diary, a handwritten account of Amorez's dragon quest."

Teka blinked in surprise. "You have Amorez's diary? How did you get it?"

"I don't remember."

I sat on the edge of the bed and watched her. She simply stared at the book in awe.

"Your hair and eye colors… You can't be Hume."

Teka shook her head. "Not fully."

"I hope you're not Dákun Daju. I don't think I can stand to be so close to one after—"

"Feykin."

I blinked. "What?"

"I'm half Feykin."

"You…you're a…a– "

"You've never met a Feykin before, have you?"

I shook my head. "Not that I know of. You're nothing like what the books I have read described."

Teka quirked an eyebrow. "Oh? And how did they describe us?"

"One said Feykin were deadly intelligent and more aggressive than Dákun Daju. Another also said they have wings, but you don't."

"At least they got something right. Most Feykin are very aggressive due to their forced seclusion from the rest of the world. And I cannot grow wings, because I am only half Feykin. Though I am stronger and faster than Humes, I'm extremely weak compared to a pureblooded child Feykin."

"How come you're not with the rest of the Feykin?"

"Because I'm not really accepted amongst either Feykin or Hume. I survive by trading to Demons and Dákun Daju."

"So even the Feykin are racist. Gods! Why is everyone so against peace amongst the races?" I punched a pillow.

"It has been that way since the time of the Earthic Landings. And I can assure you, several people wish for peace amongst the races."

"Sure, everyone wishes for it, but no one does anything about it."

"What would you do?"

I thought about her question for a bit. "I don't know."

Our conversation lapsed into silence.

Finally, she sighed. "So what are your plans?"

I shook my head. "No idea."

Truth was I was too scared to return to the Temple in case the fake Valaskjalf was still there waiting to kill me. And the haunting memories of Ríhan's murder would probably drive me to insanity. I had nowhere else to go and no one to turn to.

"I don't suppose you know any Kinös Elda?" Teka asked.

"Not really. Why?"

"I was just thinking, maybe you should find out what that book of yours says. That way you will know why you were almost killed for it."

"Can you read it?"

"I can read the modernized runes but not the old ones that your book is written in."

"So where do I go to find a translator?"

"Only place I know would be the Sorcerers' Isle."

I gawked at Teka. "Say what?"

She smiled. "The Sorcerers' Isle."

"It's real?"

She laughed. "I was born there."

I thought about her proposition. I could go to the Sorcerers' Isle and get the diary translated while at the same time possibly learn more magic. Maybe if I studied under a Sorcerer for a little while I could come back and defeat those two Dákun Daju and avenge Ríhan.

"Okay. Let's go to the Sorcerers' Isle."

Teka smiled at me.

"How do we get there?"

"We'll sail there on my ship, Shadow Dance."

"How soon can we leave?"

"Soon. But first I'll have to get you some new clothes."

I looked down at myself to discover I was dressed in only a white smock.

"Your old ones were rather chewed up, so they were discarded."

"But I…"

Teka looked at me quizzically.

"I don't have any money."

"Don't worry about money." Teka tossed me a robe.

I sighed and donned it before collecting what was left of my effects. Teka lead the way out of the clinic.

Sindai was a quaint little town built on the banks of the powerful Anakor River. Most of the buildings were crafted from bricks of hardened river mud, but a scant few were entirely wooden. They were arranged in spirals around the heart of Sindai, a red marble obelisk from the ancient times.

"Verd is this way," Teka said, pointing down an alleyway.

She took the lead, and we meandered our way to a grassy hill just outside town. A miniature, wooden fence guarded a portion of the hill and surrounding area. A well-tended garden of flowers and strange vegetables grew inside the fence and a gravel walkway lead to a tiny wooden door.

"This is a shop?"

Teka only smiled. She walked up to the door and knocked thrice.

"Verdelite, you home?"

I heard a commotion from within; then the door creaked open. I could not see the being in the doorway, but a gnarled, pale hand reached out to beckon Teka inside. I followed slowly.

The interior of the hill was lit blue by strange stones along the walls. It was surprisingly warm, despite the lack of a fire. Furniture and knickknacks were strewn everywhere in the room, each only half the normal size. I could not help but wonder just what sort of creature lived here.

"Sit. Sit. Sit. You too tall for Verdelite." The creature's voice was barely above a whisper, but I could not pinpoint the source.

Teka sat cross-legged on the floor by a table and motioned for me to join her.

As I sunk to the floor, the creature entered the room with an armload of snacks, which were deposited on the table. The little thing stopped and stared at me with huge, dark eyes as I stared back, taking in all the details.

I figured this creature must be a she, for she wore something similar to a dress. Her skin was an extremely pale blue and covered in what looked like fur. Her face was small and broad with a wide nose. I could barely see her tiny ears through her thick mane of dark hair. And she was tiny, standing only about a third of my height at most.

"Verdelite, this is Xyleena." Teka's voice was barely above a whisper as she spoke. "Xyleena, this is Verdelite. She is a member of an ancient race known as the Wakari."

"I have never heard of the Wakari." I kept my voice low, figuring loud noises would probably hurt her ears.

"Wakari no like bright balls in big blue. Stay underground. Safe." Verdelite poured some sort of the hot drink into small cups as she explained.

"So you don't like sunlight." That explained her ashen complexion. "Then why are you on the surface, Verdelite?"

She handed me a cup. "Verdelite no know how Verdelite come. Teka save Verdelite. Verdelite live Sindai."

"You must have a history of saving people, Teka." I smiled at her as I took a sip of the drink. It tasted like a medley of berry juices and honey– delicious!

Teka shrugged. "What can I say? I have a soft spot. Say, Verd, Xyleena here is in need of some new clothes for a journey we will be leaving for soon. Do you have anything?"

"Teka come for garm? Verdelite have much garm. Yes. Yes."

She darted away from the table, moving faster than I expected with her short legs. A moment later, she returned to the table with an armful of clothes.

"Xyleena like Verdelite garm. Garm of all color. What Xyleena like?"

"I-I'm not sure."

Verdelite snorted at my answer and began drooping clothes over my shoulder. I could barely feel the cloth, even as I ran my fingers over it.

"What do you make these with? They're amazing."

"Verdelite sing stone. Stone weave to garm."

"You make clothes from stone and they're lighter than air? How is that possible?"

Verdelite just smiled at me as she rummaged through the pile. "Wakari secret."

"The Wakari believe they are living stones that their god, Arx-Omani, adored," Teka explained. "They have amazing talents for stone crafting. I believe their songs are actually some sort of slow-working spell."

"Xyleena take garm. Match eye color." Verdelite held a tunic to me.

I could not make out the color at all due to the blue lighting from the crystals along the walls, but I nodded in agreement anyway. Verdelite returned to digging through the pile again. She squeaked when she found something and pulled it out. Another tunic was draped over me before she went back to rummaging. Two more articles of clothing were laid in my arms.

"Garm for queen. Look better on Xyleena."

"Thank you for your generosity, Verdelite," Teka said with a chuckle. "How much do you want for these?"

The Wakari waved her hand. "Xyleena take gift. Good make new friend."

"That is so sweet of you. Thank you very much, Verdelite." I wanted to hug her for her kindness but was rather wary of alienating her. Instead, I hugged the clothes she had given me.

"I'll be gone for a while, Verd. If you need anything, just ask Jakk. He'll help you." Teka got to her feet and stretched.

"Verdelite ask Arx-Omani watch Teka. Keep safe. Verdelite light stones for Xyleena. New friend to Wakari."

"Thank you again, Verdelite. It was a pleasure meeting you." I bowed to her as I stood.

She grinned and moved to inspect my hip sack.

"Xyleena need new. Verdelite sing. Make new. Make of diamond. Never break."

"Wow. I look forward to seeing it."

"Is there anything you need while I'm abroad, Val?"

"Verdelite like more tea. Where Teka get?"

Teka chuckled. "That, dear friend, is a Feykin secret."

We were lead to the door and wished many a fond farewell. Finally, I could see the clothing Verdelite had given me– amethyst, diamond, ruby, emerald, obsidian, gold, and silver. I felt like the richest person in the world! How am I ever going to repay her?

"Now then, we'll head out. It should take us about eight days to reach the Sorcerers' Isle. Then we can get your book translated and decide on a path from there."

"Don't you feel guilty taking these clothes from her?" I asked as I fell into step behind Teka.

"She'll often give things away like that. She has no real need for money because she sings most of what she needs from nature. Wakari are a peaceful race. It's a shame that they're not really known."

"How will I ever be able to repay her?"

"The same way I do. Bring her gifts like tea or art. That is all she really wants– friendship." Teka stepped on the dock and gestured to the ship before us.

"Wow." I gawked at the ship.

It was fairly small, only about eight wyvern-lengths long and two wide. Almost everything about it was as black as night, yet it shimmered in the light of the suns. The two masts were of clear crystal, which refracted all light into countless rainbows. It was gorgeous!

"This is Shadow Dance, a ship sung from onyx and diamond. Verd gave it to me when my last ship was swallowed by a storm– the same storm I pulled her out of."

Teka lead the way to the main deck and barked orders to her crew, who immediately jumped to their chores. I was shown to a room on one of lower decks, allowed to change, then given the grand tour of the Shadow Dance.

Magic was what they named the mutagenic powers that had developed in the Bedebian survivors. No one understood precisely what had caused the mutation, but they managed to narrow down the source to some form of radiation in the atmosphere of Bedeb.

– FROM "THE CHRONICLES OF ITHNEZ, VOL. IV"
BY ORN TERSON, COURT HISTORIAN

Dimitri's ruby eyes watched as Godilai paced the room, impatient for news. Their search of Sindai had resulted in no sign of the girl, so the duo had gone to the team's designated meeting place. The shabby tavern reeked of fish and booze and something Dimitri did not want to think about. The entire place made him sick, but not nearly as sick as the thought of losing the girl. If the Anakor River swallowed her, then the Dragon Diary was lost as well. That very thought distressed Dimitri beyond words– the diary was the key. If it was truly lost due to the incompetence of two Dákun Daju women, there would be Régon to pay.

Dimitri sighed and relaxed into the pillows propped up against the headboard of a lumpy bed. His gaze continued to follow Godilai. Truth was, he wanted to get to know her more, but she was in no mood for conversation. So he admired her from afar.

Her long, shapely legs made pacing the room rather quick work. He was sure she would wear out what was left of the tattered rug. Godilai froze mid-stride and drew her swords a heartbeat later. Dimitri heard it, too, but made no move to arm up; he knew those footfalls. The door burst open as a burly sailor was thrown through it. Luna and Vincent stepped in a moment later.

"What is the meaning of this?" Godilai yelled, pulling the sailor to his feet by his hair.

"He has seen the girl," Luna answered, sealing the door.

Dimitri smirked and looked the sailor over. "Has he now?"

He was tall and muscular with skin worn from the winds. He sported shoulder-length blond hair and a full beard.

"How long ago was the girl found? Did you get her name?"

The sailor's blue eyes met Dimitri's in a fierce gaze. "What does it matter to you?"

"Very well. What is your name?" Dimitri asked, getting to his feet.

"Jakk."

"Well, Jakk, the girl has something in her possession that belongs to me. Now tell me what happened to her."

Jakk crossed his arms defiantly. "What if I don't remember?"

Godilai's blade was on his neck a second later. In a whispered hiss, she said, "I suggest you start remembering."

Jakk slowly unfolded his arms. "She washed up on shore this morning. Teka and I brought her to a healer where she made a rapid recovery. Then I left for my crabbing. I never learned the girl's name. I caught a glimpse of Teka's ship sailing away when I returned to port. Where she went? I do not know. I don't even know if the girl is with her."

Dimitri stared at the man as he thought things over. The mystery girl had the diary, and chances were high that she could not read the runes within. She would need to go somewhere… particular to get it translated, and there was only one way to get to that island. Finally, Dimitri asked, "And what kind of ship does this Teka own?"

The sailor seemed to grow extremely uncomfortable with the subject. "It's…uh…one of a kind."

Dimitri scowled. "One of a kind does not help me. What is the name of the ship, and what does it look like?"

"It's black. Two masts. Silver sails. Really hard to miss."

"And the name?"

The sailor did not answer. Godilai dragged her blade over his neck, leaving a crimson line. He got the hint. "Shadow Dance," Jakk whispered and hung his head, ashamed.

"So now we are searching for a black ship called Shadow Dance and captained by someone named Teka. And which direction was the ship headed?" Dimitri asked, turning his back on the sailor. He grabbed his father's diary from the hidden pocket of his coat and began to flip through the pages.

Jakk sighed. "I don't know. North?"

"Perfect. That was most helpful, Jakk."

"What do you want from the girl?"

Dimitri growled at the inquiry.

A sudden thud followed a gurgling noise. Dimitri looked over his shoulder. Godilai was cleaning the blood of her sword and the sailor lay dead on the floor, his neck sliced wide open.

"Why did you kill him?" Vincent asked, sounding very annoyed.

"He outlived his usefulness," Godilai answered, returned her sword to its sheathe. "Besides, if we stay here talking any longer, we will miss our ship."

"Indeed we will," Dimitri mumbled. "Where did you two find him, anyway?"

"He was dropping off a load of crab when the ferry from Beldai landed," Vincent explained. We figured he had been away when you two went about, so we asked. We got lucky."

"I am curious," Luna began, "what lies to the north aside from Arctica?"

"The Sorcerers' Isle," Dimitri answered with a smirk.

"And just how do you know that?" asked Godilai.

Dimitri flipped to a page in Agasei's diary and showed his team the spread– a hand-drawn map of the world. Just west of the country of Arctica lay an ellipse with the words "Sorcerers' Isle" scrawled in standard.

"There's no way in Havel that that diagram is accurate," Godilai muttered.

Dimitri winked at her. "It depicts a force field around the isle. My father could not figure out how to break it, but I know how."

Godilai frowned.

Luna sighed. "And just how do you know you can get through?"

"A few centuries of research will make you well schooled in several things." Dimitri slapped the diary shut, returned it to his pocket. "It doesn't matter at the moment. We need to get out of here before the ship leaves without us."

"You really think the brat is headed to the Sorcerers' Isle?" Vincent asked, helping Dimitri gather some belongings.

"I hope she is. And as soon as I find her, I am going to kill her myself to make sure it's done right."

"Let's get going!" Godilai shouted, shoving her way past the others.

I shall never forget the words spoken by Thedrún that day, "It is only in sorrow that the storm masters us; in elation we face the storm and defy it."

– FROM "CONVERSATIONS WITH DRAGONS"
BY DJURDAK ZA'CAR

My arms were heavy. My legs were sore. My whole body begged for sleep. But haunting visions kept me awake. There was nothing I could do to force myself into a dreamless rest. Therefore, I once again found myself on the main deck of Teka's ship sparring with shadows. I had rehearsed the battle dance Zhealocera and I had barely begun to practice until each movement became instinctive.

As I repeated the dance for the sixteenth time this night, I thought about the mess my life had become. I was on the run from an enemy I knew little about, headed for an island long thought myth, and my best friend, Ríhan, had been murdered– all for a stupid book!

I grumbled at the thought of that book, the Dragon Diary. Everything that had happened to me in the last two weeks was because of that cursed book. I wish I could just throw the cursed thing overboard and be done with it. But every time I tried to dispose of the book, something, like a spectral whisper in my ear, stopped me.

I sighed and began the routine again. Who am I trying to fool, anyway? I am nothing more than a teenage girl who cannot remember an inkling of her past. Why could the diary not find its way to someone more worthy to uphold the legends within? Someone…stronger.

"Amorez, why don't you do this yourself?" I whispered to the wind.

"Land ho, Cap'n!" The cry of the boy in the crow's nest yanked me from my thoughts.

I glanced up and followed the direction he pointed. A shadow formed just over the predawn horizon. I stared at it as we drew nearer. Soon enough I could make out mountains piercing the sky behind a curtain of tall trees. It looked so…normal. Not at all what I was expecting the Sorcerers' Isle to look like.

"We should be landing within the hour, Xyleena," Teka said, suddenly beside me.

I nodded but otherwise did nothing.

"Maybe you should have something to eat before we disembark. You look weak."

"I'm fine."

I heard Teka click her tongue before she walked away. I sighed and continued to watch the island grow. I could not shake the feeling of familiarity, almost as if I had seen the island before. I scoffed and finally looked away. Yeah right.

As Teka predicted, the Shadow Dance made landfall in just under an hour. I was surprised to discover that Teka had beached her ship on the white sand beach of the island instead of anchoring a few leagues out and rowing ashore. She explained that high tide made the beach almost disappear, making it easier to leave the island. Plus the ship was safer beached as it was instead of anchored out at sea.

Teka, two of her crew, and I were the only ones to leave the ship.

"Too many visitors would send the Feykin into a defensive frenzy. We want them to listen to us, not kill us," Teka explained as she led the way up a path to the trees.

"I don't know if I want to meet them now," I muttered.

Teka chuckled.

"They're not bad," one of the crewmembers replied. "They're just protective of their land and their people."

The other crewmember patted me on the shoulder as he spoke. "Trust me, lass. I'd rather deal with ten Feykin than an angry wyvern during breeding season."

I smiled but found no comfort in their amusement. Try as I might, I could not escape the heightened sense of awareness that washed over me. We are being followed.

I cast my gaze around the lush foliage that surrounded us. Plants of all kinds grew wild and dense, completely untouched by man. Multicolored flowers, ferns, and grasses made the forest absolutely breathtaking to behold.

A gentle rustle of wings had my heart in my throat. I slowly moved to grasp the tessens from my bag. I breathed slowly like Zhealocera taught me, trying to calm myself. A twig snapped. I spun around to block any attacker but found none. A bird cawed angrily and took flight. I watched it for a moment as I exhaled slowly.

"Just a dahma bird," Teka muttered, a tinge of disappointment in her voice.

I turned to face her in time to see her sheath a dagger. She winked at me before turning in the direction we had been headed.

"So are we going somewhere special?" I asked, falling in step behind Teka.

I heard her smile. "Not really. You see, we cannot enter any of the Feykin towns without their permission. So we have to find them first."

"I don't understand. How do we find the Feykin if we don't go to their town?" I frowned when her chuckle reached my ears.

A dozen bodies suddenly burst from the foliage and surrounded us. Teka and her crewmembers made no move to fend them off, but I flipped open my tessens just in case.

"Like that," Teka answered as she rested a hand on my arm.

I sighed and allowed myself to relax.

"Kahs gözandí, fratime," Teka said. "Eo ík Teka Loneborne."

"Aké la ja chee?" One of the older-looking men in the group surrounding us stepped closer.

He and Teka conversed while I studied our captors.

Though styled in different ways, their hair was always silver. The only way I could tell them apart otherwise was their eyes, which varied in as many exotic and strange colors as the Dákun Daju. They were clad in strange garb that looked like it had been woven in eccentric patterns from various plant life.

Snow-white and pearled wings extended from the backs of each Feykin. I noticed that the tips of their feathers were tinted to match their eyes. A strangely crafted silver armor ran the length of each of their wings and made them look fierce and dangerous. Yet overall, they looked…well, human. Nowhere near as exotic as I was expecting.

"We are to follow them to Thorna and speak to the Council of Elders," Teka announced in Standard.

I turned to face her. "Is that normal?"

"No. But because they do not know you, they are demanding that you be judged by their Elders before they offer any assistance." Teka nodded to the older Feykin she had been speaking to.

He uttered a command in Kinös Elda, and the Feykin started through the trees. Teka, her crewmates, and I followed a moment later.

"What would happen if these Elders decide I am not worthy of their help?"

Teka sighed. "They will kill you."

"That's comforting," I muttered.

We must have trekked miles upon miles through the dense forest– over hills and under a noisy waterfall where we all paused to drink. I had no idea exactly how long we traveled, as the foliage blotted out the suns. On many occasions, we caught sight of large deer herds. The Feykin took note of their location, probably to return later for a hunt.

Just when I thought I could not take another step, one of the younger boys in the group escorting us let out an excited whoop. He burst forward with enough speed to rival a Dákun Daju and used his wings to thrust him forward faster. Some of his companions laughed at his antics and gave chase. How they could have so much energy after such a long walk was beyond me. I began to wonder what had suddenly got them so riled up. At the crest of a sizable hill, I had my answer.

Looming over us were the largest trees I had ever seen! Each one must have grown to at least a league high, if not more. And nestled among the branches were hundreds of platforms and bridges, creating a wondrous maze through the giant trunks of the trees. Many of the platforms had huts built on them, and women were about doing various chores. Children ran across the bridges playing and laughing.

I continued to gape at the splendor overhead as our guide lead us up a spiraling walkway and into the heart of the canopy. We caught the attention of many inhabitants as we paraded past them. Some of the younger children joined the parade. One of the children, a small girl with lavender eyes, grabbed my hand and walked beside me.

The parade ended just outside an insanely wide tree that had been hollowed out. Our guide ushered us inside. Teka thanked him in Kinös Elda and lead the way over the threshold. I blinked, waiting for my eyes to adjust to the brightness within.

We were in an enormous, round room. The walls were lined with floating orbs, which glowed in varying colors of light. In the center of the room was a wooden bench that stood before five raised platforms. Seated on each of the platforms was an ancient-looking Feykin flanked by trident-wielding guards.

Teka bowed to the five Elders before taking a seat on the bench. Her crewmates and I mirrored her actions. The old Feykin were silent as they studied us for a long while. I took this time to observe them.

The oldest man in the middle wore a dark-green, pointed hat that flopped to one side of his head. His grey eyes were half hidden by small spectacles and white-silver hair. His face was gentle but wrinkled and sporting a long beard. His four companions were similar, but upon closer inspection, I noticed two were women.

"Kíen la ja süm, Teka Loneborne?" The man in the middle spoke in a strained whisper.

I began to wonder exactly how old he was.

"Estéz karétez la meo micallaz, bó et kanójo wa Xyleena."

The conversation continued, keeping its quiet tone. I found myself wishing once more that I knew a bit of Kinös Elda.

"Xyleena?"

The old man's voice yanked me from my thoughts. I looked at him, confused.

"It ja nan hakaní estéz tantúre?"

"Uh…"

My vacant expression made him smile.

"Hoko bemum Thera Onyx." He flicked his wrist, and a guard ran from the room.

Upon learning that this girl, who had proven herself to be the Dragon Keeper, was a Priestess of the Temple, I grew concerned; not for her, but for the rest of the world. In all honesty, I feared that she lacked the resolve to do what was necessary to save us.

– FROM "THE SECOND KEEPER"
BY THERA ONYX

We must have sat there in silence for a good hour before the guard returned with a young woman in tow. Unlike the other Sorcerers I had seen so far, she wore jet black, which matched the ebony feathers of her wings. Her silver hair fell past her shoulders and covered one of her deep, violet eyes. She dared a glance at me before bowing to the five Elders.

"Núl wa de ja du bemum meo po, Ujak?" Her voice was like water– gentle, yet hiding an untamable ferocity.

The old man in the middle platform motioned toward me and said something in Kinös Elda. I felt foolish being talked about in a language I did not know.

"My uncle says you do not understand the Ancient Tongue. Is this true?"

I smiled nervously at the girl and nodded. I wondered how she had learned Standard in a society that seemed to know only Kinös Elda. I watched as she said something to the old man, her uncle. He said something in return, and the girl faced me again.

"He wishes to know why you have sought us out."

"I thought Teka explained that to the man she spoke to in the woods."

I looked at Teka for an answer, but she only shrugged. I sighed and returned my attention to the girl.

"I came here to find a direction, I guess."

"So you are lost?" The girl crossed her arms. "Why would you risk your life and come to Feykin lands to ask for directions?"

"You probably won't believe a word I say." I sighed. After a moment, I rummaged through my satchel and pulled out the strange book. "I am being hunted by two Dákun Daju women, a high prince wannabe, and an ugly judge all because of this stupid book. It is written in runes that I cannot read. Teka cannot read them either, so we came here to get it translated and come up with a direction to take with it."

The Feykin girl betrayed no emotion as she looked at me. Without a word, she turned away to translate what I had said. The five Elders grew ever more shocked as the translation went on. When at last the girl finished, the Elders excused themselves and disappeared.

"They have gone to decide what to do with you," the girl explained. She waved her hand and muttered something. A stump suddenly grew from the floor. "I am called Thera, by the way," she said, sitting.

"Nice to meet you. I am Xyleena."

Thera's intense gaze held mine, leaving me feeling awkward.

"You...remind me of someone." Finally, she looked away.

"Who?" Teka asked quicker than I.

Thera waved the question off. "An old friend of the family."

"I hope you don't think me rude, but how did you learn to speak Standard?"

Thera chuckled, looked at me again. "My mother taught me after she returned from her adventures."

"Your mother must have been brave to leave the safety of the isle," one of Teka's crewmates replied.

Thera smiled "Thernu Onyx was brave, as brave as the companions she traveled with."

"Thernu? Where have I heard that name before?" I mumbled.

Had Ríhan been beside me, he would probably laugh before stating the answer as if it were obvious. I lamented at that thought.

"Thernu was the Necromancer who brought life to Amorez's Twelve," Thera said proudly.

My jaw fell slack in surprise.

"Wow!" exclaimed Teka's crewmates.

"I am honored to meet the daughter of a legend." Teka bowed her head in respect to Thera.

"But that happened almost four hundred and fifty years ago," I pointed out.

"Time does not flow as quickly here as it does beyond the island," Thera explained. "For each year here, seven pass outside."

"That means only about sixty-four years have passed here since the days of Amorez and Agasei," Teka's crewmate explained.

Thera nodded.

I took a closer look at the Feykin girl. She could not have been more than twenty, which I found odd given the amount of time that had passed. Surely Thernu was not in her sixties when Thera was born."Do Feykin age slower than Humes, too?"

"I do not know enough about Humes to say for sure."

"Amorez was a Hume," Teka stated matter-of-factly.

"Yeah, but an immortal one," I muttered, earning a chuckle from Thera.

"That is true. In all the time Amorez spent here, she did not age."

I could not help but wonder about the Dragon Keeper. The false prince had called her out at the Festival, but she had not shown herself. How did he know she was even alive? "Say, Thera, do you know what Amorez looks like?"

"Of course. Red hair. Green eyes. Sometimes wears glasses. Stands about your height."

That description reminded me of someone I had recently met, but I had to be sure. "Does she wear a white cloak, black leathers, and silver armor emblazoned with scrollwork?"

"On occasion." Thera's brow creased. "Why do you ask?"

I was amazed. The mysterious Judge Zamora and Dragon Keeper Amorez were one in the same! "You're not going to believe this, but a woman by the name of Judge Zamora came to the Temple of Five Souls a while ago. The first day I really got to meet her, she was in black leathers and silver armor. She had a duel with Freya, the Wolf Demon subst– "

"Ah, dear Freya." Thera smiled.

"You know Freya, too?"

"Oh, yes. Amorez's entire team– Djurdak, Freya, Amorez, Moonwhisperer, Artimista, and Mother– spent many a fortnight here."

"I have never heard of Moonwhisperer or Artimista," I said.

"Moonwhisperer was Kadj-Aramil's chosen name. He was the alchemist who also helped birth the dragons. Artimista was Kadj's older sister and only surviving family member. Both were Dákun Daju."

"That is probably why I've never heard of them. Dákun Daju are often written out of Hume history." I sighed and vowed to never forget their names.

"I could get you one of our history books," Thera said. "But you would have to learn the Ancient Tongue to read it."

"At this point I think it would be wise if I did learn. And I would love to read an accurate account of history."

It was then that the five Elders filtered back into the room. They eyed me as they once again took their places at their respective platforms. Thera stood and waited for them to speak.

"Meoja ker dumakunga…" The voice of Thera's uncle continued in a wheezy drawl.

Thera nodded and turned to face me.

"They have decided to declare you friend, and they have a gift to present to yo—" She spun back to the Elders. "Iríjhone Reshé?"

"Vero, Thera." Her uncle nodded, bemused. He pointed at me. "De wa et nena ni Amorez."

"I should have known," Thera muttered and turned to face me. "They have a gift for you, Dragon Keeper."

"Dragon Keeper?" Teka and her crew exclaimed.

My mouth fell open in surprise. Then the words of Zahadu-Kitai came back to me, You will begin to realize who you are then. After a while to recover from the shock, I said, "There is no way that I can be a Dragon Keeper. I cannot… I am not strong enough or smart enough. I couldn't even protect the person I loved."

"I know you are Amorez's daughter; you look just like her," replied Thera in an obvious tone. "Besides, do you think Amorez was instantly battle forged when she first rose against Agasei?" She asked, crossing her arms. "She had to learn, and she lost many friends on the battlefield. It is not an easy job. It is, however, a necessary one."

Teka placed a hand on my shoulder. "She's right, Xy. I'll bet my boat that the guy chasing you is Agasei's descendant."

"That would explain a lot," I muttered, looking at my feet.

Thera suddenly knelt in front of me. She extended her hand, revealing a gorgeous necklace. It was elliptical in shape with gold and silver filigree around an amber jewel that looked like the eye of a lizard. Twelve empty sockets were hugged by the filigree and appeared as if jewels had fallen out of them.

"This was Amorez's dragon eye amulet. She left it with us to protect until it was needed again. It is the key to summoning the Dragons of Light."

Thera clasped it around my neck, and a strange sensation of being tugged in different directions overcame me.

"How does it work?" I asked, admiring the amulet.

"I am not sure how it works. Amorez never said." Thera stood and turned to face the Elders.

They conversed in Kinös Elda again while I tried to figure out why I felt like I was being tugged in so many directions. Could it be the dragons calling to me?

"Well, looks like we have a new traveling companion."

Teka's voice called me out of my thoughts. I looked up to meet Thera's violet gaze.

"The Elders want me to teach and protect you while you quest for the Dragons of Light."

I slowly looked up at the Elders, then to Thera. "Is seeking the dragons really necessary? I mean, why not just take out the bad guys now?"

Thera gaped at me. "You said yourself that you are not strong enough. You will need the Twelve to make you stronger. Plus, what if your attack on the Dark Keeper fails, resulting in him winning the Dragon Diary and releasing the Shadow Dragons?"

"With the help of the Feykin, an attack on him shouldn't fail," I pointed out.

"We have no real reason to get involved," Thera answered quietly.

Her answer left me confused.

"Agasei's heir has made no move against us. Therefore we do not see him as a worthy threat to stand against him."

"But if he gets the Shadow Dragons he's sure to wipe out every non-Dákun Daju. Isn't that reason to—?"

"No," Thera curtly answered. "Chances are likely that he does not know the location of our home. Therefore he is no threat to us."

"What if you're wrong and he does know where to find the Sorcerers' Isle?"

Thera shrugged. "Hopefully you will be on your dragon quest by then."

I sighed. "I think we should take him out of the picture now before he can amass any sort of arm—"

"Why are you afraid to go on this journey?" Thera interrupted.

I looked up to meet her gaze once more. "There are a few reasons..." I muttered, looking away.

"Such as?"

I sighed and stood up in such a rush that the guards jumped as if expecting an attack. "First, I just lost my best friend, and I need time to myself. Second, I have never seen the world outside the Temple walls. I would not know what to do or where to go. Third, I am not strong enough. And lastly, Amorez is alive, so I am not needed."

Thera shook her head. "The killing of your friend is reason enough to become stronger. Do you not want to avenge him? And I know that seeing the outside world is an exciting idea. I have never left the Sorcerers' Isle, and I would love to see what lies in the world beyond. Amorez might be alive, but for some reason the dragons are looking to you to be their Keeper. Questing for them will make you stronger."

"Thera's right, Xy. You need this," Teka replied.

Her crewmates nodded in agreement. I sighed and met the gaze of each of the Elders. They simply stared back. I closed my eyes and tried to imagine what Ríhan would say at a time like this.

Do it, Xy! Think of how much you could learn! It will be exciting! His voice echoed in my mind.

As much as I wanted to fight it, I felt myself giving in. This quest would be to avenge him; him and everyone else that false prince and those Dákun Daju murdered. I exhaled slowly and opened my eyes.

"When do we leave?"

I followed Thera out of the hollowed tree that served as the Elders'
chamber. Thorna had grown dark, lit only by more of those strange, floating
orbs. Few people wandered the bridges and platforms. Night had descended
quickly.

I cast a glance skyward only to see thick foliage and no sky. Disappointing.
Just when I wished to see the familiar constellations, they had become
obstructed. That small comfort would have been welcome in this strange
place.

Teka's voice pulled me from my reverie.

"Return to the ship and tell the crew we will be staying a few days. I'll
send word should anything change."

"Aye, Captain." Her two crew members left.

"May I see the Dragon Diary, Xyleena?" Thera asked after watching the
two men vanish into the darkness of night.

I quickly pulled the old book from my sack and handed it to the young
Feykin. She began to flip through the pages, and a frown etched its way across
her features.

"It will take me some time to convert these ancient runes to Standard. You
are welcome to stay with me while I work on this."

"Very generous of you, Thera. Shíkai ja," Teka replied as she and I
followed the young Sorceress over a bridge.

"Gratíe."

Thera stopped mid-step, causing Teka to almost bump into her.

They both faced me.

"Eo du capel ja nan lig Kinös Elda."

I stared blankly at Thera as she studied me for a long minute.

"It ja hakaní?"

I crossed my arms in irritation. "What?"

"Xy, you said thank you informally in Kinös Elda," Teka explained.

"Really?" I uncrossed my arms.

"You truly did not know?"

I shook my head. "Honestly, I do not recall anything about my life. I am
not sure what happened to me, but I was found washed up on the beach by the
Temple of Five Souls. When I woke, I had no memories of who I was or
anything. It is possible that I really do know Kinös Elda, I just cannot be
certain."

Thera and Teka looked at each other then back at me. It was Teka who
came out of the shock first. "Have you spoken other Kinös Eldic words

before?"

"Well… I have used heile pricé once befo—."

"Wait a second!" Thera exclaimed. "You have used magic before but you are not trained? Do you have any idea how dangerous it is to attempt such a thing?"

"I just repeated the things that I heard Ríhan and Zhealocera use, among others."

"Who is Zhealocera?"

"A Dákun Daju warrior at the Temple of Five Souls."

I watched as Thera pondered over my words.

"I did not know a Dákun Daju lived there," Teka muttered. "What is she like?"

"She's actually really nice, but she can be rather intimidating when you aren't used to Dákun Daju like I was."

"Though some Dákun Daju are adept with magic, it is best to learn from an experienced Feykin or not at all," Thera said rather haughtily. She turned and once again started across the bridge. "What do you know of magic, anyway? Aside from the few phrases you overheard others use."

A voice from an old memory suddenly flooded my mind. I repeated the words as if I had heard them a million times. "There are three rules. One, the caster must know enough Kinös Elda to summon an element and command it. Two, the amount of magic summoned cannot exceed the limits of the caster or the caster will die. Three, magic, like most things, is best learned through time and experience."

"Wise words. I am impressed that you know so much." Thera was silent as she led us around a platform. She stopped in front of a hut and pulled aside the curtain hung in the doorway. "This is my home."

"Thank you again for letting us stay here," I replied as I followed Thera and Teka into the hut.

"Luminös!" At Thera's command an orb of light formed in the center of the room, forcing the shadows of night to retreat and momentarily blinding us. "Pox is late."

"Pox?"

"My younger sister, Piper. Pox, affectionately. Please make yourselves comfortable." Thera disappeared behind a curtain to another room.

I took in the features of the room I stood in. It was so plain that I could not believe I was in a house on an island long thought nothing more than myth. I had imagined all sorts of magical knickknacks and instruments. Instead, there were only plain walls with a few shelves laden with books, strange crystals, and bottles. A long couch occupied one wall, and a woven rug lay on the floor before it.

"Did you find these crystals on the beach here, Thera?" Teka asked as she admired a particularly large sample on a shelf.

"No. Mother brought them back from a Hume city…Gesa, I think." Thera returned from the other room, arms heavy with blankets, which she laid on one end of the couch.

93

The curtain leading outside was suddenly pulled aside, and a young girl, no more than twelve, walked in. She looked similar to Thera, but her silver hair fell to the middle of her back, and her eyes were jet black– the same as her wings.

Thera frowned. "Ja lah tarlé, Pox. Da du la ja?"

"Kíen la déoja?" The girl I figured was Pox pointed at Teka and me.

Thera hissed at her.

"Eo dur ir né et izvucí tig Tarik bó Valadri."

Thera sighed. "I thought I told you to stay away from Tarik."

"You are not mom! Stop telling me what to do! And who in the name of Régon are these two?" Pox crossed her arms and glared at me.

"Xyleena is the new Dragon Keeper. And you should remember Teka," Thera answered as she faced me.

"What happened to Amorez? I like her. She should be the only Dragon Keeper."

"Silence, Pox! You're being rude."

Pox pursed her lips in a pout. "I wish mom were still here so you can stop acting like a bossy ta– "

"Nan vocé!" Thera shouted, waving her hand in Pox's direction.

The younger sister stomped her foot and shoved her way past Thera. She disappeared into a room behind a curtain.

Thera sighed. "I apologize for Pox's behavior. After mother died, her attitude changed drastically."

"I understand," I muttered.

"It's fine, Thera," Teka said as she took a seat on the couch. "What happened to Thernu? I have not heard any news."

"She was on her way to Saathoff on Arctica's western shore when a storm blew up. The storm destroyed the ship she was on. It has been almost a year now, and there have not been any reports of survivors." Thera sighed and sunk into a seat on the couch. "Pox has hated me since. It wouldn't surprise me if she turned into a Necromancer."

"This is where I get confused." I said. "What is the difference between a Sorcerer and a Necromancer?"

Thera smiled briefly. "There are two castes in our society: Sorcerer and Necromancer. Sorcerers use the elements in the world around them, while Necromancers delve into darker magic that often deal with curses, soul breaking, and the undead."

"How many Necromancers are there now?" Teka asked. "Last I was here, there were only sixty-seven."

"Their numbers have grown at an alarming rate. There are now almost four hundred."

"How many Sorcerers are there?" I asked.

"Many more." Thera smiled.

She shot Pox a warning glare as she passed through the room only to disappear behind another curtain. I could hear the girl rummaging around for something, and then a soft spell was muttered. Shortly afterward, I could smell something cooking.

Thera suddenly stood and moved to one of the shelves. She skimmed the titles of many books before removing one and returning to her seat on the couch. She snapped her fingers, and Dragon Diary materialized before her.

"That was impressive."

"A simple summoning spell. It only works short range," Thera muttered as she flipped through the ancient pages of the Dragon Diary. "Interesting."

"What does it say?"

> *Dear Diary,*
>
> *I chuckle slightly as I write those words, for I cannot think of another way to begin this tale of my life. The past few years have proven to be a great challenge, not only for me but for everyone involved. You see, we created dragons! Twelve of them, to be exact. Twelve to counter Agasei, the evil force that has washed over our world like a great flood. Within the depths of these pages, I shall tell you the story from its benign beginning to its historic ending.*
>
> *The year was AR 39, my twenty-first since birth. I was studying for the test of Monkhood when he came to the Temple of Five Souls. He had come for two reasons, the obvious being the Festival of the Ixys. Little did anyone know, he was actually at the Temple for an extremely rare item– the Phoenix plume.*
>
> *Let me backtrack a minute to explain who he is– Agasei DéDos, a young Sage from Cah on the Southern Stretch. He was not bad looking, to be honest, sporting unruly black hair and gorgeous blue eyes that I could lose myself in. He was tall, well built, and intelligent. Nevertheless, I could never escape the bad feelings I got when he was close...*

Pox cleared her throat, effectively stealing our attention. "I made some dinner. It's ready if you are."

"Thank you, Pox," Thera said as she stood and stretched.

She returned Dragon Diary to me as she led Teka and me into the other room. It turned out to be a small kitchen complete with a table set with royal-purple dishes, hearth, sink and more lighted orbs. Thera summoned four chairs from the floor and motioned for Teka and me to sit.

"Your dishes are beautiful."

"Gratíe, Dragon Keeper. They have been in our family for generations," Pox said as she dished out some meat and vegetables for me.

They smelled so good that I could not wait to taste them. Pox and Thera sat down when the plates and cups were full.

"Enjoy," Thera said, taking up her knife and fork.

Teka thanked her and dug right in.

"What kind of meat is this?" I asked, cutting into it.

"Siminea," Pox answered quietly.

"Lion," Thera translated.

Teka chucked at my expression. "They wander into Thorna all the time. If they are not killed and eaten, the lions will attack."

"The last time one attacked was a few years ago. A big male got into Feyd's Smithy and mauled one of his children before it was killed," Pox said as she spread soft cheese on her bread. "As I recall, Feyd's family got to keep the lion's meat. And they turned the skin into a rather lovely rug."

"Is his child okay?"

"Welmitek is fine. He brags about the scars all the time." Pox chuckled.

Thera rolled her eyes. "I smacked him for it one day, and he bragged about that!"

"Yeah. He survived a battle with a Druid!"

"Laugh it up, Pox. Laugh it up."

We lapsed into silence as we ate. My mind was preoccupied with what Thera had read aloud from the diary. Amorez's description of Agasei was almost identical to the man pretending to be Valaskjalf. I figured that they had to be related. And by the way Amorez wrote, it was almost as if she was in love with Agasei at one time. If that were the case, then I could not help but wonder if the affair had spawned a child.

Daughter of Amorez. That is what the Elder Feykin had called me earlier. Somewhere in the back of my mind, I knew it was true. I was Amorez's daughter. But…who was my father? My hair was as black as night, the same as Agasei, not Amorez. Her hair was auburn red. Could I possibly be the heir to both sets of dragons? That thought disturbed me.

"Are you okay, Xy? You look upset." Teka gently touched my hand, and I forced a smile.

"I was just thinking of…something."

"Your friend Ríhan again?"

"Not exactly." I sighed. "I was thinking of something Thera read from the book."

"Speaking of which, what were you reading?" Pox asked, looking to her sister for an answer.

"Amorez's diary," Thera replied after a moment's thought. "Xyleena came here to get it translated."

"Oh." Pox looked at me. "So you don't know Kinös Elda? No wonder Thera is speaking Standard."

"There is a Professor at the Temple that teaches Kinös Elda." I bit my lip as memories of Ríhan resurfaced. "I never signed up for the class. Now I wish I had."

"Spending your life regretting your past choices will get you nowhere," Thera replied softly. "Live for tomorrow."

Teka nodded. "I agree."

"Speaking of the diary, how about we get back to work on it?" Thera stood from the table, bowed to her sister, and left the room.

Teka and I followed shortly afterward, leaving Pox to clean up.

The four of us spent the next several hours reading page after page after page of the diary, marking the pages that needed translating from the older runes. We would return to those pages later in hopes of finding some sort of clue as to what Agasei's descendant was after. It was not until the wee hours of the morning that sleep overcame all of us.

The longer humans lived on Ithnez, the further from Arcadia we dared to venture. In doing so, we discovered and catalogued many of the native animals and fauna. This, of course, caused some problems as the Ithnezian creatures won out over the ones transported to this world from Earth. Within the first year, we were forced to utilize the native animals in place of the ones we lost.

– FROM "THE CHRONICLES OF ITHNEZ, VOL II"
BY ADJIRSÉ DÉDOS

I awoke with a start and bolted upright. I breathed a sigh of relief as memories of where I was returned to me. I was in Thera's home in Thorna, sprawled out on the living room floor in a tangled mess of blankets. I did not recall ever falling asleep the night before. We were so busy reading what we could of Dragon Diary that we had stayed up almost all night.

Amorez's firsthand account on history was terrifying to listen to. It was very different from what the history books had taught us. They always depicted Amorez as a fearless woman who could do anything. But she was left terrified and clueless many times, according to her own words. She and I were more alike than I had first realized.

My thoughts were interrupted as Thera pulled back the curtain that lead out of the hut. She looked like she had not slept a wink, but she smiled anyway.

"Good morning," I said.

The young Feykin pursed her lips for a moment. "Kahs gözandí. That is good morning in Kinös Elda. Kahs nóc is good night."

I repeated the phrases several times to hopefully remember them later. "What is hello?"

"Tanda." Thera smiled. "'Tíc it eo lig standard words den Kinös Elda?' Remember that phrase any time you want a translation."

"I need to write that one down."

Thera laughed.

"Did you get any sleep last night?"

"No. I was too involved in those ancient runes."

"Any progress?"

"You have no idea." Thera beamed and summoned a chair. "Amorez was bound and determined to hide a great deal of information, especially when it came to the Dragons of Light. She wrote a riddle in a language that has not been used on Ithnez since before the Earthic Landings. Then she scrambled the letters and converted all of it to the ancient runes."

"How in the name of the Five Souls did you figure all of that out?"

"It wasn't easy. The good news is I've deciphered a great deal of the pages we couldn't read last night, including a page titled 'Riddle of the Twelve.'"

Thera began leafing through the diary until she found the page she sought. "The weird thing is, the handwriting on this page is different than the rest of the diary. And the ink looks quite a bit fresher."

"Interesting," I murmured and scooted closer so I could see the page she was looking at. Thera's pretty handwriting in violet ink stared up at me from the page.

In this mystery must you delve,
To find my sacred dragons twelve,
And vanquish evil from this land.
Now listen close the clues at hand:
Vortex the Wind, on water borne;
And west of magic castle lore.

"Holy Souls! You converted much more than I thought."

I read the lines over and over again. I kept going until my eyes started to cross. Then I began to wonder what the fifth and sixth lines were talking about. What could this Vortex the Wind be? Could it be referring to one of the dragons?

"Vortex is one of the Dragons of Light," Thera answered as if reading my mind. "The wind elemental if memory serves me. So Vortex the Wind must be naming the dragon."

"That is exactly what I was thinking. But," I felt really awkward saying this, "I don't understand… Why would this point to only one of the dragons? All twelve of them should be together, shouldn't they?"

Thera stared at me for a moment. "You really do not recall anything from your past?"

I shook my head.

"Very well, I shall remind you. When the battle against Agasei was over, Amorez imprisoned the Shadow Dragons beyond what is known as the Dragons' Gate. The Dragons of Light, however, were hidden away throughout Ithnez in order to protect them from those who would seek to use them unjustly. This portion of riddle only points to the first of the Twelve; the other eleven will follow. I just need to work on the conversion and translation."

"Okay," I said as I let everything sink in. "So… where do we find this Vortex?"

Thera set the diary on the floor open to the page of the riddle and simply stared at it as if her gaze alone could scare it into giving up its answers.

West of magic castle lore… That line had to be the key to this Vortex the Wind. That got me wondering, "Hey, does the Sorcerers' Isle have any castles?"

Thera never looked away from the open page. "Our capital city, Thuraben, has the only castle in all our lands."

"What lies west of there?"

Thera thought a moment. "More forest, a river that empties into the sea, a few more cities, and some mountains."

A river that empties into the sea west of the Thuraben castle? Vortex the Wind, on water borne. Water borne... That has to be it! I smiled. "I think I got it!"

Thera's gaze was instantly on me.

So I explained, "The sea west of your castle of magic, long thought lore by everyone on the outside. Vortex on water borne. The dragon must be somewhere on the sea close to the Sorcerers' Isle."

"I'm impressed." Thera nodded for emphasis. "So what is the plan?"

"How far is Thuraben from here?"

Teka's voice called out from the spare bedroom, "Roughly fourteen days." She pushed aside the curtain to join Thera and me in the main room. After a huge yawn, she continued, "By wyvernback it would be more like eight or nine. I heard you two talking, so I decided to get my lazy bones out of bed."

"I am not certain if I have ever ridden a wyvern before," I admitted.

Thera shrugged. "It is very easy to learn how. The problem is paying for their use."

Teka clicked her tongue. "How much does renting wyverns cost here in Thorna?"

"A full seven days for three wyverns may cost around fifteen hundred crowns."

"That's about thirty-seven hundred bits," Teka replied.

I whistled. "That's quite a bit."

"I can cover the fee, but—"

I shook my head in a hurry. "Don't spend all of your money on me, Teka."

She sharply shushed me. "I was going to say I will cover the fee if you promise to pay me back once you've saved the world."

"Say what?" I blinked in surprise.

"Become the Dragon Keeper, beat the bad guys, and save the world. That will be your payment to me in return for my services." Teka extended her hand for me to shake. "Deal?"

"But... I'm not even sure I can pull any of that off."

"I believe in you." Teka smiled.

I slowly reached up to grasp her hand. "I hope your belief is well placed."

"You will do great. Remember, Amorez didn't think she could save the world either, and look what she accomplished."

"You're right." I felt my confidence growing. For the first time since this whole fiasco started, I was beginning to believe I could do it. I could save the world.

"So"– Thera clapped her hands together– "when do we leave?"

Artimista did not look up from her task as she said, "When deeds speak, words mean nothing. Do not just talk about what you intend to do to Agasei once you meet face-to-face; You must act."

– FROM "THE UNSUNG"
BY J'VAC TAIG (TRANSLATED BY B'REG KUNGA)

Dimitri's crimson eyes scanned the land around him. There were no signs of life in this grey and barren desert. There were only rocks, craters, mountains. Long shadows seemed to come alive, stretching, reaching. Moving his gaze skyward, he found the blackness of night dusted with a million stars. Two planets hung in the void, giving light to the desert. He thought he recognized them both, but his mind was drawing a blank.

"Where am I?" he wondered aloud, his own voice seeming leagues away. He returned his gaze to the endless horizon. "This place is teeming with magic…"

This way.

Dimitri whirled around, ready to defend himself against the source of the otherworldly whisper. There was nothing. Nothing at all. Had he imagined it?

What are you waiting for?

Dimitri blinked in surprise and shook his head as if to clear it. The ground suddenly cracked beneath his feet, almost toppling him before he regained his balance. A black smoke hissed into the atmosphere from somewhere in the depths below. The smoke converged into a single, transparent form; A man, tall in stature, with hair that matched the night and eyes like sapphires. Dimitri knew this man though they had never met.

"Father?"

The greatest treasure lies not far away. The ghost of Agasei pointed the way.

"The Dragons' Gate…" Dimitri took off at a full sprint. He had done it! He had found the Shadow Dragons!

"Heile pricé!" a girl's voice cried out.

Before he knew it, a giant tornado of fire spawned right on him. He screamed in agony as the flames devoured him. It felt like forever before the storm vanished and dropped him to the ground. His last image was that of a girl with dragon-green eyes and obsidian hair.

"Dimitri!"

He could hear Godilai now. Funny how his last thoughts would be of her.

"Dimitri, wake up!"

He groaned as he opened his eyes. Godilai's gorgeous face hovered over him, her cyan eyes betraying her worry for him.

"Am I dead?"

"Dead?" Godilai retreated from her position but continued to stare at him. "What did your dream reveal to you?"

101

Dimitri sat up in the small bed and glanced about. He was in a room so small he doubted a single wyvern could stand in it. The floor, the walls, the ceiling, even the cot he was on was all craft from wood; dark-stained jávi from the looks of it. Godilai was in the corner, sitting on the floor under the only window. He finally remembered where he was. "We are on the ship."

"Where did you go when you dreamed?" Godilai asked softly, hugging her knees to her chest and leaning her head against her arms.

Dimitri found the pose rather arousing.

"Dimitri?"

"Oh! Uh…" He felt heat rush to his face. "I do not know where it was, but my father was there. He pointed me to the Dragons' Gate. That was when Amorez's daughter hit me with a fire storm."

"I see." She was quiet for a while, and Dimitri could not help but stare at her. "Do you think it was a premonition?"

"If it is, then I will have to be more prepared for that little wretch. She will become stronger with each dragon she finds, while I won't achieve my full power until I can unlock the Dragons' Gate."

Godilai sighed. "So it is a race then. And we are lagging behind."

Dimitri threw the covers off and got out of bed. "We have to get Amorez's diary at any cost."

Godilai watched him pace the small cabin. "Maybe someone to infiltrate her team, gather info, and then steal the diary for us."

"That is a great idea, but it cannot be any of us. If we try to infiltrate her team, she will probably recognize us and kill us before we get a second chance."

"Hire a desperado. It'll cost you quite a bit, but—"

"It'll be worth it in the end." He grinned maliciously. "I like the way you think."

Godilai un-tucked herself and stood up. "The best place to find desperadoes is in Zadún. There is a tavern there called Thief's Paradise."

"How do you know that?" He turned to face her only to see the door opened and swinging slightly back and forth in time with the waves. He sighed. "I need to learn how to do that."

A short time later, Dimitri left the bowels of the ship. He made his way out on the main deck, squinting as the suns' light blinded him. A cry from the crow's nest above had many relieved whoops coming from the crew. Dimitri rushed to the ship's bow railing and watched as the land mass on the horizon drew closer.

"Not at all what I was expecting," Vincent said, suddenly beside him.

Dimitri smirked. "And what were you expecting?"

"I heard from sailors that there is an island in the north inhabited only by naked women. And the beach is covered in jewels the size of my fist."

Dimitri rolled his eyes. "Right."

"Just imagine landing on that island and seeing all those ti—"

"Captain says we get off here," Luna said, smacking Vincent upside the head.

Dimitri quirked an eyebrow. "Something wrong?"

"Yeah. He refuses to get any closer to the Sorcerers' Isle." She tapped her foot in irritation. "Something about attacks on other ships that got too close."

"What are we supposed to do then? I can't swim!" Vincent shouted.

"Silence yourself, fool," Godilai hissed as she walked up. "We'll use a row boat."

Dimitri looked back at the island and estimated the distance to shore. "That will be a long row. Luna, what if I pay him extra to get closer."

She snorted. "Good luck. Superstitious fool will not budge. And he says he'll be leaving as soon as we're off his ship."

Dimitri sighed. "Fine. Let's be rid of these fools."

"What are you planning?" Godilai asked.

Dimitri made his way to the helm. He conversed with the captain for a moment and handed over a leather pouch. Moments later, Dimitri was at her side again.

"You paid him?" Luna's voice betrayed her fury, though her face and eyes remained void of emotion.

Dimitri smirked and raised a hand to silence her. "Just wait."

A heartbeat later, an explosion erupted from the captain's quarters. The crew instantly rushed to put the fires out.

Dimitri smirked. Stupid Humes made such easy targets.

"Hydor esso!"

Water converged in Dimitri's outstretched hand before launching at the crewmembers in a rapid succession of spheres. Each water ball struck with enough force to crush bones. By the time the spell ended, only seven members of the original crew remained.

"I will have to remember that one," Luna muttered.

Dimitri flashed her a crooked smirk before staring the crewmen down. "You seven will obey my commands now or join the others in Havel."

One of the men launched himself at Dimitri, shouting. "I'll send you there first!"

In a rush of inhuman speed, Godilai struck, cleanly slicing him into three. Godilai sheathed her swords as each portion of the sailor thudded to the deck. She stared at the remaining six crewmen, daring them to make a move.

"Anyone else want to play?"

"Wh—what are your orders?"

"Simple." Dimitri pointed his thumb at the island over his shoulder. "Land the ship on the Sorcerers' Isle."

The sailor swallowed nervously. "Yes, sir."

As the remnants of the crew hopped to their tasks, Dimitri's team conversed. Together they developed what they thought would be the perfect lie to gain the trust of the Sorcerers. Dimitri silently prayed to Régon that the plan succeeded.

A little more than an hour later, the ship was beached on the hot white sands of the Sorcerers' Isle. As Dimitri's team disembarked, the crew members approached.

"Any orders before you leave, sir?"

Dimitri glanced at them over his shoulder. "Mind the tide."

When they were out of earshot, Godilai punched Dimitri's shoulder. He hissed in pain and shot her a death glare. "Not going to kill them?"

"We may need an escape route," he reasoned.

Godilai pursed her lips in thought for a moment. "What makes you think they will stick around? After the way we dispatched the rest of the crew, they will leave while we are gone."

"Good point." Dimitri turned to cast another spell but froze. Before him stood a beautiful silver-haired woman in a sage-green dress. Giant swan-like wings tipped with silver armor were spread wide as if she were ready to take flight. Suddenly, Dimitri's entire team was surrounded by winged warriors with silver hair.

"Are these guys Sorcerers?" Luna asked, gripping the handle of her giant sword.

"Let's find out." Dimitri raised his hands in surender, stepped forward.

The woman in green simply observed.

"Meo namae wa Dimitri Renoan. Kíen la ja?"

She hesitated, glanced at the other Feykin in the group. "Eo ík Habanya-Ürg. Aké la ja chee?" Her voice was as soft as the wind.

"Eo nan lig Kinös Elda. Eo ík guídes."

The silver-haired maiden who called herself Habanya-Ürg stared at him for a moment, judging him. She folded her wings, pointed at Dimitri's group. "Drop weapons. Follow."

Dimitri nodded. To his team he said, "Put your weapons down."

"Yeah, then they'll take us somewhere to kill us," Vincent muttered, gripping the handle of his axe even tighter.

"Just drop it," Godilai hissed as she put her swords and daggers on the ground.

Luna grumbled and did the same. Dimitri's dual sword was added to the pile a moment later.

"Just do it, you idiot. Who knows what they will do to you if you refuse," Luna reasoned.

Finally, the old Judge gave in and gently laid his axe on the ground.

Habanya-Ürg barked orders in Kinös Elda. The other silver-haired warriors grabbed the discarded weapons and motioned for Dimitri's team to follow. Habanya-Ürg took point as the long trek through the dense forest began.

It was not an easy road, even after Xyleena had taken it up. There were many times I thought about giving in and returning home. I am certain she felt the same, yet her determination kept her pressing on. And, somehow, she even managed to keep all of us together.

– FROM "THE SECOND KEEPER"
BY THERA ONYX

Dimitri felt insanely awkward under the gaze of the old man with the pointed hat. He had been eyeing Dimitri and his team suspiciously ever since they had been lead into the Chamber of Elders. After it had been revealed that no one in Dimitri's team spoke Kinös Elda fluently enough to answer questions, a guard had been sent to fetch a translator.

After what felt like hours, the guard reentered the chamber. He was followed by a young girl with jet-black wings and onyx eyes. She bowed to the Elders and sighed impatiently as the old man spoke in a slow drawl. Dimitri took a liking to the young girl right away.

"I'm Piper Onyx. I was summoned here to serve as translator between you and the old ones. They want to know why you are here."

"It is nice to meet you, Piper. I am Dimitri Renoan. My team and I have come here seeking assistance."

Piper translated word for word as he spoke, making it difficult for him to concentrate.

"Assistance with what?"

"There is a young girl going around claiming to be the daughter of Amorez and the next Dragon Keeper. She is in fact the Dark Keeper, and she has stolen my mother's diary to find and unlock the Dragons' Gate. My team and I have come to warn you of her treachery and ask for help in stopping her." Dimitri watched the faces of the Elders to judge their reaction to his story.

The old men betrayed no emotion; instead, they simply uttered two words in Kinös Elda and left the room to speak in private.

Piper turned to face Dimitri. "This girl you speak of, is her name Xyleena?"

"I am not sure what her name is, but she has short, black hair and green eyes." Dimitri watched as her expression grew ever more worried. "Is something wrong?"

"She calls herself Xyleena, and she left with my sister at first light the day before."

Dimitri jumped to his feet and grasped the girl's shoulders. "Do you know where they were headed?"

"Thuraben. They said something about taking the river boat to the coast and something great hidden farther west."

Dimitri's heart skipped a beat at the news. He slowly released the grip on Piper's shoulders and sunk into his seat. "This is terrible."

"Is my sister in danger?"

"That girl will do anything to have her way," Godilai replied. She was impressed by Dimitri's acting skills and immensely glad that they seemed to be working.

"We were on our way here to ask for help translating the runes of the Dragon Diary when she attacked us. She killed most of our crew, stole the diary, and rushed here."

"But Teka was with her…and she seemed so nice. It's hard to believe that she is the Dark Keeper." Piper began to pace the floor. "It doesn't make any sense. She kept going on about how she was not strong enough to do the dragon quest. It was as if she did not want to go. And Teka vouched for her."

"It is possible that Xyleena used some sort of mind control on your sister and friend," Dimitri explained, trying to keep his lie alive. He had to think quickly to get the girl back to believing him.

"Aren't there ways to counteract mind control spells, Dimitri?" Luna winked at him, leaving the perfect opening for his trickery.

"I've found some artifacts to ward off the effects. One is that bracelet you wear, Luna. I have this ring. In addition, I gave Godilai and Vincent small charms. I only have this necklace left." He pulled the ancient necklace from the pouch strapped to his belt.

Piper gawked at it. "Amorez had that same necklace!"

"My mother gave it to me when I felt the call of the dragons." Dimitri watched as a frown etched its way across Piper's lips.

"You're lying. The Twelve don't call the second-generation Keeper. And Amorez wouldn't give that necklace away to anyone."

Dimitri swore a silent oath. "I'm not lying, Piper. I swear that Amorez, my mother, gave me this necklace."

Piper crossed her arms. "If that's true, then tell me what Amorez looks like and what she said when she gave you the necklace."

"She is a little shorter than I am. She has green eyes and red hair that she styles in spikes. She fights with dueling blades and wears black leathers covered with light silver plate similar to the armor on your wings. And she only said, 'Take this to keep your mind clear,' when she gave me the necklace." Dimitri smiled as the girl's suspicions were obviously extinguished.

"My apologies." Piper turned away.

"It's all right. After the trickery the Dark Keeper has played on you and your kin, I understand your wariness."

"She would come in very handy if she could join us to defeat this Xyleena," Godilai murmured to Dimitri, just loud enough for the Feykin to hear.

Piper looked at her in surprise. "My sister would be more useful. She is a Druid. I am merely a Mage."

Godilai shook her head. "Ranks do not matter. It is how you think and react that make you useful."

"I agree." Luna nodded. "You are smart. You take in details. And you are quick. We should bring her with us, Dimitri."

"What better way to save your sister than to travel with the ones trying to prevent the world's destruction?" Vincent added, also trying to convince the girl.

Piper met Dimitri's gaze. "If I can save Thera, I'm coming."

"That's what I like to hear!" Dimitri smiled and stood up again. He extended a hand to her and presented the ancient necklace. "You will need this to prevent Xyleena's spells from affecting you."

"Thank you, Iríjhone Reshé." Piper admired the necklace for a moment before donning it. She scratched her head in confusion a heartbeat later.

Dimitri sneered. "What will you tell the Elders when they return, Piper?"

The young Feykin tilted her head to the side for a moment. "You are the real Dragon Keeper, and you require fast transportation in order to catch up to Xyleena. You will get the diary back and continue with your dragon quest."

"That is exactly what I had in mind." Dimitri laughed and took his seat again as the Elders returned from their discussion.

Each took their places in the five platforms before the oldest spoke the decision aloud.

"My uncle said that they want you to hunt down the Dark Keeper and kill her. He will provide you with anything you require." Piper awaited Dimitri's response.

He stood up and bowed to the Elders. "Tell him I am grateful for his generosity and that I will require your presence as well as his fastest mounts."

Piper translated back and forth a few more times before Dimitri's team was allowed to leave. They were immediately rushed to the stables and given silver wyverns. Piper led the way to Thuraben.

When Amorez had fallen to her knees in despair, it was Zenith who was the first to go to her. The great dragon wrapped his tail around her in a hug, then I heard him quietly say, "It is never too late to be what you might have been."
— FROM "AN ONLOOKER'S JOURNAL"
BY THERNU ONYX

"Meo namae wa Xyleena. Eo ík et Iríjhone Reshé," I repeated for probably the fiftieth time.

"Good!" Thera cheered. "Now, count from zero to twenty."

I laughed. "That's easy. Na. San. Sku. Teh. O. Ven. Mé. Im. Lin. Bin. Ra. Sanra. Skura. Tehra. Ora. Venra. Méra. Imra. Linra. Binra. Skucóra."

"Perfect." Thera applauded. "What is one hundred?"

"Mehnt," I answered without a second thought.

"And one thousand?"

"Shréva."

"Very good. List the colors."

As I recited them, I thought about everything that I had learned in the last five days we had spent on the road. First was learning how to ride a wyvern, which was definitely awkward for both the wyvern and me. But by nightfall on the first day, I was riding as if I had been doing it every day for my entire life.

On the second day, I learned that Ekvinöj, the name of my wyvern, was Kinös Eldic for Equinox. Later that morning Thera began giving me lessons in magic. First it was learning some beginner spells like forming orbs of light, healing small wounds, and bending the natural elements—just a few things that could come in handy should I find myself in an emergency.

Then she began teaching me how to actually speak Kinös Elda. I picked everything up incredibly fast, surprising both Thera and Teka. I felt like I was not actually learning; I was remembering.

Thera's voice interrupted my thoughts. "Okay. Enough review. Time to start with body parts."

I smiled, eager to begin. I repeated each new term aloud as she listed off more and more. The day continued with me learning countless new words and phrases. Ríhan would have been proud of me.

A thought suddenly occurred to me as I remembered him. "Thera, is there a spell that will let the caster speak to the dead?"

"Yeah. It's called suicide," Teka bluntly answered.

Thera glanced from her to me and sighed. "Talking to the dead is something only a Necromancer can teach, and even they are not quick to do it."

"Why is that?"

"Summoning the dead in any way is never a good idea. They have a nasty habit of hanging around for the rest of the caster's life. That is, of course, if they have survived the experience to begin with."

"It kills you?"

"Summoning a soul from Havel means trading places with that soul. The caster can easily overspend their life force in that way, because they no longer feel any pain or discomfort. And if the caster dies while the summoned soul is still in the mortal world, that soul will grow vengeful and attack the living."

"Like I said, best way to talk to the dead is to die," Teka said. She slowed her wyvern enough to fall in step beside me. "Don't try it."

"I won't. I was just curious."

"If you plan on having any sort of afterlife, I would strongly suggest avoiding dark magic. Atlidmé won't allow your soul to rest comfortably in Havel if you do," Thera explained.

"So any magic dealing with souls, death, and curses is dark magic?"

Thera nodded.

"Okay."

"Good. Now, recite the words I just taught you."

I chuckled. "You are a strict teacher."

Thera smiled at me, and I began my recitation. She continued drilling me until nightfall. We stopped our wyverns by a riverbank and set up our camp.

"Heile!" I lit the wood Teka had collected with one of the simple spells Thera had shown me. "How much farther is it to Thuraben?"

"About a day and a half backward." Thera laughed as she pointed her thumb over her shoulder—in the direction we had just come from.

"I thought we were hopping a ferry in Thuraben?" Teka quirked an eyebrow at the young Feykin.

"We are making much better time on the wyverns." Thera shrugged. "We will reach the boat house on the western shorn late tomorrow as opposed to waiting for the ferry to arrive, refuel, and then leave again."

"Boat house?"

"Yes. The ferry stops there to drop off passengers who want to go to Tamilyt. They can also rent boats for fishing on the open sea."

"And late tomorrow is when we get there. That is good timing."

"Only seven days instead of the usual ten. I am impressed by these wyv—"

A loud screech from farther in the woods had us jumping to our feet in an instant. I gripped my tessens firmly, ready for anything. Silence was our reward for our quickness.

"That was a wyvern call," Thera said quietly. "It is highly unusual for wild wyverns to be out here. They keep to the mountains farther east."

"Do you think we're being followed?"

Teka got no answer.

"I'll take that as a yes."

"We should keep watch," I said as I scanned the trees for anything suspicious.

"Or we could keep going tonight."

"I cannot see in the dark, Teka. And lighting orbs will only give away our position to whoever might be following us."

I nodded in agreement to Thera's reasoning. "Can you set up some wards around our camp?"

"Yes."

"After the wards are set up, one of us will remain awake and on guard. We will trade guard posts every few hours—one awake, two asleep."

The three of us did just that. Thera set up multiple and complex wards to prevent any intruder from overtaking us while we slept. Then we split the night into separate shifts. My shift was the first—uneventful. I was kept entertained by the amusing snoring coming from Ekvinöj. When my shift reached its end, I roused Teka from her sleep. I watched her get comfortable before I let my own exhaustion pull me into the dream world.

I was awakened the next morning by Thera roughly shaking me. We packed up the camp quickly, choosing to break our fast while on the road. I was hoping that we had roused early enough to slip past whoever it was that might be following us. I prayed we were just being paranoid, that the would-be prince could not find the Sorcerers' Isle.

Noon came and went. We were leagues away from our camp, and still none of us spoke a word. I ran through all of the Kinös Eldic terms I knew, repeating them again and again, over and over until I was sure I had them memorized.

The suns were low in the sky when a small hut came into view. It sat a good distance from the riverbank where a few skiffs were tethered to a short dock. Thera stopped her wyvern at a hitching post set up outside a rudimentary fence. We dismounted our steeds just as a handsome young man exited the hut.

"Good gozavé!" He waved as he called his greeting.

"Hello, Kínashe. I din ormá né alú a amyíac."

Thera and he continued their friendly exchange for a minute more. Try as I might, I could only catch a word or two of what was said, for they were simply speaking too fast for me to keep up. I looked to Teka for help with the translation, but she was too busy unloading our packs from the wyverns to pay attention.

With the little details regarding the boat's use worked out, the man led us down to the water's edge where five green wood rafts were tethered to a small dock. The rafts themselves looked like the leaves of an yggdraberry tree—complete with the long curl at the front, which held a small lantern and a rudder in the shape of a stem. He guided us to one of the leaf-shaped skiffs and even helped load some of our gear. I hopped in and sat on the small bench toward the front and admired the craftsmanship even further.

"Tic kahl wah…?"

"Nai. Nai, Thera." He smiled sweetly as he turned down her money. "Nír irím, bó kerím ska."

"Shíkai ja, Kínashe." Thera smiled as she untethered the skiff from the dock.

He gave the dinghy a shove to get it away from shore and waved farewell.

"He was nice about not charging us," said Teka as she took up a leaf-shaped paddle and began to move us down the river.

"Kínashe is always nice like that." Thera smiled. After a moment, she turned to look at me. "So were you following the conversation?"

"Believe it or not, I understood a few of the words you haven't taught me yet, but I wasn't able to follow the whole conversation."

"Interesting." Thera stared at me, and I could tell she was lost in her thoughts.

"What do you know about your life, Xy?" Teka asked after a moment of silence.

I looked her in the eye as I answered. "I washed up on the beach outside the Temple of Five Souls. A boy named Ríhan discovered me and had me moved into the medical wing where I spent the next week recovering. When I finally woke up, it was discovered that I had no memories of who I was or where I had come from. So the Palavant took me into the Temple's care, and I lived there ever since, hoping and praying to one day learn who I was."

"Apparently, you do remember quite a bit from whatever kind of life you lived before you ended up at the Temple," Thera replied. "You have picked up a difficult language far faster than any other person with no experience in it, and you have mastered the simple spells I taught you only days ago. If I were of rank to take apprentices, I would say you would be graduated to Mage, if not Druid already."

"Wow." I could not suppress a grin.

"I believe you were already taught all of this stuff—fighting, magic, languages, and whatnot. Then for whatever reason, you lost your memory. Now it only takes a small insight into what you already know to have those memories come flooding back."

I was quiet as I mulled this over in my mind. What Thera said was true. I was starting to remember far more advanced words in Kinös Elda than what she had already taught me, while magic and fighting came to me as easy as walking. I began to wonder what had happened that caused me to lose my memory in the first place.

I freed the Dragon Diary from my hip sack and began flipping through pages. Maybe the answer to my past was written somewhere in the ancient runes. I tried in vain to spark a memory that would reveal to me the words written on the crinkled parchment. Eventually I gave up, choosing instead to further study the drawings within.

One drawing in particular captivated my attention. It was a map of the world, but it looked different from the few others I had seen. There were islands, rivers, and lakes on this map that should not exist. And it included a detailed outline of the Sorcerers' Isle.

Teka jerked my attention away from the map. "Well, we are definitely out to sea now."

Our blue sun, Rishai, had already vanished below the horizon, while Aruvan just kissed the tops of the mountains on the small island in front of us.

"Ah. I love how the sunset reflects off the water like that," Thera whispered.

"Vero," Teka said quietly. "It's beautiful."

I blinked at them. "What water?"

My companions stared at me.

Finally, Thera pointed toward Aruvan. "That water."

"That is an island."

Thera and Teka glanced at each other then back at me.

I chuckled at the look on their faces. "You don't see the island?"

"We see only water, Xy," Teka explained.

"Luminös!" I made a small orb of light form in my hand so I could see the map in Dragon Diary again. The island I was seeing in front of me also appeared on the map. I pointed at it as I tilted the page so my companions could see. "The island is right there. You don't see it?"

"That is a blank spot," Teka replied after she had leaned in for a closer look.

"Okay. Relax," Thera spoke gently. "Maybe the island is protected by a field that only a Dragon Keeper can see through. If that is the case, then we probably just stumbled upon the hiding place of the first dragon."

"You will have to tell me if I am on course," said Teka. "I cannot land a boat on an island I cannot see."

"Okay." I stood up and hurled the globe of light as far as I could. It splashed down on the water not far from the island and faded away.

"It vanished." Thera smiled. "That means I was right about the field protecting it."

"Thank the Gods. I was beginning to think I had gone insane." I sighed as I sat back down. "Keep heading in the direction of Aruvan, Teka. We should reach the island in a few moments."

"Aye aye!"

I chuckled at Teka's enthusiasm as I tucked the diary back into my hip sack. A few minutes passed as I watched the pair, waiting in eager anticipation for their expressions to betray the moment they saw the island for themselves. It felt like forever before Teka's eyes went wide and her jaw dropped.

"Oh, wow!"

"It's huge!" Thera exclaimed, her expression a mirror of Teka's.

I smiled as I turned away to look at the island a little more closely. It was slightly bigger than the island home of the Temple of Five Souls, and much wilder in appearance. A trio of jagged mountains capped with the lingering snow of a winter storm dotted the interior. Enormous plants, each beginning to glow with a medley of bio-luminescent colors against the darkening night, grew thick and untouched over almost every inch of the island. Where plant life did not grow, strange crystals of heights varying from a half meter to five meters sprang up. Each of them glowed a magnificent blue that seemed to pulse as a heartbeat.

Little spots of cerulean and white light flickered between the foliage, moving en masse like glow bugs around the shore and climbing higher. As I watched the glowing mass move upwards, I caught a glimpse of something dark floating high above the island – tucked safely between the mountains as if they were its guardians. As my gaze lingered on the floating shadow, something within me seemed to whisper, "I feel you…"

"I thought it would be a minuscule island." The sound of Thera's voice yanked me back, and I lost my concentration on the floating shadow. "For Amorez to shield one of this magnitude, she must have had help."

"Either that, or she was more talented in magic than she let on." Teka offered as explanation. "How do you think it was done?"

Thera cupped her chin in thought. "I think it works similarly to the field surrounding the Sorcerer's Isle. We breached a field of magic projected to guard the island from intruders. Anyone who wasn't deemed worthy of entry was just warped around the island without their knowledge."

"It's strange…" I heard Teka murmur. "I've come this way countless times and never once did I see this island."

I shrugged. "Maybe you are seeing it now because I am here with you."

"What is that?" Thera pointed at something behind us.

I turned around to see what she had spotted but could not see anything in the waning light as Aruvan disappeared completely.

"I hate to say it again, but I don't see anything." Teka squinted, hoping to see something.

Thera stood and flicked her wrist as she cast her spell. An orb of light erupted over her target, revealing my worst nightmare. A split second later, the spell was countered, restoring darkness to our pursuers.

"We have to hurry!" I exclaimed, trying to urge Teka to go faster.

"Who was that?"

"He is the Prince Valaskjalf wannabe who is after the Dragon Diary. And he brought some ugly old Judge and those two Dákun Daju women I fought at the Temple. The Godilai one is the one who murdered Ríhan."

"I think Pox was with them." Thera frowned.

"Great," Teka muttered. "We better come up with a plan to fend them off pretty darn quick."

"We have to reach the dragon first. Who knows what those guys will do if they reach him before we do," I said, watching the shore grow ever closer.

I am coming, Vortex.

"I don't understand why they would take such a tiny skiff this far out into the open sea," Luna whispered.

Dimitri scoffed and continued to watch the dinghy in front of them as it sailed toward sunset.

They had caught up to the trio a few days ago. He had expected to obtain the Dragon Diary easily, but the young Feykin proved to be quite adept at defensive wards. Therefore, he chose to wait for another opportunity to present itself. Thus far, his patience had not rewarded him.

"I think they spotted us," Godilai announced.

A globe of light suddenly erupted overhead. A heartbeat later, Piper cast a spell to counter the magic.

"Curse that girl!" Luna hissed. "I cannot wait to see her dead."

Dimitri rubbed his eyes and blinked, trying to readjust to twilight. Finally, his eyes cleared, and he searched the horizon for the girls. What he saw shocked him. "Was that island always there?"

"What island?"

Dimitri pointed to where he could barely see the shadows of the girls against the outline of the island. They were scrambling to reach the shore. He would bet all the money in the world that there was a dragon somewhere on that strange island. "Get us there. Quick!"

Vincent panted as he tried to force the skiff in the right direction. "The tide has turned against us, Dimitri."

"Hold on to something," Piper said, standing suddenly. She did not wait for the others to comply. "Aero bíraw!"

A great surge of wind and water lurched the skiff forward on a wave. But it stopped too short to get the team to land. Piper repeated the spell another time and another. Four more spells and Dimitri's team could finally beach the skiff on the island, right beside the one they were following.

Xyleena's team was nowhere to be seen.

We could not help but gawk at the beauty of the island as Thera, Teka, and I pushed our way through the wyvern-sized foliage. Though I had taken the lead, I could not tell where it was that I was heading; I merely followed the mysterious pull I felt. It was as if something within me was guiding me to the place I needed to be; the place I knew I would find Vortex waiting.

"Aero bíraw!"

My attention was stolen for a moment as one of our pursuers cast the spell.

"Time to go!" I took off deeper into the overgrown wild faster than before. Thera and Teka were right behind me. As we shoved past leaves the size of tables, I heard Thera casting multiple wards. I prayed that they worked or at least bought us enough time to obtain the aid of Vortex.

The thick vegetation ended abruptly, and I came to a sudden stop. Thera and Teka barely managed to avoid running into me as I stood there, staring in wonder. They were both about to ask why I had stopped, when they realized what had won my attention. A crystalline archway stood before us, forming a doorway to a glowing, rainbow staircase. I traced the stairs as they wound their way through the trio of mountains and upwards, to a shadow floating about five hundred meters above the ground. Without a word to Thera or Teka, I rushed to the stairs and began the climb to the top. Teka took off after me while Thera lingered a moment to cast a spell.

Thera laughed as she landed on the stairs in front of me and folded her wings. "That one will be a nasty surprise."

I wondered what kind of spell she had just set up to keep our pursuers busy.

My sides were burning, and my legs begged for rest by the time we reached the halfway point of the stairs. As much as I tried, I could force myself to run no farther. I slowed to a stop to catch my breath before continuing at a brisk walk.

The sounds of a battle wafted up from the stairs below. I glanced down to the base of the stairs to see the would-be prince's team trying to fend off a strange plant. The plant appeared to be winning.

"That one yours, Thera?"

She grinned at me and nodded. "I call it crazy weed."

"I like it." Teka clapped Thera on the back. "Teach me that one sometime."

A moment more of watching and we were on our way again. Many minutes passed, and the stairs still did not end. My legs were burning. My lungs could not seem to get any air. And my feet felt too heavy to lift another step. Nevertheless, I had to press on. I had to get to Vortex!

I gasped for air and forced myself onward. The sounds of the battle died away. I had a feeling that the Dákun Daju had finally beaten the crazy weed. I heard Thera start another spell as the final steps came into view at last.

I paused to study a black dragon statue that guarded the castle's entrance. Its wings were folded along its back, and its tail curled around its feet. Ancient runes were embossed in the dais the dragon stood on.

"I wonder what it says." I tapped the dais.

Thera glanced at it and shook her head. "There isn't any time. The Shadow Keeper will overtake us if we don't hurry."

I followed her and Teka into the castle.

The entrance hall spilled out into a huge circular room with easily one hundred corridors. And each one of the corridors veered off in a different direction. The floor was some sort of grey stone slab with a glow emitting from the joints, but the walls were all opaque crystal. More rainbow stairs wound their way upward into darkness.

"Okay, Xy, time to break in those new Dragon Keeper senses." Teka sighed.

"I…" I slowly began to walk the circumference of the room, pausing by each corridor. "I don't know!"

"Calm down," Thera said softly. "Clear your mind and feel it out just like when you cast a spell."

I nodded and took a deep breath. I let my eyes drift shut as I circled the room again. I felt a strange pull toward one direction. I followed it until it changed direction again. I opened my eyes and looked at the doorway I would need to take.

"The floor?" Teka sounded skeptical, not that I could blame her.

However, the crystalline oculus I stood on did look familiar. I stepped off the oculus and willed a memory of it to return. I knew it opened, but how?

"I don't see a lever or switch," Thera announced as she searched the room. "Then how does it open?"

A word sprang from my memories, and I snapped my fingers. "Infé!"

As soon as the word was uttered, the oculus vanished, revealing another rainbow staircase.

Teka laughed and clapped me on the back. "Nice one, kid."

I smiled and led the way down the new stairs. Thera fell behind just long enough to set up a ward and seal the doorway. As soon as the oculus was back in place, we were plummeted into darkness.

"Luminös!" I lit two orbs in my hands. I dropped one down the stairs to gauge how far it was to the bottom. "Thank the gods this isn't another hour-long venture."

"I don't think I could take another set of a million stairs like that last one," Teka muttered.

About halfway down this set of stairs, a bright light flooded down from the room above. A heartbeat later I was sent flying as a body struck me. The two of us plummeted to the floor and hit hard. It felt like several minutes before I could breathe again. By then my opponent was already on his feat, sword drawn. His crimson eyes glared at me.

"Your adventure ends here, Xyleena."

I forced myself to my feet and freed my tessens. With a flick of my wrist, the fans opened, revealing their razor-sharp blades. "You know my name, but I don't know your real name."

He laughed darkly. "Dimitri DéDos."

"Why did you kill Valaskjalf?"

A huge gust of wind nearly knocked both of us off our feet. Luckily, I maintained my balance.

Dimitri scowled. "Quit trying to stall, girl! If you are afraid to fight me, then hand over Dragon Diary, and I will spare you."

"I seriously doubt that. Remember? I was there when you slaughtered all of those innocent people at the festival." I sank into the fighting stance I had practiced time and time again on the deck of the Shadow Dance.

Dimitri appeared amused. "You want to fight like a Dákun Daju?"

This is a Dákun Daju stance? I hoped I did not betray my surprise to him at his words. "I was trained by one of the best." I really hoped he would believe that and back down.

Instead he just quirked an eyebrow. He sneered as he sank into a fighting stance of his own. "So be it. Can't say I didn't try to spare your life."

Another gust of wind howled through the room.

The Haven had flown right past both of the stars in the system while en route to the habitable sister planets. The leadership committee had unanimously agreed to name the largest sun, a white-blue Main Sequence F-type star, Rishai in honor of the system's discoverer. The other, a yellowish G-type similar to Earth's Sol, was named Aruvan after Rishai's wife.

– FROM "AN UNTITLED SCIENCE LOG"
BY UNKNOWN

I could see the burning hatred teeming in his crimson eyes as he glared at me. I glared right back, trying to ignore the sounds of the battle on the stairs above. I had to focus on my opponent, just as Freya had taught me. My heart beat loudly in my ears. My breath came in deliberately slow, measured breaths. My hands were sweaty. I was nervous. And he could tell.

Dimitri slowly advanced to his left. I stepped right, keeping the distance between us the same. He smirked. Another step. Then another. I matched him step for step, circling the room almost twice.

He struck, fast as lightning and much stronger than expected. I screamed as he jerked his sword free of my shoulder. A warm flow of blood crept down my arm and pooled at my feet. He sneered, obviously enjoying the pain he caused.

"How do you like that, little girl?"

I said nothing, electing instead to allow my latent battle instincts to take over.

Another gust of wind rampaged through the room as I sunk back into my fighting stance. Dimitri scoffed and raised his sword over his head. With an enraged cry, he brought it down. Our blades met in a resounding clash that made sparks rain. Again and again he attacked. I successfully blocked each attempt. Finally, he backed off for a moment.

"Block this!" He raised his hand over his head as if grabbing energy then thrust his hand forward. "Daréta suahk!"

I barely managed to throw myself out of the way before a red bolt of lightning ripped though the room. Dimitri covered his ears as the boom of thunder echoed off the stone walls. I used this short respite to heal my wound and cast a protective barrier around myself. I rose to my fighting stance as the last echo of thunder faded into oblivion.

Dimitri glared at me through gangly bangs and lunged. I managed to dodge all of his attacks and even land a few blows of my own. I spun around and smote him across the face with the blades of one of my tessens. He recoiled and howled in pain. Taking advantage of the situation, I quickly spun again, striking two more times before dropping to the ground to kick his feet out from under him.

I stood over him as he groaned in pain.

Above the dueling Dragon Keepers, another battle raged on. Thera and Teka found themselves against two Dákun Daju assassins and a powerful Judge. Teka confronted each opponent head on with clawed fists and a whip. Thera, on the other hand, fell back just far enough to avoid their weapons. The young Feykin fired off one spell after another.

"Thera!"

The cry of her name made her freeze. Turning to search for the source, she found it near the top of the spiraling staircase.

"Pox?" Thera blinked, hoping she was imagining her sister. It was no illusion; she was really in league with the enemy. "Pox, what are you doing here?"

"Thera, stop this foolishness!"

Thera cast another rapid string of spells to assist Teka before confronting her younger sister again. "What foolishness?"

"You are in league with the Dark Keeper!" Piper cried.

Thera's blood ran cold.

"You're wrong, Piper!" Teka shouted as she dodged a blow from the Judge's heavy axe. "Xyleena is a good kid! There is no way she could be the Dark Keeper!"

"Dimitri is the true Dragon Keeper!" Piper shouted back. "His mother is Amorez, and he needs the Dragon Diary to prevent Xyleena from freeing the Shadow Dragons!"

"Shut up, girl!" the magenta-haired Dákun Daju hollered.

Thera sent a spell after her before daring a look below. Xyleena looked terrified, while the man she figured was Dimitri sneered. He was enjoying the pain and fear he inflicted. There was no way that he could be Amorez's heir.

"You're wrong," Thera whispered. She sighed and turned an angry glare on her sister. "You are wrong!"

Piper frowned. "I am always wrong to you. I cannot do anything right in your eyes. And now that your mind has been stolen by the Dark Keeper, I will be forced to destroy you!"

"No, Pox!" Thera watched, horrified, as Piper gathered energy for a spell. "Don't do it, Pox!"

"I don't take orders from you!" Piper launched a ball of red energy at her sister.

Thera barely managed to leap out of the way before the energy struck. It blew a huge portion of the wall and stairs away as it exploded.

Debris rained down on the duelists below.

I heard the explosion and dared a glance upward. Thera was in the air, held aloft by her midnight wings. Just opposite her, a gaping hole in the stairs still smoldered from the energy that had struck. Pieces of the wall and stairs fell to the ground a little ways away from where I stood. I had a split second to wonder what was going on up there before Dimitri struck again.

I growled out of annoyance and struck back. Our blades collided in a vibrant ring. I swung my other fan beneath his blockade, cleanly slicing across his thighs and almost unmanning him.

"You wretch!" He shoved me away and managed to heal himself before I regained my balance.

The moment I did, Dimitri lunged for me. I spun away, narrowly avoiding the edge of his sword.

I was growing weary from the fighting, but there was one tactic I had yet to try. I summoned energy and focused it in my hand. Dimitri gawked at me as I aimed the magic at him.

"Daréta esso!"

The crackling ball of electricity launched at my command. It slammed into Dimitri with enough force to hopefully break bones while successfully knocking him back several meters. He slumped to the ground, unconscious. I breathed a sigh of relief and sunk to the floor.

"Impressive spell, girl, but it seems to have drained you of all your energy."

My heart stopped, and a cold chill ran up my spine at the voice behind me. I looked over my shoulder to see the Godilai Dákun Daju standing on the final step.

"You!"

She sneered. "Still mad about your little friend, I see. Do not fret. I will send you to him!"

"No!"

I barely blocked her sword in time. The blow was so strong that my arm went numb clear up to my shoulder. Godilai growled and kicked me in the gut hard enough to send me skidding across the floor. I collapsed, barely able to breathe as I clutched my stomach in agony.

"A futile effort, Hume. Now you d—"

A deafening roar cut off the last of her words. I was too weak to block my ears from the onslaught of the sound.

"Who dares disturb the peace of my Sky Castle?" A male's voice boomed from somewhere behind me.

I groaned as I managed to roll myself over to see who he was. All I could see was a pair of glowing amber eyes floating in the shadows beneath the stairs.

"Vortex?" I managed to whisper.

The amber eyes lost much of their fierceness as they focused on me. "It is nice to see you again, hatchling."

I stood with Amorez on the crest of that hill, watching as a storm grew on the horizon. On this, the first day of peace after Agasei's reign, the storm seemed a bad omen… at least until Vortex changed our minds, "Clouds have come floating into our lives, no longer to carry rain or usher storm, but to add color to our sunset sky."

– FROM "CONVERSATIONS WITH DRAGONS"
BY DJURDAK ZA'CAR

A giant foreleg slowly emerged from the shadows, revealing gorgeous cerulean scales that refracted light as if they were sapphires. Long, ivory claws dug into the stone floor as the dragon took another step, then another, until at last he had fully entered the light.

I gawked at him, this dragon called Vortex. He stood easily sixteen meters high at the shoulder. Thin, cream-colored wings lay folded across his back, which was armed with ivory spines. His long neck held his wedge-shaped head aloft. And he stared down at me with gentle amber eyes that were protected by a ridge of bone and long, ivory horns.

A joyful whoop echoed down from the stairs above. Vortex followed the sound and snorted at the five that were there. The dragon lowered his gaze to Dimitri, who had finally come to and was trying to sneak away unnoticed.

"You will fail, Dark Keeper, just as your sire failed."

Dimitri flushed at the dragon's words before scrambling up the stairs. Godilai was not far behind him. Vortex watched their retreat, greatly amused, before returning his attention to me. "Are you injured, hatchling?"

"That Dakun Daju woman kicked me pretty hard, but I'll be okay. I just need to regain some energy." I forced myself to sit up, trying to ignore the painful protest of my muscles at the movement.

"Take some of my energy," Vortex said as he sat on his haunches. "Believe me, I have enough to spare."

"I thank you, Vortex, but…"

He lowered his head until he was almost touching me. "But?"

I resisted the urge to reach out and stroke his snout. "I am not sure how to do that."

The dragon stared at me, confusion and worry growing in his amber eyes. "You cannot remember?"

"Remember what?"

I heard Vortex snarl, but it was not directed at me. Over my shoulder, I could see Thera and Teka as they descended the last few stairs. Both sported cuts and bruises but were otherwise fine. Thera bowed to the dragon as he snarled again.

"We are friends, great dragon. I promise."

Vortex leaned in and sniffed the air around Thera.

"You look like Thernu, but you smell different."

"Thernu was my mother. I am Thera."

"She has gone to Havel?" Vortex sounded disappointed.

"The sea swallowed her a year ago."

Vortex was silent a moment. "I am sorry."

"As am I," Thera whispered. She knelt beside me to begin helping me heal as Vortex turned his attention to Teka.

"You are completely new to me."

Teka chuckled. "I am just the ship captain who brought you your new Keeper. My name is Teka Loneborne."

"You have an important role, Teka Loneborne. One that is far from over." The dragon straightened his neck and watched the three of us for a moment.

"What happened to Dimitri and his team?" I asked as Thera finished healing my wounds and moved away to start on Teka's.

"I am not sure," Teka admitted with a shrug, "but I think the appearance of Vortex caught them with their pants down. They rushed out of here faster than Thera and I could catch them."

"And Pox blew up most of the remaining stairs with a spell." The fury in Thera's voice was as obvious as the wings on her back. "I could have followed... I should have followed."

Teka gripped the young Feykin's shoulder tightly. "But we needed you."

"Why isn't Amorez here?" I blurted, successfully redirecting the conversation.

Vortex tilted his head to the side. "She is otherwise occupied."

"No. I mean, why is she not your Keeper? Why did you pick me? Amorez is stronger and far more experienced."

Vortex studied me. "Xyleena Renoan, why do you doubt yourself so? You are much stronger than you realize."

Renoan? That's right. That was her full name, Amorez Renoan. I frowned. "You did not answer my question."

The dragon snorted. "You are the Dragon Keeper because you agreed to it."

"What?" Thera, Teka, and I asked in unison.

Vortex sighed and closed the distance between us. "You and Amorez met and agreed that if a Dark Keeper ever rose to power again, you would be the one we turned to and called our Keeper. Do you not remember anything?"

I hissed through my teeth in frustration.

"Please, great dragon, try to understand," Thera began. "Something happened to her. She was found washed up on the shores outside the Temple of Five Souls. When she awoke later, she could not remember anything."

Vortex grew ever more worried by her words. "You really have no idea who you are and what you have done? This is disturbing news."

"You're telling me." I muttered, hugging my knees.

"You know nothing of what you have been taught—fighting, magic, the ancient tongue, and the locations of each of my brothers and sisters. You could have easily defeated every one of that would-be Dark Keeper's team without a second thought if only you could remember."

"Can't you teach her?" Teka pleaded.

"Zenith of Space and Time could easily replace her missing memories, but I cannot. I can only tell you what I know. I am afraid it will not fill in many blank pages in your history, but maybe it will help you find yourself."

"Find myself." I chuckled. "Zhealocera said the same thing."

"I guess she knew more about you than even you realized," Thera murmured, sitting beside me. "So what is Xyleena's story?"

Vortex looked me in the eye as he spoke. "Xyleena Renoan, you were born four hundred and twenty-eight years ago. Your mother is obviously Amorez, while your father was Djurdak, the former High Prince of Ithnez. He renounced his title when he married your mother.

"You were taught magic, alchemy, fighting, and languages at a young age. Some time after your one hundredth year, Amorez introduced you to us, the Twelve. That was the last time we were ever summoned by Amorez.

"It was you who secreted us to places all around the planet in hopes of protecting us. And you wrote the 'Riddle of the Twelve' so you would not forget where to find us."

"Merciful gods!" I cried and buried my head in my hands.

Vortex curled his tail about me in a gentle hug.

I sighed, feeling defeated. "Anything else?"

"The last time I saw you was when you summoned me here and told me to await your return to the Hidden Plains. That was almost sixty years ago." Vortex was quiet for a bit. "Your mother came alone a few years ago. She was distraught and hoping to find you."

"I guess she didn't." I sighed and rubbed my temples. "What about my father? You sure his name was Djurdak?"

Vortex eyed me for a moment. "Agasei had been dead for almost a decade when you were born, hatchling. And Djurdak has been in Havel for a little more than three centuries now."

Feeling numb, I could only nod in understanding. I was missing so much of my life, and everything I thought I knew about my past was all wrong. Granted, I was grateful to know I was not the spawn of Agasei, but I could not escape the feeling that so much more was missing. The truth about who I was lay before me now on a path I once walked. There was no turning back.

"Okay." I got to my feet. "We need to find the other eleven dragons before Dimitri can find the Dragons' Gate."

Thera smiled at me. "We can do it."

"Sure we can!" Teka clapped both of us on the back.

"The black dragon statues are the keys to the Dragons' Gate," Vortex explained. "There are twelve statues placed outside each of our hiding spots. Should Dimitri find all twelve statues, he will unlock the route to the gate."

"And the only way to find the Dragons of Light is in the Dragon Diary." I patted my hip sack. "That means we have to keep Dimitri from getting his grubby little hands on it at any cost."

"Agreed." Teka nodded.

"You should be on your way then, hatchling," Vortex said as he stood.

"You will need to stay ahead of him to prevent the release of the Shadow Dragons."

I looked up at Vortex. "You are coming with us, aren't you?"

"You truly have forgotten much." Vortex sighed. "I shall be within the dragon eye, awaiting your summons."

"Wait! How do I—"

I watched as the dragon faded into wisps of blue. They danced around me, creating a whirlwind before shooting into the amulet around my neck. One of the empty sockets turned blue.

The dragon of wind was mine.

Dimitri mumbled a long string of curses as he led his team out of the bizarre castle. He could not understand how such a young and terrified girl could cast a complicated spell like the thunder ball that hit him. He would have to be extremely careful the next time they met in battle.

He stopped just outside the castle gates and examined the black dragon statue. He knew there was a key to the Dragons' Gate on the statue, but where?

"Dimitri, quit playing with that thing and let's go!" Luna shouted.

"No." Dimitri examined the statue, running his fingers along every nook and cranny. Still, he found nothing that resembled a key.

Vincent sat down on the stairs to watch. "What are you doing?"

"A key to the Dragons' Gate is on this statue, but I cannot find it."

Godilai moved to stand behind him, allowing her cyan gaze to scan the entire statue. "Are you sure it is an actual key you are looking for?"

Dimitri faced her. "I read somewhere about keys on black dragon statues. With all twelve keys, the route to the Dragons' Gate will be revealed."

Godilai flashed a smirk, earning an evil look from Dimitri. "Are you sure you are looking for a key like the kind used to unlock doors? Perhaps you are mistaken and the keys are hints that point to a location."

Dimitri sighed. "What did you find?"

Godilai pointed. "Look at the dais."

Dimitri mumbled something incoherently as he moved to stand beside Godilai. He followed the invisible line drawn by her finger. Ancient runes were embossed into the black marble just under the dragon's front claws.

"Baah!" Dimitri knelt before the dais and ran his fingers over the runes. "What in Havel does it say?"

"The greatest secret lies," Piper said slowly as she translated the runes.

Dimitri quickly scribed the translation into his father's diary.

"Thank you, Piper. Now, let's get out of here."

Dimitri led his team down the rainbow stairs at a brisk pace. As they descended, Dimitri formulated their next plan of action. As soon as he was back on solid ground, he initiated the plan.

"We should destroy their skiff," Luna said, making a beeline for the beached dinghy.

"Do not touch it!" Dimitri ordered.

Luna shot him a dirty, albeit confused, look.

"They have to get off the island somehow. And when they do, they will try to find the next dragon."

Godilai crossed her arms. "You want them to find the next one?"

Dimitri smiled at her. "Relax. You are going to follow them on foot once they return to mainland. Listen to their conversation closely. If they uncover the location of the next dragon, return to me with the information immediately."

Godilai frowned. "And if they should find me before then?"

"You are a Dákun Daju. I think you can handle those three girls."

"Not if they summon that dragon."

Luna scoffed. "Aren't you forgetting something, Dimitri? How do we sneak past the girls as they make their way to the Sorcerers' Isle?"

"Simple." Dimitri laughed and put his hands on Piper's shoulders. "An invisibility spell."

Piper smiled proudly. "That's an easy one."

Vincent pointed toward the top of the stairs. "I suggest using it quickly, because I think that's them exiting the castle."

Dimitri jumped into their skiff. "Time to go!"

Godilai, Luna, and Piper followed his example while Vincent just sort of fell into the boat, much to the amusement of the others. Dimitri shoved the boat away from shore.

"Dasai nagarésayo!" Piper cast the invisibility spell the instant the boat reached open water.

The team lingered there, waiting for Xyleena and her friends to leave the island.

Several minutes passed before Xyleena and her team reached their skiff. The girls looked it over, probably to see if it had been sabotaged. When they deemed it worthy of travel, they pushed off from the beach.

Dimitri allowed them to pass his team before he took the oar and followed the girls back to mainland.

*When I asked if he could pull off this impossible feat of
creating dragons, Moonwhisperer would only smile and say,
"What better way is there to find the limits of the possible than
to go beyond them and into the impossible?"*
                                    – FROM "THE DIARY OF AMOREZ"
                                           BY AMOREZ RENOAN

It was after midnight when Thera, Teka, and I returned to Kínashe's
boathouse. We tethered the skiff to the dock and gathered our belongings as
quietly as possible. The last thing we wanted was to alert someone to our
presence, as I was certain Dimitri had not given up on his goals that easily.

We unhitched our wyverns and took off into the forest. After about an
hour's hard ride, we came across a clearing next to the riverbank. Thera gave a
signal. We reined in our wyverns and dismounted. Teka and I set up our camp
as Thera placed wards around the clearing.

I took the first watch. It proved to be a rather chilly night, but I would not
dare light a fire for warmth. Therefore, I found myself huddled between the
three sleeping wyverns, staring up at the stars and listening to the sounds
around me. The rhythmic soft breathing of my comrades mixed with the gentle
gurgling of the river a few meters away. It was a sweat lullaby.

"I remember a night like this…"

I bolted upright and immediately scanned the clearing. Everything
appeared normal… except… A few meters away, a strange man was sitting
before a raging fire. I quickly rubbed my eyes, attempting to clear them. He
was still there and I drank in his image. His hair was long and black, tied back
in a low tail. He was dressed in a plain, blue tunic and brown, leather pants.
Something about him seemed familiar.

"Don't you remember? It was a few days after your twenty-third birthday.
You had been so angry about something and avoided everyone as much as
possible. Then I came back." the man grinned and stirred the fire. "I took you
to our favorite hill and we looked at the stars for hours. I don't know what it
was, but something about them seemed comforting to you."

"Are you…real?"

"Later that night, I treated you to your first pint of ale." He laughed at a
memory. "You should have seen your face. You looked like you had just taken
a lick of the sourest bitterpome in the bunch."

"Please answer me." I felt tears stinging my eyes. "Who are you?"

His blue eyes finally focused on me and he smiled.

Hatchling!

I gasped as my eyes flew open. An instant later, I was sitting up and
searching my surroundings. Thera and Teka were sound asleep. There was no
fire, no blue-eyed man.

You were dreaming.

"Who's there?" A quick scan of the perimeter again revealed nobody, nothing.

There is no need to fear, hatchling. It is only me.

"Vortex?"

I heard laughter echoing in my mind.

"How can I hear you if you aren't here?"

I am always here. You can hear me in your mind, because we are linked to each other through the dragon eye.

"Can anyone else hear you?"

I would have to be released from the eye to speak to others.

"I see." I yawned and rubbed my temples. "How long was I asleep?"

I cannot say. Vortex was quiet for a moment. That dream disturbed you. Perhaps it would be wise for you wake one of the others so you can get some rest.

"You knew what I was dreaming?"

When I am in the eye, I see what you see and feel what you feel. I know that the man you saw in your dream was very close to you…and he is in Havel. The dragon sounded saddened by that, as if he knew the man. He sighed. Please, hatchling, get some sleep. You need it.

"Right," I muttered as I got to my feet. A shiver ran through me as the cold of night swept away the heat of the wyverns' bodies. "I just hope I don't have another dream like that one."

I roused Thera from her fitful slumber and helped her get situated for her turn at the watch. I bade her good night and curled up between the wyverns again. I watched her for a while, wondering what was going through her mind to give her young face such a dark look. After a few minutes, I caught a glimpse of a tear as it crept its way down her cheek. She sniffled and wiped it away, almost angrily.

She must be thinking of her sister's betrayal. I thought.

Vortex quietly agreed.

I diverted my attention then, giving Thera as much privacy as I could allow. As I gazed up at the stars one more time, I thought of that man. His name was on the tip of my tongue, yet – like everything else I tried to remember – I could not coax it from my past. I sighed and prayed to the Souls for peace. Finally, I let my eyes drift shut and was asleep in no time.

Daylight. I stood alone within a forest of glimmering, snow-white trees. Silver mist clung to the ground and danced in a gentle breeze. Before me loomed an ancient stone ruin that had long ago been overgrown with white vines and other foliage. I knew this place, though I could not recall exactly when or where I had seen this building before. I remembered it when it was new. It had been beautiful.

The soft fluttering of wings from behind me stole my attention. I looked over my shoulder to see a phoenix perched in one of the trees. She watched me intently, so I turned to her and bowed.

The phoenix suddenly burst into flames. A nude woman slowly stepped out of the fire. With a flash of light, she was clad in a simple, pale-yellow dress. She stared at me, and I stared back in awe.

I had never seen the Goddess of Fire in human form before. She was beautiful. Her silken hair cascaded down her back, almost to her feet, and shifted from red to golden yellow. Her striking blue eyes held a depth of knowledge that no one could possibly hope to achieve. She was shorter than I imagined, standing about my height. And she carried herself regally.

I finally broke out of my stupor and smiled. "Tanda, Zahadu-Kitai. Núl cistrena ja chee?"

"Last we met you could not speak a word of the ancient tongue. You are learning quickly."

I chuckled. "From what I heard, I already knew Kinös Elda. I just needed to remember."

She was quiet for a minute before she nodded. "What you say is true."

"Can you tell me how I lost my memories?"

Her eyes locked on mine for a long, quiet moment. Finally, she sighed and stepped past me. "You fell," she simply stated.

I shook my head. "What did I fall from?"

Zahadu-Kitai smiled at me over her shoulder. "The Dragons' Gate."

I had not expected that. For me to not only know the location of the Dragons' Gate but to attempt to open it was a huge shock. What could I have possibly been doing? I hoped I was not up to anything bad.

The silence between us had apparently grown too long, and the Daughter of Fire started walking away.

"Thank you, Zahadu-Kitai. You have been a great help."

She looked at me over her shoulder. "You are welcome."

I watched as she walked away and disappeared in a wink of crimson light. I sighed and looked back at the collapsed building. I could not help but wonder where I had seen it before.

I awoke with a start and shivered from the cold. Thera stood over me, looking concerned, while Teka knelt by my side.

"Thank the Gods." Thera breathed a sigh of relief and dropped the blanket. I promptly sat up and wrapped it around me again.

"We thought you would never wake up."

Between chittering teeth, I managed, "Why did you think that?"

Teka frowned. "We've been trying to wake you for over an hour!"

"Oh." I stretched, pulled the blanket tighter, and finally stood up. "Well, if you were in the middle of an important conversation, you wouldn't want to wake up, either."

"What?"

"A conversation with whom?" Thera asked as she helped me pack up my sleeping roll.

"Zahadu-Kitai told me how I lost my memory. It was a rather disturb— what?"

Both of them looked absolutely bewildered.

"The Goddess of Fire spoke to you in a dream?" Teka asked.

I nodded. "That isn't anything new. She has been coming to me in my dreams for a long while now."

"Okay…" Thera cleared her throat, returned to her task. "So what did she say?"

"She told me how I lost my memory."

As I retold the events of my dream, Thera and Teka grew ever more shocked. When I had finished the story, they were both quiet.

Finally Thera spoke. "Do you know why you were at the Dragons' Gate?"

"Believe me, I wish I knew. I really hope I wasn't on a mission to free the Shadow Dragons."

"Maybe you were there just to see if the gate was still locked," Teka suggested.

I shrugged.

"Well, what would it mean if you had gone there to release the dragons?"

I seriously doubt you had gone there to unleash that kind of evil unto the world, hatchling.

"That's what I'm hoping was the case." I sighed. I noticed the weird stares from my comrades. "I forgot. You guys can't hear Vortex speak while he is in the amulet."

"Wow," said Teka. "Scared me there for a minute."

"You can hear him?" Thera asked.

I nodded.

"What is it like?"

I clicked my tongue. "It's hard to describe. Imagine having someone whispering in your ears, but it echoes as if there are about seven people speaking at once."

Teka laughed as she mounted her wyvern. "Sounds like it will drive you mad."

I grinned. "Probably."

Vortex snorted.

Thera hopped into the saddle of her own wyvern while I rummaged through my hip sack. "Xyleena, may I see Dragon Diary again? I'd like to work on the riddle some more while we ride."

I gave the young Feykin the diary before mounting Ekvinöj.

"Do let me know if you remember anything about the riddle. It would make this quest much easier."

"I hear you on that one."

Let them know if you remember anything, even if it is as seemingly unimportant as the origins of that ruined building in your dream, Vortex said.

I nodded, even though he probably could not see me.

After taking a moment to gather our bearings, the three of us were back on the trek east.

Thera woke us from our sleep much earlier than usual. She seemed very excited, which was odd considering her lack of sleep the night before. When Teka and I were finally awake, the three of us gathered around the small fire to prepare breakfast. Thera explained her excitement.

"Great Kkaia of Rock I took, and hid away on isle that shook." Thera smiled proudly.

"Oh! It is the next part of the riddle. Say it again, Thera." I listened as Thera repeated the fragment she had finally converted. "Kkaia of Rock on isle that shook."

"What could that mean?" Teka said between yawns.

My sister Kkaia is of earth. However, I have never heard of an island that shakes, Vortex announced after what sounded like a huge yawn.

I relayed the message.

"Blast. I was hoping he knew the answer so we didn't have to spend the next unknown span of time thinking of an answer." Teka muttered thoughtfully as she chewed her food.

"It could be worse. We could be searching for these dragons without any clues to their locations," Thera muttered.

Teka snorted. "Think, Xy. Try to remember the 'Riddle of the Twelve' back when you wrote it. Maybe you will discover the answer."

"I'll try, but I can't guarantee anything. I don't even remember when I originally wrote the riddle or why I put it in my mother's diary."

So it would never be lost? Vortex offered.

I suppose that would be the best place to keep the key to all twenty-four dragons. I thought.

Vortex's chuckle echoed in my mind.

"How about we think on the road?" Teka asked. "I don't know about you two, but I'm dying to sleep in a bed that doesn't include rocks." She rubbed her back for emphasis.

"How long until we reach Thorna?"

Thera looked skyward as if she could gauge the distance by the thickness of the forest canopy. Maybe she could, I realized. After all, she was the native to this land. Who would know it better?

"We should pass Thuraben later today, so I'd say we were still six days out of Thorna. But if we ride hard today, we could be there in three or four."

"I like that idea," Teka said as she packed her belongings and tied them to her saddle.

I quickly scarfed down the remainder of my breakfast and began packing my own things up. Minutes later, the three of us were speeding through the underbrush.

Great Kkaia of Rock I took, and hid away on isle that shook. I repeated the portion of the riddle for probably the thousandth time.

Vortex was just as lost as I was when it came to discovering an answer. Had Ríhan been here, he probably would have laughed and given me a long list of geographical locations in the world with islands that experienced earthquakes.

That is it, hatchling! Ask Teka if she knows of any islands with abnormal geographic activity.

I relayed Vortex's message as requested.

"I have been thinking the same thing," Teka answered. "The only place I can think of that would frequently cause earthquakes is along Zarconia's Fault. But it's mostly just open sea, no islands."

"Or at least none that you could see," Thera replied, slowing her wyvern enough to run stride for stride with mine.

She passed me Dragon Diary, and I quickly turned to the hand-drawn map. There was only one island along the entire fault line.

That has to be it!

"Have you ever seen an island here?" I pointed at the island while Teka looked at the map.

She shook her head after a moment.

"Then that is where we will find Kkaia's Shaking Island."

"Straight west of Aissur and along the fault. That should be easy to find."

Thera urged her wyvern faster. "Then let us hurry to Thorna so we can leave."

Teka and I followed her example. The rest of the day and well into the night, the three of us rode our wyverns as they sprinted onward to Thorna.

The only weapons that seem to work against these Dákun
Daju are the Mercury 2 plasma cannons. The problem with
using those is the cells won't last forever and we have no
replacements, nor do we possess the technology to make more.
We need to develop some other type of weapon to take these
savages down.

– FROM "A LETTER TO THE KING"
BY AN UNKNOWN SOLDIER

Godilai silently cursed the topography of the Sorcerers' Isle. Due to the thick underbrush, she was having a rather difficult time keeping up with Xyleena's team as they moved eastward. She had almost lost the trio a few times in their driving sprint and was ultimately forced to change tactics to keep up with them. Now she sprinted along the riverbed, matching stride for stride with their nimble wyverns.

Though she found herself several meters away, Godilai could still hear the conversations of the three girls. They were quiet now, but a little earlier they had been excited about cracking part of a riddle that dealt with the dragons, something about a rock on an island that shook. As soon as they could figure out what that clue meant, she could return to Dimitri and relay the information.

The Feykin girl slowed her wyvern to match Xyleena's pace. Godilai reduced her speed and focused her attention on their conversation.

"Have you ever seen an island here?" The Dragon Keeper pointed at something in the diary and earned a negative answer from her grey-haired comrade. "Then that is where we will find Kkaia's Shaking Island."

"Straight west of Aissur and along the fault. That should be easy to find."

Godilai froze in her tracks, plowing a trench in the river mud as her feet dragged to a stop. Finally! She knew where the next dragon clue led. With a smile on her lips, Godilai turned west.

Dimitri stepped from his tent, stretched and yawned. By habit, he glanced around at the meager camp he and his team had established late last night. They were by the river, surrounded by trees and fauna so thick it was like a shield. The wyverns had been tied up at the fallen tree on the east side of the camp; they were content to hum as Luna fed them fish. A small fire pit was a ways away from the reptilian mounts. Tents had been set up in an arc around the heat source and Vincent and Pox were tending the fire. Everything was in order.

Dimitri yawned again as he crossed the few steps from his tent to the fire. Vincent was quick to hand him a cup. He sniffed the steaming concoction as he sat; it was more of that herbal mix that Pox seemed fond of. Dimitri looked

134

across the blaze at the Feykin girl. He could still feel her mind at the very back of his, and he knew that she was thinking of her elder sister. He sipped the drink thoughtfully, then delved deeper into her mind. After a moment of searching, he found what he was after: Her repertoire of magic. Though not as extensive as he imagined, it was far more than what he knew. So he started memorizing her spells as if they were his own.

Only moments passed before the warble of the wyverns stole his concentration. Hearing footsteps rapidly approaching from the trees, he and the trio were quick to react. They armed up and waited with bated breath for what felt like hours. Only when a flash of white appeared between the thick foliage did they relax. A moment later and Godilai leapt over the fallen tree. She glanced sidelong at the wyverns when they hissed at her. Then she strode between the tents and came to a stop a few paces from the fire pit.

"I take it you return with good tidings, Sortim."

Godilai nodded to Luna. "They finally learned the next location. It is somewhere along Zarconia's fault west of the city of Aissur."

"Follow the Fault westward from Aissur?" Dimitri quirked an eyebrow at the information.

"Yes." Godilai nodded for emphasis. "A hidden island exists somewhere along the fault line, and the next dragon to be found is nesting there."

Dimitri was silent as he removed his father's diary from the hidden pocket. He quickly flipped to the page he sought and stared at the map. There was quite a bit of open water between Aissur and the Lescan coast, even following along Zarconia's Fault the entire way. However, if his team could reach the island first and set up an ambush, he could win the diary from that cursed girl. It was a big if, but it was still too good of a chance to pass up.

"Hey, Pox." Vincent caught the attention of their Feykin ally. "Is there a way you can get us to Aissur really quick? Like, using magic or something?"

She frowned. "I could use a warp spell, but I would need to see where I was going before it would work right. And I have never seen the lands outside the Sorcerers' Isle."

"What would happen if you just tried to warp?"

"We could warp into a wall or the bottom of the ocean or a thousand other places."

"What if you used someone else's memories to see the place you need to warp to?" Dimitri asked, looking up from the map at last.

"I have never tried it that way, but it could work if the memory was clear enough."

Luna scoffed. "I don't even remember the last time I was in Aissur."

"Same here," said Godilai.

"I was in Aissur a few years ago," Vincent offered.

Pox winced. "So much can change in only a few years. I do not think it would be wise to—"

"I was there two months ago, right before I hired Godilai to break into the Imperial Library," Dimitri said.

"That would probably be the safest vision."

"Okay, so here is the plan then." Dimitri returned his father's diary to the pocket, clapped his hands and rubbed them together. "Pox warps us to Aissur, and we hire another ship and crew to sail us along Zarconia's Fault. Once we find this Shaking Island, we locate the black statue and copy the clue down. Then we will set up an ambush for Xyleena's team."

"I think we should check to see if her dragon is there first. That way we can verify that we beat her to the island."

"Yes. Good idea, Godilai." Dimitri smiled. "Okay, so once we spring the ambush, kill whoever you must, but get Amorez's diary."

"I have noticed that Xyleena usually keeps it in the sack on her hip. If it is not there, the Feykin, Thera, will have it," Godilai explained. Her cyan gaze shifted to Pox for a moment to read the girl's reaction to the idea of killing her sister; there was none. "And I suggest finalizing the details of the ambush once we have seen the terrain of the island."

"Of course." Dimitri rolled his eyes at the obviousness of the Dákun Daju's suggestion. "Now that we are all clear on that… Pox, how about that warp?"

The young Feykin nodded. She stood up from her spot, grabbed a cup, and made her way towards the river. At the bank, she dipped the cup into the river water. Once the cup was full, she made her way back and held it before Dimitri. She told him that he needed to concentrate on the time he spent in Aissur. While he concentrated, Pox cast a spell to reflect his memory on the surface of the water. After a few moments of studying the projected image, Pox ended the spell and tossed the cup away.

It took the team a few minutes to pack up the camp and loose the wyverns. Once they were ready, Pox ordered everyone to hold on to her. When she felt all four sets of hands gripping her, she concentrated on Dimitri's memory of Aissur. With the image clearly in her mind, she uttered two words. In a flash of light, they were gone.

They had told the hatchlings to call me Master; it was a title I did not want. Instead, we sat together to invent a more appropriate title. Queen was suggested, as was Summoner, but Dragon Keeper... That was the one that stuck. I had become the Dragon Keeper.

– FROM "THE DIARY OF AMOREZ"
BY AMOREZ RENOAN

It was late in the morning on the sixth day after discovering the location of Vortex. We had been on the road for almost fourteen days now and were desperate to get back to Thorna. Thoughts of warm baths, hot meals, and soft beds kept us at a hard and rapid pace. Even our wyverns seemed eager to return to their home.

The weather, on the other hand, saw fit to keep us delayed. A great squall had blown in during the early hours of the morning and showed no signs of letting up any time soon. The three of us took shelter in a hut forged by Thera's magic and traded stories over the small fire.

"So, Thera," I started as I poked the fire with a stick, "why is it you and Pox have black wings while the other Feykin have white ones?"

Thera shrugged. "My mother was born with white wings. For some yet unknown reason, she returned from her adventures with Amorez with black wings. The people say that it is a mark the dragons left on her when she gave them life. Anyway, Pox and I were both born black-winged."

"That's right. I forgot Thernu was the Necromancer whose magic helped birth the Dragons of Light."

I watched as Thera slowly ran a finger over the feathers of one of her wings.

"Are you okay?"

"I am fine." Thera smiled and crossed her hands in her lap. "I just miss mother and Pox."

"I know that feeling," Teka muttered. "My mom was murdered because she loved a Feykin and bore his child. I was seven when we lost her. My father raised me until he, too, was murdered. Nothing like finding yourself alone on the streets at the age of twelve."

"Try living for centuries and seeing loved ones come and go like the wind while you stay young."

Thera and Teka looked at each other then at me. I gasped, suddenly realizing what I said. "I'm sorry. I...I don't know why I said that."

Vortex snorted. *Yes, you do.*

"Xy, did you just remember something from your past?"

I frowned. "I – I am not sure."

Tell them about the ruined building from your dream, Vortex suggested.

Why? Do you think it is connected with people who have been dead for who knows how long?

I felt Vortex's presence recede from my mind, and I sighed.

I am sorry for being short with you. Not knowing my own history is getting on my nerves, especially when I am constantly asked if I remembered something.

They only wish to help you, hatchling. And if it bothers you, tell them so.

I sighed and gave in. "Do you two remember the other day when I told you about my dream?"

I watched as Thera and Teka nodded before continuing.

"Well, something has been bothering me about it."

"Oh?" Teka leaned in to listen.

"There was a building in my dream overgrown with vines, and it was falling apart. I can clearly remember seeing it when it was new, but I can't tell when or why."

"Do you remember where it was?" Teka asked.

"I was standing in a forest of glowing white trees, and the building was in front of me. I have dreamt of that forest many times before. I know it is ancient, but I do not know where it is."

"It is true that the forest is from bygone times," Thera said. "My mother told me about it once. If I remember correctly, the White Woods are on one of the islands close to the southern tip of Mekora Lesca. She said something about a city lo—"

"A city long forgotten where the ghosts of the first victims still remain."

I shook my head as if waking from a dream. Thera was gaping at me while Teka glanced between us in confusion.

Thera hid her surprise with a serious look as she spoke. "I was just about to say the same thing."

"I...I remember hearing that somewhere."

Somewhere in the back of my mind, Vortex laughed. I told you it was important.

Oh hush. I could not suppress a smile. Thank you, Vortex.

"Well, if Thernu was there once and Xy remembers the place, maybe there is a dragon hidden there." Teka wiggled her eyebrows suggestively.

"Are you saying we should scour the White Woods for who knows what on a hunch?"

"You never know. It might help jog Xy's memory in the process."

"I say we think about which path to take while we are en route to Kkaia. In the mean time, how about we pack up and be off." I pointed outside with my thumb. "The rain has finally stopped, and I am in a mood for a hot, relaxing bath back in Thorna."

"Oh! I like the sound of that!" Teka exclaimed as she stretched.

She and I began packing up our things while Thera quickly geared up the wyverns. Minutes later, we were speeding through the forest once again.

Several hours had passed in rapid transit eastward. It was well past sundown, and Thera's floating orb lit our path between the dimly luminescent plant life. A few minutes ago, she told us we would reach Thorna within the hour.

There had been little talk between us on this portion of our trek, probably due to the debate about visiting the White Woods. I was torn over a decision. On one hand, if seeing the forest in person could restore my memory, then it was well worth going. On the other, I needed to find the other eleven dragons.

Thera whistled, robbing my attention from inner demons. She slowed her wyvern to a slow walk and finally stopped, and the other wyverns were obliged to follow. Teka and I glanced at each other, both of us wondering the same thing. Before we could utter a word, Thera began casting protective barriers around us.

A beam of energy shot out of the forest, aimed straight for me. Thanks to Thera's barrier, the beam reflected skyward.

"Núl wa et shríldu ni esté?" I shouted at the trees.

An instant later, several angry Feykin surrounded us. Thera tried calming them down to find out what was wrong, but they would not listen.

Summon me! Vortex shouted.

Do you know what has them so upset?

No, but they will kill you if you do not hurry.

Before I had a chance to do anything else, we found ourselves prisoners. Thera had surrendered us under terms I did not know. I could only hope that whatever she had planned saved us from whatever fate the Feykin had in mind.

When Solahnj told me she was with child, it brought back
memories of my beloved and our child who could never be. I
hurt. I hurt a lot. And that hurt further fueled my rage. Hidden
beneath that anger and pain, I felt a sense of pride; I was to be
a father. I prayed that this time, the child could live.

– FROM "THE DIARY OF AGASEI"
BY AGASEI DÉDOS

We were bound and gagged, forced to walk at spear point as the Feykin
lead us into Thorna. I watched the scant few inhabitants out this late as we
were paraded through the town. Many of the men glared at me while the
women quickly disappeared inside various huts.

Our armed escort led us up the bridges and walkways until we arrived at
the hollowed-out tree that served as the chamber of elders. We were promptly
shoved inside and forced to sit on the wooden bench before the five empty
platforms. We waited.

I sighed. What have we done to deserve this?

I do not think it was anything you did, hatchling.

You think Dimitri was here?

Vortex was quiet for a moment. Yes, I believe he was.

That explains everything, then. What do you suggest we do to get out of
this mess? I glanced about at the guards—seventeen were in here with us and
several more were stationed outside the chamber. Each one of them was armed
and exceptionally talented in magic. Not great odds.

Attempting to fight your way out would only get you killed, hatchling.

I nodded slightly.

The only thing you can do for now is wait and hope that Thera can sway
the minds of her kinsmen. However, should you get the chance to do anything
in your defense, make sure you summon me.

I promise that will be the first thing I do.

Therefore, we waited. Several hours must have passed before the curtains
leading outside were pulled aside. I sat up straighter in my seat as I watched
the Elders file into the room. Unlike before, they did not take their seats on the
raised platforms. Instead they faced us, and each looked at me with utter
disdain burning in their eyes.

Thera stood from the bench and bowed low. Her uncle waved his hand, and
the gag vanished from her mouth.

"Shíkai ja, Uncle."

My mind instantly began translating every word of their conversation into
Standard. And I listened closely, hanging to every word and hoping against
hope that Thera could sway their minds.

"Why have you requested to stand before this honorable council, Thera?"

Thera stood to her full height and stared straight into her uncle's eyes.
"Please, Uncle, tell us why you seek to kill Xyleena and her allies."

"She has deceived you into believing she is Amorez's heir when in fact the young man known as Dimitri Renoan is the Dragon Keeper." The old man pointed at me as he spoke. "She has stolen the diary needed to unlock the Dragons' Gate and intends to free the Shadow Dragons."

Thera shook her head. "I am sorry, Uncle, but it is you who has been deceived. The man who came here, Dimitri, is Agasei's heir. He has murdered several innocent people, enslaved my little sister to do his bidding, and is hunting Xyleena because she is the true Dragon Keep—"

"She has placed a spell on you, Thera!" the old man shouted. "She wants you to believe that she is good because she needs your power to fend off the Dragon Keeper!"

"That is not true!" Thera screamed as tears beginning to roll down her cheeks.

"Screaming at us will not help you, child," one of the other Elders said.

Thera took a long, steady breath and wiped her tears away with her sleeve.

"I can prove Xyleena is the Dragon Keeper."

From somewhere in the back of my mind, I heard Vortex shout, Get ready!

"How so?"

Thera waved her hands in my direction, and the bindings and gag vanished. The Elders cried out and guards surged forward. My hand flew to the dragon eye amulet and brushed the jewel that marked Vortex's presence. A strange, numbing sensation spread through my fingertips as I threw my hand in the air and shouted.

"Vortex!"

A navy light exploded from my hand, and a strong gust of wind burst forth from the amulet. The gale surrounded me in a dizzying whirlwind. I could not breathe as the wind whipped and spun around me, slowly turning navy blue. A heartbeat later, the wind shot upward and converged, solidifying into the sapphire-scaled Vortex. The dragon of wind roared and flared his wings to make a slow descent to the floor.

From the corner of my eyes, I saw the Elders fall to their knees. I ignored them for a moment to walk up to Vortex and pat him gently on the forearm. He craned his long neck to look at me.

"Hello, hatchling."

"I can't believe I remembered how to do that."

Vortex chuckled. "I knew you would."

"Xy," said Thera, "the Elders have expressed their deepest apologies and ask for your forgiveness."

I turned and looked past Thera at the Elders. They still knelt on the floor, staring in awe at Vortex. The guards too were kneeling. A few wept.

I nodded. "Ja lah tído guídemavet."

Relieved cries echoed in every corner of the room. The Elders slowly rose to their feet and beckoned Thera to come. I freed Teka from her binds as Thera conversed with them.

"Thank the gods you were quick to summon him." Teka pointed her thumb at Vortex. "I thought we were goners there for a minute."

I could not help but smile. "Me, too."

"So what do you think the Feykin will do now?"

"Let us go," I said as I observed the interaction of the Elders and Thera. "I do have a quest to get back to."

"Have you thought about taking a little detour?"

"You mean, have I thought about going to the White Woods to see if it restores my memory?"

Teka nodded.

"I have thought about it, but I think there are more important things to take care of first."

"Yeah, I guess you're right."

Thera came bounding back to us, a huge grin on her face.

"What are you so happy about?"

"I have just been promoted to Occultist."

"That's great!" I exclaimed.

"Congratulations!"

"Thank you." Thera bowed to us. "The Elders suggested we walk with Vortex down to Amorez's old hut. It is down on the ground level of town and has room enough to fit three dragons. It is, however, a little dusty from lack of use."

"The room sounds fine, but I'm not sure the walkways and bridges can support Vortex's weight."

"Then I will just have to fly down," Vortex said with a laugh.

"Can you even get out of the door?" Teka asked.

Vortex snorted and faded into wisps of blue. The wisps swirled around for a moment before shooting out of the door. I lead the mad rush outside just in time to witness Vortex reform and slowly glide to the ground. The few Feykin awake at this hour cheered at his presence, and I could not suppress a smile.

"Show off!" Teka called after him.

"I don't know about you two, but I am ready for some long overdue sleep. Come on." I started walking the maze of bridges and walkways.

Moments later, Thera and Teka caught up to me, and the three of us made our way to the ground level.

*After reading many logs and even Agasei's own journal, I
fully understand why he did what he did. The loss of a wife
and unborn child would send anyone into a blind rage, but
then to be sentenced to death in prison because he went
against orders to try to save her? No wonder people say he
went insane when Raiza was murdered.*
– FROM "A TYRANT'S HUMANITY"
BY PRINCESS UNÉ SHARVÍN

I woke to an exceedingly annoying knock at the door. With a heavy sigh, I
peeled back the covers and left the warmth of my bed. I grumbled about how
Thera and Teka could sleep through such a racket as I yanked the door open.
Thera's uncle Ruwviti greeted me with a smile.

"Kahs gözandí, Iríjhone Keeper. How are you?" Once again, my mind
translated the Kinös Elda.

"I am awake," I said after a huge yawn.

"I apologize if I woke you, but I have something important to speak to you
about." Ruwviti ushered me out of the hut that had once been Amorez's.

I paused to admire all of the gifts that had been laid outside while I slept.

Ruwviti chuckled. "Tokens of admiration and apology. It would seem our
people have taken a liking to your presence."

"Better than the alternative," I muttered.

Ruwviti smiled wryly and led me on a slow walk around Thorna.

"I know you will be leaving soon, Dragon Keeper, and I wish for you to
take my niece. If there is anyone who can restore Pox to her senses, I know it
is Thera."

"I was hoping she would be coming anyway. I still cannot translate the
keys to the Dragons of Light on my own, and Thera is proving to be more than
capable of handling the task."

"So I have heard." He smiled. "And know this, if you require anything to
aid you in your battle against Agasei's heir, please let us know. We will be
more than willing to help in any way."

"I'm glad to hear that, Elder Ruwviti. I may need all the help I can get."

He nodded in understanding. The two of us continued walking in silence
for a few minutes. Just when I was beginning to wonder what he was thinking,
he stopped outside a sizable hut.

"There is another reason I wanted to speak to you alone before you set off."

"Oh?"

Ruwviti nodded and pulled back the curtain of the hut. I quickly ducked
inside, and he followed. When my eyes adjusted to the lighting within, I
realized I was standing in a classroom. Several young Feykin glanced up at me
from their desks. And the woman at the front of the room stopped her lecture.
She bowed to Ruwviti as he and I strode up the aisle.

"This is Q'veca, one of the finest Menta teachers in all our lands. Q'veca, this is Xyleena Renoan, heir to Amorez's Dragons of Light."

Q'veca smiled. "It is a pleasure to meet you, Dragon Keeper."

I touched my fingers to my heart, then my forehead, before extending them outward as I bowed slightly in the honorable Feykin greeting Thera taught me. Gasps escaped several of the children, and Q'veca's smile widened.

"I brought you before Q'veca today to fill a request from my niece," Ruwviti explained. "Thera said you had learned much about magic and its uses and suggested having you take the Menta examinations. Should you pass Q'veca's test, you will be graduated to Menta status."

My heart skipped a beat. "You mean I can be apprenticed to a Sorcerer if I pass?"

Q'veca nodded. "That is correct."

I exhaled slowly to calm myself. "When do we start?"

"Recite the rules of magic."

I thought of that strange memory with the rules and smiled. "One, the caster must know enough ancient tongue to summon the desired element and direct it as he or she wishes. Two, the amount of magic summoned should not exceed the limits of the physical body that summons it, or the caster forfeits their life. Three, magic, like many things, is best learned through time and experience."

Q'veca glanced at Ruwviti before turning her attention back to me. "What spells do you know?"

"Do you want me to show you or just list them off?"

Ruwviti chuckled, and Q'veca blinked at me in surprise.

"Um…just list them for now."

"Heal, light, fire, silence, fire storm, thunder ball, thunder bolt, wind gust—"

"Okay, that's enough." Q'veca shook her head and faced Ruwviti. "I don't think she should be graduated to Menta."

He and I both frowned.

She raised her hand to prevent any remarks. "She has been using more advanced spells than even some Mages are capable of. Therefore, it is my opinion that Xyleena be graduated to Mage status…if not higher."

Elder Ruwviti nodded in agreement, and I had to bite my lip to keep from cheering.

"Thank you for your time, Q'veca."

She bowed and watched as the two of us exited her classroom.

Outside, Ruwviti faced me with a smile. "Congratulations on becoming a Mage, Xyleena."

"Thank you, Elder Ruwviti."

"Now, if you will excuse me, I have another matter to attend to. I trust you can find your way back to your hut?"

"Yes, sir." I watched him walk away before turning in the direction that would lead me back to Amorez's old hut. I laughed and took off at a full sprint, racing down the walkways and bridges.

I burst through the door of the hut, causing Thera and Teka to jump and scream. I stood in the doorway breathless and smiling. Thera quirked an eyebrow at me while Teka grumbled incoherently.

"Where were you? You left without saying anything," Vortex said, snaking his head into the main room from where he was bedded.

"I'm sorry. You were all sleeping, and Elder Ruwviti showed up and led me to a classroom."

"Ah. My uncle took you for the Menta exam." Thera nodded. "How did it go?"

"I am a Mage."

Thera blinked in surprise while Teka fell off her seat.

"Yeow!"

"So you surpassed the expectations of a Menta?"

I nodded and helped Teka up.

"That's great! I had a feeling you would. Did my uncle tell you who you are apprenticed to yet?"

I shook my head. "No, but he had to leave in a hurry. I guess he was on his way to find me a teacher."

"Hopefully you won't end up with Valadri. He is a horrible teacher," Teka muttered.

Thera laughed and nodded. "How he ever made it to Sorcerer rank is beyond me."

Vortex huffed. "I hate to spoil this cheery atmosphere, but we have some important planning to do."

Teka stuck her tongue out at me. "That is what we were doing before Xy scared me out of my wits with barging in through the door like that."

"What have you come up with so far?" I asked, taking a seat at the long table. A chart from Teka's ship had been laid out over the surface.

"Well, it would be quicker to sail straight to the Shaking Island instead of stopping in Aissur. But we would need to restock supplies, so we would almost have to sto—"

"Restock here," I said as I fished for the map within Dragon Diary.

Teka sighed. "I'm not allowed to."

"Why not?" Thera asked.

I laid the diary map up on the table and compared the two maps while I listened on the conversation.

"I have never been allowed to trade or request goods from any part of the Sorcerers' Isle because I am not Feykin."

"You are half. I don't see what the problem—"

"There isn't a problem," I interrupted. "Elder Ruwviti said the Feykin would help me in any way I needed. If my team needs supplies to continue on this quest, I'm sure they would be willing to give them." I picked up a charcoal pencil and sketched the Shaking Island onto Teka's map using Dragon Diary as reference.

"Well, that's a relief." Teka sighed and leaned in to study the addition to her map.

"Someone is coming," Vortex announced.

Seconds later, a loud knocking came from the door. Thera sighed and answered the door.

I heard a young woman's voice from the doorway. "Tanda, Thera. Tic la ja?"

She and Thera continued talking for a few minutes while Teka and I sorted out the details of the maps. Finally, Thera said good-bye and returned to the table.

"You have another gift, one I think you will appreciate greatly."

I glanced sidelong at Teka, who shrugged. After a moment, I put down the pencil and moved toward the door to join Thera. Curiosity got the best of Teka, and she quickly followed.

"Apparently the smithies worked on it all day and half the night."

"What is it?" I stared at the large wooden crate set on the floor and watched as Thera broke into it.

A smile slowly crept across her lips as she removed the lid. "Armor."

She picked out a piece of the plate and handed it to me. I was expecting it to be heavy like the armor of the Temple Knights, but this was extremely light, almost weightless. It was shining silver with beautiful filigree stamped into it, similar to the one I had seen on Zamora... Amorez.

"And it came with these."

I handed the plate to Teka, who seemed eager to examine it, and took the metal bars from Thera. I chuckled, instantly recognizing the design, and flipped them open.

"A new set of tessen fans."

Teka whistled. "Wow!"

Wow was an understatement. The fan blades were emblazoned with an image of each of the twelve Dragons of Light surrounded by the elements of their birthing and tapered to a razor-sharp edge.

"I love them." I breathed. I ran my fingers over the designs—seamless, beautiful craftsmanship. "I wish I knew how they did this."

"Each item is imbued with magic. The armor can never be destroyed, and the tessens will never go dull," Thera explained. "And they also added special wards to the metal as they crafted them. I am not sure exactly which wards, but I am sure they will come in handy."

I returned to the other room to show Vortex, who seemed pleased about the gifts.

"Finally, something you can use."

We all laughed before setting about on the business of sailing to the Shaking Island. By the end of the day, we had a route planned and a list of supplies drawn up.

Thera delivered the list to her uncle, and Teka went off to prepare her crew for travel. I remained in the hut with Vortex to pack for the days to come.

*Instead of continuing to the old, Earthic principals of
currency, we implemented a barter system. And with the
barter system came the individual castes. Masters of these
castes took on students and created different levels to describe
their progress in the craft. It was no longer apprentice,
journeyman, master; Now there were many levels of
progression and learning.*

– FROM "THE CHRONICLES OF ITHNEZ, VOL. I"
BY ADJIRSÉ DÉDOS

I watched Vortex play with the dolphins as Teka oversaw the task of loading the supplies. He splashed and rolled, dove deep, and terrorized fish– not at all what I was expecting a dragon to act like, but who was I to kill his fun? After all, he had been locked away from the rest of the world for who knew how long.

I smiled and turned to see what Teka was up to. She had been here since before the suns came up, stocking supply crate after supply crate. The Feykin had been very generous with the supplies they donated. I yearned to thank them with a gift but was not quite sure what to give them.

The suns were almost halfway through the sky when the last crate was loaded onto the ship and stored in the decks below. I watched as Teka thanked the Feykin for their help before she disappeared into her quarters. Minutes later, she reappeared in fresh clothes and with the charts in her hand. She winked at me as she strode to the helm to meet with her first mate and helmsman.

Thera sighed, suddenly appearing beside me. "Well, that was boring."

I nodded in agreement and turned my attention back to Vortex. I snickered, seeing him floating on his back and basking in the sunlight.

"By the way, once we leave the force field around the island, don't be surprised if things are very different from when you arrived here."

I frowned at her. "Why is that?"

"You have spent sixteen days here. Outside our force field, about one hundred and twelve days have passed."

"What?"

"I told you. Time passes differently here."

I sighed. "I didn't expect that much time to pass."

A little over three months had gone by outside the Sorcerers' Isle. It would now be the time of the Rising of Nahstipulí, I realized. Ríhan's birthday would soon be here.

"Are you okay? You look depressed."

"I'll be okay. I just realized my best friend's birthday is coming up." I looked down at my reflection in the water. "Neither of us will be there to celebrate it."

Thera put a hand on my shoulder. "I am sorry, Xy."

"I'll be okay. It just takes time to get over the pain."

Thera nodded knowingly.

"We have a little bit of a problem," Teka announced as she walked up behind us.

Thera muttered something while I sighed and turned to face Teka.

"Shadow Dance is so heavy with supplies that we will have to wait until nightfall when the tides are deepest to take off."

"No, you won't," Vortex said with a laugh. He bounded out of the water and shook himself off before continuing. "All you need is a little push."

I laughed. "That is a great idea."

"Um…this ship is laden with enough supplies to last the next six to eight months, if not longer. Can you move that much weight?"

Vortex snorted indignantly and braced his head against the bow of the ship. With a grunt, he dug his claws into the beech and gave a huge shove. The Shadow Dance jolted, sending people flying. Vortex repeated the process once more to force the ship into deep enough water for it to start floating on its own.

"That is the last time I ask a dragon if he can move something heavy," Teka muttered and turned away to check on her crew.

Vortex snorted again. He flared his wings and beat them to send a blast of wind at the ship. Shadow Dance rode the waves and wind out to the open sea.

"Okay, that is making me nauseous," Thera said as she sat down on the deck.

Vortex lunged into the water and swam beside the ship.

"I apologize, Thera."

The young Occultist nodded.

"This is your first time on a ship, right?" I asked, sitting beside her.

She smiled wryly.

"Don't worry. The sea sickness will wear off in a bit."

"I am more worried about a repeat of history." She pushed her hair from her face. "I really hope we don't find ourselves in a storm."

"Ah." I had forgotten Thera lost her mother in a storm at sea. "I'm sure nothing like that will happen."

"If I sense a change in the winds, I shall alert you," Vortex said.

Thera smiled at him. "Thank you."

"Are you planning on swimming alongside the ship the entire way to the Shaking Island?"

"That is a long way, hatchling, and even I don't have that much energy. When I tire I shall return to the eye."

"Then how can you monitor changes in the winds?" Thera frowned.

"Do not fret, young one. I can still feel them while I am within the eye."

Thera's worry appeared abated for the moment. "Well, seeing as how I have never been on a ship like this before, I think I will go have a look around."

"Have fun." I watched the young Feykin disappear below deck. I closed my eyes and leaned back against the railing.

"Are you okay, hatchling? You seem upset."

"I'm okay. I just wish Ríhan was still here."

"He is, Xyleena," Vortex said gently. "His spirit will always watch over you."

I nodded solemnly.

The day flew past, and I watched everything from my spot at the railing. Vortex had grown bored of swimming and had returned to the eye, yet I could still feel him watching me. I wished I could feel Ríhan the way I did my dragon.

After the suns were set and the sky was dusted with the first stars, I finally moved from my spot. I quietly crept down to the lower deck where my quarters were and threw myself onto the bed. I sighed and let sleep take me.

I awoke with a jolt and wiped tears away. Ríhan had danced in and out of my dreams, and the last had disturbed me greatly. I took a deep breath in hopes of calming my emotions, but it did not work. So I crawled out of bed and once again returned to the top deck.

It was still night out. Bedeb floated high in the sky, its rings casting midnight rainbows in the heavens above. Two of the moons were just above the eastern horizon, while the third had almost sunk below the western side. Countless stars dusted the sky.

It was a beautiful summer night, but I was in no mood to appreciate it. Instead, I found myself leaning over the railing, staring at my darkened reflection on the water.

I sighed. "Atlidmé, if you can hear me, please take care of Ríhan in Havel. I hope he has found peace in your realm. He is a good man and very wise. So if he is chosen to be reborn some time later, I can vouch for him. And if you see him, tell him… Tell him I love him…and I miss him."

I finally cried.

*'The Ghosts of the Firsts'. That is what they are calling the
people that were killed when I sent Demona to sack the city.
Thousands were killed, and more swore fealty to me and my
cause. The sacrifices were necessary, though I did not intend
for so many to perish.*

– FROM "THE DIARY OF AGASEI"
BY AGASEI DÉDOS

It had been over a month since Dimitri's team arrived at the Shaking
Island, and they continued to endure the long overdue appearance of Xyleena's
team. They knew she had not been there yet, as the dragon was still here and,
thankfully, asleep. However, nasty earthquakes were happening more and
more frequently and steadily increasing in magnitude. If Xyleena's team did
not arrive soon, he would be forced to give the order to evacuate the island.

Dimitri stood alone atop a cliff overlooking a thundering waterfall. From
this vantage point, he could see the entire island and the ocean surrounding it.
The whole island was rich with fauna. Many creatures roamed in tiny herds,
flocks, or packs as if the constant threat of earthquakes did not exist.

Dimitri took a deep breath, enjoying the mingling scents of the deep woods
and salty sea air. He exhaled slowly and cast one more look at the horizon.
Still no sign of another ship. Dimitri clicked his tongue and turned to begin his
descent from the cliff. Godilai was there, watching him as she had been the
last few weeks. He could not suppress the smile at seeing her again.

"She isn't here again?" Her voice was like the wind.

Dimitri sighed and shook his head. "The captain said he and his crew will
have to leave within the next few days, or they will not have enough supplies
for the return trip to Aissur."

"I will deal with them later."

A look of curiosity flashed across Godilai's face. "What do you have in
mind now?"

"You."

She frowned.

"I want to know more about you."

Godilai crossed her arms. "That is not what you meant."

Dimitri smiled and walked right up to her. He watched the way her cyan
eyes hardened. She was steeling herself, trying, albeit in vain, to keep her
distance.

"Tell me something, Godilai," he whispered to her. He had a burning
question to ask, one that had been plaguing him for weeks now. But now, face
to face, he had lost his nerve to ask. "Why have you been watching me?"

She scoffed. "You asked me that the other day. What is really on your
mind, Dimitri?"

He sighed and turned away from her. It was either now or never, he
realized. He had to ask her. "What would you do if you were to become high

queen of Ithnez?"

She was quiet for the longest time, and he feared that she had walked away, leaving his question lost on the winds. He looked over his shoulder to see her standing, unmoved. Her cyan eyes had softened, and her lips were slightly parted– beautiful.

Finally, she answered. "If I could do anything, I would enslave the Humes and force them to serve the Dákun Daju. But, Dimitri…"

"Yes?"

"What are you planning?"

He smiled and turned to face her completely. "I intend to overthrow the royal house of Za'Car and reclaim the throne that once belonged to my father. And I want you at my side…as my queen."

"Wha—What are you saying?"

"When you are gone, I crave your presence. And when you are with me, I just want to hold you close and tell you…tell you how much I love you. I want to marry you, Godilai."

"I…I'm not sure what to say." She turned away from him, but he was sure he caught a glimpse of a blush on her cheeks.

He nodded and stepped closer to her, placing his hands on her shoulders. "Just think about it for now, then."

She nodded, unsure of what to say. Rapid footsteps approached, and Dimitri promptly removed his hands. They both sunk into fighting stances, ready to attack whoever was running toward them. Luna burst through the foliage headed straight for the duo.

"She's here! She's here!" Luna exclaimed and skidded to a stop in front of Godilai. "Another ship just appeared over the horizon; a black one with silver sails."

Dimitri smirked. "Finally!"

"I will get everyone in position for the ambush," Godilai said, looking into Dimitri's eyes.

"And I will have Pox hide our ship in an invisibility field." He winked.

The trio rapidly descended the cliff to prepare for their enemies' arrival.

Once back with the rest of their team, the plans were quickly reviewed and set into motion. The traps were checked, weapons were gathered, and they veiled themselves in the foliage and mud. All that was left to do was wait a little longer.

Unnoticed by anyone, a pair of amber eyes bore witness to everything.

There are other… creatures… on this planet. At first, we only
caught glimpses of them; tufts of hair, ever watchful eyes,
fangs, talons. Then, one day, one of them revealed itself. It
was humanoid, but looked like a wild animal – something very
similar to the ancient, Egyptian god Anubis.

It did not speak, just looked at us as we looked at it. Then, the
creature vanished into the surrounding swamp. It has been a
fortnight since it appeared, and we have yet to see it again.
Others have started calling it… them… Demons.

– FROM "HISTORY OF BEDEB, VOL I"
BY ACASIA FLEMENTH, MAGISTRATE ELECT

Thera and I sat together at a table in a lone corner of the ship's galley. Having finally pulled the young Feykin away from her meditations, I had suggested that she and I spend the afternoon playing various games – a fun way of learning other cultures. I had already shown her an old game of cards that the Temple Priests taught me. Once she had mastered that, she began to teach me a Feykin game involving several hand sized clay rods, which were painted black and white, and five tiers of wooden boards that were emblazoned with a grid of squares.

We were about half way through the complex strategy game when a soft rumble echoed through the galley, and the Shadow Dance rocked on a violent wave. I met Thera's gaze. I could tell she was thinking the same. A moment later, both of us ran from the room. We gathered our weapons and burst onto the top deck, expecting to be under an attack. Instead, we found the crew was busy with their normal tasks. I located Teka at the helm and moved to join her.

"What was that?" Thera asked as she and I reached the top step.

"The rumble?" Teka glanced up from the charts in her hands to see us nod. "That is what an earthquake sounds like at sea."

"We must be getting close then," Thera said, glancing at me.

I clicked my tongue and moved to the railing to scan the horizon. Nothing. I sighed and closed my eyes.

Vortex whispered to me from the back of my mind. Feel it out, hatchling. You know where to find the island.

I slowly opened my eyes. There! Just over the southeastern stretch of ocean, the shadow of an island brushed the sky. I whooped and pointed toward it.

"Now we're talking!" Teka laughed. "Come and turn Shadow Dance so that we sail straight for the island."

I blinked in surprise. "You want me to steer the ship?"

"No one here but you can see our destination," Thera pointed out. "We could sail right past it without you directing us where to go."

"Good point," I said and moved to the wheel.

"Okay, steering the ship is fairly easy," the helmsman explained, stepping aside to teach me. "Each one of the knobs on the wheel represents ten degrees, like in a circle. The silver one is zero degrees, which means that if that one is at the top of the wheel, as it is now, the ship will go straight. The blue knob marks ninety degrees, meaning the ship will turn starboard, or right, if you move the wheel so that knob is on top.

"The green knob marks two hundred and seventy degrees. That will turn the ship to port, or left. You basically just turn the wheel in the direction you want to go. Keep in mind that it doesn't take much to turn the ship in a wide arc."

"Okay, so the island is slightly south of us, so I would need to turn right...er, I mean starboard."

The helmsman nodded and moved to allow me to steer. I calmly took the wheel and turned it one... no, two knobs towards the blue. Moments later the bow of the Shadow Dance was pointed straight at the island. I straightened the wheel and watched until I was sure the course was correct. I nodded and allowed the helmsman to take the wheel again.

"I centered the bow on the island, so just keep going this way."

You did great! Vortex exclaimed.

I could not suppress the proud smile that grew on my lips.

"About how far away does it look?" Thera asked, looking eagerly over the bow.

"I'm not completely sure, but it will be at least a few hours. We'll get a better idea once we've breached the field protecting the island."

Teka smiled. "I can't wait to meet the next dragon."

I nodded in agreement and watched as the Shaking Island crept closer. A bad feeling washed over me, and I shivered.

I had been slightly off on my guess. Almost five hours later, we finally broke the field around the island. The crew whooped upon seeing the long-lost isle, and a few clapped me on the back. I could not bring myself to spoil their good mood with a warning of danger, which had been eating away at me since I first laid eyes on the island.

Teka decided to anchor the ship about a league out, as she did not know what lay beneath the surface of the water. For all anyone knew, there could be rocks or coral surrounding the island. Therefore, we loaded up a few rowboats and began the final trek to shore.

Teka had been right to worry about rocks hiding in the shallows. The rowboats barely managed to sneak over them. No doubt that Shadow Dance would have grounded long before even reaching the shore.

It was sunset by the time we found ourselves standing on the rocky beach. I shivered again, unable to suppress the bad feeling I got when I looked at the scenery.

You are right to worry, hatchling, Vortex whispered in my ear. *Something is not right here.*

Will Kkaia attack us?

I doubt that. She should be able to recognize you, even after all the time that has passed since last you saw us.

I hope you are right. I began making my way up the rocky beach.

"Wait." Thera hissed.

Everyone turned to face her. She muttered something I could not hear and stared at her ribbon staff. A soft lick of wind caused the ribbons to dance, revealing to Thera something that made her gasp. A heartbeat later, she cast a spell, and a force field melted away, exposing another ship.

"It's a trap!" I freed my tessens and flared them.

An instant later, we found ourselves surrounded. Thera quickly took flight and cast defensive barriers around us. Pox shot out of the trees, headed straight for her sister. The two collided mid-air and plummeted. I rushed to help Thera, but the Dákun Daju on Dimitri's team stopped me.

"Now, you will die." Luna growled, brandishing her giant sword with practiced ease.

I sunk into a fighting stance. "I don't think so."

Godilai laughed darkly. "You can't beat both of us, girl."

"That's what you said last time, before I sent you running like a pair of frightened neerie birds."

The Dákun Daju exchanged a look then lunged for me. I slid my left foot further back, widening my stance as some unknown teacher had taught me. When the duo was a mere blink away, I brought my war fans up in front of me, forming a shield that forced their blows to graze harmlessly away with a metallic ring. As they reeled around for another combined strike, I ducked low and swept my fans in a wide and fluid arc. I felt the blades tear at the clothing on their legs and heard them hiss in pain as I somersaulted away.

They were both upon me before I could get to my feet again. Godilai loosed a furious sound as she brought her sword down for a killing stroke, but a field of magic deflected the blow. I silently thanked Thera for her spell work as I launched telekinetic spells to knock the Dákun Daju away. Luna recovered faster and crossed the space between us in a flash, swinging her sword in a circle that would have caught me just below the knee had I not back flipped away. I barely had time to react as Godilai hurled something at me. I deflected the object with a fan and heard a loud thunk as it sank deep into the wood of a nearby tree. Half a heartbeat later, several more of the small, shiny objects were heading for me. I brought my hand up in front of me and uttered a spell. The objects, which turned out to be a menagerie of small knives, froze midair. I cut the magic and let them fall harmlessly to the ground.

I took up my stance again, and stared the duo down as they prepared to strike.

Dimitri danced away from the swings and parries of the sailors' blades before blasting them away with a fire spell. He could not help but smirk at the pained yowls that the spell tore from the sailors' lips. It felt so good to be able to cause that much pain to these pathetic Humes with so little effort. Of course, he owed much of his new knowledge of magic to young Pox. Without her teaching, he was sure he would still be straining to form even the simplest spells.

He dared a moment's respite to set his crimson gaze on the young Feykin, finding her high above the treetops several meters away and locked in a heated exchange of spells against her sister. Pox's onyx eyes were burning with barely contained rage as her older sister tried in vain to bring her back to her senses. Pox wanted none of it, and blasted the area with a spell powerful enough to vaporize a radius of trees. The sister managed a defense, and countered with a ferocity that rivaled a Dákun Daju. Dimitri had to admire the Feykin. They were ferocious and powerful in battle—the perfect ally for any Dákun Daju warrior.

A loud thunk by his ear caught him unprepared, and Dimitri was forced to quickly break his concentration on the ducling Feykin. He glanced first over his shoulder to see what had caused the sound, only to discover Godilai's whittled jawbone stuck deep into the wood of a tree. He turned to scan the area in front of him, finding Godilai and Luna double-teaming Xyleena just meters away. He watched their exchange, formulating a plan to defeat the girl while admiring the skill she had to fend off two highly experienced Dákun Daju Assassins.

After a minute or two more of watching, he had his plan worked out.

I glowered at the murderous duo as I took up another fighting stance. Luna surged toward me with a burst of speed I could barely follow. Less than a meter away, she dropped and slid across the ground while swinging her sword in a climbing arc. I blocked the blade with little effort but barely managed a defense as Godilai sped in from my blind spot. Just as I shoved their blades away from me, a fourth body suddenly entered the fray, leaping clear over the kneeling Luna to attempt a killing stroke from above. I instantly recognized the new fighter as Dimitri himself. They had tried to trick me, but all they had succeeded in doing was infuriating me. I launched a series of spells in rapid succession. The first of which rammed into Luna and forced her back several meters, while the second sent Godilai airborne for a few seconds before she crashed into a tree. My third spell was reflected away as Dimitri countered it almost with practiced ease.

I quivered as the magic drained my energy, and watched in silent fury as the Dákun Daju quickly recovered from the magic I had hit them with. As much as I tried to hide it, Dimitri and the Dákun Daju realized just how weak I had become. They smirked maliciously as they closed in, and I knew that I had to end this soon.

Xyleena!

I flinched at the echoing shout from the back of my mind, a bit annoyed at myself that I had completely forgotten I was in possession of a dragon. I brought my hand up to brush against the jewel of Vortex, and felt the tingling creep through my fingertips. Before I had a chance to finish the summoning, Godilai and Luna struck a combination of rapid sweeps that would have left me without any limbs had Thera's protective magic not been in place. I tried to retaliate with blows of my own, but I was too slow, and the evil trio laughed as they easily countered each strike. Before I knew it, they had disarmed me and forced me to my knees.

Dimitri closed in for the kill, a look of absolute euphoria on his face. His blade flashed, catching the sunlight as he raised it higher and higher. Just as he began the downward swing, the whole island rumbled and the ground churned and shifted. Dimitri lost his footing and staggered back a ways before the upheaval laid him out flat on the ground with a violent shake. Godilai swore venomously as she too was jostled by the quake. I however, used the tremor to my advantage and kicked Luna's kneecap as hard as I could. She screamed in pain as the joint over extended and she went face first into the dirt. I was on my feet and running faster than any of them could react.

As I retreated for safety, I freed my new war fans from my hip sack. I had hoped to not break them in so soon, but with the loss of my old ones, I had no choice. I heard Dimitri's roar even over the angry rumble of the ground, and spun around to reflect the spell he sent after me. Instead of reflecting the oncoming rush of razor-sharp wind, the tessens sent out an energy all their own. The energy cut right through the deadly spell and divided it into two parts, which flew harmlessly past me and crashed through the trees.

I took off running again, hoping to get far enough away to summon Vortex before my enemies caught me again. The violent quake was finally receding and I was grateful for the calming, but regretted it at the same time. I had barely crossed a few meters before Godilai and Dimitri caught up to me. In a frenzy of flashing steel and limbs, the duo once again had me pinned with no hope of escape.

"Die!" Dimitri shouted as he prepared to deal a finishing blow.

A spiked chain wrapped around his blade and yanked it away. A heartbeat later, another body slammed into Godilai, sending her tumbling away from me. I scrambled to gather my tessens and swung at the new body only to be blocked by a sickle.

"Take it easy!"

I knew that voice. I lowered my tessen to reveal the face of the one who spoke. Her amber, wolfish eyes sparkled with amusement.

"Freya?"

The Wolf Demon smiled.

"What are you doing here?"

"Saving your life." She spun around me and launched her spiked chain at

Dimitri.

He barely managed to block it with a spell before Freya attacked again. While she was occupied with Dimitri, I faced Godilai.

The look in her cyan eyes sent shivers down my spine. "You are going to pay for the cheap shot you caught Luna with."

I was about to respond when a flicker of movement out of the corner of my eye stole my attention. I jumped out of the way just in time to avoid being crushed by Luna's enormous sword as she leapt out of nowhere. She was quick to recover from the failed attack—too quick for anyone with a hyper extended knee. Realizing she must have healed the wound, I backed away and brushed my fingers against the dragon amulet. The tingling sensation returned in an instant, but Luna and Godilai lashed out at me before I could finish the summoning again.

Luna roared as she and spun around to strike again. I deflected Luna's heavy sword with a spell. It ricocheted and struck Godilai's shoulder, leaving a deep wound. She cried out in pain and fell back slightly.

Before she could heal the wound, I landed a kick to her head and sent her sprawling across the ground. I was about to permanently remove her from the fight when the ground shook violently and knocked me off balance. A huge mound of earth surged upward, separating the fighters. With a load roar, the rocks and mud exploded outward, leaving a bronze dragon in their place.

We - as the remnants of humanity - go there, to a planet which now bears my father's name, to live on... and live strong. Two hundred and ninety-seven light-years from Earth, a new chapter in human history waits to be written.

– FROM "SHIP'S LOG: HAVEN"
AS SPOKEN BY NORALANI ITHNEZ

I stared in awe at the dragon before me. Her scales were brown and bronze but shifted to gold in the light. Ivory horns protruded from her skull and curved forward slightly. A spiked frill guarded her neck, and long, sweeping spines covered her back and tail.

Her great wings were flared, and she hissed at Dimitri. Without warning, Kkaia flicked her tail, sending large chunks of earth in his direction. Luna was barely quick enough, shoving him aside to take the hit. She cried out as a spike of stone impaled her just below her ribs on her right side. Godilai swore and rushed to her comrade's side. Dimitri took a quick assessment of the situation and ordered the remnants of his team to come to him. As he helped Godilai gather Luna, he glared at me.

"This isn't over."

Kkaia snarled at him and sunk her talons into the earth in preparation to launch herself after him. He quickly uttered a string of words and a thick, black cloud immediately descended on the whole area. I heard a young voice recite two words, and then there was silence. Minutes later, a voice I recognized at Thera's rang out.

"Nevoa cäipe!"

At her command, the black cloud rolled away. I quickly searched my surroundings for any sign of Dimitri or his team, but found nary a sign of them.

I sighed in relief. "They're gone." Teka was suddenly beside me, weapons raised against Freya. The Wolf Demon chose to ignore her.

"See, Kkaia? I was right," Freya said, thumping Kkaia on the side.

The dragon snorted and folded her wings.

"Who is this...woman?" Teka asked, looking to me for an answer.

Freya! Vortex shouted in the back of my head.

I could feel his happiness surging through me, and I could not help but laugh. "Well, Freya's not an enemy, so you can lower your weapons. Aside from that, I'm not really sure."

Teka faced me "You know her name and say she's not an enemy, but you're not sure about anything else?"

"I have no idea what she is doing here or how she even got here to begin with."

Freya laughed. "Simple. This is my island."

Kkaia snorted again and sat on her haunches. "Oh, hush! It was my home long before it was yours."

159

"How so?" Teka finally relaxed enough to lower her guard.

"It is a long story," said Freya. "All you need to know right now is that Agasei exterminated most of my clan when he discovered this island was the… Well, it was important. What remained of my clan never returned here."

"Freya!" Thera landed in a rush and ran up to the Wolf Demon, catching her in a tight hug. The embrace was returned with equal enthusiasm. "Oh! It is so good to see you again. How have you been?"

"Wait a second!" Teka furiously shouted.

I looked at the demi-Feykin in shock at her outburst. Freya and Thera broke their hug to gape at her as well.

"How do you know her?"

"Remember? I told you Freya and Amorez stayed in Thorna for many, many years." Thera laughed at Teka's dumbstruck expression.

"Speaking of Amorez…" I said suddenly. "Where in the names of the Five Souls is she?"

"Do not fret over her, Xyleena. She is fine," Kkaia answered, lowering her head so she could speak to me eye to eye.

I sighed.

Amorez is on her own mission, Vortex explained.

"Zamora is Amorez, right?"

I watched as Freya slowly nodded.

I shook my head. "Figures."

"Don't be upset, Xy," Freya said.

She stepped past Teka to offer her hand to help me up. I sighed and allowed her to help me to my feet.

"There is something I don't understand. How did you escape the Temple after Dimitri attacked the festival?"

"Amorez, Zhealocera, and I managed to warp off the island before he had taken complete control of it," Freya explained. "Zhealocera returned by herself shortly afterward to see if you had been captured. I cannot say for sure what happened in the Temple since the attack, but she relayed to us that you had not been found. Therefore, I came here, hoping that I had not missed the opportunity to catch up to you. When I discovered Kkaia was still here, I knew you were on your way…especially after the idiot showed up."

"Is there a particular reason you were looking for her?" Teka asked. "Aside from just seeing if she was alive and well?"

"Xy is the Dragon Keeper. Without her the Dragons of Light will never be found, and the Dark Keeper will rise to power once again."

"Couldn't Amorez find them?" Thera asked, leaning on her staff.

"She knows not where her twelve were hidden," Kkaia whispered sadly. "And we dragons cannot find our brothers and sisters the way our Keeper can."

"So now that you have found me, what do you want?" I asked.

Freya quirked an eyebrow at me. "I mostly just wanted to see if you were alive. But now that I know you are, and on a quest to free the dragons, I can help you."

"Help me how?"

"A clansman of mine resides in Zadún. I believe he will be very helpful in this venture you are on."

"What skills can he bring to the table to help us?" Teka asked, crossing her arms.

"He is a Fox Demon– quick, agile, resourceful, and deadly. I taught him how to fight, and he is very capable of handling himself against your Dákun Daju and Feykin opponents," Freya said over her shoulder to Teka.

"I like him already." Teka muttered sarcastically and rolled her eyes.

I sighed. "I guess we can take a slight detour and stop at Zadún while we translate the next part of the riddle."

Freya faced me. "Riddle?"

"Yeah. The 'Riddle of the Twelve' is the key to the Dragons of Light. Apparently I wrote it years ago, but something happened, and I lost my memory."

"That explains why Amorez and I couldn't find you," Freya said thoughtfully.

I nodded in agreement.

"So…Zadún is almost straight north," Teka announced. "And since it is summer, the ice shelf that usually surrounds Arctica will be melted. That means we can be there within two weeks or so." She clicked her tongue and started for the rowboats.

"While en route maybe you can fill me in on some details."

Freya nodded. "I can try. I was on the Sorcerers' Isle for most of the last three centuries, so I can't fill in all the blanks for you."

"Something is better than nothing," I muttered.

"Maybe you can fill me in on what happened to you that made you disappear."

I shook my head in agreement, and then glanced up at Kkaia. "Were you going to swim with the ship or rest in the eye with Vortex?"

"You have obtained Vortex already?" Kkaia sounded excited.

I nodded and watched as golden energy crackled around her. An instant later, she levitated and melted into bits of earth. These bits swarmed around me before shooting into the dragon eye. A bronze jewel filled in one of the empty slots of the amulet.

His wings beat like roaring thunder, stirring the air into great,
quivering waves. His scaly hide glimmered in the suns' light
like a million sapphires thrown upwards into a midday sky.
Ivory talons and a crest of horns of lengths greater than any
man was tall gave the beast a ferocious look. But his eyes...
his eyes, though burning like hot fire, seemed as friendly and
welcoming as a babe's. He was intimidating, but absolutely
spectacular to behold!

– FROM "MY MYSTICAL ADVENTURES, VOL VII"
BY DAHM THE BARD

Dimitri sighed. It had been just over two weeks since their embarrassing retreat from the Shaking Isle. They had struggled to keep Luna alive long enough to seek an expert healer. Though Pox was great with small wounds, she had been unable to help Luna. The spike meant to end his life had embedded itself deep within Luna, and there was no way for the young Feykin to heal her.

They had rushed Luna to the healer in Zadún, hoping against hope that something could be done. The healer took one glance at the wound and faced Dimitri with a grim expression. There was no way to save Luna.

The healer had given her some kind of herbal mix before leaving the room. Godilai sat at Luna's side, holding her hand. It was the most emotion Dimitri had ever seen either Dákun Daju show.

Luna closed her eyes and took a ragged breath. "I…I want…"

"Shh, Luna-Sortim," Godilai whispered. A tear slowly rolled down her cheek.

"Please…kill her. Kill the Dragon…Keeper." Luna finally exhaled and remained very still.

Godilai nodded and placed a kiss on Luna's brow. "I will, meo sortim. I promise. In your name I will kill her." Godilai took a knife from her belt and held it to her arm.

Dimitri left the room. He knew the Dákun Daju ritual for honoring the dead– an hour of bloodletting. He had done the same when his mother died. It was something best handled in private. So he would leave Godilai alone with her grief.

Vincent and Pox approached him as he walked toward the exit of the small clinic. Dimitri could tell they were eager to hear about Luna's condition. He simply shook his head and continued walking. Vincent and Pox hung back, neither daring to follow him in his current mood.

Dimitri pushed the door aside and walked into the frigid night air. He shivered as he reached for the knife on his belt. He unsheathed it and held it to his arm. In one fluid motion, he dragged the blade over his flesh and watched as his blood flowed unabated.

He walked on, letting droplets of blood splatter on the frosted cobblestones.

When he felt the flow cease, he took the knife to the wound. Again and again he repeated the process until the hour had passed. He put his knife back in its sheath and looked around.

He had wandered into a shabby-looking part of Zadún. Several buildings looked as though they had seen much better days. They were unkempt with windows shattered, walls falling apart, doors hanging askew and tough plants overgrown about them.

There was one building, however, that had lights on and merry music blaring from within. Dimitri read the sign out front: Thief's Paradise. He snickered and stepped inside.

A scantily clad bar wench with voluptuous curves met him at the door. She attached herself to Dimitri's arm and walked with him as she spoke. "Ye come for drink or pleasure, sir?"

"Drink," he answered flatly.

She frowned in disappointment and escorted him to the bar. While he took a seat, she dodged rowdy customers and scurried back to the door.

"What's your poison?" the bartender called out.

Dimitri blinked at the sight of him. The bartender was a Demon with rich, amber eyes and fox-like ears half hidden in an unruly mane of lavender and jet-black hair.

Dimitri cleared his throat. "Lescan yellow ale."

The bartender shot him a rather bored look before he turned to pour the drink. Moments later a large mug was set on the counter. "Five even, man."

"What?" Dimitri blinked.

The Demon rolled his eyes. "Oi! Five bits for the drink."

"Oh." Dimitri quickly dropped the coins in the bartender's clawed hand.

The Demon clicked his tongue and walked to a livelier group at the other end of the counter. Dimitri stared at the wound on his arm as he sipped the ale.

"Hey, Kitfox! Fix me up with another round!" A man with a strange accent took a stool at the bar not far from where Dimitri sat. Dimitri studied the man out of the corner of his eye. He was tall for a Hume, and dark skinned. A forest-green coat that fell to the tops of his knee-high leather boots and tight leather breeches made up his outfit, which was accented with several sashes and leather belts which holstered pistols and sheathed a fancy rapier. A triangular-shaped hat sat atop the man's head, and a ribbon held his long blonde hair in a neat tail.

The Demon bartender waved in acknowledgement and poured the drink. The glass was then sent sliding down the bar to the waiting hand of the patron.

"Thanks, mate!"

"Yeah! Yeah!" Kitfox turned his back on the dull end of the bar.

"Bloody Demons," muttered the blonde man.

"I heard that!" Kitfox shouted over his shoulder.

Dimitri snorted.

"Well, at least your kind is better than those Dákun Daju bas– "

"Watch it." Dimitri growled.

The blonde-haired man quickly met his gaze and winced. "Sorry, mate.

Thought you were Hume."

"You thought wrong." Dimitri took a long draft from his ale.

"That explains a few things," Kitfox said as he walked over.

Dimitri glared at him through a veil of black bangs.

"You reek of blood."

"Got a problem with that?"

Kitfox snorted. "Not if you like smelling like fresh bait to other Demon clans. It'll be fun watching them tear you apart and eat you." The Demon smiled, revealing extremely sharp fangs.

Dimitri scoffed. "If any of your Demon friends want to try killing me, I wish them the best of luck."

"Right." Kitfox laughed and walked away.

"I'd pay to see a good fight like that," muttered the blonde.

"You can't afford anything!" Kitfox called back.

"Okay, fine! If I had the money, I would pay to see a Dákun Daju fight a clan of Demons."

"How broke are you?" Dimitri asked, taking another draft of ale.

The blonde fixed him with a strange look. Finally, he sighed. "Broke enough that I need to avoid almost every guild on two continents."

"Including this one!" Kitfox added.

"Oh, shut up!"

Dimitri chuckled. "Did you gamble it all away or something?"

"Nah, mate." The blonde moved a few stools closer so he could speak quietly. "I'm a pirate, and I lost me ship and me crew in a raid from a rival guild. I need to pay them back to drop the bounty on me head but can't find any work or crew to assist in such a manner."

"So you'll do just about anything for money?"

"Aye. Pretty much."

"How about working for me, then?"

Dimitri whistled as he walked the streets back to the clinic. He was in a great mood after leaving the company of the blonde pirate. Finally, he had a plan in the works to bring Xyleena down. All he had to do was bide his time and hope his man worked his magic.

"We'll go in the morning. It's too late to see him now, Xy."

Dimitri froze in his tracks.

"Well, at least Thera managed to translate the clue to Atoka. If not for that, this day would be a total wash."

Dimitri quickly ducked behind the side of a building as the voices drew closer. He chanced a peek and smirked as he recognized the faces of Xyleena and her team.

"Here's the inn. Do not worry about affording the rooms. I'll take care of it."

"When does Thief's Paradise open tomorrow?"

"Not until sunset, but we'll meet up with Kitfox at noon so we don't need to–"

The voices cut out as the door of the inn closed behind them.

So Xyleena and her team were in Zadún, and it sounded as if they had discovered the location of the next dragon. Dimitri was elated by this happy turn of events. All he needed to do now was follow Xyleena's team. He already knew where they were staying and when they were leaving. It was almost too easy.

Dimitri snickered and waited a few minutes more to make sure the coast was clear. When he deemed it safe, he sprinted from his hiding spot. He had to tell his team of this discovery.

*It had been twenty years since a Hume had last set foot on
Arcadian soil, the site of my son's first attack. Nothing was the
same. The once luscious forest and fertile fields were nothing
more than wastelands. Test after test resulted in the same
outcome: Life would never – could never – exist here. Thus,
Arcadia was officially abandoned.*

– FROM "THE CHRONICLES OF ITHNEZ, VOL. II"
BY ADJIRSÉ DÉDOS

Say it again, hatchling.

"Deep in ice, Atoka I bound, just north of arctic castle found," I whispered the clue to Atoka's location for probably the one-hundredth time.

My two dragons and I had spent the better part of the morning trying to solve the riddle. We were no closer to finding an answer than we were when Thera had first announced her completion of the translation the day before.

There aren't any castles in the whole of the Arctican continent. Kkaia sounded annoyed and frustrated. At least, there weren't any one hundred and seventy years ago.

That is provided, of course, that the riddle does not speak of snow castles built by children, said Vortex.

It does not, I assured them.

And the map in the diary does not show any hidden locations farther north?

I sighed as I pulled Dragon Diary out of my hip sack again. Once more, I found the world map and scoured over every little detail while comparing it to the normal map pinned to the wall of my room at the Zadún Inn.

I sighed. "Nothing."

Three hard raps at the door made me jump. I caught my breath before getting up from the bed and walking to the door. I flipped open my tessens and pressed my ear to the hardwood.

"Yeah?"

"It's Freya."

I unlocked the door and opened it ever so slightly before backing away. Freya pushed the door open and glanced at my flared weapons before I put them away.

"What was that about?"

"Can never be too careful," I muttered and walked back to the bed. "I take it we're about to leave?"

"Yes."

"Good. I need to do something besides pick three brains for an answer." I returned Dragon Diary to my hip sack and grabbed the scant few other trinkets that I called mine before joining Freya at the door. She was staring at me, a curious expression on her features.

"What's wrong?"

"You are so much like your mother."

Before I could ask her to explain, she was out the door. Moments later, I was following her out of the inn.

"Ah! Good. Everyone is here," Freya said as she and I met Thera and Teka outside. "Now, the tavern I'm taking you to is in a rough part of town. A rather rambunctious guild of Demons controls the area, so watch yourselves. Should we come across any Demon besides Kitfox, do not speak, and whatever you do, do not meet their gaze. Doing so could prompt an attack."

"I can't wait," said Teka.

"Should I cover us in barriers, or will that send the wrong message to this violent Demon guild?" Thera asked, trying to ignore the stares of the citizens that passed by. It was clear to tell from their expressions that they had never seen a Feykin before. If their staring was bothering Thera, she certainly did not betray her discomfort. I was impressed.

"No magic unless they attack us," Freya said, turning to leave. "Let's go."

Thera, Teka, and I followed Freya as she briskly weaved her way through the streets and alleys. While we walked, Kkaia and Vortex continued talking about the riddle to Atoka. I, on the other hand, could not shake the feeling of being followed no matter how many times I checked behind me.

Freya's pace slowed remarkably, as we entered a derelict part of town. She kept sniffing the air and would stop occasionally to stare down a dark alley or behind us. Then with a growl or snort, she would start walking again. Finally we reached the only building in the vicinity that looked halfway decent. I read the sign out front: Thief's Paradise.

I watched as Freya banged thrice on the heavy wooden door beneath the sign. A few moments of waiting, and nothing happened. She banged again.

"The bar isss closssed."

I spun around at the raspy voice behind me. An instant later, Freya was between me and the other Demon that had slunk his way in behind us.

"Leave." Freya growled.

The other Demon did not oblige.

Freya freed her kusarigama and snarled at him. "Leave!"

"Thisss isss not your turf, Wolf. You do not order me about."

"Get out of here, you slithering bastard!" a woman's voice screeched.

I glanced over my shoulder to see a nearly naked woman in the doorway of the tavern. I immediately returned my attention to the unknown Demon.

"Make me, wench!" He hissed and shoved Freya aside in a mad dash to the doorway.

I gasped as I caught a full view of him. He had the torso and head of a man, but the rest of him was a black snake.

"Get out of here, Naga!" A new Demon stood in the tavern's doorway, shielding the nearly naked woman.

He was tall and handsome, dressed in a loose-fitting pants and a sleeveless, white tunic that revealed tattoos of symbols on his muscular biceps. A messy mane of lavender and jet-black hair fell to his waist. Fox-like ears grew atop his head, and deep, amber eyes bore into the Demon before him. He bared his fangs in warning, and the Snake Demon backed down.

167

"I will not forget thisss." With a furious hiss, the Snake Demon slithered away.

"You taking in strays now, Kitfox?"

I glanced at Freya as she spoke, then back at the Demon in the doorway. He smirked and glanced at the woman he guarded before stepping into the street. I noticed his bare feet were clawed like Freya's, but—unlike her—he wore no armor.

"It looks like you are, too." His amber gaze fell on me for a moment as he walked past.

I scoffed.

Thera giggled. "You have a really poofy tail."

Freya and Teka snickered. The Fox Demon turned slightly to glance at his lavender-and-black tail before looking at Thera.

"The babes dig it." He wiggled his eyebrows suggestively, making Thera blush.

Freya promptly smacked him upside the head.

"What was that for?"

"Being you."

"Either you hit harder than you used to, or I've got a soft spot for you." He grinned and rubbed the sore spot on his head.

Freya rolled her eyes. "Kitfox, this is Xyleena, Teka, and Thera." She pointed to us respectively. "They are the ones I told you were coming."

"Wait a minute." Kitfox pointed at Thera. "You're Feykin, right?"

"Yes. Is that a problem?"

"Not at all." He shook his head, grinning. "I just wasn't told I would be teaming up with a Feykin. Should prove interesting."

"Freya, you're not seriously forcing him on us, are you?" I looked at her, pleading. "He acts more like a child than a warrior."

"Aw! I'm not that bad!"

"Trust me, Xy, his battle skills make up for his...personality."

Freya snickered when Kitfox sent her a hurt look.

"Anyway, I have things which require my attention, so why don't you three fill Kitfox in on what's going on."

"Wait a minute!" I shouted. "You're leaving? Just like that?"

"I have to," Freya replied with a simple shrug.

"I thought you were here to help," Teka said accusingly.

Freya frowned. "I have, and I still am. Trust me. We will meet again very soon. But there is something important I must do before then."

I sighed and waved her off. "Fine."

"Don't be like that, Xy."

"Just go, Freya." I met her gaze. "Like you said, we'll meet again soon."

"Good-bye." Freya bowed slightly then turned and walked away.

I watched her until she disappeared from my view.

"So...uh, Xyleena was it?"

"You can call me Xy."

"Okay. Xy," Kitfox paused as if testing the taste of my nickname, "do you and your friends want to come inside? You can tell me everything that's been going on over some lunch."

I nodded. "Thank you, Kitfox."

He clapped his hands and ushered us inside the tavern. The bar wench set all four of us up at the bar with some hot stew and cider before disappearing. Thera, Teka, and I spoke for hours about recent events, filling Kitfox in as much as possible. He never once interrupted as he listened.

Finally, we reached the end of our tale and a long silence followed. Kitfox sat in the stool, simply nodding as he mulled everything over. Then he looked at me and took a deep breath. "So you are the Dragon Keeper, and you wrote a riddle to remind you where you hid the Dragons of Light, but you somehow have amnesia and cannot remember a thing. You recently relocated two of the twelve dragons, and now you are here looking for a third dragon frozen in ice north of town. Got it."

"Woah! Woah! Wait a minute." I waved my hand to stop him from further rambling. "How do you figure the next dragon is north of Zadún?"

"Simple!" He laughed. "The last line makes it clear as day. Just north of arctic castle found. There is an ice sculpture in the central square not far from the inn you were staying at. Guess what the sculpture is."

I sighed. "A castle?"

"Yup." He grinned. "It's been there, frozen, for at least the last century. It doesn't even thaw in the summer when temperatures reach fifty or sixty degrees."

"I like this guy!" Teka said, slapping the bar.

Kitfox looked at her and chuckled.

"I guess he does grow on you after a while." Thera admitted with a soft smile.

"Aw, that's sweet of you."

"Okay, Kitfox. So what do you say you show us to this ice castle so we can begin hunting for the third dragon?"

"Sure. Just give me a few minutes to pack some things and tell Toya she needs to be scarce for a while. I won't leave her here unprotected with the Warinarc guild hanging around." Kitfox left his stool and vanished through a door at the far right of the bar.

"If Freya trusts him, it means we can. Right?" Teka asked, glancing over my shoulder at the door.

"I don't sense any animosity or evil intentions from him, Xy," Thera added. "I think everything will be okay."

"I hope you two are right."

Minutes later Kitfox returned with Toya in tow. He gave her some money out of a chest behind the bar and pocketed the rest. As we left the bar, he locked the door and ran his fingers along the sign over the door.

"For luck," he said with a crooked smile.

We escorted Toya to Kitfox's and Freya's guild house, which was not far from the tavern, and headed off to find the ice castle and Atoka.

*Many things are ravaged by time, even those deemed immortal
or indestructible. Time is a slow killer; slower than any
poison. It is a torturous thing to endure. I sit here and watch
as year after year and century after century pass by. I remain
unchanged, but friends and loved ones have long turned to
dust.*

Time is killing me.

– FROM "THE DIARY OF AMOREZ"
BY AMOREZ RENOAN

A thousand curses streamed through Dimitri's head the instant he realized Xyleena had just recruited another team member. And a Fox Demon to boot! With this new addition, he would have to be wary of the Demon's heightened senses of smell, hearing, and sight. Dimitri's tactics were suddenly in desperate need of changing.

With a frustrated sigh, Dimitri continued stalking the other team. They had gone from their meeting in the tavern, which he himself had had a drink in last night, to some heavily guarded building. Then from there they headed back toward the inn. He had to wonder what on Ithnez they were up to.

"That Demon…" Godilai spoke barely above a whisper. "I believe he is a member of the Tahda'varett guild."

"What is the significance of that?" Vincent asked as he scratched the back of his head.

"It is the same Demon guild that Amorez's Demon companion, Freya Latreyon, belonged to," Pox answered. "I heard it is the largest and strongest Demon guild on the planet."

"Could Amorez be somehow guiding that little wretch?"

"Quiet!" Dimitri hissed. The Fox Demon's ears were twitching, and more than once he had glanced in their direction. Thankfully, Pox had covered them in a field of invisibility. It seemed to be working until the Demon's senses managed to detect them.

Dimitri swore when the Fox Demon smelled the air and turned to face them head on. He broke away from Xyleena's team and continued to sniff the air as he meandered closer.

"What do you smell, Kitfox?" Thera had called to him from farther away.

Kitfox stopped and stared directly into Dimitri's eyes. Dimitri could hear the Demon's low growl.

"Blood." Kitfox did not break the stare even as he answered his Feykin teammate.

Dimitri winced, remembering how Kitfox had pointed out the smell on him when they had met in Thief's Paradise.

"It's probably from the butcher down the street," said Xyleena, turning slightly to walk away. "Come on, boy! I'll get you a bone later."

171

Kitfox rolled his eyes in annoyance. Then he smirked. "I'm not moving for anything less than ten bones!"

"What?" the girl hollered in rage.

"Come on, Xy. Don't be mean to him." Teka put a hand on the young Dragon Keeper's shoulder.

Xyleena grumbled something. "Five bones!"

Kitfox sighed. "Fine! But they better have a lot of meat on them!"

"Yeah! Yeah! Can we get moving now?"

"Listen well, for this will be your only warning." Kitfox's growl of a whisper was barely audible even by Dákun Daju ears. "Stop following us, or I will tell her you are here, Hume-aju. Then we'll see how long you really last in a fight." With a snarl, he turned away and strode back to the others.

"What the? Did he see us?" Dimitri glanced sideways at Pox.

She quickly shook her head.

"His senses are even keener than those of a pure-blooded Dákun Daju," Godilai admitted begrudgingly. "If we are to continue this charade, I suggest we change tactics now."

"What do you suggest we do?" Vincent grumbled.

"With you here? Nothing. You are too old and fat to be taking the rooftops."

"Then why don't we just change our location so the wind doesn't carry our smell toward the fox?"

"Whatever we decide to do, I suggest doing it quickly," Pox said. "They are about to leave our sights." She pointed in the direction Xyleena's team was headed.

"Forget the fancy stuff," Dimitri said. "Just try to stay upwind from Kitfox while we follow them. First chance we get, steal the diary. Take Xyleena's whole hip sack if you have to." He rushed after Xyleena's team.

"I'll take her head." Godilai vowed and immediately followed Dimitri.

Pox and Vincent followed moments later. The four of them managed to catch up to Xyleena's team when they stopped to admire an ice sculpture in the bustling main square.

"Godilai, can you hear what they're saying?" Dimitri whispered.

"There are too many people here."

"Xyleena just took Dragon Diary out of her hip sack," Pox announced.

Dimitri returned his attention to the black-haired girl. Indeed, she was turning pages in the ancient book until she got to one in particular. A moment later, her face lit up with delight.

"I think that sculpture is a clue to another dragon."

"What's the plan, Dimitri?" Vincent asked, watching as the Dragon Keeper excitedly pointed to something in the book she held.

"We keep following them. They will lead us to the next clue."

"Same rules apply. Steal the diary if there is an opening," Godilai added.

"It looks like they're heading north. There's nothing up there except an ocean."

"Have you forgotten already, Vincent?" Dimitri rolled his eyes as he led his team after Xyleena's. "Their first two dragons were hidden on islands that only the Dragon Keeper could see. I'm thinking the third dragon was hidden in the same manner."

"Be quiet or the Demon will hear you," Godilai hissed.

Dimitri's team continued to follow Xyleena out of the city of Zadún and beyond. Though it was summer, the ground and trees were still covered in a thick layer of snow and ice. It made trailing Xyleena's team tricky and cold. Still, they managed to trek a few leagues without being noticed.

By nightfall, the temperature had dropped well below freezing. Xyleena's team finally stopped. While the girls set up a rudimentary camp, Kitfox wandered off into the woods. Dimitri held his breath, worried that the Demon might have gotten scent of his presence. He breathed a sigh of relief when Kitfox returned minutes later with a few freshly killed hares.

Dimitri's team slipped away to set up their own camp. Godilai elected to keep watch over Xyleena's team in case they snuck away in the middle of the night. Some hours later Dimitri returned to Godilai's side with hot drinks. They sat in silence, watching their enemies as they slept.

"What did I learn from this ordeal?" There was a hint of laughter in Artemista's tone. After a contemplative moment, she said, "I learned that all of the races – Hume, Dákun Daju, Feykin, and Demon–can get along; especially when the world is depending on them."

– FROM "THE UNSUNG"
BY J'VAC TAIG (TRANSLATED BY B'REG KUNGA)

I barely got any sleep. The night was too cold, and no matter how many times I wrapped the blanket around me, I could not stop shivering. Too frustrated to try to sleep any longer, I got up and quietly left the tent I was sharing with Thera and Teka.

It was not even dawn yet, I realized when I stepped outside. Not only that, but our camp was void of our guard, Kitfox. I surveyed the forest around our camp, looking for the Fox Demon. He was nowhere to be seen, and I felt a wave of panic wash over me.

Where could he be? I asked my dragons. Could he have gone to report our location to Dimitri?

They did not answer.

"You okay?"

I instantly swirled around, swinging my fist at the head of whoever snuck up behind me.

Kitfox caught it easily and frowned at me. "I knew you didn't like me, but that was a little extreme. Don't you think?" He released my arm and walked over to what was left of the fire.

"I'm sorry, Kitfox. You surprised me is all." I sighed and moved to sit beside the glowing embers.

He scoffed. "You should look up more."

"What do you mean?"

"I was in the tree." He pointed at the one that loomed over our tent. I studied it to realize a branch almost half-way up the tree was void of snow and icicles. The others around it were leaden with the signs of winter. Suddenly I felt guilty about thinking all those bad things about him. "You would have seen me if you had bothered to look up."

"Oh."

We lapsed into an awkward silence. I watched as Kitfox laid some wood on the embers and coaxed a fire from them. He then sat down in the snow and looked anywhere except in my direction.

"I don't mean to be rude to you."

His ear turned toward me. "Something about me bothers you."

I sighed and looked away from him. "What gave you that idea?"

"The 'Come on, boy! I'll get you a bone later' comment burned me. Just because I'm part fox doesn't mean you have to treat me like I'm your dog."

174

I closed my eyes. I had not even realized I had done that. With a sad sigh, I opened my eyes again. Kitfox's beautiful amber gaze was fixed on me.

"I don't know what to say apart from sorry. Yet it doesn't feel adequate enough for the insults I paid you."

He blinked in surprise. "I wasn't expecting that."

"Hmm?"

"I had a feeling you would apologize. You seem like the type. I just didn't know you'd do it so...nicely." Kitfox scratched his cheek and tried to explain. "Most Humes I have come across wouldn't give half a mud lump about my people. In fact, many Humes prefer to hunt us or oppress us. You are...different."

"I hear that a lot." I flashed a small smile. "I have a Dákun Daju friend who is like you. The students at the Temple beat me up because I refused to treat her like dirt."

"I'm impressed."

"What about?"

"You befriended a Dákun Daju. You are now traveling with a Demon. You have a half-Feykin sailing you around the world free of charge. And you have a pureblooded Feykin willing to protect you even at the cost of losing her sister. You are a very rare person, Xy."

I could feel the heat rush to my face. "Thank you."

"So who is this Dákun Daju friend of yours?"

"Zhealocera. She's from Katalania where her cousin is queen."

"No kidding?"

I nodded. "I met Zhealocera in my battle class the same day I first met Freya. Freya assigned me as her sparring partner because I had chosen dual wielding weapons, just like her. Anyway, Zhealocera obviously already knew how to fight, but battle classes are required to become an Enforcer. So she would spend the class period teaching me how to fight."

"See, Freya taught me almost everything I know about fighting. I would have listened to her." Kitfox chuckled. "Then again, I am sort of biased to my own people."

"Well...with Zhealocera's teaching, I was able to fend off two Dákun Daju and even send them running."

"Really?"

I nodded.

"Not bad for a Hume."

"What about you?"

"What do you mean?"

"I mean, you know more about me then I know about you. So..."

"Oh." He chuckled. "Well, my name is Kitfox Latreyon. Freya took me in as a cub after she found me abandoned in a back-alley dumpster in Gesa. During my thirteenth year, I was officially adopted into the Tahda'varett Demon guild. Now that I am in my twentieth year, I am eligible to lead a small order of the younger members of the guild. Should I prove to be a worthy pack leader, I could be chosen to join the Alphas."

"That sounds exciting."

"What are you two doing up so early?" a sleepy voice muttered.

Kitfox and I looked at the tent to see Teka step out.

"Did we wake you?"

"No, the cold did." She plopped down next to the fire with a shiver. "I can't wait to find this dragon. Afterward, I'm going to the bar to have me a hot butter ale or…six."

Kitfox licked his lips. "Good idea."

"How long until we reach the northern coast anyway?"

"We should be there by noon today if we break camp soon." Kitfox's ears twitched, and he quickly looked over his shoulder. A moment later, he sniffed the air.

A feeling of dread washed over me at his reaction, and I hoped I was just over reacting. "What is it?"

"The wind carries the smell of old blood." Kitfox stood suddenly, his back to Teka and me. "Tell me something. What does this Dimitri guy following you look like?"

"He's tall with messy black hair and crimson eyes and– "

"He's Hume-aju?"

I nodded slowly in answer.

"Crap. Wish I had known that sooner."

I got to my feet. "What's wrong?"

"I think he's been following us since yesterday." Kitfox looked over his shoulder at me. "I smelled him before we reached the ice sculpture. I think he was hidden by some kind of magic field. I told him not to follow us, but it smells like he did anyway."

"Wait a minute. You told him to stop following us? Why not just attack him?" I asked as I watched Teka duck into the tent to rouse Thera.

"I thought he was just some sick stalker. I didn't know he was your enemy." Kitfox faced me when I sighed. "I'm sorry."

"It's okay. It's my fault anyway because I didn't tell you beforehand."

Kitfox smiled and shook his head. Together he and I put the fire out and cleaned up while Thera and Teka packed up the tent. Minutes later, we were back on the trail northward.

While we trekked through the snow, I kept an eye on Kitfox to gauge his reaction to various sounds and smells he might have picked up. If he did detect anything, he certainly was not giving it away. Both of his ears suddenly perked up, and my hands immediately found their way to the tessens on my belt.

"We've reached the coast," Kitfox announced and pointed ahead of us.

The evergreens thinned out, revealing an icy gravel beach and sapphire water.

"There it is. Atoka's island." About a league away from the coast was an island I knew the others could not see.

"I wonder how we can get there," Thera said as she looked up and down the coast.

"Swimming is out of the question. The water will freeze you to death in under three minutes," Kitfox replied. "You could fly over there if you could see it. What about a spell?"

Thera looked at me. "How far away do you think the island is?"

"About a league. Maybe more."

"Too far for me to cast anything that would help. And I can't warp us there, because no one has seen"– she paused to look at me– "or can remember the island in detail."

"We'll just build a raft, then," Teka said, retreating to the trees.

Minutes later, she returned with a large trunk floating behind her. She muttered something, and the trunk dropped to the ground with a thud.

"I need at least two more trunks like this. Want to see if you can find them?"

"Sure."

Kitfox led me into the forest to hunt for trunks while Thera and Teka started on the raft. Several minutes passed in silence before we found a trunk buried in the snow.

"This one looks good."

"It's under, what, two meters of snow?"

Kitfox chuckled. "This is how you solve that problem."

He dug his claws into the wood and gave a rough yank. The tree gave out and sent him flailing into the snow. I burst out laughing, while he dug himself out.

"That didn't work as I had planned."

I offered my hand to help him to his feet. "Want to try it my way?"

Kitfox sighed and took it. "What is your way?" he asked as he shook himself from snow.

"Levítum!" I waved my hand, and the giant log shook then floated off the ground.

Kitfox's jaw dropped. I laughed.

"You know magic, too?"

I smiled proudly. "I was recently graduated to Mage."

"Nice."

Kitfox and I returned to Teka and Thera with the log and were promptly put to work on piecing the raft together. After a good two hours' steady work, the raft was ready. Teka set it adrift in the water and tested it before she deemed it worthy of travel.

I caught Kitfox staring over his shoulder, ears perked in opposite directions and a frown on his lips. "What do you hear?"

"I think we had better get a move on. The Hume-aju is making quite a bit of noise. I think he, too, is building a raft to get to the island." Kitfox looked at me.

"We should get the drop on him before he does the same to us."

Thera nodded. "I agree with Teka."

I glanced at Kitfox. "Get ready to see some of the greatest creatures in history."

He smirked coyly.

I brought my hand up and gently brushed my fingers against the jewels of the dragon eye. Instead of the usual tingly feeling that signaled the start of the summoning, I felt nothing. I sent Thera a look of panic over my shoulder, and tried again. Still, the summoning did not activate. Thera frowned in a mix of worry and bewilderment. Teka reflected the Feykin's unease at the situation. Kitfox, however, was at a loss.

I turned away to focus my thoughts inwards. Kkaia? Vortex?

Nothing.

Where are you guys? Still they did not answer my calls. "What in Havel is going on?"

"What indeed?" I ignored Kitfox's question and tried calling my dragons again.

Silence was my only response.

"Forget it!" I seethed, silently hoping that nothing bad happened to my dragons. "I'll figure it out later."

"Let's hurry and get across," said Kitfox, moving towards the raft. "We can mount a defensive on the beach over there if we have to. But while we're en route, keep working on your necklace thing."

I nodded and stepped onto the raft.

Once Thera, Teka, and I were aboard, Kitfox gave the raft a push out to open water then hopped on. He shivered and shook the water from his shoeless feet. Teka took the oar she had fabricated and sliced the water with it while I directed her to the island.

About a quarter of the way to the island, a biting wind picked up. Kitfox sniffed the air and growled. A heartbeat later Thera summoned her ribbon staff. She looked through the jewel atop and frowned. She shook her head, muttered a spell, and waved her arm. Another raft appeared in the water not too far behind us.

"Is that the bad guy?" Kitfox pointed his clawed thumb at the other raft.

I nodded.

"Yeah. He is the person I smelled yesterday. He also came into the tavern the night before. He looked miserable."

"Incoming!" shouted Teka.

I glanced up to see a fireball headed straight for us. Before anyone could react, the ball of fire froze in midair and splashed into the water not far away. Thera and I looked at each other then got to our feet. While she summoned her spell, I launched mine.

"Hydor esso!"

"Hydor sibatín!"

Both of our spells struck Dimitri's raft simultaneously and froze solid in moments.

"Nice shot." Kitfox clapped me on the shoulder.

"Teka, try to get us to land quickly. We cannot make a stand on open water like this."

A heartbeat after Thera spoke, another of Pox's spells was inbound.

"Nagaré!" I waved my hand at the ball of slowly freezing water.

It vanished and reappeared a moment later, headed in the opposite direction. Pox managed to catch it and send it back.

"Aero bíraw!" Thera clapped her hands behind us, and a sudden gust of wind formed a wave that propelled us forward just enough to miss the frozen water ball.

"We've breeched the field!" Teka exclaimed.

I turned away from Dimitri's raft to check out the island up close. It was nothing more than a frozen wasteland. No trees. No life. Just rocks and snow.

"How in the world could someone hide an island this big?" Kitfox asked.

"That's nothing compared to Vortex's island." I suddenly felt two presences touch the back of my mind. Kkaia? Vortex? Is that you?

We are here, hatchling.

Kkaia's soft voice echoed in my mind a heartbeat later. What is wrong?

Where in Havel have you two been? I frowned. We have trouble!

We slept.

I could tell they were hiding something. Tell me later. Dimitri is close and I have been trying to summon you.

We are ready, hatchling.

Be careful.

"Kkaia and Vortex are finally ready," I said. I brushed my fingers across both jewels of the amulet, and they tingled with power. "As soon as we land on the island, I'm summoning them. I'm tired of Dimitri's attempts to gang up on me."

Kitfox grinned. "I can't wait to see these dragons."

I grinned back. "They won't disappoint."

We were still several meters from the icy shore of Atoka's island when
Thera suddenly took flight. I watched as moments later she landed on the bank
and held her staff aloft to cast a string of spells. By the time our raft was
beached in the icy gravel, she had set up several wards in hopes of deterring
Dimitri and his team.

The instant my feet were on the island, I threw my hand in the air and
shouted the names of my dragons. Wind and earth erupted from the dragon eye
amulet in spectacular flashes of light. A heartbeat later, the separate elements
solidified into their respective dragons. Their roars echoed off the barren
landscape.

Kitfox covered his ears and winced as he gawked at Vortex and Kkaia.
"You were right, Xy. They don't disappoint."

I smiled at him before returning my attention to our pursuers. They were
still several minutes out and too far beyond my spell range to use magic. They
were, however, well within Thera's range. She wasted no time summoning
another water spear and hurling it at them. Pox was not quick enough to
counter the spell, and the water pierced their raft and froze solid.

Another two water spears were sent their way. These froze solid before
striking their raft, damaging it enough to cause it to start sinking. Thera hurled
another spell. It struck the fat judge and knocked him into the freezing water.
He tried to get back on the raft but only succeeded in flipping it. The rest of his
teammates went under, and their raft sunk shortly afterward.

"That was almost too easy," Vortex remarked and sat on his haunches.

"I concur." Kkaia flicked her tail in agitation.

"Hmm…" Kitfox knelt and stared at the water.

"What's wrong?"

He looked up at me. "It has been over three minutes. They'll be frozen to
death by now."

"I doubt they were that easily defeated," Teka muttered.

I nodded and glanced sideways at Thera. She had collapsed to her knees
and held her head bowed toward the water. Her ebony wings drooped, and her
silver hair shrouded her face.

"Thera?"

She turned away from me. "We should find Atoka's nest." Thera sounded
miserable.

I looked to Teka for help. She sighed and shook her head then walked over to Thera. I barely heard their murmured conversation as I joined Kitfox and my dragons at the water's edge.

The Fox Demon sighed and stared out across the water. "The Feykin on that raft was her sister, huh?"

"Yes," Vortex answered plainly.

"May her soul find peace in her mother's embrace when she arrives at the Gates of Havel." My fingers gently touched the water as I spoke the prayer aloud. A tear fell and rippled the water's mirrored surface. "Atlidmé, watch over her."

Kitfox gently laid a hand on my shoulder. I wiped my tears away and looked into his somber, amber eyes.

"I see why you can befriend Dákun Daju, Feykin, Demon, and Hume alike. You are passionate and honorable, even to your enemies."

"Many would see that as weakness," Kkaia said.

Kitfox looked up at the dragon of earth with a frown.

"It isn't a weakness," he said firmly. "It is strength, pure and simple."

Kkaia snorted and lowered her head so she could stare straight into Kitfox's eyes. "Your versions of strength and weakness are backward, Demon."

"You are wrong, dragon." Kitfox growled. "A mother's love for her children or husband may be her weakness, yet she would lay down her life to protect them if need be because of that love."

Kkaia stared at him and remained silent. With a grunt, she rose to her full height. "I like you, Kitfox. You have a strong heart."

Kitfox gaped at Kkaia then looked at me.

I could only shrug. "I have no idea what that was about, but I tend to agree with her."

"Oi!" Teka called. "Let's find Atoka so we can leave this frozen wasteland."

I glanced at Thera as I got to my feet. She seemed calm, almost numb, yet I could see misery swimming in her eyes.

I sighed and looked up at Kkaia and Vortex. "You two staying here or returning to the eye?"

"I am certain you do not need us to help you find our sister." Vortex stood and began to fade away.

A moment later Kkaia followed his example. Wind and earth swirled around me and was absorbed into the amulet. The jewels marking the places of both dragons sparkled with the power of their elements.

"So…where is this dragon exactly?" Kitfox asked with a shiver.

I closed my eyes and focused on the pull emanating from somewhere on the island. A moment later, I knew where to find Atoka.

"Follow me." I took off at a brisk walk, following the pull of Atoka.

I could hear the ice and snow crunching under the feet of the others as they walked with me. Moments later, we were carefully treading across the slippery surface of a long-frozen lake.

"It doesn't make sense!" Thera cried.

I stopped in my tracks and turned to look at her.

"Pox could have easily blocked all of those spells I cast against Dimitri's team. She did not even try! Why didn't she try?"

Teka sighed and moved to comfort the young Feykin. I watched for a moment as they whispered to each other in Kinös Elda. Then I turned my attention to Kitfox. He shivered while he watched the scene before him.

"You're cold," I muttered.

He finally looked at me. "Don't worry abo—" His ears twitched.

An instant later, he spun around just in time to block the blow from Godilai as she crashed into him. Half a heartbeat later, Dimitri smashed into me. The four of us fell to the ice hard enough to crack it. Before any of us had a chance to do anything, the ice gave way, and we plummeted into the darkness below.

I groaned as I forced myself to sit up. Kitfox was already on his feet and standing guard over me. Godilai and Dimitri were sprawled out a little ways away and were quickly recovering from the fall.

"You okay, Xy?" Kitfox extended a hand to help me to my feet.

I took it gratefully and surveyed our surroundings. We were in some kind of cavern under the ice. It was warmer here than on the surface, yet drifts of snow and huge icicles were in abundance all around us. Sounds of a battle echoed down from the surface.

"I'm fine."

"You won't be for long," said Dimitri. His crimson eyes twinkled with malice.

Kitfox snarled back and flexed his claws. "You'll have to get through me first, Hume-aju."

"Don't waste your life protecting that weak fool, Demon." Godilai hissed and released her swords from their sheaths. She sunk into her fighting stance.

"I'll throw those words back at you."

"Wait!" My shout echoed off the walls of the cavern we found ourselves in.

"What do you want?" Dimitri hissed through his teeth.

"I just want to know why you are so bent on freeing the Shadow Dragons."

He looked stunned at my question.

"Tell me why you want to release that kind of evil on everyone!"

"No." Dimitri shook his head. "Not everyone. Just those responsible for causing this misery I've found myself in." His hands turned to fists. "You Humes took everything away from me! You destroyed my father…my mother…my home. I will unleash evil on every Hume and annihilate them all!"

"That happened centuries ago!" Kitfox shouted back. "Get over it!"

"Never!" Dimitri lunged for Kitfox.

The Demon was much faster, blocking Dimitri's feral attack and slamming him into the floor. While Dimitri wheezed for air, Godilai lashed out. Kitfox managed to push her away. She stumbled to the floor and somersaulted past him. Kitfox snarled and grabbed her by her hair. He yanked her back, tearing a scream from her, and slammed her into the wall.

"You will pay for that, Demon!"

Kitfox snorted. "It will take much more than a Dákun Daju and a half to make me pay for anything."

I laughed when Godilai remained silent, glaring at Kitfox.

"I like you more and more, Kitfox."

"Glad to hear it."

"Heile suahk!"

Kitfox cried out as Dimitri's spell struck him and sent him flying into the wall hard enough to crack it.

Godilai wasted no time and lunged for me. I barely managed to avoid her swords during the initial few seconds, when her attacks were wild and driven solely by rage. She swung her swords in obvious hopes of taking my head off, but they were so easy to avoid or deflect that I felt like I was dueling a clumsy child, not a proud Dákun Daju Assassin. I dipped under another of her wild swings and moved fast, closing the distance between us. I do not know what compelled her to turn her back to me, but I took advantage of her position. Using just the tips of my fingers, I quickly jabbed her spine in several locations. She cried out as if kissed by a hot iron poker, and she went limp and fell to the floor in a heap. While I kicked her swords out of her reach, I looked at my fingers in shock—trying to remember where I had learned that paralyzing technique.

Dimitri shoved himself off the cavern floor just enough to perform a sweeping kick. Distracted from trying to recall the memory of learning that bizarre technique, I did not have time to react. Mere seconds later I found myself laid out on the ground, wheezing for air. Dimitri did not grant me any time to recover, and brought his dual sword down for a crippling blow. I stopped him the only way I knew how—a hard kick to the groin.

His face flushed red and he fell away with a groan. As he fell, he clocked his head on an icicle and was rendered unconscious. I took a moment to finally recover from my fall, and then quickly flipped to my feet. I rushed over to check on Kitfox, and managed about half the distance before a small knife whistled past my ear. It sunk deep into an icicle, and flakes of snow showered down. I turned to glare at Godilai just as she prepared to throw another of her knives. I closed the distance between us in a few strides and stole the small blade from her hand. I stared down at her, watching her struggle to get up and return to the battle. As much as I hated this woman for killing Ríhan, seeing her so helpless made me feel... feel sorry for her.

I sighed and buried the blade of the knife in the wall. "Stop this, Godilai."

"N-Never!" She struggled even harder to get to her feet.

"If you don't stop, you will die."

She laughed darkly. "A w-weak Hume... like you... could never..."

"Shut-up." I hissed in annoyance. "I could kill you right now if you weren't so pathetic."

"Whatsss stopping you?"

I shrugged, though I doubted that she could see the action from the floor. "I guess it's because I'm not without compassion. I don't attack people who are weaker than me, and I certainly don't kill people in cold blood." I glanced sidelong at Dimitri as he finally started to stir. "And I definitely don't kill because someone else orders it."

She rambled something in a language I did not know, and then was still.

I sighed, both in relief that she had finally passed out and to expel some of the built up stress. Then I turned to deal with the more pressing task at hand— stopping Dimitri permanently. I had not even taken two steps before Godilai exploded from her slumped heap with a roar. Taken aback at her sudden recovery from that crippling technique, I did not have time to defend myself as she lashed out at me with a barrage of punches and kicks. Several of her blows landed to my face and torso before I began to defend myself.

As before, her technique matched that of a child's, and it was easy for me to overwhelm her. She tried to kick my feet out from under me, but a quick jab to her stomach made her think otherwise. I followed that punch with several others to her midsection and even one to her chin despite having to jump to reach. Before long, I had her bested yet again.

I heard Dimitri groan, and caught a glimpse of him moving. Before I knew it, he rejoined the fray. It was then that Godilai's sloppy technique turned graceful and deadly accurate.

Had she just been toying with me this whole time? I wondered as I struggled to fend the duo off.

"Now you will pay for Luna's death!" Godilai kicked me in the chest so hard I barreled into the wall, cracking it further.

I slumped to the ground beside Kitfox and gasped for air. My mind swam in and out of awareness. Dimitri sneered and bent over me. I felt him rummaging through my hip sack and finally pulling something out of it. I could barely make out my dragons screaming at me to get up.

"N—No…" I tried to take back the book he stole.

He scoffed and slapped me before turning away. He paused to skim over pages in the book and laugh darkly. I felt tears sting my eyes.

"Now you can kill her, Godilai."

Kitfox erupted from his position and smashed into Dimitri. The book was dislodged from Dimitri's grasp and landed at my feet. I listened to the battle as I stared at the book, trying to regain my strength. My dragons were whispering to me, trying to urge me to do something.

Everything in the cavern suddenly grew quiet. I looked up as someone knelt before me. My vision slowly cleared to reveal Kitfox, worry clearly evident on his features. He gently stroked my sore cheek. I did not have the strength to do or say anything. He backed away, and I let my eyes drift shut.

I returned to consciousness some unknown time later. Thera was standing over me, healing all my wounds, while Kitfox and Teka looked on. We were still in the cavern, I realized. I felt an excited buzzing at the back of my mind, and I could tell Vortex and Kkaia were relieved to see me well. A minute later Thera sighed and backed away.

"Done." She sounded exhausted. "You were lucky, Xy. A few minutes more and you would have been beyond my help. Thankfully Kitfox sent Dimitri's team running away screaming."

I looked up at Kitfox. Half of his tunic had been torn away, revealing burnt flesh and dried blood. Other smaller wounds were evident all over him. I met his amber gaze. He winced as he shivered.

"You should let Thera take care of that for you," I muttered, pointing to the deep wound on his ribs.

Kitfox smirked. "She didn't have enough energy to heal the both of us. And you needed her attention more than me."

"Kitfox told us that Dimitri managed to get his hands on Dragon Diary," Teka said as she moved to kneel beside me.

I felt my stomach sink at her words and immediately searched my hip sack for the book.

"I managed to get it back from him, but I think he found the page with the riddles on it," Kitfox said. He winced as he held the diary out to me. I grabbed it and hugged it to my chest.

"Thank you, Kitfox. Thank you so much."

He smiled at me and nodded. I quickly stuffed the book back into my hip sack.

"You feeling up to finding this dragon or do you need to rest more?"

"I'm feeling just fine, but I'm worried about you," I said as I got to my feet. My legs wobbled and gave out.

Kitfox caught me and grunted in pain.

"I'm sorry. I'm so sorry."

"It's okay." He made sure I could stand on my own before letting me go and stepping away.

I caught a glimpse of the wound before he hid it with his hand. Blood had started gushing from it, staining his belt, pants, and what was left of his tunic.

"Please let me heal that for you."

Kitfox looked at me. "I don't think you have the strength to."

"Xy might not, but I do," Teka said, stepping closer to the Demon.

Kitfox sighed and moved his hand away from his wound. Teka made a face and gently touched her fingertips to the deep gash in his side. He yelped and dug his claws into the wall to keep from lashing out at her.

"Medícté!"

I watched as the wound slowly healed itself. Before it was completely closed, Teka stopped and dropped to her knees in exhaustion. "I'm sorry. That's…that's all I can do."

"Yeah." Kitfox grunted and rested his head against the wall. A minute later, his ears perked up. He quickly ripped his claws from the wall and backed away with a growl.

"What's wrong?" Thera and I were at his side a moment later.

"I heard a heartbeat," he said, looking at me. "It was very faint and slow, but it was there."

Teka looked up at me. "Is it Atoka?"

"Deep in ice, Atoka I bound." I smirked and glanced about the frozen cavern. "This is about as deep in ice as we can get."

"All right. So how do we free the dragon from the ice?"

"Simple." Kitfox grinned. "We break it." He slammed his fist into the ice. The impact cracked the ice but left no damage otherwise.

"That will take a while."

Kitfox looked over his shoulder at me. "How about we try it your way then?"

I smiled at him as he moved away from the wall. Vortex, Kkaia, please lend me some of your energy.

Take all that you need, hatchling.

I felt a wave of serene energy wash over me. "Gaia Semít!"

A spike of earth erupted from the ground. Before it could sink back from whence it came, I cast another spell.

"Levítum!"

The spike of earth levitated, and I flung it toward the ice wall. It struck with a resounding crack and stayed there.

"That didn't work out so well," Kitfox muttered.

I walked up to him and laid my hand over his wound, making him yelp in surprise. A moment later, the gash was fully healed. By the time I finished healing him, the spike of earth had dissolved into sand. It left a gaping hole in the ice wall big enough for all of us to crawl through.

Teka's jaw dropped as she gazed into the room beyond. "Wow."

Thera, Kitfox, and I moved around so we could see through the hole. A pale-blue dragon stared back at us from atop a bed of snow and jewels of ice.

"I was beginning to wonder when you would appear again, my Keeper." The dragon rose to a sitting position and flicked her spiked tail happily. "I must say, you did make an awful racket out there."

"It's good to see you again too, Atoka." I smiled and crawled through the hole in the wall. "How have you been?"

"Completely and thoroughly bored out of my mind." Atoka watched as the others crawled through the hole. "You seem to be traveling with quite a strange menagerie of people. Who are they?"

"Not…what I was expecting," Kitfox muttered.

Atoka snorted and craned her neck so she was eye to eye with the Demon. "And just what were you expecting, Fox?"

Kitfox glanced my way before answering the dragon. "I always imagined you dragons were as wise as you were powerful. You, Atoka, are more like an impatient cub."

I had to bite my tongue to keep from laughing as Atoka stared Kitfox down. Vortex and Kkaia, on the other hand, guffawed so loud I felt I would go deaf.

Finally Atoka laughed. "What is your name, Demon?"

"Kitfox Latreyon."

"You are the son of Freya?" Atoka's liquid voice was full of surprise.

"Not exactly. She adopted me when I was a cub."

"I see." Atoka finally stopped scrutinizing Kitfox to move on to Thera. "You look like—"

"Thernu." Thera smiled sadly. "She was my mother."

Atoka nodded in understanding. "She was mine, too."

"What?" Kitfox's expression made me laugh.

"Thernu Onyx was the Necromancer who brought the Dragons of Light to fruition."

"Oh! Right. Right. I forgot about that."

Teka bowed to the dragon as she looked her over. "I am Teka Loneborne, Atoka. It is a pleasure to meet you."

"A demi-Feykin. Interesting." Atoka stood to her full height. "I am the dragon of eternal winter."

"Are you the reason Arctica is so cold?" Kitfox asked, crossing his arms.

Atoka snorted but did not answer.

"Atoka."

The dragon looked at me.

"Not to be rude or anything, but how do we get out of this cavern?"

"That's easy, Xy." Kitfox laughed. "Behind some of the snow piles and icicles in the last room there are some stairs and a statue."

"Let me guess. The statue is a black dragon."

"How did you know?"

"Those statues mark the location to the dragons' nesting places."

"Don't forget, Dimitri can unlock the route to the Dragons' Gate with the clues from all twelve statues," Teka added.

Kitfox scratched his head. "Aren't the Shadow Dragons supposedly locked behind the Dragons' Gate?"

"So they say," Atoka said.

I whirled around to face her. "What is that supposed to mean, Atoka?"

"Come now. You are all cold. You should be some place warmer." The dragon faded into snowflakes and ice crystals that whipped out of the room through the hole.

I silently fumed and followed Atoka. Thera, Teka, and Kitfox were hot on my heels as I located the hidden stairs. Atoka greeted us as we ascended to the surface of the hollow lake.

"So, are the Shadow Dragons in the gate or not?" I asked as I walked up to Atoka.

Do not fret over such things, young one, Kkaia whispered to me.

I frowned. "What are you three hiding?"

Teka rubbed her chin. "Kkaia and Vortex won't answer either, huh?"

Thera nodded. "Very suspicious, indeed."

Atoka sighed. "Truth be told, we cannot be sure if our dark brothers and sisters are still within the gate."

"Why not?"

"They are not our brethren, but born of another power." She snapped her jaws shut several times, and I could tell she was having trouble trying to explain. "We of the Light can sense each other when close as we were born from the same source—hence the strange pull you started feeling when you donned the amulet. Those of Shadow, we cannot detect as they were not made alongside us."

"How could they have escaped?" Kitfox asked. "I thought the Dragons' Gate was designed to keep them locked away forever."

I felt an uneasy feeling wash over me, and I looked up to Atoka.

"Did I let them out?"

"What?" Thera, Teka, and Kitfox exclaimed in unison.

Atoka sighed again.

Why would you say that, hatchling?

"Because Zahadu-Kitai told me how I lost my memories!" I cried. "I fell from the Dragons' Gate! I released the Shadow Dragons!" I fell to my knees. "I released the Shadow Dragons."

Kitfox was at my side an instant later. "No, you didn't, Xy." He cupped my chin in his hand and forced me to look at him. "If you had, the world would be in shambles. The influence of the Shadow Dragons would be seen everywhere if they had been freed. They are still locked up. Isn't that right, dragon?"

"It is true that the Shadow would bring destruction everywhere they went." Atoka replied thoughtfully. "It would be obvious by now, three years after their suspected release."

Kitfox smiled and looked at me again. "See? The bad dragons are still locked up."

As I stared into his soft, amber eyes, I could see an emotion there that I could not place. I somehow knew everything he said was true. Finally, I looked away and nodded.

"Thank you, Kitfox."

"No problem." He stood and extended a hand to me.

I took it and allowed him to help me back to my feet.

"Now, how about we get out of this place? I don't know about you, but I'm freezing my tail off."

I laughed humorlessly. "I don't have a tail, but I'm freezing something off."

Atoka walked beside us as the four of us made our way back to the rocky beach.

"It looks like Dimitri's team stole our raft," Teka announced. "I had a feeling they would."

"I'd still like to know how they survived."

"Pox said something about me falling for her illusion," Thera admitted quietly. "It is a mistake I will not make again."

"Teka's right," I said, scanning the beach. "Our raft is gone."

"Then how do we get back to mainland?" Kitfox asked. "I haven't seen any trees here to use in making another."

Atoka snorted. "You little things worry too much." She walked right up to the water's edge and touched her nose to the surface. She exhaled, and I watched in amazement as frost crept along the surface of the straight. An instant later, the entire distance between the mainland and us was frozen solid.

"Sweet!" Kitfox thumped Atoka on the foreleg. "I like your style, dragon."

"The ice won't last forever. Best to move along while you can. And when you get the chance, I'd take a closer look at Amorez's diary." Atoka faded into snowflakes and ice crystals again.

Her power whirled around me, chilling me to the bone, before shooting into the dragon eye. A pale-blue jewel formed in one of the vacant spots.

The dragon of eternal winter was mine.

I think that being a female hero is a tough job. No one expects
a woman to be strong enough to pull off the same feats as a
man – especially if one is to lead an entire army to victory.
They would find themselves quite surprised at a woman's
drive and dedication to perform those same feats.

– FROM "THE DIARY OF AMOREZ"
BY AMOREZ RENOAN

Two days after acquiring Atoka, we finally made it back to Zadún. I could not wait to get back to the inn and warm up with a large mug of hot tea. I could tell Thera and Teka had similar plans. However, Kitfox seemed to have another destination in mind.

The Fox Demon led us down streets that took us farther and farther away from the inn. Just when I was about to ask him what he was planning, he stopped. Kitfox grinned at us over his shoulder and knocked thrice on a heavy oaken door of a rundown building. A slot in the door opened, revealing another pair of amber eyes. Kitfox muttered something I could not hear, and the slot was closed. A moment later, the door was unlocked and pulled aside.

The Demon in the doorway bowed and ushered us past. "Welcome to the Tahda'varett guild house."

Kitfox nodded and stepped over the threshold. Thera, Teka, and I hesitated before following him into the warm and dimly lit hallway.

"Are you sure we're allowed in here?" Thera asked, nervously looking at the black-haired Coyote Demon behind us.

"We take in people all the time, but we refuse to help rival guilds like the Warinarc and Serpehti."

"So…you live in a rundown house?" Teka asked, her voice thick with skepticism.

The Coyote Demon snorted, and Kitfox met Teka with a bored stare and pushed aside a door.

The room beyond was lavishly decorated in the Tahda'varett guild colors–black, red, and gold. A long bar was on one side of the room attended by a few Wolf Demons. The other side of the room was filled with tables and sofas. Several Demons were lounging on the furniture talking, joking, or playing games. Only a scant few looked toward the open door.

"Does this look rundown to you?" Kitfox asked as he walked into the room.

"You got me there."

Teka and I followed a moment later.

Thera was a little more reluctant to enter the room. "You are sure no one here will attack a Feykin?"

Kitfox smiled over his shoulder at her. "I promise, Thera. No one here will attack you or anyone else unless they are provoked into doing so."

With a sigh, she finally entered the room.

"Hey, Rahvel, I need six hot butter ales and two large pots of tea."

A burnt-orange Fox Demon behind the bar gawked at Kitfox. "Who beat you up?"

Kitfox laughed. "Nobody worth mentioning at the moment."

"Right." Rahvel shook his head. "You look like something the cat dragged in, and you expect me to believe nobody important kicked your a—"

"Add some food to my order too. And bring everything to room seventeen." Kitfox smirked. He smacked the bar and backed away. "It's open, right?"

"Last I checked it was," Rahvel muttered and disappeared through a door.

"Follow me." Kitfox waved to a few Demons as he led the three of us down a short flight of stairs.

"Is everyone in the Tahda'varett guild of canine descent?" I asked as another Fox Demon walked past us up the stairs.

Kitfox made a face while he thought for a moment. "'Tahda'varett' means honorable canines in a language predating the Earthic Landings so, yeah; almost everyone in the guild is of canine descent. There are a scant few exceptions, though."

"How long has this guild been around?"

"Much longer than all of the other Ithnezian Demon guilds combined." Kitfox grinned and opened a door marked seventeen. He ushered us through and sealed it behind us, plummeting us into blackness. "Hang on. I'll light the fire."

"You can see in the dark?"

He laughed. "Of course."

I saw sparks as he ran steel over flint. A moment later, a spark combusted the tinder, and a small fire was burning in the pit. Kitfox placed a few logs on the fire and backed away.

"There we go."

I looked around the room. There were two beds, side tables, a desk with a potted plant, and a chest of drawers. The fireplace was on the wall opposite a door left slightly ajar. The Tahda'varett guild emblem was emblazoned on the wall over the desk.

"Not bad, Kitfox. But why are we here?" Teka asked as she sat on one of the beds.

"The inn charges too much, whereas the guild house is free for members." He chuckled. "Plus it is covert enough that we can freely discuss things requiring secrecy."

A rapid knock made me jump. Kitfox chuckled and moved to open the door. Rahvel and another Demon were there with trays of food and drink. Kitfox stepped aside to let them in and watched as they set the trays on the desk. Kitfox slipped Rahvel some coins before he left the room.

"So, let's have some dinner and take a closer look at this diary. I'm dying to know what Atoka meant by taking a closer look at it."

Hours later Dragon Diary was spread out on the floor between the four of us. We had gone through every page at least three times now, searching for something out of the ordinary. Every page was the same– worn parchment with fading ink. Only when we turned to the "Riddle of the Twelve" did the ink change, but that was due to Thera's translations. There was nothing outstanding to be found in the book.

Okay, Atoka, a little hint would be great right about now, I muttered.

What you are looking for is hidden amongst the riddle.

Does it need to be decrypted?

No.

I sighed and turned to the page with the "Riddle of the Twelve" scrawled over it. "Whatever we are looking for, it is on this page."

"Let me see it a second," Kitfox said, plucking a leaf from the plant on the desk.

I handed the diary over and watched as he rubbed the leaf over the page. A moment later, he grinned and rubbed more vigorously.

"Looks like Freya's handwriting, and it's in Kinös Elda."

I leaned in to see what had been revealed on the page. "'Xyleena, seek out the royal Dákun Daju.' And it points to the next two encrypted lines of the riddle."

"Okay...what is the point of telling us that?" Teka grumbled.

"I think Freya is trying to tell you about a person who might know the answer to the next portion of the riddle," Kitfox said as he passed Thera the diary.

"Who is the royal Dákun Daju? That is the question," Thera said, reading the clue.

"There is only one Dákun Daju sovereign." I smiled. "Zhealocera's cousin, the queen of Katalania."

Kitfox laughed. "So we are off to Kamédan."

Teka yawned. "Uh. Let's wait until morning to start another venture. I'm too tired to move right now."

"Okay, so the plan is to leave tomorrow morning after breakfast and head straight for Kamédan."

I received nods in answer. A few minutes of arranging sleeping sections later, and the four of us were sound asleep.

Kitfox led us past the ice castle on our way to the harbor. A huge crowd was gathered around the fence that protected the sculpture, talking in growing alarm and anger. Kitfox looked at me for a moment then pushed his way through the crowd. He returned several minutes later with a grave look on his face.

"The ice castle has almost melted."

"What?"

"I thought you said it never melted."

All three of them looked at me for an answer.

"The only thing I can think of is Atoka somehow played a part in keeping the castle frozen."

"Well, whatever happened, it sure is angering several of the people in town. And several others are scared that this is a sign of the end of things," Kitfox said as he looked over his shoulder at the crowd.

Atoka, can you do anything to restore the castle?

I felt a cold chill wash over me as the dragon's mind melded with mine. You would have to summon me so I could use my power.

I sighed and nodded solemnly. "Atoka could restore it, but I would have to summon her here."

"Great!" Kitfox smiled.

"I don't know if that is such a good idea," Thera said, gauging the crowd. "We don't know how these people will react to a dragon."

"Yeah, but obviously the sculpture is of great significance to these people. I think it would be worth summoning her if it could be restored," Teka argued.

What do you three think? I asked my dragons.

The way I see it, one of three things will happen, Kkaia said. The people will run away screaming. The people will attack you out of fear. On the other hand, the people might cheer at the arrival of the Dragon Keeper.

Hopefully it will be the latter reaction, Vortex replied.

I nodded. Get ready, Atoka.

As you wish, my Keeper.

"I'm summoning Atoka." I brushed my fingers over the jewel that marked the dragon's presence within the amulet. I felt ice-cold energy wash over me as I thrust my hand into the air. "Atoka!"

A pale-blue light exploded from the dragon eye, and the crowd immediately silenced and turned to look at me. The light changed into snowflakes and ice crystals and whirled about the town square before they took on the form of the dragon of eternal winter. She roared as she solidified from her element.

Atoka paused to observe the reaction of the crowd. No one screamed. No one ran. They all stood there, watching in silent awe as the dragon took a step closer to what remained of the ice castle sculpture.

"Totally not the reaction I was expecting," Kitfox whispered in my ear.

I nodded as I watched Atoka snake her neck around the sculpture to examine its remains. A moment later, she backed away and sat on her haunches. Her eyes flashed blue, and she exhaled a great breath. Ice and snow whirled around the sculpture and solidified. A minute later, the ice castle was back to its previous splendor.

"It is done," Atoka replied and looked at me. "I instilled a fraction of my essence into it, so it should remain frozen for all time."

The crowd cheered. Kitfox clapped me on the shoulder and ran toward the dragon. I smiled as several people turned and applauded or thanked me graciously.

"The Dragon Keeper has returned!" several cried out.

"Amorez is back!"

"Hooray for Amorez!"

I found myself frowning at their cheers for Amorez. I am not Amorez. How could they think that I am?

Correct them, hatchling.

Let them know who you are.

Are you sure that is wise?

They apparently thought it best not to answer.

I sighed and raised my hands over my head. "Listen! Listen to me! Please!"

The crowd continued to cheer. Atoka roared long and loud. Immediately the crowd quieted.

"Thank you, Atoka."

"You are welcome." She nodded her great wedge of a head.

I returned my attention to the crowd. "Please listen. I am not Amorez Renoan."

Almost everyone gasped.

"I am her daughter, Xyleena."

"Why do you have the dragons?" a voice in the crowd called out.

"My mother passed the Dragons of Light on to me so that I may protect you."

"Protect us from what?" shouted another voice.

I looked at Thera, Teka, and Kitfox. All three of them nodded in agreement.

"Agasei's son is bent on releasing the Shadow Dragons from the Dragons' Gate. I am trying to prevent him from achieving that, but it is proving to be a difficult task."

"Can we help?" asked a child who stood before me.

I stared at her, unsure of how to answer.

"At this point we are not sure exactly how any of you can help us, but any assistance is much appreciated," Thera explained, placing a hand on my shoulder.

"Xyleena Renoan." An old man in a uniform stepped forward from the crowd. He smiled and bowed to me. "I am Zhaman Verrs, the Magistrate of Arctica. I would like to extend my deepest gratitude for restoring our ice castle, a priceless heirloom, to our city. It would be my honor to repay your favor by fully financing and supplying you in any way needed."

"I thank you, Mr. Verrs. Teka, would you like to speak to him about supplies for our journey?"

The first winter we experienced on Ithnez was a hard one. The weather was biting cold, and it seemed to drop several meters of snow every night. We ran short on food as many of our crops from Earth did not take well to this alien land. Eventually, we were forced to consume more of our livestock than intended.

At least we survived.

– FROM "THE CHRONICLES OF ITHNEZ, VOL. I"
BY ADJIRSÉ DÉDOS

Two weeks had passed at sea, but it felt like much longer. Much of my time was spent with Kitfox as he taught me a few new tricks to use in battle. Thera, on the other hand, worked on translating the next portion of the riddle. We kept ourselves as busy as possible to stave off boredom.

As I stared out at the open, moon-kissed water, I thought about recent events. I was proud of myself and the people who had become a huge part of my life. I hoped that news of our actions in Arctica spread and worked as a deterrent to Dimitri's plans.

"What are you thinking about?" Kitfox's voice made me jump. He chuckled and apologized.

I nodded and turned my back to the railing to talk to him. I marveled at how his eyes sparkled like the stars overhead.

"I was just thinking about everything we've done so far. We've obtained one quarter of the twelve dragons, defeated Dimitri and his team in battle time and time again, and then we helped the people of Zadún by restoring their heirloom." I counted things off on my fingers. "I am very proud of all of it."

"Glad to hear that." Kitfox smiled and leaned on the railing.

We lapsed into a comfortable silence. He gazed into the water's depths, while I looked up at the stars.

"You know, I'm kind of nervous about meeting this Dákun Daju queen."

I looked at him over my shoulder. "Why is that?"

"I haven't had the greatest luck when it comes to getting along with Dákun Daju. Do not get me wrong, I try. I just end up saying something that burns them, and then they try to kill me."

I laughed. "That sounds about right."

Kitfox frowned at me.

"Look, if the queen is anything like her cousin, I'm sure you'll be fine."

His ears perked up as the cry from the crow's nest went out. We both looked beyond the bow of the ship to see the multicolored lights of Kamédan come into view.

"I hope you're right."

Teka, Thera, Kitfox, and I disembarked from the Shadow Dance a little over an hour later. The smell of spices and wildflowers filled the air as we meandered through the busy streets. People dressed in festive colors smiled openly as we passed them. Chains of colored lights and streamers of green and brown hung from almost every building.

"What are they celebrating?" Thera asked when we came across a square filled with dancing people and loud music. Those that were not dancing or playing music were gathered at the exhibitor stalls that lined the square— bartering for all sorts of trinkets or food. There was even a large wine stall with a game of dice being played at a corner table. I expected to see a head of violet hair among the people gathered around, but the only Dákun Daju there had pink hair.

"It is the summer solstice," I answered, looking away from the festivities.

Fireworks suddenly burst into the air above us, and sparkles rained down amid cheers and applause.

"They are celebrating the Rising of Nahstipulí."

"Humes certainly have an interesting way of celebrating," Thera said as she watched the fireworks.

We continued walking through the crowded streets and past several vendors barking for us to buy something from them. Thera eagerly checked out a particular stall claiming to be selling authentic Feykin knickknacks. She was extremely upset when she realized that the vendor was selling only junk. She had given him quite an earful before Teka and I pulled her away.

Eventually we had to stop and ask for directions to the castle. A young boy happily guided us through the city until we found ourselves at the gates of the castle. I whistled in awe as the lighted fountains erupted, nearly overcoming the gate's prominence. The castle looked like a giant quartz crystal formation. A strange platform hovered above the tallest spire as if suspended on the air itself. The platform was lit in blue, and long ribbons floated to the ground amid lush gardens and sparkling fountains.

A guard tapped the gate, stealing my attention away from the beautiful vista. "Can I help you?"

"We need to speak with the queen on an important matter," I replied.

The guard scoffed. "I hear that one a lot. Sorry, girlie, but I can't let you in."

"Please! I really need to speak with her."

The guard shook his head and started walking away.

"How about her cousin, Zhealocera? Is she here?"

The guard froze mid-stride and looked at me over his shoulder. "You know the queen's cousin?"

"I went to school with her. If she's here, please tell her Xyleena is at the gate."

His jaw dropped. "You're Xyleena?"

"Yes." I nodded.

"Why didn't you just say so?" The guard quickly unlocked the gate. "Please, come with me."

"Thank you."

The four of us followed him straight up the cobblestone walkway and into the crystal castle. He kindly asked us to wait in the lobby and disappeared through a gilded door.

"Interesting castle," Kitfox muttered as he looked about the room.

Moments later, I heard feet running through the room beyond. Suddenly the door burst open. A violet-haired Dákun Daju stood in the doorway, and I smiled upon recognizing her.

"Zhealocera!"

"Xyleena!"

Before I knew it, she clobbered me in a hug. I returned the embrace with equal enthusiasm.

"Oh! I am so glad to see you! Where in the world have you been?"

"In places I've never dreamed of."

"And who are these three?" Zhealocera pointed her thumb at the trio I called my team.

"Thera Onyx is the Feykin. Kitfox Latreyon is the Fox Demon. And Teka Loneborne is the demi-Feykin. They are the people who have been helping me find the dragons."

"So that is what you have been up to. We were so worried. When we found Ríhan, we feared the worst for you."

My smile faltered slightly at the mention of Ríhan's name. It did not go unnoticed by the Dákun Daju warrior.

"He was a good man, Xy. He left our realm too soon."

Tears stung my eyes. Just when I thought the wound had finally closed up, here it was being torn open again. "He is in Havel. If Atlidmé asks, tell him I'll vouch for Ríhan so he could be reborn again later."

Zhealocera nodded solemnly. "Ríhan was right, you know."

"What are you talking about?"

"Zamora is Amorez. Ríhan was right the whole time."

"I know." I smiled. "He's never wrong. What happened at the Temple anyway? I heard something about you barely managing to escape."

Zhealocera's expression turned grim, and she sat on one of the lounge chairs with a sigh. "After the fake Valaskjalf blew up the Festival of the Phoenix, his lackeys tortured and killed many of the Priests and Knights there. Several students were murdered during the ordeal… all for the purpose of learning where the dragons were hidden.

"What?"

Kitfox growled. "I really don't like those guys."

"I did hear that Serenitatis has become Palavant in our absence, but the school is all but shut down. Too many students and their families were murdered in the attack."

197

I shook my head as Zhealocera's words sunk in. I could not believe things had gotten so bad.

"So what about you? What sort of adventures have I missed out on since last we met?"

"More like attempts against my life," I said sourly.

I sat in a seat across from Zhealocera and began to divulge everything that had happened since the Rising of Zahadu-Kitai. It took me over an hour to fill her in on everything. Once I had finished, she stared at me in obvious astonishment.

"Gods! I wish I could go with you on your quest." Zhealocera sighed. "Alas, I cannot."

"Why not?" I frowned. "We could really use you."

"Freya left me with an important mission. It will take me quite some time to complete it."

Kitfox's ears perked up. "Freya was here?"

Zhealocera nodded. "Here and gone."

Kitfox's ears drooped, and he muttered something.

"What mission did she leave you with?"

She regarded me carefully. "I am to gather an army of Dákun Daju to join the fight against Agasei's heir."

My breath caught at this news.

"Freya is off gathering Demons. And the gods only know where Amorez keeps herself."

Thera smiled. "Knowing her, she's gathering the Feykin. Needless to say, after the trick Dimitri pulled on my people, it will be easy to sway them to join us."

"So the world's races are uniting for the first time in centuries." Teka's happy laughter was contagious. "I can't wait to see that."

"I agree. I just wish it would be under better circumstances than the ones we face," Zhealocera said and covered a yawn.

It must have been well past midnight, I realized.

"I hate to say it, but I'm ready to pass out."

"I'm already asleep," Kitfox mumbled, making me laugh.

"When can we meet with your cousin the queen?" I asked. "Freya told us to get in touch with her."

"Shazza will have retired for tonight. So in the morning at the breakfast table you will meet her."

"Is there anything in particular I should know before I meet her? I'd hate to accidentally insult her."

"Shazza is as forgiving on others as I am. You don't need to worry." Zhealocera got to her feet and stretched. "Come on. I will show you to some rooms where you can spend the night in comfort. It sounds like you have been lacking that recently."

I smacked Kitfox on the arm to wake him. He growled lightly and glared at me, earning a laugh from Zhealocera. She ducked out of the room through the gilded door with the four of us right behind her. We followed her up a few flights of stairs and down a long hallway until she stopped between two sets of doors.

"These four rooms are open. I will tell the maids that you will be spending the night. They will supply you with some fresh garments and blankets. Sleep well, friends."

I watched as Zhealocera walked briskly away before I opened one of the doors. A huge stateroom was on the other side. With an exhausted sigh, I stepped in and threw myself on the bed. Sleep quickly overtook my mind.

Believe it or not, the quest wasn't the hardest thing I have ever had to do. No; the hardest thing was keeping the team together for nearly two years. Not an easy thing when they are different races who all want to kill each other.

– FROM "CONVERSATIONS WITH AMOREZ"
BY DJURDAK ZA'CAR

"Xy! Xy! Wake up, you lazy lump of dung!"

I groaned and rolled over. I felt the bed shift as someone crawled into it. The owner of the voice started shaking me in the attempt to force me awake.

"Xy. Xy. Xy! Wake up, Xy! Xy!"

"Oh, shut up already!" I grabbed the arm of the person shaking me and gave a good yank.

With a loud yelp, the owner of the arm rolled over me and hit something with a loud thud. An object fell to the floor and shattered. I sighed contently and rolled onto my other side. An instant later, a body was on top of me, pinning me to the bed with a fierce growl

"Wake up!"

My eyes burst open at the angry snarl. Kitfox humphed triumphantly and started tickling me. I squirmed and begged for him to stop.

"Oh, no! This is revenge for throwing me into the nightstand!"

"I'm sorry!" Tears welled in my eyes from laughing so hard as I fought against his tickling.

With a sigh, he finally stopped his torture and rolled off me. I caught my breath before I looked at him.

"You are evil."

He smirked. "In its purest form."

"You might want to work on it," I muttered and sat up on my elbows. "I think Dimitri has you beat in the evil department."

Kitfox snorted. "You got me there." He finally crawled out of bed and turned to stare at me. "Hurry up and get out of bed, you lazy lump. We have a queen to meet, remember?"

"Why were you the one to wake me up?"

"Teka and Thera were too scared. Now that you've thrown me into the nightstand, I know why." He chuckled. "You're scary."

I laughed. "Okay. I see your point."

"I'll see you at breakfast." He waved and strode from the room. With a content sigh, I flung the blankets off me and prepared for the day.

Thera, Kitfox, and Zhealocera were already at the breakfast table enjoying a wide variety of delicacies when I finally found the room. I thanked the maid who had escorted me and joined my friends at the table.

"I heard you gave Kitfox quite a beating when he tried to wake you."

I blushed at Zhealocera's words, making Kitfox burst out laughing.

"Who are your friends, Zhealocera-byö?" A gentle voice came from the door.

I looked over my shoulder to see who had spoken. It was a Dákun Daju woman with lime-green hair done up in a bun with tails that fell over her shoulders. Brilliant orange eyes fixed on me for a moment before looking at the others. She wore a remarkably simple dress adorned with minimal gold armor.

Zhealocera got to her feet with a smile. "Shazza, may I introduce you to Xyleena Renoan, the Dragon Keeper, and her teammates, Kitfox Latreyon and Thera Onyx. Everyone, this is my cousin, Shazza Hoshino, the queen of Katalania."

"It is an honor to meet you," I said as I rose to my feet. I bowed then raised my head to expose my throat in the customary Dákun Daju greeting.

"So you are the one we've been waiting for. Lady Freya said something about you coming to see me."

"So why did Freya want us to meet exactly?" I asked.

Shazza shrugged and strode to the table. "I was told you would know the reason when you arrived."

"Helios sings to free his light. Past the dead long lost must you fight." Thera announced, stealing the attention of the entire room. "Freya's note in the diary said to seek out the royal Dákun Daju and pointed to those lines. I'm guessing that you know the location the clue is referring to."

"The dead long lost, you say?"

Thera nodded.

"Interesting riddle."

"You have to solve riddles for each dragon?" Zhealocera stared blankly at me.

"Yeah, after converting the riddle from a language so old no one speaks it anymore," I explained.

The queen cupped her chin in thought.

"The riddle could be referring to the Tomb of the Lost," Shazza said. "It is a hidden tomb for unnamed Dákun Daju warriors lost to an ancient war."

"And you know where it is, don't you? That's why Freya told me to find you."

Shazza smiled at me. "Exactly."

"How far away is this tomb?" Kitfox asked.

"Far northeast of here. Probably over a month's worth of travel by wyvern."

"That is going to be a rough trip," Kitfox sighed, closing his eyes as if to remember something. "Northeast of here are mountains, thick forests, part of the fault line, and open plains."

"What about sailing there?"

"The coastline is littered with sharp rocks and shallows," Shazza explained. "No ship could pass safely."

Thera sighed. "And Teka's crew is eager to return to their families in Sindai. That is why she is with them instead of here with us. I doubt she can persuade them to continue on this voyage. Sorry, Xy, but it looks as though it's down to just the three of us now."

I shrugged. "I can understand the yearning for family. If they really want to return, I say let them."

"Okay, so we're taking it by wyvern?" Thera asked.

Shazza nodded. "I will set up everything. After breakfast, I will lead you to the Tomb of the Lost. Until then you are welcome to rest here."

"Wait a second," I gawked at the queen, "you're going to lead us there?"

Shazza nodded. "The Tomb of the Lost is sacred Dákun Daju ground. I must go with to ensure that the spirits of the fallen are not enraged by the appearance of non-kin."

"Thank you, Shazza-sortim." I bowed to her as she turned to leave the room.

"I will be leaving after breakfast as well," Zhealocera said.

I sat down and looked at her across the table.

"Now that I know you are here and where you will be heading, I have to begin my mission to amass the Dákun Daju against Dimitri."

"I wish you the best of luck and hope you have a safe journey, Zhealocera." I raised a glass of juice to her.

She smiled and raised her own glass. "And I wish you the same, Xyleena-sortim. May we meet again in the face of victory."

We drank long drafts.

It was almost midday when Kitfox, Thera, and I were summoned to the castle stables. Shazza was already there, dressed in the more traditional Dákun Daju garb of light armor and leathers. She was saddling up seven gold wyverns while giving an aid a list of instructions to be completed while she was absent from the capital. Finally, she turned to greet us with a smile.

"These are some of the fastest wyverns in the whole of Katalania. They should get us to the Tomb of the Lost without any trouble." She thumped one of the wyverns on the shoulder and tightened the riding straps. "I trust you all know how to ride."

"I prefer to run," Kitfox muttered and crossed his arms.

Shazza smiled over her shoulder at him. "As do I. But even Dákun Daju and Demons get tired."

"Why are there seven of them?" Thera asked as she reached out to stroke the eye ridges of one of the wyverns.

It cried in delight and licked her arm.

"Zhealocera-byö will be taking two of them on her journey, and we will

---

take the other five." Shazza dug a scroll from one of the packs bound to the saddle of a wyvern. She unrolled it on a portion of the fence to show us the map of Katalania. "We will circle Preséo Lake and head straight north until we reach the cliffs that mark Zarconia's Fault." Her finger pointed at every landmark she named off. "Once we've passed the cliffs, we turn slightly east and follow the peninsula to the very tip. That is where we will find the Tomb of the Lost."

"The cliffs will be the hardest part of this little venture," said Kitfox. "I hope you packed a lot of rope."

"Do not fret over the supplies, Demon. I have everything covered." Shazza returned the scroll to the pack and thumped the wyvern affectionately.

"So when do we leave?" I asked, placing a hand on Kitfox's arm to silence his growl.

"Right now," Shazza said as she mounted a wyvern. "Zhealocera-byö will leave on her own once she has returned from informing Teka of your leave."

"Okay." I nodded and hopped into the saddle of another wyvern.

Kitfox sighed and took the reins of another before giving them to me.

"What ar– "

"I will run." He winked at me and smiled.

I sighed.

"You really should ride the wyvern," Thera asserted as she mounted up.

Kitfox rolled his eyes.

"Don't complain when we leave you in the dust," Shazza said as she urged her wyvern forward.

Thera and I followed a moment later. Kitfox jogged beside us until we reached the gate. The guards bowed to their queen and quickly unlocked the gate. Kitfox bolted ahead of us, and I watched in shock as his form shifted into the shape of a lavender-and-black fox. He stopped a ways ahead and turned to look at us. I could almost see the smugness in his amber eyes.

"Okay, I was not expecting that." I laughed and urged my wyvern to follow him.

Thera whooped and took off after me. Shazza was soon to follow.

By the end of the first day, we were already at the foothills of the Ahgberor Mountains. Shazza pulled her wyvern to a stop just after Aruvan disappeared behind the snowcapped mountains. Thera and I helped her set up camp for the night, while Kitfox hunted. He returned in his near-Hume form shortly after we had gotten a fire roaring.

"I am impressed you managed to keep up, Demon," Shazza said.

Kitfox snorted and dropped the five birds he had caught at her feet. She glared down at him.

"Don't for one second mistake me for a weakling." He growled and walked away.

After a moment, Shazza grinned at his back. I sighed in relief. It looked as though they were finally getting along.

We woke early the next morning and packed up camp quickly. Once again, Kitfox refused to ride a wyvern and took off in his fox form. We managed to catch up to him when we reached the road that ran from Aissur to Puukan. He allowed Shazza to take the lead after that.

Four more days passed in pretty much the same fashion. On noon the fifth day, we reached the cliffs Shazza had warned us about. We spent the rest of the day thinking of a way to ascend the sheer faces.

On the morning on the sixth day, we began the dangerous climb up the cliffs. Kitfox made it look easy as he bounded from rocky ledge to rocky ledge in his fox form. Thera and Shazza had an easier time than I did when it came to leaping from rock to rock. Agitated and frustrated at being left behind, I finally broke down and used a spell to levitate myself and my wyvern to the top of the cliffs. Kitfox joined me at the top a few minutes later and peered over the edge to watch the others.

"I shouldn't have used that spell," I mumbled groggily.

Kitfox looked back at me and wagged his tail sympathetically.

"Wyverns are heavier than they look. I'm tired now." I yawned.

An instant later the near-Hume form of Kitfox sat down beside me. He sighed and rubbed my shoulders. "It was better than being left behind by those two. I never realized just how much alike Feykin and Dákun Daju are."

"Hmm." I closed my eyes and leaned into his shoulder.

He chuckled slightly and wrapped his arm and tail about us. I do not know how long I dozed, but Kitfox woke me when Shazza and Thera reached the top of the cliffs. The nap refreshed me enough to continue on riding for a few more hours. At nightfall, we finally set up our camp.

The seventh day saw fit to drench us in rain from sunup to sundown. We set up camp early that night and tried in vain to dry off around the fire. That night was the first night I spent curled up next to Kitfox. His fluffy lavender tail proved to keep me warmer than my blankets.

I awoke the next morning to Kitfox's light snores and his arm draped over my waist. He looked so adorable when he slept that I almost did not want to wake him. But when his amber eyes fluttered open and focused on me, I could not help but smile at his blush.

The sky was grey again that day, and the winds slowed us down greatly. Shazza finally gave in to the brutal weather and set up camp well before evening. That night I prayed to the gods to give us good weather for the rest of our Katalanian trek.

Amazingly, the next three days were sunny and warm. We easily managed to make up for the time lost during the storm. Nonetheless, I was eager to reach the end of our journey.

It was late in the evening on the fourteenth day when we came across the first grave marker. Shazza immediately slowed her wyvern down. We progressed slowly as the gravestones grew more and more cluttered.

"Be careful here. Bandits frequent the area to rob the graves," Shazza said as she pulled a contraption from the pack on her wyvern.

With a click, the item unfolded to become a highly decorated bow. Shazza then shouldered a quiver of arrows and knocked one.

"I thought Dákun Daju always fought with close-range weapons," Thera said.

Shazza glanced over her shoulder. "Not always."

Kitfox yipped, effectively capturing our attention. An ancient iron gate loomed on the path before us. Its metal was twisted into dangerous spikes that conveyed the message, "Keep out." Behind the gate stood even more gravestones– some damaged, others worn by wind and time. Several bleached bones littered the ground.

Shazza slipped out of her saddle and strode to the gate. With a gentle push, it screeched open on rusty hinges. She looked back at us. "Tie the wyverns up here. The path beyond is too narrow for them."

"And hope no one gets the urge to steal them," Kitfox muttered as he transformed back into his near-Hume form. He sniffed the air and growled slightly.

"What do you smell?" I asked as I tied my wyvern to a part of the fence.

He faced me with a grim expression. "Death."

I nodded in understanding and freed my tessens from my belt. Thera muttered the spell to summon her staff. Then the four of us passed through the gate.

"Does anybody know who is buried here?" Thera asked, attempting to read the names on the gravestones.

We walked in silence amidst the graves before Shazza answered.

"Most of those buried here are Dákun Daju warriors lost to a war predating the Earthic Landing. However, I'd wager some other races have laid their dead to rest within these grounds."

"I hope their souls aren't angry at us for treading this holy ground," I said quietly.

Shazza sighed and looked at me over her shoulder. "You're a Priestess?"

I nodded in answer.

She shook her head and walked on.

"What's wrong with being a Priestess?" Kitfox asked quietly.

"Nothing. Just a pointless occupation."

"To you."

"Stop it, both of you," Thera snapped. "Xy, can you feel Helios yet?"

"Hang on." I closed my eyes and focused on the nine remaining pulls I felt from the dragons. One was far stronger than the others… and close by. I slowly nodded and opened my eyes. "Follow me."

I led the others around the headstones at a brisk pace. After a few minutes, we arrived at the sealed door to an ancient tomb. A black dragon stood guard over the door, and I knew I was in the right place.

"Yeow. That stone slab has to weigh, what? Five tons?" Kitfox said as he ran his hand over the door's surface.

"It is far too heavy for me to levitate with magic," I said and looked at Thera.

She shook her head.

"I don't think I can move it either, but let me try."

Lightning crashed overhead. We both looked up at the darkening sky as thunder rolled.

"Terrific."

"Give it a shot, Thera," Shazza said as she backed away slightly.

The young Feykin nodded and cast the spell. A spark of light bounced off the tomb a second later. Nothing else happened.

"What does that mean?"

Thera looked at me then at Shazza. "There is a ward protecting the tomb. No magic can be used on or within it."

"I love this place," Kitfox muttered. His ears went flat against his head and he growled as rain began to fall.

The four of us quickly set up a shelter and camped beneath it as we tried to come up with an idea to move the stone slab.

About an hour had passed when Kitfox suddenly smacked himself in the forehead. "We are such idiots!"

"What?"

"We are?"

"Speak for yourself, Demon."

Kitfox looked at me with a sigh. "Xy, just summon a dragon to move the slab."

I groaned. Why hadn't I thought of that before? I stepped out into the rain and brushed my fingers over the jewel marking Kkaia's presence in the amulet. A warming sensation crawled up my arm as I threw my hand in the air.

"Kkaia!"

Golden-brown light exploded from the dragon eye. Sand and pebbles flowed out of the amulet and amassed into the form of the dragon of earth. Kkaia roared upon her revival.

"Amazing!" Shazza whispered as she gawked at the dragon.

Kitfox snickered. "Wait until you see her other ones."

"Kkaia, can you move the stone slab that seals the tomb?" I asked as I thumped her foreleg.

She looked down at me then at the tomb. With a snort, she raised her front paw to the stone slab. The instant she touched it a shock of energy blasted through her frame, causing her to loose a pained and furious roar.

"No good," Thera said with a disappointed sigh.

"Dark magic protects this tomb. You would need either Abaddon or a Necromancer to break through it," Kkaia said as she licked her front paw.

Kitfox sighed. "We don't have either of those."

"Thank you for trying, Kkaia."

I watched as she nodded and faded into her element. Sand and rocks swirled around me before reentering the eye.

I turned to look at my team. "Any other suggestions?"

"Know any Necromancers?" Shazza looked at Thera for an answer.

I, however, watched as Kitfox examined the tomb more closely.

"Plenty, but they are all back in Thorna."

"That rules that out." Shazza sighed. "Who or what is Abaddon, anyway?"

"Amorez's dragon of death," I said over my shoulder. I turned my attention back to Kitfox as he jumped to the top of the tomb and stood beside the dragon statue. "Well, I guess the dragon would belong to me now."

"Aha!" Kitfox exclaimed and ducked behind the statue. A moment later, I heard a loud click. Then the slow scraping of stone over stone reached my ears. Kitfox leaped to the ground as the stone slab slowly sunk into the earth.

The Fox Demon looked at me over his shoulder. "I, uh, found the doorknob."

I clapped him on the shoulder and laughed as the slab disappeared with a loud thud. "Good job."

"Well then…" Shazza stood and re-knocked an arrow. "Let's get going."

Thera quickly fabricated some torches and lit them with her magic. I took one and led the way over the threshold. Together, we plunged into the Tomb of the Lost.

The light from our torches scattered the darkness as we descended an ancient stone stairwell. The air in the tomb was clammy and reeked of decay. The farther we plunged into the tomb, the more pungent the smell got. I could barely breathe as the stairs leveled out into a narrow corridor. Each side of the passageway was lined with skeletons stuffed into countless recesses.

I shuddered. Kitfox gently laid a hand on my shoulder and smiled as I looked at him. With this small comfort, I pushed myself onward. After several meters, the passageway forked left. A sickly green mist crept along the soggy floor as I led the way past the corner. My instincts told me not to go that way.

"What is that light?" Kitfox whispered in my ear and pointed toward the end of the corridor.

An ethereal light glimmered in midair. For each step we took toward it, the light moved away a pace.

After several meters the corridor widened into a round room. The strange light floated at the opposite end where an angry-looking iron gate guarded the next portion of the corridor. I took one step into the round room, and the light sank to the floor and vanished with a puff of smoke.

"What was that all about?" I heard Thera mutter as I dared to venture farther into the room.

Like the rest of the tomb, the walls here were lined with skeletons, some of which had fallen from their recesses to litter the ground.

"Living mortals at last have come to this place where all is numb."

I froze midstride as the gruff whisper reached my ears. I flared one of my tessens and scanned the room. Excluding my team, the tomb was void of life.

"So…it wasn't just me who heard that voice, right?" Shazza whispered as she too scanned the room.

"What the– " Kitfox pointed toward the gate.

The smoke the strange light had left behind swirled and danced, forming an apparition. A moment later the form solidified into the last creature I ever expected to see.

"A sphinx," I whispered.

It had giant wings that looked as though they were taken from an eagle. Its body was that of a lion, and a tail curled about its four clawed feet. The head of a black-haired woman stared straight at us, its eyes teeming with a mix of curiosity and wisdom.

"Oh, this isn't going to be good," Thera said, bringing her staff before her as if it were a shield.

"In hopes to pass my riddle gate, do you dare to test your luck at fate?" The sphinx slowly looked at each of us as it spoke. "Answer right, my test of four, to pass through this iron door. Answer wrong and here you'll lie with this gate forever nigh."

"What does it want?" Shazza asked, her voice thick with annoyance.

"We have to solve its riddles to get past it. Four riddles, one for each of us. Answer wrong and it will kill us."

Kitfox smirked and took a step toward the creature.

"All right, Sphinx, I'll play your little game."

"I don't think that is such a great idea, Kitfox," I said and grabbed his arm.

"I for one do not want to rest my fate so firmly in the hands of a Demon."

Thankfully, Kitfox chose to ignore Shazza. He looked at me with a gentle smile. "Don't worry, Xy. Freya and I used to toss riddles back and forth all the time, so I've had quite a bit of practice." He looked at the sphinx and nodded. "All right, what is your first riddle?"

The creature's eyes swirled with red light as it took a breath. "I welcome the day with a show of light. I stealthily came here in the night. I bathe the earthy stuff at dawn, but by the noon, alas! I'm gone."

Kitfox chuckled. "Too easy, Sphinx. The answer is the morning dew."

The sphinx was quiet for a moment, brooding. "One shall pass and three remain to play my game once again."

"What is your second riddle?"

"Always wax, yet always wane, I melt and succumb to the flame. Lighting darkness with fate unblessed, I soon devolve to shapeless mess."

Kitfox was quiet for a moment, long enough that I began to worry. Finally, a smile crept over his lips. "The answer is a candle."

"Two are free. Save two more. Then all shall pass through my door."

I breathed a sigh of relief at the sphinx's words.

"No legs have I to dance. No lungs have I to breathe. No life have I to live or die. And yet I do all three."

Kitfox bit his bottom lip as he thought. He suddenly snapped his fingers and looked into the sphinx's eyes. "The answer is fire."

"One remains to save all four. Does he who speaks still want more?"

Kitfox laughed. "You bet I do."

A menacing grin etched its way across the sphinx's face, and I got a sudden sinking feeling.

The sphinx took a breath. "With potent, flowery words speak I of something common, vulgar, dry. I weave webs of pedantic prose in effort to befuddle those who think I wile time away in lofty things above all day. The common kind that linger where monadic beings live and fare. Practical I may not be, but life, it seems, is full of me!"

Kitfox winced as the sphinx's words died away. He swore silently and turned away from the sphinx to think. I glanced at the creature, the wicked look still plastered on its face as it sat there.

"You," I whispered.

The sphinx tilted its head, the smug look completely drained from its face.

"The answer is you, a riddle."

The sphinx hissed and vanished in a puff of smoke. The gate to the next portion of the corridor creaked open.

Kitfox laughed and hugged me. "You are brilliant!"

"Um...guys? I hate to crush the good mood, but I think we should be running now!" Thera exclaimed as she pushed passed Kitfox and me.

We glanced back at the corridor we had just come from to see the sickly green mist filtering into the room. And with it came a horde of armed skeletons.

"Time to go!" I shouted and quickly turned on my heel.

The four of us bolted through the gate and tried to seal it, but the mist reached us before we had the chance. We sprinted down several meters of crumbling corridor. The clamor of the skeleton soldiers echoed off the walls, and I knew they were gaining on us.

The corridor came to an abrupt end. I swore and spun around to face our enemies. Kitfox quickly began to search the bricks, while Thera, Shazza, and I prepared to fight the army of undead rapidly approaching.

An arrow split the air between us, narrowly missing Kitfox as it dug into the wall. Shazza wasted no time in firing an arrow in return and knocking another. Her arrow embedded into the sternum of a skeleton but did nothing to phase it. Thera tried a spell but only succeeded in creating sparks that slowly sank to the floor.

"Hurry, Kitfox!" I shouted as I dodged a spear. "We won't stand a chance against those things if they get any closer!"

"One second!"

"At this rate we might not have that long!" Shazza hissed and fired another arrow.

This one plunged deep into the eye socket of a skeleton. A moment later, it collapsed and did not move again.

"I can't...reach!" Kitfox hissed.

Suddenly a loud click echoed in the corridor. I glanced behind us in time to see the wall shift to the side. Another corridor lay beyond– this one much narrower than our current one. The stone door slowly began to move back.

"Move! Move! Move!" I shouted.

Kitfox lead the way; Thera followed. Shazza slipped in behind me just in time to avoid being crushed as the wall sealed itself.

"That was way too close," Thera gasped as we took a minute to catch our breath.

"Makes you wonder," Kitfox said between breaths, "just how in the names of the Five Souls we are supposed to get out of here."

I groaned. "I really hate you for saying that."

He grimaced. "Sorry."

"Okay, let's move on before those undead learn how to open that door," Shazza muttered. "We'll figure a way out of this place as soon as we get this dragon."

After a moment more of resting, the four of us began our trek through the cramped passageway.

The constricting passageway continued for several meters until it finally emptied out into a gargantuan room. A crumbling stone bridge lay before us, stretching over a vast chasm. The sickly green mist swirled and rolled and almost boiled as it churned in the chasm. My eyes followed the bridge to an island of ragged stone at the very center of the room. A grim-looking ancient citadel sat atop the island, and a brilliant white light radiated downward from the top.

"There! That has to be Helios!" I pointed toward the light.

"Fantastic," Shazza muttered. "Just how do we get all the way up there?"

"Simple. We walk," Kitfox said as he took the first step out onto the bridge. He hesitated a moment to see if the bridge would hold. When it did nothing, he took another few steps. "I think it's safe."

I nodded and took a few steps after him. Shazza sighed and took a slow step out. Thera, on the other hand, took flight and hovered close by. The four of us slowly advanced on the citadel. More than once a piece of the bridge gave out and plummeted into the green mist.

Roughly halfway to the island, the bridge dipped and disappeared into the mist. I watched in horror as skeletons spawned into existence within the sickly, twisting fog. The instant they were within range, they attacked.

"What do we do now?" Shazza shouted as she fired two arrows into the horde of skeletons.

"Duck!" Thera cried as she swooped down low.

She used her staff to bowl through the skeletons, knocking them out of the way to clear a path. Without a second thought, I sprinted after her. Kitfox was instantly behind me, and Shazza followed a heartbeat later.

We ran as fast as we could to escape the mist and the undead army it spawned. After a good five hundred meters, we burst out of the mist, coughing and sputtering. We slowed to catch our breath only after we were certain the undead were no longer chasing us.

"I am never coming here again," Kitfox managed between coughs.

I chuckled and wholeheartedly agreed with him.

"Come on. Let's get this cursed dragon so we can be done with this place," Shazza grumbled and knocked another arrow as she marched onward.

I sighed and followed with Kitfox.

We trudged along the remaining portion of the bridge in silence. At long last, we stood at the base of the dreary citadel. I craned my neck to see the apex and the white light that burned there. I followed a stairway that wound its way around the girth of the citadel from top to bottom. Though some of the stairs were damaged or missing, the way up looked sturdy.

My attention was stolen by a low growl. I looked to Kitfox. He looked back at me, his face contorted in fear. He swallowed and slowly looked over his shoulder. I followed his gaze and gasped.

A great rotting beast glared at us with glowing green eyes. It snarled, revealing sharp teeth, and took a step toward us. Pieces of dangling, putrid flesh swayed to and fro at the movement.

"Here we go again," I said softly as I slowly inched away from the dire beast.

"Get to the stairs," Kitfox whispered as he moved to stand between the beast and me. "Go. Now."

"Not without you." I grabbed his arm.

He smiled at me over his shoulder but kept his eyes on the beast. "I'll be right behind you."

I nodded and turned away to lead Shazza and Thera up the stairs. The beast roared. I glanced back in time to see it tackle Kitfox to the ground. I screamed his name.

"Run!"

"He can handle it!"

Shazza yanked my arm, while Thera shoved me. Together they half dragged me up the stairs. I took another glance back at Kitfox to see that he had morphed into his fox form and was leading the dire beast away from us.

"Stay ahead of it, Kitfox. I'll come back to save you," I whispered. I broke free of Shazza's grip and sprinted up the stairwell as fast as I could.

Several hundred meters above the base of the citadel Kitfox suddenly sprang onto the stairs in front of me and slumped. He lay there, whimpering from a deep wound that ran the length of his body. I cried as I picked him up and cradled him in my arms. Filled with anger and desperation, I ran on.

The dire beast was hot on our heels when the stairs finally ended. The apex was empty, save for a white glowing crystal in the center. Shazza swore as she and Thera turned to face the beast. I fell to my knees.

Hugging Kitfox close to me, I cried out, "Helios!"

The white light exploded. It washed over the citadel like a raging torrent, turning the beast to dust. An instant later, the light faded away, leaving only a regal white dragon where the crystal once stood.

Helios's blue eyes focused on me, and the dragon bowed. "Well met, Keeper Xyleena."

I completely ignored the dragon, choosing instead to devote my attention Kitfox as he whimpered weakly.

"Don't you dare die on me, Kitfox." I sobbed.

Thera knelt in front of me and let her hands hover over Kitfox's wound. A moment later, her hands glowed with golden energy.

"Medícté!" The cry of her spell echoed in the colossal room.

Seconds passed like hours as the spell began to take its effect. Slowly but surely the wound running the length of Kitfox's body healed. Thera moved her hands away with a sigh. Kitfox's amber eyes fluttered open, and he yipped. I hugged him even tighter, making him grunt.

"I hate you."

I laughed as he licked my tears away. I finally released him from the hug. He took a few steps and morphed back to his near-Hume form.

"I hate you, too." Kitfox smiled and rubbed his side.

Shazza walked up behind him and smacked him soundly with her bow. He swore loudly and clutched the back of his head.

"What were you thinking, you idiot? That thing almost killed you!"

"You don't say? I never would have known that without you here to explain it to me!"

"Those two seem to be getting along fine," Helios said flatly.

I sighed and turned my attention to the dragon.

"I am never coming here again."

The dragon snorted at my outburst.

"Ever!"

"I can't say that I blame you." Helios sat on his haunches and glanced about his surroundings. "This place makes the punishment pits of Havel look like paradise."

"Hey, dragon, explain something to me!" Kitfox strode right up to Helios and stared him down. "How in the names of the Five Souls do we get out of this place?"

Shazza crossed her arms. "I am more curious to know how it is Thera can suddenly use magic again. I thought the ward placed on the tomb prevented it."

"Uh…the…um…the crystal was the ward," Thera stammered. "As soon as it shattered, I felt the ward lift. And it didn't shatter until after Xy broke it by summoning Helios."

"As for leaving this tomb, it is much easier than entering it," Helios said. "This citadel's apex is a special platform that will lift all those atop it to the surface with but the uttering of a simple spell." Helios looked at Thera. "I believe you know the one to which I am referring."

Thera thought about it for a moment then smiled. "Anybody want to vacation here? No? Good. Let's go!"

She uttered the spell, and the platform rumbled, shook, and then slowly rose.

> I watched as the triplets – now merely a great mess of pitted bones and tattered ligaments– began to stir. And then, with a horrid cry, the undead rose again; an invincible force from whom the living would suffer.
>
> – FROM "AN ONLOOKER'S JOURNAL"
> BY THERNU ONYX

Warm sunlight, fresh air, and the annoying buzzing at the back of my head that signaled the presence of the three dragons– when these three things fell into place, I cheered. We were finally free of that wretched tomb! Kitfox, Thera, and Shazza all laughed at me, but I could tell they were just as happy to get out of there as I was.

Thank Khatahn-Rhii you are safe!

We were so worried when we felt you disappear, hatchling.

What happened in the tomb?

I scratched my ear and shook my head as all three dragons spoke at once. They continued to rant while I got my bearings. We may have made it out of the Tomb of the Lost, but we were still in the cemetery surrounding it. I sighed. Relax. Everyone is fine. The tomb was a nightmare, but we made it out, Helios included.

"You okay?" Kitfox asked, helping me off the platform as it finally came to a complete stop.

I pointed to my head with a smile. "Dragons."

Kitfox rolled his eyes at my answer.

"They were worried, huh?" Shazza inquired as she watched Helios step off the platform.

"Oh! Immensely."

We heard that! Atoka snorted indignantly.

I giggled. I know.

Are we wrong to fret over you, hatchling?

No, Vortex. But laughing is the best way to relax after such a stressful– I froze when Kitfox stopped suddenly and sniffed the air. "What is it?"

Kitfox turned his head and continued to sniff the air. Then he looked at me. "I recognize this scent, but I can't remember where."

"Is it Dimitri?"

"How could he have followed us here?" Thera asked.

I shrugged and kept my eyes on Kitfox.

"No. No, it's not Dimitri." Kitfox breathed in deep. "It smells Hume, though."

"Maybe a bandit here to rob the graves?" Thera offered.

Shazza quickly knocked an arrow. "If it is a bandit, I will skewer him and feed his guts to the undead!"

"Do not be so hasty," Helios muttered and sat on his haunches. "The intruder could be an innocent bystander."

"Right," I muttered and flared my tessens. "Forgive me for being a bit paranoid. You see, I have this Shadow Keeper following me around, trying to kill me."

Helios snorted. Kitfox growled and sunk low to the ground. He crept his way across the ground without a sound, making it at least five meters before he dropped behind a grave marker. There, he waited. A moment later, he pounced. A man screamed in surprise and swore. Minutes passed to the sounds of a scuffle in the dirt. Finally, Kitfox reappeared, dragging a blonde man unceremoniously over the ground.

"Oi! Come on, mate! I did not mean anything by it! Lemme go!"

I watched as Kitfox threw the blonde man into a headstone and pinned him there.

"What are you doing here, Kkorian?" Kitfox snarled as he rested his claws against the man's throat.

"Take it easy there, Kitfox. You know I don't mean any harm."

"Do I? Last time I saw you, you were all buddy-buddy at the bar with the Hume-aju who's been trying to kill me and my friend over there." Kitfox jerked his head in my direction. "Why should I trust you?"

"Crikey, mate! You think I liked that whacka? I was just being nice to him since he bought me a few rounds. I swear it!"

"You left with him!"

"Sure. We left at the same time, but I do not know where he went. I haven't seen him since that night!"

Kitfox snarled.

"Okay! Okay! I lied! I have seen him. He's with a hot little Dákun Daju sheila somewhere near here."

"What?" Kitfox dropped the man and leaped to the tallest tomb he could find.

"Bloody, stupid mongrel," the blonde mumbled as he got to his feet and dusted himself off. He picked his hat from the ground and dropped it on his head before looking around. His blue eyes fell on me, and he cleared his throat.

"So...you two know each other?" Shazza asked.

The blonde glared up at Kitfox. "Aye. And I wish I didn't!"

A moment later, the Fox Demon landed on him and pinned him to the ground.

"I didn't see anyone." Kitfox rested his claws at the blonde's throat again. "You better come up with a reason for me to keep you alive real quick."

"Stand down, Kitfox!" Helios shouted.

Kitfox growled and looked up at the white dragon.

"I sense no evil in this man."

"Yeah! Listen to the bloke, you dumb bitzer!"

Kitfox snorted and slowly let the blonde up.

"You had better be right, Helios," the Fox Demon muttered as he moved to join me.

"Thanks...mate." The blonde's eyes practically exploded from his skull at the sight of the dragon.

Helios chuckled and bowed his head.

"What do we call you?" I asked as I folded my tessens and returned them to my belt.

The blonde just stared at Helios wide eyed.

"His name is Kkorian McKnight. He is a failed pirate, so you cannot believe a word that he says," Kitfox said and crossed his arms.

"There's a difference between a failed pirate and a broke one, mate." Kkorian finally came out of his stupor and got to his feet. "How'd you get the dragon?"

"We outsmarted a sphinx and fought off countless undead in a tomb far beneath your feet until we reached the citadel where I had hidden him a little over a century ago."

I chuckled when Kkorian's jaw fell slack.

"Just another normal day in the life of a Dragon Keeper."

Thera burst out laughing. "You call that normal?"

Shazza snickered. "I'd hate to see it when you are busy."

"Let me get this straight in me head. You"– Kkorian pointed at me– "are the Dragon Keeper. And you have a member from every race helping you? How did you pull that off?"

I shrugged. "It just worked out that way."

"The suns will be setting soon, young ones," Helios said as he got to all fours. "I think it is best not to linger here after dark."

"Yeah, I would like to leave the cemetery. I think I've seen enough of one to last me several lifetimes," Thera complained and took the lead as we meandered our way through the graves.

"Hey, wait a just tic!" Kkorian grabbed my arm to get my attention and earned a fierce growl from Kitfox.

I put my hand on the Fox Demon's shoulder to calm him as I looked at Kkorian. "What did you want?"

"I was just wondering if I can come with you."

I frowned. "I don't know…"

"Are you kidding?" Shazza laughed and punched Kkorian in the arm, making him grimace in pain. "Anyone who can so easily get on the nerves of that Demon is well worth having on the team."

Kitfox bared his teeth at Shazza before looking me in the eye. "Don't accept him, Xy. We can't trust him."

"But Helios said there isn't any evil in Kkorian's heart. And since he's a pirate, I think he could be a valuable member to this team," Thera said.

Kkorian faced her with a happy albeit lopsided grin. "Thanks, sheila!"

"What's a… sheila?"

The pirate guffawed.

"Girl." Kitfox said flatly. "He means girl. The idiot speaks with words no one else knows."

I nodded and looked Kkorian in the eye. "I'll think about your request for now. You'll have my answer in the morning, Kkorian." I walked away.

Kitfox sighed and followed after me. "Please, Xy. Don't bring him on."

"I haven't decided anything yet." I looked up at him. "Because you saw him with Dimitri and therefore don't trust him, neither do I."

Kitfox nodded and draped his arm around my shoulder as we continued to walk. "I never did thank you for saving me back there."

"You mean when that beast nearly killed you?"

He blushed and nodded.

"I still hate you for that, by the way."

He chuckled. "Yeah."

We followed the path between the graves in silence, listening as Shazza and Thera filled Kkorian in on the day's adventure. We reached the main gate of the cemetery just as the suns kissed the horizon. I watched, bemused, as Helios bounded over the gate before I passed through it.

"Where are our wyverns?" Shazza demanded.

Everyone instantly rounded on Kkorian.

He raised his hands in defense. "I swear I didn't touch them!"

"Yeah rig– " Kitfox froze and sniffed the air. With a growl, he turned and jumped onto Helios' back and scanned the surrounding land. He groaned in defeat. "There they go, ridden by you-know-who and his gang."

Thera spread her wings and took flight only to land on the highest point of the gate. Shazza soon joined her, using her Dákun Daju height and strength to boost her to the top. I frowned, wishing for the same vantage point. Helios's tail suddenly snaked around me and lifted me up so that I was beside Kitfox. The Fox Demon held me steady and showed me where to look.

"Yup, that's them." I sighed. "Great."

"It is going to be a long walk back to Kamédan," Shazza muttered.

"Why walk?" Helios looked at me over his shoulder. "You have four dragons to ride."

I stared at Helios, dumbfounded, as the others whooped.

"I never even thought of that."

Kitfox chuckled and squeezed my shoulders. "Don't worry, Xy. None of us did."

The four of us returned to the ground and faced Kkorian. After a round of apologies to him, we set about making a camp for the night. Helios instructed us on how to create rudimentary saddles for dragon riding. Then we ate, and the five of us fell asleep beneath Helios's wings.

> *I was once told 'bravery is stupidity that gets a statue after'. I must be pretty stupid, because this is the bravest thing I have ever done.*
>
> – FROM "CONVERSATIONS WITH AMOREZ" BY DJURDAK ZA'CAR

Long after the suns had vanished and the three moons came out in full, a shadow snuck away from Xyleena's camp. Once safely out of hearing range, the shadow whistled a bird's call. An answer came from farther ahead. The shadow ran along until it reached a rocky outcrop. It paused to catch a breath as two more shadows silently joined it.

"Here's what you were after," whispered the first shadow, handing over a scrap of parchment. "You better get a move on. They're flying back to Kamédan in the morning via dragon back."

"Blast!" The second shadow hissed. "I need you to stick with them for a while longer."

"Fine. But me price just tripled."

"What? Why, you ungrateful– "

"Hey, mate, you didn't tell me I'd be dealing with a Tahda'varett Demon and a Dákun Daju. Not to mention all the crazy thingos they go through on a day-to-day basis. That's why me price went up."

The second shadow growled. "Fine. But if you don't get my any useful information on them, I will gut you."

"No worries, mate. I'll get you what you need."

The second shadow tossed him something. "Take this."

"What is it?"

"A mirror. Pox enchanted it so we can communicate through it. It works as a simple pocket mirror until you utter 'Dasum meo Dimitri' to it."

"Dasum meo? That's Kinös Elda, isn't it?"

"Of course. Now be gone," the third shadow ordered as it briskly walked away.

The second shadow followed a moment later.

"Bloody Dákun Daju rats," the first shadow muttered. Then with a sigh, it raced back to Xyleena's camp.

"Do you really think we can trust that moronic Hume to finish the job?" Godilai whispered as she watched Dimitri pace before the fire.

He paused to flash her the slip of paper and took to pacing again. "Kkorian got the runes from the black statue. That means we have four of the twelve keys to unlocking the Dragons' Gate." Dimitri removed his father's diary from his backpack and turned to the page with the handwritten clues scribed across it.

"'The greatest secret lies just beyond Human eyes on an isle.' And this last one, 'Moving by day.' What is it pointing to?"

Godilai sighed unhappily. "I neither know nor care at the moment."

Dimitri froze in his tracks and glared at her.

"The individual pieces aren't going to make sense until we acquire more of the riddle. Plus, I am more concerned with Xyleena having obtained a third of her dragons."

"I am aware of this, Godilai."

"Then why don't we do something?" she roared.

The pair was quiet, listening as Vincent snored loudly and rolled over while smacking his lips. Godilai shook her head and rolled her eyes in annoyance.

"What would you suggest? Hmm?" Dimitri moved to stand in front of her. "Taking them in their sleep? They have a dragon watching over them right now. We would not stand a chance. We have tried and tried and tried to steal the diary, and each time we have come up short. Ambushes do not work, because the Feykin brat and the Demon can sense them. So what should we do, Godilai?"

The Godilaied Dákun Daju glared at him, then spat and looked away. "There isn't anything we can do. At least not until we've found the Dragons' Gate."

"And that is why I've hired Kkorian. He can slip us the information we need to keep up with Xyleena's team, which was your idea to begin with." Dimitri knelt and took her hands in his.

She slowly looked at him again.

"Please, Godilai, bear with me. We will come up with a plan soon, but for now at least we must be patient."

"I just hope we can trust this Kkorian moron to uphold his end of the bargain." Godilai stood.

Dimitri nodded in agreement. "Wake the others. We'll have to warp to Kamédan in order to keep up with Xyleena's team." Dimitri kissed her hand and stood. "I will release the wyverns. No sense in taking all nine of them with us."

Godilai nodded and ducked into the tent where Vincent and Pox slept. Dimitri, on the other hand, looked skyward and whispered a prayer to the stars.

I had to keep her from giving in to despair. So I cornered her, stared her down, and said, "A dream does not become reality through magic or because you wish it so; it takes sweat, determination, hard work, and, yes, sometimes failure. You want to know what your greatest weakness is, Amorez? Giving up. You cannot do that now; you must not! Always try just one more time; you will either find a way, or make one!"

It worked.

– FROM "AN ONLOOKER'S JOURNAL"
BY THERNU ONYX

I woke just as dawn was beginning to break. In the pale-blue light that filtered through Helios's wing, I could see Kitfox fast asleep. I admired him as he sighed contently. He hugged his tail with one arm, while I used the other for a pillow. I frowned and quietly snuck out of the shelter made of Helios's wings.

I shivered as the cold air washed over me. With a sigh, I moved away from our small camp. I did not go very far, just far enough so that I could watch the suns rise over the ocean.

"It is the sixteenth day after the summer solstice," I whispered to the wind as Aruvan slowly rose. A sad smile made its way to my lips. "Happy birthday, Ríhan."

"Are you all right, Xyleena?" Helios's inquiry carried over to me.

I was quiet as I glanced at the white dragon over my shoulder. "Hey, Helios, can I ask you something?"

"You may ask me anything."

I looked back out over the ocean. "What advice would you give to a person whose heart is torn in two? One half is dedicated to her first love, the one who died, while the other half is growing fond of another."

"So you are confused about your feelings for Kitfox and Ríhan."

I gasped and looked up at Helios. His blue eyes sparkled in a mix of understanding and sympathy. "I saw how you reacted when Kitfox nearly died while saving you from the dire wolf. You care deeply for him. Yet it is not the same as the love you shared with Ríhan."

"I know I can never get Ríhan back, but I just can't seem to let go." Tears welled in my eyes. "I'm not sure I want to let him go."

"Xyleena." Helios's tone turned firm, almost scolding. "It makes no sense to be in love with someone who is no longer alive. To have fond memories of that person is fine, but clinging to them as if they are still alive is a waste of your life. You have been through that before and I would hate to see you suffer through it again. Please, for your sake, you need to move on."

I frowned at the dragon's words. "What if I can't?"

Helios sighed. "What went through your mind when you saw that you might lose Kitfox?"

I was quiet for a while as I recalled the event that nearly ended the Fox Demon's life. The tears began to roll down my cheeks. "When I saw Kitfox like that I...I panicked."

"You thought it was Ríhan all over again. Another man was sacrificing himself to save you– a man you have come to love almost as much as he loves you."

I collapsed to my knees as the dragon's words sank in. I knew it was true, but I did not want it to be. I did not want to love Kitfox, because...because I could not stand the thought of losing him. I hugged myself and bawled openly. Strong arms suddenly surrounded me, rocking me gently.

"Shh. Shh. Everything is okay."

I gasped at Kitfox's voice and looked up at him. With an anguished cry, I threw my arms around him and cried into his shoulder. He just sat there, holding me.

It was several long minutes before I calmed down. Kitfox continued to hold me, slowly rubbing my back. I sighed and backed away slightly to look into his eyes.

"I'm sorry, Kitf—"

"You don't have to apologize, Xy." He smiled sweetly and wiped away my tears. "Are you okay?"

I nodded. "Thank you."

"Do you think you are ready to face the others? They've been worried about you for the last twenty minutes." His ears twitched and turned to listen to the others behind us.

I glanced over his shoulder. Kkorian was staring at us wide eyed, while Shazza and Thera spoke quietly to each other.

"I'll have to eventually." I sighed. "I just don't want to answer a thousand questions about this."

Kitfox chuckled. "Me neither, actually."

"So what do we tell them?"

"Hmm..." Kitfox slowly got to his feet and helped me up. "Do you think a bad dream will work on them?"

"I hope so."

Together Kitfox and I made our way back to the others. To my surprise, none of them asked about my little breakdown. They just inquired about how I felt.

"I'm fine, really. Just an overreaction to a bad dream."

"Okay," I could tell Thera did not believe the explanation I offered. Thankfully, she chose to hold her tongue instead of putting a voice to her thoughts. "Are you feeling well enough to travel?"

"Are you kidding? I can't wait to get out of here," I said, glancing sideways at the twisted iron gate that guarded over the tomb.

"The feeling is mutual," murmured Shazza.

"So let's get a move on." Kitfox strode past me to start cleaning up our camp.

I nodded and moved to help him, but Thera grabbed my arm.

"Are you sure you're all right?" She stared into my eyes.

I slowly smiled and clasped her hand. "I will be fine. I just need something to get my mind off of the things that haunt me."

"I recommend dealing with your problems quickly." Thera finally released my arm. "They will drag you down so far that you will not be of any use to us in this quest or the fight against Dimitri."

I frowned at her words. Though I knew what she said was true, I was angry about being coddled, especially since she did not know the whole truth about my problems.

"I'll deal with it."

"I hope you do," Thera whispered and walked away to help the others pack up.

I turned and brushed my fingers across the jewels of the amulet. A moment later, I threw my hand in the air.

"I release you all!"

Wind, earth, and ice erupted from the dragon eye. The three elements separated as they whirled around and then congealed into their respective dragons. The roars ripped the air.

"Gods! That was bloody amazing!" Kkorian exclaimed.

"And loud," Kitfox complained as he rubbed his ears. "Every time you dragons do that, I get a headache."

"Plug your ears," Kkaia replied.

Kitfox growled at her.

Helios chuckled as he moved to join the other three dragons. "Now, now, sister. Play nice."

Kkaia snorted and sat on her haunches. "So why have you summoned all of us?"

"I thought you guys could hear everything I hear when you are in the eye." I quirked an eyebrow at the four dragons.

"That is true, hatchling. But we only hear and see everything you do when we enter your mind." Vortex lowered his head to my height as he spoke. "When we are completely within the dragon eye, we cannot hear anything."

I shook my head. "Okay, so you didn't hear our plan to fly back to Kamédan?"

Atoka chuckled. "We did now."

I rolled my eyes.

"When did you want to leave?"

A little over an hour later, all nine of us were airborne. The four dragons flew in a formation so close they nearly brushed wingtips. To my left Kitfox whooped in obvious enjoyment of the flight astride Atoka. To my right Kkorian clung tightly to Shazza in fear of falling from Kkaia's back as she beat her wings. Thera, on the other hand, worked on translating the next portion of the riddle while she rode on Vortex.

"I remember the first time we flew together like this," Helios said with amusement.

Vortex chuckled. "We were still hatchlings, probably about as long as Shazza is tall."

"That was so long ago. I'm surprised we can remember it like it was yesterday," Kkaia replied. "It was shortly after Amorez had finished her year-and-a-half-long dragon quest."

"No. Remember? She called it the dragon hope," Atoka said.

"Why did Amorez call it that?"

I barely heard Kitfox's question over the rush of wind.

"We were the last hope to ending Agasei's evil reign," Helios answered. "Had we failed to stop him and the Shadow Dragons, the world would have been completely swallowed by darkness."

"Agasei was so bent on revenge that the dark power from the Shadow Dragons was choking life from the entire planet," Atoka added. "During the Dark Keeper's reign, so many people were either murdered or dead by disease and famine that the population dwindled to almost nothing."

Vortex nodded slightly. "It took the planet centuries to recover from that devastation."

"When we finally faced Agasei in battle, the Shadow Dragons were much older and stronger than we were, but we were still able to defeat them!" Kkaia exclaimed. "The people of this planet rejoiced, and we were declared heroes for all time."

"Your story is still told," I replied. "But I'm afraid that many of the details of the battle have been lost or forgotten."

"That is depressing to hear," Helios said, glancing back at me for a moment.

I nodded in agreement and chanced a glance downward just as the cliffs marking the fault line whipped by. We had just covered five days of travel via wyvernback in a little over two hours.

I smiled. "At this rate we should be back in Kamédan by nightfall."

We passed the time listening to the four dragons tell stories about their adventures with Amorez.

It was shortly after sunset when the crystal castle of Kamédan came into view. Shazza suggested having the dragons land in the royal gardens. The dragons obliged, back-winging and landing in perfect formation amidst the fauna and fountains.

Once the five of us dismounted, I thanked the dragons for their help. I watched as the four of them faded into their elements and swirled around.

They entered the dragon eye amulet with flashes of light, and the four jewels marking their presence shone with their essence.

Cheers of joy made me freeze. I looked over my shoulder toward the gate. Hundreds of people were pressed against it, cheering and applauding happily.

"Wave," Kitfox whispered in my ear.

I blushed and slowly raised my hand to wave to the people at the gate. Their cheers grew even louder.

"I wasn't expecting this kind of reaction," Shazza muttered, staring in awe at everyone gathered.

"If it's any consolation to you, I wasn't expecting it either," I said with a goofy sort of smile.

Shazza flashed a halfhearted smile.

"I think the crowd is growing," Thera chuckled and glanced at the Dákun Daju. "I hope your royal guards can hold the gate."

"Likewise." Shazza nodded. "I'll send some reinforcements once we are inside the castle."

"Wait a second!" Kkorian exclaimed. "You are the queen?"

Kitfox smacked the back of Kkorian's head. "Don't you know anything? Of course she's the queen of Katalania."

"That hurt, mate." Kkorian rubbed the back of his head. "And no, I didn't know that Shazza was the queen. If I did, I wouldn't have enjoyed the ride so much."

Shazza rolled her eyes. "Let's go. Do whatever you want inside until we meet again at the table for some dinner. Once the cooks are notified of my return, it should be only an hour or so before a meal is served."

"Thank you, Shazza-sortim," I said as I turned to follow her inside.

Thera and Kitfox were at my side a moment later. Kkorian took one last, long look at all the people at the gate before he followed after us.

I sighed contentedly as I sank into the hot water. The maids had drawn me a bath to relax in, complete with scented salts. I let the spicy-sweet scent wash over me as I closed my eyes and let my mind wander.

The water was cold when a loud knock on the door pulled me back into reality. I did not even recall falling asleep. I quickly gathered a towel and wrapped it around me before I answered the door.

Kitfox took one look at me and blushed completely before closing his eyes tightly. "I'm so sorry! I was only coming to tell you that dinner is ready."

I laughed and caressed his cheek. He cracked an eye slightly to look at me. "Don't worry about it. I'll be down in a minute."

"O-okay." He chuckled nervously.

I watched for a moment as he briskly walked down the hall before I closed the door. I dressed in one of the dresses the maids had left me and brushed my hair before I left my room.

I managed to find the dining room on my own this time. Kitfox looked up at me as I entered and blushed again. I smiled sweetly at him.

"You look good in dresses, Xy," Thera said as she looked between Kitfox and me.

"Thank you."

I took a seat at the table opposite her just as Shazza and two of her aids walked into the room. To my surprise, the queen was still dressed in the clothes she had worn on the journey to the Tomb of the Lost. She sighed as she took a seat at the table and waved her aids away.

"I apologize for my appearance. I have been too busy catching up on matters of the state to get washed up for dinner."

"It is perfectly all right, Shazza-sortim," I said with a smile.

She dipped her head in a nod, and the cooks stacked mountains of food on the table.

"How go the translations of the next part of the riddle, Thera?" Kitfox asked, placing a good portion of meat on his plate before passing it on.

Thera groaned slightly. "You are not going to like this part of the riddle."

"Oh?" I glanced at her as I dropped some vegetables on my plate. I even snuck a few onto Kitfox's plate, making him stare at me in disbelief. "You should eat them. They're good for you."

He snorted and moved the vegetables back to my plate. "You eat them for me."

I moved them back. "Just shut up and eat them."

He frowned and pushed them to the side of his plate. "I am a carnivore, Xy. I don't touch vegetables."

"You two are getting weirder and weirder the longer you are together," said Shazza. "Thera, what were you saying about the riddle?"

"The next part is four lines, two dragons. I've managed to translate most of it, but the rest will take a little while longer," Thera answered as she continued looking between Kitfox and me. "I should have all four lines done by morning."

"Sounds good to me," Kkorian said between bites. "Say, Shazza, how did your guards do against the huge crowd at the gate?"

"I had to send out fifteen more to calm the people down. They spent almost the entire hour explaining to them that the Dragon Keeper was in fact back. Now there are even more people gathered around the gate."

Kitfox whistled. "Wow. Xy's getting popular."

I frowned. "That is what worries me."

Kkorian looked at me, confusion burning in his blue eyes. "Why? Don't you want to be popular?"

"I want news of my presence to spread, but I'm not sure if it is a good idea to have so much attention. I'm worried about how Dimitri will react to this." An image of the Festival of the Phoenix flashed in my mind. "I don't want him to murder more innocent people."

Kkorian frowned. "What did he do?"

I sighed as I met his gaze. "He cast a fire storm spell on the people gathered at the Temple of Five Souls during the Rising of Zahadu-Kitai."

Kkorian was shocked at this news, even angry.

I looked down at my plate. "He killed thousands with that spell."

"I didn't think he was that powerful," Shazza said quietly. "That settles it, then."

I looked up at her. "Settles what?"

"I'm coming with you." She smiled at me. "I wasn't sure if I should, given my responsibilities here. But with a madman like that running around, I think it would be wise to assist you in taking him down. That is, of course, provided you'll have me."

"Are you kidding? I'd love to have you join us."

"Me too!" Kkorian exclaimed.

Kitfox rolled his eyes as he chewed on a piece of meat. Shazza chuckled.

"Well then, we'll rest here tonight and decide what to do tomorrow once Thera has had a chance to finish the translation."

I smiled. "That sounds good to me."

I looked at Xyleena – really studied her– after the ordeal in the tomb Helios called home. She was changed. Stronger. I do not mean physically, but mentally. Her will to overcome these hardships had grown stronger; she would be the Dragon Keeper.

– FROM "THE SECOND KEEPER"
BY THERA ONYX

I thanked the maid as she closed the door behind me. I turned to see Kitfox, Thera, and Shazza standing at a table in what I figured to be Shazza's office. They waved me over and pointed to the map spread out before them. When Kkorian finally joined us, Thera read off the translation.

"Wildfire the Blaze will come back when water falls upon attack. Riptide the Torrent points the way to fire beneath dragon bay."

"Wow, Amorez certainly didn't make it easy to find her dragons, did she?" Kkorian muttered and crossed his arms.

"I wrote the 'Riddle of the Twelve,'" I replied as I looked at the map on the table.

Kkorian blinked at me in utter disbelief.

"If you wrote it, then why don't you know the answers?"

"She fell and bumped her head. Now she can't remember anything from about four years ago and back," Thera replied as she turned to the map in Dragon Diary and placed it in front of me. "Xy, do you see any differences between the maps?"

"Hang on." I took the next few minutes to compare the two maps.

Kkorian scratched his head. "Why would she see any differences?"

"She can see the dragons' hiding places, but no one else can," Kitfox answered.

Kkorian nodded and quieted down so I could concentrate.

After a few more minutes, I sighed. "I don't see anything different."

"Bugger." Kkorian crossed his arms. "Hey, what was that riddle again?"

Thera quirked her eyebrow at him. "Wildfire the Blaze will come back when water falls upon attack. Riptide the Torrent points the way to fire beneath dragon bay."

"Dragon bay, you say?"

Thera nodded.

Kkorian looked at the map and smiled. He pointed to a body of water on the continent of Katalania. "This is Dragon Head Bay. I bet you a million bits that that is where you need to go. It is not a very safe place to sail a ship, though. Too many shallows."

Kitfox gawked at Kkorian. "How did you figure that out?"

"Simple." Kkorian smirked. "Years ago there was a rumor of untold treasure somewhere in the bay. I took me ship and me crew there in search of it. It proved to be a very bad idea."

Kitfox laughed. "You really are an idiot."

"Enough, boys." I sighed and looked at the Dragon Head Bay on the hand-drawn map in the diary. Though nothing appeared as I watched it, I had a good feeling about it. "Kkorian is right. That is where the next two dragons are hidden."

"So what is the plan?" Shazza asked as she rolled up the map and placed it in a drawer.

"I thought that was obvious," said Kitfox. "We take the dragons to the bay and figure out how to get under it to find the other two."

I focused my thoughts inward until I felt the presence of the four dragons. Do you guys mind flying us again?

We live for flying. Vortex replied a moment later.

Yes! Let's fly! Let's fly! Atoka laughed.

"The dragons are ready to fly us again," I announced. "When do you guys want to leave?"

"I have some tasks that require my attention before we can leave," Shazza replied. "Maybe by either late afternoon today or early tomorrow."

"I actually like that idea," Kitfox said. "We can rest up a little bit more and think of some battle tactics should we run into Dimitri again."

"Or more undead," Thera said in an undertone.

I heartily agreed with her.

"Okay, one more day of rest before we head out again. Sounds good to me," Kkorian said with a smile.

Thera, Kitfox, Kkorian, and I left Shazza to her work.

We gathered in the library to discuss battle plans and other things. We met late that night for dinner and revealed our plans to Shazza. She seemed impressed and told us that she had everything set up for her departure from the capital. She even had her aids gather the various supplies needed for the long quest. Everything was set for our journey.

After a hearty breakfast the next morning, the five of us strode out to the royal gardens. I summoned all four of my dragons again, drawing attention and cheers from the people who passed by the castle gates.

I waved to the people as I mounted Helios. With a great flourish of wind and wings, the four dragons took to the air. We circled the crystalline castle once before turning southward toward the Dragon Head Bay.

The story will continue in

Selena Inali Raynelif Drake is an American author best known for her paranormal mystery series, The AEON Files. Drake is a martial arts enthusiast, a Wiccan with Cherokee roots, and an award-winning artist. Her love for writing started when she was eight, and she has won a number of Editor's Choice awards and a Shakespeare Trophy of Excellence for poetry. Her works have been published in Thrice Fiction Magazine, Emerging Authors 2018, and Emerging Poets 2018. She currently lives in Minot, North Dakota with her dog, Pipsqueak, where she continues to work on more books.

You can find out more about Selena by visiting sirdwrites.com

Glossary

A note from the author:
I realize that the language of Dragon Diaries is extremely confusing. Most readers will probably just glance over the words, but for those (like me) who enjoy learning new things, here is a little bit of a guide to the language known as Kinös Elda. Hopefully it will help.

Kinös Eldic Phrases

Tabiki ni heile. — Wall of fire
Esté imlít lerra rité mertuác jidó. Arx et cólaz ni Kohnbenai rahn. — This great world will die soon. As the acts of Darkness spread.
Meo resuko. — My diary
Meo namae wa Agasei DéDos. Esté buko wa meo resuko bó et tel né rité sterim et Nírigone Súl. — My name is Agasei DéDos. This book is my diary and the key to finding the Dragons' Gate.
Sortim — Sister
Kahs gözandí — Good morning
Ja lah shikenó — You are welcome
Iríjhon Resuko — Dragon Diary
Kahs gözandí, fratime. Eo ík Teka Loneborne. — Good morning, brothers. I am Teka Loneborne.
Aké la ja chee? — Why are you here?
Kíen la ja süm, Teka Loneborne? — Who are you with, Teka Loneborne?
Estéz karétez la meo micallaz, bó et kanójo wa Xyleena. — These men are my friends, and the girl is Xyleena.
It ja nan hakaní estéz tantúre? — Do you not understand these words?
Hoko bemum Thera Onyx — Please call Thera Onyx
Núl wa de ja du bemum meo po, Ujak? — What did you call me for, Uncle?
Meoja ker dumakunga — We have decided
Iríjhone Reshé — Dragon Keeper
Vero — Yes
De wa et nena ni Amorez — She is the (female) child of Amorez
Shíkai ja — Thank you
Gratíe — Thanks (informal)
Eo du capel ja nan lig Kinös Elda — I thought you did not speak Kinös Elda
It ja hakaní? — Do you understand?
Ja lah tarlé, Pox. Da du la ja? — You are late, Pox. Where were you?
Kíen la déoja? — Who are they?
Eo dur ir né et izvucí tig Tarik bó Valadri — I went to the river with Tarik and Valadri.
Siminea — Lion
Kahs nóc — Good night
Tanda — Hello
Tíc it eo lig "standard words" den Kinös Elda? — How do I say "standard words" in Kinös Elda?

Meo namae wa Dimitri Renoan. Kíen la ja? — My name is Dimitri Renoan. Who are you?

Eo ík Habanya-Ürg. Aké la ja chee? — I am Habanya-Ürg. Why are you here?

Eo nan lig Kinös Elda. Eo ík guídes — I do not speak Kinös Elda. I am sorry.

Meo namae wa Xyleena. Eo ík et Iríjhone Reshé — My name is Xyleena. I am the Dragon Keeper.

Na — Zero

San — One

Sku — Two

Teh — Three

O — Four

Ven — Five

Mé — Six

Im — Seven

Lin — Eight

Bin — Nine

Ra — Ten

Sanra — Elven

Skura — Twelve

Tehra — Thirteen

Ora — Fourteen

Venra — Fifteen

Méra — Sixteen

Imra — Seventeen

Linra — Eighteen

Binra — Nineteen

Skucóra — Twenty

Mehnt — One hundred

Shréva — One thousand

Kahs gozavé — Good afternoon

Tanda, Kínashe. Eo din ormá né alú sa amyíac — Hello, Kínashe. I would like to rent a boat.

Tic kahl wah — How much for

Nai — No

Nír irím bó kerím ska — Now go and have fun

Infé — Open

Tanda, Zahadu-Kitai. Núl cistrena ja chee? — Hello, Zahadu-Kitai. What brings you here?

Núl wa et shríldu ni esté? — What is the meaning of this?

Ja lah tído guídemavet — You are all forgiven

Tic la ja? — How are you?

Byö – Cousin

Eo rité res meo ligto. — I give my word.

Dasum meo… — Show me…

Dasum meo nishi. — Show me everyone.

Kahs gözandí, Xy-sortim. — Good morning, my sister Xy.

Nevoa cäipe — Fog disperse

Et Sleiku ni Sango — The Dance of Blood

Meo sortime, meo fratim, illam durus. — My sisters, my brother, live strong.
Iktanilla — Immortal
Silentium — Silence; Be quiet
Symbilla et Illa-Arnaxu sornipé; Ten Sutétim isila con strujaz ni ponet —
Symbilla the Life-Bringer dreams; On Southern isle with golden streams.
Ja la mishi, nena. — You are lost, child.
Ja la nan mert. Iram ger. — You are not dead. Go back.
Ligam ni Skura bó inferom. — Speak of Twelve and enter.
Hyerjam — Shatter, break

Spells

Aero bíraw (air-oh bee-raw) — Wind gust
Daréta esso (da-ray-ta eh-so) — Thunder ball
Daréta suahk (da-ray-ta soo-awk) — Thunder bolt
Dasai nagarésayo (da-sigh na-guh-ray-say-oh) — Sight reflection
Dasum meo (da-soom may-oh) — Show me
Heile esso (hail eh-so) — Fire ball
Heile pricé (hail pree-kay) — Fire storm
Heile suahk (hail soo-awk) — Fire bolt
Hydíca semít (hi-dee-kuh sem-eet) — Ice spike
Hydíca tabiki (hi-dee-kuh ta-bee-kee) — Ice wall
Hydor esso (hi-door eh-so) —Water ball
Hydor sibatín (hi-door see-bat-een) —Water spear
Kósa sibatín (koh-sa see-bat-een) —Chaos spear
Levítum (lay-vee-tum) – Levitate
Medícté (med-eek-tay) – Heal
Nagaré (nah-guh-ray) – Reflect
Nan dasai nevoa (non duh-sigh ney-voh-uh) — Blinding mist (literally "no sight
mist")
Nan vocé (non voh-kay) — Silence (literally "no voice")
Luminös (loo-mihn-ahs) — Illuminate, Light
Uerto palaso (oo-er-tow pah-lass-oh) — Poison arrow

Names and Places

Aadrian (ey-dree-ahn) (city) — Lesser capitol city of Mekora-Lesca
Aadrian Ithnez (ey-dree-ahn ith-nehz) (person) — The man who ultimately saved
the human race from extinction and helped found the planet which bears his name
Adoramus (ah-dohr-ah-muhs) — Shadow Dragon of Light who was killed in the
final battle between Amorez and Agasei
Agasei DéDos (a-guh-sigh day-dose) — The original dark Dragon Keeper and
creator of the Shadow Dragons
Aidana Wovril (ahy-deyn-ah wohv-ril) — Feykin Elder and one of the Generals
leading the Army of Light
Aissur (a-soor) — A major city on Katalania

Amorez Renoan (ah-more-ez ray-no-ahn) — The original Dragon Keeper and creator of the Dragons of Light

Aruvan (ah-roo-vahn) — The smaller, yellow sun

Atlidmé (at-lid-may) — God of water, death, and winter (giant serpent)

Bakari-Tokai (buh-kar-ee toh-kahy) — The grand capital of Ithnez

Bangorian Mountains (bahn-gohr-ee-an) — Prominent mountain range running the southern spans of the Mekora-Lescan continent

Bedeb (bay-deb) — Ithnez's ringed sister planet

Beldai (bell-dahy) — One of the twin cities on the banks of the Anakor River

Breccia (bresh-ee-uh) — Shaman of the Wakari Corundum Tribe

Cah (kaw) — A city in the Southern Stretch

Cosín (coh-seen) — A small town on the Southern Stretch

Dákun Daju (day-koon da-joo) — Extreme race of elven-like beings

Djurdak Za'Car (jer-dak zuh-kar) — Amorez's husband and the former high prince

Feykin (fay-kin) — Preferred name of the Sorcerers

Freya Latreyon (fray-uh luh-tray-in) — Wolf Demon and teacher to Xyleena

Godilai Locklyn (god-il-lahy lok-lin) — Dákun Daju warrior

Havel (ha-vell) — The name for the realm of the dead

Ithnez (ith-nehz) — The planet where the adventure takes place

Jetep (jay-tehp) — City of outlaws and mercenaries on the southwest coast of Mekora-Lesca

Jítanath Locklyn (jee-tuh-nath lok-lin) — Only son of Dimitri De'Dos and Godilai Locklyn

Jormandr (johr-man-dohr) — Gargantuan rock serpent that terrorizes the Wakari

Kamédan (kah-may-dan) — The capital of Katalania

Khatahn-Rhii (kah-tawn ree) — God of wind, evolution, and autumn (dragon)

Kinös Elda (keen-ahs el-duh) — The ancient tongue

Kkaia (kuh-kay-uh) — Dragon of earth

Kkorian (kuh-kor-ee-an) — Hume pirate

Kula (koo-luh) — Shadow Dragon of Earth

Kúskú (koo-skoo) — Dragon of Illusion

Luea (loo-ee-uh) — Queen of Aadrian

Magnathor (mag-nuh-thor) — Gargantuan sea monster which haunts the waters of the Myst

Míjin (mee-jin) — One of the Feykin Generals in the Army of Light

Monrai (mon-rye) — Major city located on the outskirts of the Myst

Nahstipulí (nuh-step-oo-lee) — Goddess of earth, life, and summer (Ixys, a black unicorn)

Nemlex (nehm-liks) — Major Katalanian trade city

Nexxa (nehks-uh) — Dragon of Venom

Nír'l (neer-il) — An elder Dákun Daju who is related to Dimitri

Noralani Ithnez (nohr-aw-lawn-ee ith-nehz)— Named after Aadrian's only daughter, she is the last surviving member of the Ithnez bloodline.

Pletíxa (play-teeks-uh) — An insignificant town on Katalania

Pyrex Akregate (pie-rehks ak-rii-gate) — Wakari Alchemist who helped bring the Shadow Dragons to life

Q'veca (coo-vay-kuh) — Menta trainer on the Sorcerers' Isle

Régon (ray-gahn) — God of Chaos and Creation
Rhekja (rek-yah) — Gazelle Demon and owner of the Bird in Hand Tavern and Inn in Monrai; member of the Schaakold-Vond'l guild
Ríhan (ree-han) — Xyleena's best friend
Rishai (ree-shy) — The larger, blue sun
Ruwviti (roo-vee-tee) — Elder Sorcerer and Thera's uncle
Sauqe (sok) — Tiny fishing town on Katalania
Schaakold-Vond'l (shahk-uld von-dul) — A high-powered Equine Demon guild
Seramahli (sehr-ah-maw-lee) — Major Wakari city, home of the Corundum Tribe
Serpehti (sur-pet-ee) — Another rival guild of the Tahda'varett
Symbilla (sim-bee-ya) — Dragon of Life
Sindai (sen-dahy) — One of the twin cities on the banks of the Anakor River
Tahda'varett (tuh-dah-vahr-eht) — Kitfox's and Freya's guild
Taypax (tay-paks) — Dragon of Death who was killed in the final battle between Amorez and Agasei
Thedrún (thehd-roon) — Dragon of Thunder
Thera (ter-uh) — Feykin Occultist from the Sorcerers' Isle
Thernu (ter-new) — Thera's mother
Thorna (thorn-uh) — A major city on the Sorcerers' Isle
Thuraben (thoor-uh-ben) — The capital of the Sorcerer's Isle
Valaskjalf Za'Car (vuh-lask-jahlf zuh-kar) — Current high prince of Ithnez
Visler (vihs-lur) — Silver, dragon-shaped homunculus; also called a Sentinel
Vitaani (viht-ahn-ee) — Dákun Daju General within the Army of Light
V'Nyath (v-nee-ath) — Dákun Daju General within the Army of Light
Vronan (vroh-nahn) — Largest city on Ithnez; houses a major trading port
Wakari (wuh-kar-ee) — Dwarf-like creatures that live far underground
Warinarc (war-een-ark) — A rival guild of the Tahda'varett
Wyrd (weerd) — Shadow Dragon of Undead
Xyleena (zahy-lee-nuh) — Heroine of Dragon Diaries
Zadún (zah-doon) — The capital city of Arctica
Zahadu-Kitai (za-ha-doo-key-tie) — Goddess of fire, rebirth, and spring (phoenix)
Zalx (zahlks)— Dákun Daju General within the Army of Light
Zamora Argatör (zuh-moor-uh ahr-guh-tour) — Amorez's alias
Zhaman Verrs (zah-mon verz) — King of Arctica
Zhealocera (zee-low-ser-uh) — Dákun Daju friend of Xyleena
Zhücka (zoo-kuh) — Feykin General within the Army of Light
Zön-Rígaia (zohn-ree-gayh-yah) — High powered Feline Demon guild
Zrehla (zer-ey-luh) — King of the Southern Stretch

Other Languages:

Bakari-Tokai (buh-kahr-ee toe-kahy) — 'City of Survivors' in the Dákun Daju dialect
S'vil-Tokai (suh-vhil toe-kahy) — 'City of Invaders' in the Dákun Daju dialect
D'go-Pahngíl (dug-oh pawn-geel) — 'Blood Fang' in the ancient Demon dialect

Made in the USA
Columbia, SC
15 October 2021